When Shrimps Learn to Whistle

When Shrimps Learn to Whistle

to Whistle

SIGNPOSTS FOR THE NINETIES

DENIS HEALEY

MICHAEL JOSEPH

London

MICHAEL JOSEPH LTD

Published by the Penguin Group
27 Wrights Lane, London, W8 5TZ, England
Viking Penguin Inc., 40 West 23rd Street, New York, New York 10010, USA
Penguin Books Australia Ltd, Ringwood, Victoria, Australia
Penguin Books Canada Ltd, 2801 John Street, Markham, Ontario, Canada L3R 1B4
Penguin Books (NZ) Ltd, 182–190 Wairau Road, Auckland 10, New Zealand

Penguin Books Ltd, Registered Offices: Harmondsworth, Middlesex, England

First published in Great Britain 1990

Copyright © Denis Healey 1990

Set in 11/13 pt Ehrhardt
Printed in England by Clays Ltd, St Ives plc

A CIP catalogue record for this book is available from the British Library

ISBN 0 7181 3485 0

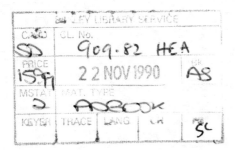

To George Kennan and all my other friends
on both sides of the Atlantic
who have helped me to understand
the postwar world.

CONTENTS

When Shrimps Learn to Whistle

INTRODUCTION

'PEOPLE MORE OFTEN need to be reminded than to be informed.' Dr Johnson was right – and never more than today. The end of the Cold War, the collapse of communism in Eastern Europe, the reunification of Germany and the disintegration of the Soviet Union are following one another at breakneck speed. The world as we have learned to interpret it over the last quarter of a century is turned upside down.

Yet once we look back beyond the mid sixties we can understand much of what is happening and how to deal with it. The twenty years after the defeat of Hitler, before the Cold War had set hard in the mould, were almost as turbulent and bewildering as the nineties promise to be. It is also worth reflecting on the lessons of earlier revolutions – in 1917, 1848, and 1789 – to gain insights into the revolution now shaking world communism.

This selection from my writings since the war is intended to throw some light on the challenge of the nineties. I have been an active observer of the postwar world ever since I left the army in 1945, and have played a direct part in many of the key decisions as a member of Labour Cabinets in Britain, both at the Ministry of Defence and the Treasury. My eleven years as a minister allowed me no time to put my reflections on to paper; however, my six years as international secretary of the Labour Party, and twenty-seven years as an MP in opposition gave me both the opportunity and incentive to express myself in print.

As a correspondent for newspapers in Europe and the United States I wrote weekly and monthly commentaries on events as they arose. I also wrote occasional reflective pieces at greater length on the issues which lay behind the news. It is mainly from such articles that I have compiled this selection of my views.

This book is in a sense a history of my own political development – a companion to my memoirs, *The Time of My Life*. On some important issues I have shifted my stance considerably from time to time, as I learned more about the facts, or as the facts themselves changed. The Russia of Gorbachev is very different from the Russia of Stalin. Military strategy in a world groaning under a fearful redundancy of nuclear missiles presents problems which would have seemed incomprehensible in 1950. The collapse of the postwar economic order in the seventies, and the revolution in the financial markets produced by information technology in the eighties, have made a nonsense of the old economic rules. In Britain itself the social changes which began under the Attlee government have undermined some of the assumptions on which Labour's postwar policies were based. Even ten years ago the looming threat to the world environment was only dimly perceived.

Nevertheless, I have been surprised and gratified to discover that there are constant themes running through my writings which are perhaps even more relevant today than when they first appeared. The force which drove me into a political career was the desire to prevent a third world war. I was born in the First World War and fought for five years in the Second. Though I had abandoned my youthful flirtations with pacifism and communism before I joined the army, I returned to Britain from Italy believing that my generation had the chance to succeed where its fathers had failed. Whereas the League of Nations had splintered at the first test, I thought that the United Nations would make a better instrument for building a world society as it was based on agreement between the most important powers.

I also believed that Ernest Bevin was right when he told the Labour Party Conference in 1945: 'Left can speak to Left.' My experiences as international secretary taught me a bitter lesson here – that the totalitarian communist regarded the democratic socialist as his bitterest enemy. Stalin did not believe in any world society which was not wholly Communist. He saw Attlee's Britain as the main obstacle to Communist control of Western Europe.

My involvement in vain efforts to save the Socialist parties in Eastern Europe from destruction rammed this lesson home. The persecution, torture, and murder of many of my friends gave a personal edge to my anti-Communism. This may have prevented me from appreciating how much Soviet foreign policy was fuelled by a historic sense of national vulnerability, aggravated by Russia's postwar weakness.

I soon realized that Stalin was not the only obstacle to my hopes. It would be difficult to build a world society even without the Soviet Union. My contacts with the socialists of Western Europe taught me that nationalism was still the strongest single force in world affairs, usually triumphing over ideology or class solidarity. I began to realize that the creation of a world society would require new political and economic structures to generate new international interests.

My support for the Marshall Plan and NATO was strengthened by the hope that they would serve as the foundation for an Atlantic community strong enough to override the nationalism of its members. I had witnessed the reluctance with which the United States finally gave its active support to Western Europe in the Second World War, and I wanted to ensure that future detachment would be as difficult as possible. If we could not get co-operation from the Communist world, perhaps an Atlantic community would provide the core round which the non-Communist world could unite.

But NATO was soon deeply divided over the role and control of its nuclear forces. Like many other young men at the time, revulsion at the prospect of a thermonuclear holocaust led me to try to understand the role of atomic weapons in strategy and diplomacy. Years of discussion with men such as Henry Kissinger and Helmut Schmidt convinced me that the moral and political problems posed by nuclear weapons are insoluble in principle, though they might be surmountable in practice. I have spent much time in the last three decades looking for ways to escape from this dilemma. The tragedy of Hungary in 1956 led me to see disengagement in Central Europe as the best way forward; many of the arguments I used then have their echoes today. Similarly the search for alternatives to the threat of suicide as a deterrent to war is now proceeding with redoubled energy in Moscow, Washington and both Western and Eastern Europe.

The idea of an Atlantic community lost its credibility many years ago, when faced with crises of the magnitude of Suez, Cuba, and Vietnam. The Carter and Reagan presidencies both undermined European confidence in the wisdom and consistency of the United States. Washington seems nowadays more concerned with the economic threat from Japan, and with its domestic war against crime, drugs, and racial conflict, than with the future of Western Europe.

As the biggest debtor in the world, which will soon owe more than all other countries put together, the United States is particularly vulnerable to the dangers created by the debt crisis and the excesses of the financial revolution. These economic problems absorbed my attention to an increasing degree after I ceased to be Chancellor of the Exchequer. They could now present a more serious threat to the Western world than the Warsaw Pact ever did.

Finally, as leader of the Soviet Union Mikhail Gorbachev has not only ended the Cold War but also explicitly invited other leaders to join him in creating 'an interdependent and even integral world'. The opportunity for creating a world society which can give meaning to the United Nations now exists for the first time since the Second World War, although the instability which has followed the end of the Cold War has made its creation at once more urgent and more intractable.

I have tried to group my essays on each of these major themes together, though in some cases they were written many years apart. They are intended to provide some signposts to the establishment of a world society, which has always been my main purpose as a politician. I do not underestimate the obstacles ahead. Adjusting policies to meet the unexpected is always difficult. In world affairs it is particularly difficult because a government which has spent years obtaining the consent of its allies and of its own people to an existing policy is naturally reluctant to start the whole process all over again on behalf of a totally different policy.

The end of the Cold War requires not only a change of policies, but also a change of ideologies. Both sides presented the Cold War as a conflict of ideologies, in which organizations like NATO and the European Community were given an absolute value quite out of character with their real role as instruments of particular policies at particular times. Changing ideologies is even more difficult than changing policies. Yet it is sometimes even more important.

I believe that Khrushchev in 1955 genuinely wanted to change Soviet policy towards the West in much the same way as Gorbachev does today. In practice that meant abandoning Lenin's doctrine of a world that was divided finally by the October Revolution into two camps which were doomed to mortal conflict. However, this was something that Khrushchev found quite impossible to do. 'We are in favour of a *détente*,' he said, 'but if anybody thinks that for this reason we shall forget about Marx, Engels, and Lenin, he is mistaken. This will happen when shrimps learn to whistle.' And thus he failed to convince the West of his sincerity.

Gorbachev has taught his shrimps to whistle. In his seminal speech to the United Nations Assembly in December 1988 he explicitly renounced those elements in Marxism-Leninism which are incompatible with a foreign policy aiming at interdependence with the West. So he cut the ground from under the feet of opponents in the West who have always been able to quote Leninist doctrine to justify rejecting co-operation with the Soviet Union.

However, ideology still restricts the Western response to the challenge laid down by Gorbachev. There are powerful forces on both sides of the

Atlantic which argue that it is impossible to co-operate with the post-Communist world unless it accepts their ideology – by which they usually mean a market economy as they imagine it was prescribed by Adam Smith in the eighteenth century, operating now in the anarchy produced recently by the globalization and deregulation of the financial markets. I hope this book may help these forces to teach their shrimps to whistle too.

CHAPTER ONE

Nationalism and a World Society

A T THE AGE OF THIRTY-FIVE, after six years as international
secretary of the Labour Party, I entered Parliament as MP for South
East Leeds. My first task was to contribute a chapter on foreign policy to a
book introduced by Clement Attlee and entitled *New Fabian Essays*. It
planned to do for the Labour movement of the fifties what *Fabian Essays*
had done in Victorian England – to provide a bible for gradualism as
against 'the Utopian or catastrophic ideas of the past'. Margaret Cole and
Dick Crossman edited the new volume in 1952; Bernard Shaw had edited
the first in 1889.

I saw the invitation as an ideal opportunity to set out the views I had
formed as international secretary, both about the problems of foreign
policy in general and about the difficulty of persuading the Labour Party
to face the realities of the modern world.

Nearly forty years later, there is little I would wish to change in my
essay, entitled 'Power Politics and the Labour Party'. Indeed, it expresses,
often better than I have later managed to do, my fundamental views not
only on foreign policy, but on socialism itself. I saw the essence of British
socialism 'not in its contingent analysis or techniques, but in its determination to apply moral principles to social life'. The thinking of Protestant
philosophers such as Reinhold Niebuhr and Herbert Butterfield had
influenced me greatly. 'The socialist,' I wrote, 'stands midway between
the liberal optimist and the conservative pessimist.'

On foreign policy I had been greatly impressed by the hard-headed
realism of American academics such as William Fox of Yale and Hans
Morgenthau of Chicago. I saw many historical changes as morally
neutral: 'It is difficult to maintain that the brotherhood of men is
better realized in Eastern Europe under a "people's democracy" than it
was under the Austro-Hungarian Empire.' Moreover, 'many of the visible

trends contradict one another. The century of the common man is also the era of the rape of the masses and of the managerial revolution.'

This was in the days when Britain was seen as one of the Big Three world powers. But I foresaw that the Korean War, in which the United States provided 90 per cent of the United Nations' forces, would produce a more self-centred American foreign policy, in which strategic interests would predominate and the views of allies count for less. Moreover 'the rise of Germany and Japan may change the nature of the Cold War . . . Britain cannot ignore the possibility that Germany may seek national unity either by war with Russia or by alliance with Russia.' Integrating Germany into some form of Western European union was no answer: 'It is already obvious that if European unity is built without Britain it will be dominated by Germany.' Finally, I predicted the possible disruption of the Stalinist bloc if China followed Yugoslavia in declaring independence from Moscow.

In 1956 I developed these themes in a contribution to *Fabian International Essays*, entitled 'Beyond Power Politics'. This was largely concerned with the advantages of the intergovernmental approach to international organization, rather than the supranational: 'The supreme advantage of the intergovernmental method is that it is less likely to produce the type of closed international society which simply raises the traditional problems of power politics to a new and more dangerous level . . . Even supranational institutions allow the possibility of secession in practice though they deny it in theory. They simply ensure that if secession takes place, it inflicts far more damage on other members of the group . . . A supranational link between the Federal Republic and her Western neighbours would create so direct and obvious a conflict between German reunification and European union that Bonn's co-operation with the West would be subjected to dangerous strains.'

Many of these points have an obvious relevance today. In another essay I wrote in 1956 for a private group, on 'Nationalism and Liberty', I carried my argument further, and applied it to the Soviet bloc as well as to the West: 'The Soviet claim to have ended national conflicts within its own camp is very far from the truth.' I pointed out that, although Moscow had sent nationalist Communist Party leaders from the constituent republics to forced labour camps, 'when the German armies reached the non-Russian parts of the Soviet Union the desertion to their side was astonishing. In 1948 the autonomous republics of the Crimean Tartars and the Chechen-Ingush in the Caucasus were both abolished and their peoples deported on the grounds that they had fought *en masse* with the Germans during the war.'

As I have so often done, I contrasted the engineer's approach to nationalism, as demonstrated by the Soviet Union, and the lawyer's approach favoured by the federalists in Western Europe, with that of the gardener, who studies the nature of the soil, takes account of the climate and the prevailing wind, and is always prepared for the unexpected drought or flood. I owed the gardening metaphor to George Kennan who has remained a friend and inspiration over more than forty years.

The views I expressed in these writings have formed the core of my thinking about world affairs ever since. I believe they are particularly relevant to the problems Europe now faces in developing fresh structures to accommodate the new democracies which have just escaped Soviet control.

POWER POLITICS AND THE LABOUR PARTY

(from *New Fabian Essays*, Turnstile Press, 1952)

That external factors would one day dominate British politics was never conceived by the founders of British socialism. Apart from one reference to the foreign policy of the Manchester School, the original volume of *Fabian Essays* never mentions the world outside Britain except to point a domestic moral. Indeed, this sort of parochialism was the Fabians' greatest strength. They found socialism wandering aimlessly in Cloud-cuckoo-land and set it working on the gas and water problems of the nearest town or village. The modern Welfare State is their monument.

But the very success of Fabianism as an instrument of domestic reform condemns it as a guide to world politics. The world as a whole has never resembled the delicately integrated democracy which Britain developed in the three centuries following the civil wars – nor have more than a tiny minority of the states within it. *Leviathan* is still a better handbook for foreign policy than *Fabian Essays*.

An understanding of the power element in politics is the first necessity for a sound foreign policy. The trade union movement, as the other main contributor to British socialism, can still, as so often in the past, go some way towards filling this gap in Fabian theory. But the trade union movement is even more afflicted by parochialism, and it tends to intervene in the formation of foreign policy to correct errors rather than to give positive direction.

The major positive influences on Labour Party thinking about world affairs have come from neither the Fabians nor the trade unions, but from the liberal-nonconformist wing with its bias towards pacifism, and the neo-Marxist wing, stemming from Continental social democracy and communism.

Because the Party as a whole lacks any systematic theory of world affairs, it has too often fallen victim to the besetting sin of all progressive opposition movements – utopianism. In particular, it tends to discount the power element in politics, seeing it as a specific evil of the existing system rather than a generic characteristic of politics as such. The liberal utopian believes that if left to themselves men will automatically act for the common interest. The Marxist utopian exaggerates the influence of economic factors on human behaviour and believes that all social evils stem from a bad system of property relations. In both cases depreciation of the power factor entails an inadequate understanding of the techniques of power.

Conservative movements which represent the ruling class have the opposite temptation. For them the exercise of power easily becomes an end in itself and the sole aim of all political activity. In Mannheim's words: 'The Conservative type of knowledge originally is the sort of knowledge giving practical control. It consists of habitual orientations towards those factors which are immanent in the present situation.' Thus it makes obsolescent administrative techniques serve as a substitute for policy in a changing world.

The foreign policies of the British parties bear out these generalizations. The Conservatives have a congenital grasp of the rules of thumb for protecting British interests as defined in the Victorian heyday. But they are slow to recognize changes in those interests and even slower to understand changes in the world within which their rules of thumb must be applied.

The Labour Party, on the other hand, has always been more alive to change in world affairs than to continuity. It is highly sensitive to the economic factors in international life. But it tends to see power politics as a disease peculiar to capitalism and to underestimate or misjudge the power factors in a given situation. At worst it is so little conscious of Britain's national interests that its attention can be attracted to world affairs only by high-flown formulas which quickly lose their relevance. Particularly when the Labour Party is in office, foreign policy becomes the last refuge of utopianism.

For the utopian, Heaven is always round the corner, every evil has a single cause and thus a single cure – there is always 'One Way Only'. Socialist attitudes to war provide many examples. Esperanto has always been popular among socialists on the grounds that nations would cease to fight one another if they all spoke the same language. Though war is at least 3,000 years older than capitalism, many socialists believe that capitalism is the only cause of war, and that therefore the Soviet Union could not commit aggression because it has a 'socialist' economy. Others maintain that the only serious danger of war springs from disparities between the living standards of the peoples; yet it is difficult to find a single war in modern times which was caused primarily by such disparities.

Between the wars this type of utopianism had a damaging influence on Labour's attitude to world affairs. Despite the contribution of the two Labour governments towards the maintenance of collective security through the League of Nations – above all in the Geneva Protocol – the first great crisis of collective security in Manchuria swept the Party into an ostrich-like policy of total war-resistance. In 1934 the trade unions forced the Party back to collective security and in 1935 Bevin led a crushing attack against the pacifism of Lansbury and the pseudo-revolutionary naïveté of the Socialist League. Yet much Labour propaganda continued pacifist in spirit right up to the outbreak of war, and the Party's attitude towards rearmament remained equivocal.

Most British socialists had been preaching for years that war was the inevitable consequence of capitalism and that no capitalist government could be trusted to use power for peaceful ends. This belief made nonsense of the Labour Party's policy for maintaining collective security through the League of Nations, which was indeed from that point of view an 'international burglars' union', as Sir Stafford Cripps maintained. But the bulk of the Party, while believing in the intrinsic wickedness of capitalism, expected capitalist states in the League to behave more altruistically than states have ever behaved in history. The League of Nations failed, as Arthur Henderson said, not because its machinery was imperfect, but because its members would not use that machinery against their own conception of their national interests. But when have states ever shown such altruism?

Parochialism also played its part. The shortcomings of British conservatism always stood between the Labour Party and the foreign scene. In the twenties many English socialists thought Britain more responsible than Germany for the First World War. In the thirties they thought the City of London responsible for Hitler. This sort of parochialism survived the Second World War: in the fifties a Labour Party Conference cheered the statement that Churchill was responsible for Stalinism in Russia. And it is not confined to socialists in Britain. Republicans in the USA maintain that the Democratic administration is responsible for communism in China.

These criticisms of the Labour Party's attitude to world affairs do not apply to the foreign policy of the two brief prewar Labour governments and still less to the postwar foreign policy of Ernest Bevin, a man with those qualities of character, judgement and imagination which go to make a great foreign secretary. But they are still valid for the bulk of the Party membership. Indeed, Bevin's foreign policy never obtained wholehearted approval from the more enthusiastic socialists in the Party, and many of those who did approve it believed that it was not to any significant degree a socialist policy. Thus the Party as a whole gave only reluctant support to the government's handling of Great Power relations, though it took genuine pride in the government's Commonwealth and colonial policy – above all, the transfer of power in India.

There is no doubt that the Labour government, because it was socialist, showed far more understanding and sympathy for the revolutionary trends in Asia and Africa than the Conservative opposition. That Britain is now the one white country with genuine friends in Asia is due to the speed with which power was transferred in India and the economic assistance which the new states received: both were opposed by the Conservatives. The government showed similar understanding for the Chinese revolution, though the fruits of this policy will be slow to mature. British influence was instrumental towards changing Dutch policy towards Indonesia. It is easy to say Britain should have done more to change French policy in Indo-China in the same way, but at the critical time de Gaulle was the French Prime Minister and British relations with France were already strained over Syria.

The contrast between achievement in this sphere and the disappointment in the wider field of world affairs is not, however, due to a sudden failure of socialist principle in dealing with power politics, for in its handling of the postwar situation the Labour government showed both an understanding and a moral strength which owed a great deal to socialist conviction.

The essence of British socialism lies not in its contingent analysis or techniques, but in its determination to apply moral principles to social life. It belongs to that stream of Christian thought which, while insisting that the individual human personality is an end in itself – indeed the only temporal end in itself – believes that all men are brothers, and must realize their brotherhood in this world by creating a society in which they enjoy an equal right and duty to freedom and responsibility. It is in this sense that our socialism is inseparable from democracy.

As a political programme, socialism developed during the nineteenth century in a number of industrialized European democracies as a protest against economic conditions which prevented working men from enjoying the freedom Liberalism claimed to have won for them in the political field. The analysis it made of those economic conditions and the techniques it invented to change them are still relevant to societies which resemble the industrial capitalist democracies of the nineteenth century, but elsewhere they have less guidance to offer. Confronted by modern American capitalism or by primitive peasant societies, socialists must make a new analysis and develop new techniques by which to fulfil their moral principles. This is even more necessary in dealing with the affairs of the world as a whole.

By choosing the phrase 'Social Democracy' to distinguish their policy from that of other parties, socialists assume that society has already realized political democracy. But in world affairs the political foundations on which the theory of social democracy is built have yet to be laid. Indeed the basic problem which socialists face in the world as a whole is almost the opposite of that which they have hitherto faced in national societies. Instead of adjusting the economic system to realize a community already established in the political field, they must adjust political relations to realize a community already existing in the technological field. They must build a world society before they can build a socialist world.

The problem is primarily political, not economic or social. It concerns the acquisition, organization and distribution of power. Power is not, of course, the only reality in world affairs. But it is a pervasive reality which has its own laws and fixes the limits within which moral criteria can operate. The central problem of politics arises from the fact that every time a political entity grows in size, strength or solidarity, it tends to obscure the fundamental brotherhood of its members with the members of other entities and thus to license immoral behaviour towards them. *Un bon père de famille est capable de tout.* 'If we had done for ourselves what we have done for Italy,' said Cavour, 'what scoundrels we would have been.'

In foreign as in domestic affairs, socialists should aim at changing the existing system so as to realize the fundamental brotherhood of all men and to check the selfish will to power. It is a fact that power tends to corrupt, but it is also a fact that men and even governments may resist corruption without sacrificing power. The urge to brotherhood is no less real a political fact than the will to power. In social as in personal life, moral progress is possible, although it is not automatic. Here the socialist stands midway between the liberal optimist and the conservative pessimist. In domestic affairs, since socialists already operate within a framework of law, they can make the necessary changes by consent through legislation. But in world affairs law is rarely able to override power and power is frequently exercised in its crudest form as physical force.

Many socialists believe that the political entities from which a world society must be built are social classes or political movements extending across the frontiers of nation states. This belief has always been a basic principle of communist theory. It was Sir Stafford Cripps' reason for opposing sanctions against Italy in 1935. It often appeared in Labour criticism of Bevin's foreign policy.

In fact, however, the world has so long been divided into geographical units, each developing at a different rate and in a different direction, that there is little basis of interest or sentiment to unite classes occupying roughly similar positions in the social pattern of their various states.

The industrial proletariat, to which this theory is usually applied, is comparatively unimportant except in Western Europe and the United States of America. Even where the proletariat is a major element in its nation state, it does not automatically agree either in theory or practice with the proletariat of other states – still less with the peasant population of its own state.

Though the majority of workers in Britain and Scandinavia support socialism, their comrades in France and Italy are Communists, while in North America they believe in free enterprise capitalism. In Argentina they form the backbone of General Perón's dictatorship. Further disagreements appear on practical problems. Italian and Polish miners can testify that trade unionists are as anxious as employers to protect their livelihood from foreign competition. The Lancashire textile worker joins the Lancashire mill-owner in opposing the common interests of textile workers and employers in Japan. Thus the popular injunction to side in all cases with the workers is no guide to foreign policy.

A policy based on socialist solidarity is still more difficult to apply. Democratic socialism is even less widespread and powerful than trade unionism and even more coloured by national interests. Every democratic socialist party aims primarily at achieving power in its own nation state and is thus obliged to consider the interests of its own state first. Indeed, to the extent that the internal structure of a given state satisfies the need of the workers within it, to that extent its socialist party will tend to put the national interest before international solidarity. It is no accident that in their approach to European unity since 1945 the socialist parties of Britain and Scandinavia have been most conservative –for they have most to conserve. Economic factors reinforce the trend towards nationalism in a governing socialist party; in a world predominantly capitalist, national economic planning may often be inconsistent with forms of international co-operation a *laisser-faire* government would be quite willing to accept.

The fact is that the nation state is by far the most important political entity in world affairs. Nationalism is the one force strong enough to defeat all comers, whether the imperialism of the past or the totalitarianism of the present.

Many British socialists share the liberal belief that every nation state is a moral entity with natural rights and duties which are ultimately compatible with the rights and duties of other nation states. But nation states are political entities, not moral entities; with interests and desires, not rights and duties. Liberal theory gives all states the right to security. But the security of Russia's western frontier is incompatible with the security of Germany's eastern frontier, and both Russia's security and Germany's security are incompatible with the existence of Poland as a nation state.

The relations of nation states are determined primarily by their power to pursue their interests, and they usually conceive their interests in narrowly selfish terms. The influence of a British Labour government in world affairs will in the first place depend on the power at its command and on the skill with which it uses that power. What then is the most helpful path towards a world society?

Orthodox Labour theory maintains that a world society can best be created by establishing the rule of law through a universal organization like the League of Nations or the United Nations; within this general framework of international order nations can be brought into closer and more lasting co-operation through regional or functional institutions like OEEC or the Atlantic Pact.

At the present time international order is at once more necessary and more difficult to establish than ever before. Modern technology has both united and shrunk the world. Nation states are becoming ever stronger and closer to one another. Events in one part of the world immediately affect power relationships in all other parts. In particular, any local war may develop rapidly into a world war in which new weapons of mass destruction threaten even the survival of the human race. All states have – and recognize – a powerful common interest in preventing war and economic crisis.

On the other hand, many parts of the world are undergoing revolutionary changes on a scale which occurs only once in a millennium. In non-Communist Asia and Africa, the peoples are growing faster than their food production. They are demanding at once national independence, freedom from white control and a rapid rise in living standards. The rest of Asia and Eastern Europe is organized under a totalitarian regime which believes itself destined to rule the world. The United States of America, economically the most powerful of all countries has leapt in a few years from isolationism to active participation in world affairs.

Socialists are by nature sensitive to these changes, as the Labour government's policy in Asia has proved. Here too, however, the besetting sin of utopianism is always offering its temptations. Too often socialists tend to imagine that changes are morally or practically desirable simply because they are changes. Men reared in the doctrine of automatic progress cannot help feeling that everything that will be will be right. But most historical changes are morally neutral. It is difficult to maintain that the brotherhood of men is better realized in Eastern Europe under a 'people's democracy' than it was under the Austro-Hungarian Empire.

Moreover, those who imagine they are jumping on the bandwagon of history often find that they have chosen the wrong vehicle. The world is going through profound changes, but it is difficult to interpret these changes rightly and impossible to predict their outcome. Many of the visible trends contradict one another. The century of the common man is also the era of the rape of the masses and of the managerial revolution. If economic man is dead in Europe he is deified in America. Most European interpretations are wrong because they use terms derived from Europe's own experience in the last hundred years. Not only the Webbs in 1935 but even Professor Carr in 1951 can describe Soviet Communism in terms of nineteenth-century European trends towards economic planning. But the striking thing about the world revolution is that everywhere the differences from European precedent are more important than the similarities. European categories crumble when applied to what is going on in Asia, Russia, and America. The same slump which produced Hitler in Europe produced Roosevelt in the USA. Keynesian economics does not explain the problem of unemployment in India.

While these great changes are still in progress there is a danger in creating international institutions which attempt to set a rigid pattern for relations between the powers. Unless international institutions allow for major changes, they will not only break down, but even increase the danger of world conflict. The juridical approach to international affairs is especially dangerous, since international law reflects a pattern of power which is changing daily. An international system must be founded on recognized common interests or a stable pattern of power – or both. It may then develop habits of co-operation which enable it to survive when the basis of interest or power has disappeared. But the development of common interests or the establishment of a stable power pattern must precede and not follow the creation of rigid legal or institutional forms.

The United Nations Assembly, for example, has assumed a universal authority, although decisions may be taken by a majority of states with little knowledge of or interest in the issues at stake and representing a minority both of people and of power. By its handling of the problems posed by Chinese intervention in the Korean War, the United Nations has already weakened its prestige throughout Asia. On the other hand when Britain asked the Security Council to uphold her rights in Persia under international law, the majority of countries were not prepared to support international law in a case which seemed contrary to their sense of justice and history. By claiming a type of authority it is unable to exercise, the United Nations risks discrediting the very idea of international order.

One way out of the dilemma is to create regional institutions linking countries which are likely to have a continuing common interest however the major changes in the world develop. This is a wise course for small states which cannot hope separately to influence world affairs. But it carries dangers for a world power like Britain, which needs close co-operation with states in every region. For regional groups can exist only by discrimination against states outside their region. A regional federation does not necessarily contribute towards the creation of a world society. Indeed, the most dangerous conflicts in the world at present lie primarily between the two great continental federations, the United States of

America and the USSR. The Commonwealth is the exception which proves this rule. Membership of the Commonwealth does not limit co-operation with states outside it precisely because the Commonwealth has no separate institutions.

Throughout its period of office, the Labour government was severely handicapped by the absolute and relative decline in Britain's power. Peace found the ruins of Britain's nineteenth-century *imperium* strewn throughout a power vacuum which was flanked by two jealous continental superstates, each immensely stronger than before the war. But for the first few years Britain's weakness was masked by the prestige of victory, by the even greater decline of other European states, by Russia's exhaustion, and by America's readiness to accept Britain's advice until she found her feet. Thus, though even Britain's survival as an independent state was in jeopardy, the skill, patience and understanding of the Labour government made British foreign policy the main constructive element in world affairs. And it was largely British statesmanship which not only carried the world through the emergencies of the postwar crisis, but also laid some foundations for a lasting world order.

The period of Bevin's main achievement was pre-eminently the period of the Big Three, a trinity to which Britain belonged more by prestige and diplomatic skill than by right of power.

Bevin saw immediately that the power vacuum between Russia and the USA presented the Soviet rulers with opportunities for expansion which if taken would make a third world war inevitable. He had become familiar with Communist aims and techniques in the course of his trade union life – the gibe that he thought the Soviet Union a breakaway from the Transport and General Workers' Union had that element of truth. But he never allowed this to obscure his appraisal of Russia's interests as a state, and he understood far better than most what dangers would follow a failure of the Big Three to create a lasting framework of co-operation while they were still the only world powers of consequence.

Filling the power vacuum by economic aid and political integration was a prime aim of his policy. For a time he believed that Britain, as the only remaining power in the vacuum, might organize it into a third force based on co-operation between Western Europe and the Commonwealth. But experience soon showed that the vacuum could not achieve either economic recovery or military security without prolonged support from the USA. Bevin's greatest personal contribution was in helping to guide America's entry into the power vacuum and in resisting Soviet expansion – largely by diplomatic bluff – until America was firmly committed there. Indeed, his achievement in peace from 1945 to 1948 was comparable with Churchill's in war from 1940 to 1941.

The techniques by which he helped to build the necessary unity against Soviet expansion – and his failures in this field, above all in the Middle East – are too well known to need recounting here. Indeed, Bevin's very achievement has encouraged the belief that in the years ahead all that is required of a Labour foreign secretary is to continue Bevin's work along the lines he himself set down.

In particular the Cold War is so prominent in popular imagination that many people see the future problem essentially as to build unity throughout the 'free', i.e. non-Stalinist, world against Soviet expansion. The conventional stereotype is somewhat as follows: the rearmament of the NATO powers, extended to cover the Middle East as well as Europe, will safeguard the frontiers of the free world against direct military aggression. The only remaining problem in world affairs will then be to protect the free world against subversion from within. Stalinist policy will aim at splitting the capitalist world by exploiting its three inherent contradictions: the conflict between classes within each state, the conflict between the imperialist states and the colonial peoples they exploit, and the economic and political conflicts among the imperialist states themselves – in particular between the victors and vanquished in the Second World War. In order to maintain unity in the free world against Stalinist subversion, the conflict between classes must be ended by social reform: the conflict between the rich white industrialized peoples of the Atlantic community and the poor coloured peasant peoples of Asia and Africa must be ended by the grant of freedom and economic aid. Internal rivalry between the non-Stalinist powers must be ended by the development of functional co-operation through organs such as OEEC and the Atlantic Pact. This picture is particularly attractive to British socialists since every element in it is consonant with socialist tradition, and Britain is well equipped to play the central part, since the Commonwealth spans the continents and Britain is a key member of both the Atlantic and the European communities.

In 1950 the Labour Party launched as the central element in its foreign policy the concept of a World Plan for Mutual Aid. The idea of raising living standards in the underdeveloped areas appeals to one of the strongest elements in socialist idealism. It is indeed the twentieth-century version of the White Man's Burden. But besides being most desirable for moral reasons, it might help to solve many political and economic problems of the world revolution.

By raising living standards in the underdeveloped areas – in itself most desirable for moral and political reasons – it would expand purchasing power to match the immense increase in the world's industrial productivity and so help to bridge the gaps in international trade. For many years most of the West European countries will need more dollars than they can earn by direct exports to the dollar area. It is far better that they should earn dollars by selling equipment to Asia and Africa than receive dollars as gifts from the USA. If America gave the underdeveloped areas dollars to spend in offshore purchases of capital goods in Europe, every dollar would do twice the work it did under Marshall Aid. Moreover, when Japanese and German production is injected into the stream of world trade, cut-throat competition will wreck the nascent political unity of the 'free world' unless markets can be expanded by some such method. Finally, the terms of trade will continue to worsen for Britain unless primary production increases to keep pace with the rise of population in Africa and Asia. Britain has thus strong reasons of national interest to urge international investment in the underdeveloped areas.

This general picture of a socialist foreign policy for Britain, besides its obvious appeal to socialist idealism, is closely adapted to the power realities of the present time. But unfortunately the present pattern of power relations is about to undergo important changes and some of the assumptions of the theory are at variance with the facts.

In the first place, the policies of welfare socialism as applied with such success in Britain and Scandinavia demand a level of civic responsibility and administrative competence which scarcely exists outside the Anglo-Saxon world and northern Europe. Under British socialism the welfare state is achieved by fiscal methods. This presumes that on the whole citizens are prepared to pay taxes and that the state machinery is efficient and honest enough to prevent tax evasion and to administer great funds successfully. This has not been the case in many parts of Europe. Most of the techniques of physical planning and control which Britain has developed during and since the war break down in a country like France, where most people see neither duty nor interest in obeying the government.

What is true of southern Europe is even more true of Asia and Africa. And if the methods of British socialism are unable to produce social justice in many parts of the world, those of American capitalism are even less appropriate. The buoyant psychology of American business has few parallels outside the USA, as the Marshall Aid administration soon discovered. The economic pre-conditions of rapid capital accumulation do not exist anywhere in Asia or Africa. There is no reason to believe that social justice in the underdeveloped areas will be built by British or American methods – if it is built at all.

In the second place, when the peoples of Asia and Africa win freedom from white control they will not necessarily cease to conflict with the white countries or with one another. All the problems of power politics which have tormented Europe for the last 600 years will then arise anew. It is already obvious that some of the new Asian states do not wish to take sides in the Cold War – the Stalinist bloc has at least as good a chance of winning their support as the democratic bloc. On the democratic side the Commonwealth is one of the most favourable factors. But South Africa's native policy is already incompatible with British policy in the African colonies and may soon become incompatible with keeping the Asian states in the Commonwealth.

The World Plan for Mutual Aid is impeccable in aim and general conception. But the difficulties of carrying it out will be immense. The scale of outside investment required to raise standards of living in the underdeveloped areas is far beyond the capacity of any combination of countries which excludes the United States. A United Nations report in 1951 estimates that an annual rise of 2 per cent in the standard of living would require an annual investment of £3,800 million pounds. Moreover, the political and administrative problems of ensuring that the money is well spent are quite as formidable as the problem of obtaining the money from America. In any case it is doubtful whether an annual rise of 2 per cent in the standard of living would by itself win Asia and Africa to the Western side. All these difficulties are no argument against doing what can be done in this direction. Every pound or dollar spent can mean the alleviation of some human misery. But the disillusion will be catastrophic if exaggerated expectations are aroused.

Most important of all, the pattern of power politics in the period ahead will differ greatly from that of the last six years. British influence was predominant in the non-Stalinist world immediately after the war because Britain was the only power in the vacuum and the United States was sinking back into an isolationism tempered by large-scale welfare activity. From 1947 onwards, when America began to use her power in Europe and other parts of the vacuums, she did so mainly as a result of British diplomacy, and her policies were fully compatible if not identical with Britain's. Except in Palestine, every American irruption into Eurasian affairs up to the middle of 1950 was co-ordinated with British policy.

The Korean War brought a fundamental change in the nature of American intervention. America provided 90 per cent of the United Nations' forces in Korea – over a quarter of a million men – and suffered heavy casualties. The average American citizen came to realize for the first time that his personal future was at stake in what the administration was doing abroad. Congress began to interfere more energetically in the formation of foreign policy. The fact that America's prime interest in Eurasian affairs is strategic rather than political or economic, together with the exigencies of party warfare in the United States, shifted the decisive influence on policy-making from the State Department to the Pentagon. The internal impact of rearmament, far greater than that of the earlier foreign welfare programmes like Marshall Aid, meant that ordinary Americans became fully conscious of the immense power their country wielded and increasingly intolerant of foreign criticism of the way they used it.

Many English socialists are watching this development with a gloom fortified by national jealousy or doctrinal suspicion. Some take the view that Britain should withhold co-operation unless her views are met, on the grounds that she is indispensable to America's foreign policy. But while America is growing in strength and independence new powers are arising inside the vacuum created by the war. Germany in Europe and Japan in the Far East offer the American strategists additional if not alternative bases for their policy in Eurasia. The fact is that even as Britain's absolute strength is growing, her bargaining power with the United States is dwindling.

The rise of Germany and Japan may change the nature of the Cold War. The point may come at which the Soviet Union will have to decide whether to seek agreement with Britain and America to protect herself from Germany and Japan or with Germany and Japan to further her designs against Britain and America. It is too soon to feel confident that Germany and Japan will feel a strong moral obligation or material interest to side with the Atlantic powers if Russia offers them tempting concessions. Indeed, Russia has far more to offer Germany than the West – not only trade, but also political unity, including if necessary the return of the territories lost to Poland.

Germany remains the most dangerous problem for British policy in future. Britain cannot ignore the possibility that Germany may seek national unity either by war with Russia or by alliance with Russia. It has been fashionable to see the answer in integrating Western Germany into some form of West European union. Britain herself has been unwilling to join such a union for fear of losing her independence outside Europe. But it is already obvious that if European unity is built without Britain it will be dominated by Germany. As Germany revives Britain may be compelled to integrate herself more deeply with Europe than is compatible with her other economic and political interests. Indeed, America is the only state with sufficient power to spare for correcting the balance in Western Europe. But many Americans believe that Germany's revival would justify their withdrawal from Europe instead of requiring them to play a more active part in Europe themselves.

Relations with the United States have thus become the central problem of British foreign policy. But material and moral factors severely limit the range of choice. Strategically Britain needs America even more than America needs Britain. Economically, though Britain might dispense with direct American aid at home, her plans for economic development abroad demand large-scale dollar aid. Politically, America's interests are far closer to those of Britain than the interests of any other present or potential ally; indeed, the Commonwealth would not survive a rupture between Britain and the USA. Morally, as a progressive democracy America is far closer to Britain than is Western Europe, southern Asia, or, of course, the Soviet Union. Anglo-American unity is indeed a condition of Britain's survival.

The final major change in the postwar pattern of power politics may come through a disruption of the Stalinist bloc. Tito's defection was premature in the sense that Russia has probably been able to eliminate the main sources of Titoism in the rest of Eastern Europe before the world situation gave them a chance of success. But the present alliance between the Soviet Union and Communist China is based on a very temporary congruence of interest. On the other hand, if China does separate herself from the Soviet Union a settlement in eastern Asia will not necessarily become much simpler.

One thing at least is certain. The situation of 1945–50, in which the Labour Party's foreign policy came of age, has gone for good. Too many minds are still dominated by the picture of two continental super-states glowering at each other over a power vacuum in which Britain is the only strong state. The emergence of Germany, Japan and China as independent powers has already changed that picture. Within a few years southern Asia, the Middle East and Africa may also take the stage in their own right. Thus the vision of a world shaped almost exclusively by Anglo-Saxon policy is fading at the very moment when it seems most likely to become reality. It is much more probable that the future will bring a return to a world of many powers in which decisions are made by the methods of traditional power politics. If this is so, conventional diplomacy will come into its own again and the adjustment of national differences by negotiation and compromise will become more urgent than the construction of international institutions or the execution of moral blueprints.

These suggestions are offered without excessive confidence. The known facts are always so small a proportion of total reality that the fruits of scientific method should never be taken as rational grounds for defeatism or over-confidence. Three predictions at least are fairly safe. Britain's influence on world affairs in the immediate future will depend more than ever on her material power to help a friend or harm an enemy. Britain's fundamental interest in unity with the United States will remain supreme. And an understanding of power politics will be more than ever necessary to a successful socialist foreign policy.

BEYOND POWER POLITICS

(from *Fabian International Essays*, Hogarth Press, 1956)

If two states have an interest in working together on one issue, they have an interest in avoiding conflict on other issues which might damage such co-operation. Thus an interest in co-operation for even limited purposes creates an interest in consultation in a much wider field. The NATO interest in European defence promoted a discussion of France's problems in Indo-China, and should also promote discussion of Britain's problems in Cyprus. Such consultation may not lead to common policies in the wider field – but it at least gives governments the opportunity for choosing policies which are compatible with those of their friends. Conflicts of policy are due as often to ignorance as to intent. Though after consultation governments will not necessarily agree, at least they will not disagree unless necessary.

Over a period of time, co-operation and consultation are likely to lead to a new relationship between the states concerned – something almost justifying the word 'integration'. The individuals concerned at both the ministerial and departmental level develop habits of working together which are increasingly hard to break. And they develop a vested interest in co-operation which may survive change in the circumstances which originally brought them together. In fact the countries in the group become increasingly interdependent.

Thus, though limited in their membership and functions, organizations such as NATO, OEEC and the Columbo Plan make an indispensable contribution towards the development of an international society. They provide the social tissue without which a sense of international community cannot survive the pressure of national interests. And they exert an influence over the behaviour of nation states which does limit in various degrees their ability as well as their desire to use their power for purely selfish ends.

The supreme advantage of the intergovernmental method is that it is less likely to produce the type of closed international society which simply raises the traditional problems of power politics to a new and more dangerous level. By its very nature the supranational or federal group creates new divisions in the world as a whole even as it removes divisions among its own members. At this particular point in history the most dangerous threat to peace would be too sharp a crystallization of the obvious division between the rich white peoples of the Atlantic basin and the poor coloured peoples of Africa and Asia. Each group stands to lose immensely by emphasizing the things which unite it internally as a community of culture instead of the things which unite it externally with mankind as a whole.

The intergovernmental method tends to discourage closed international groupings. By choosing its partners according to the specific interests it wishes to promote, a state can spread its roots far and wide throughout the world, and act as a link between other states which have no direct contact. For example, Britain's dual role as a member both of NATO and of the Commonwealth has enabled her to bring Indian and American views on Asia closer together. Similarly India's contacts with the West through the Commonwealth and with the Soviet bloc through the Bandung Conference have helped her to play a constructive role in the Cold War. Of course, commitment to one group for one function is liable to exclude a commitment to a rival or hostile group with the same function – but it does not exclude commitments to countries which are not hostile even for the same function. Britain's military commitment to NATO does not exclude her from fulfilling quite different military responsibilities inside the Commonwealth. Doubt whether the European Defence Community would have left France a similar freedom was a major reason for its rejection by the French Assembly.

At first sight the untidy complex mass of overlapping international organizations cries out for pruning and rationalization. Yet a closer study will usually show that something immensely valuable would be sacrificed by such a tidying up. For example, there was a move a few years ago to let NATO take over OEEC since the membership of the two bodies was almost identical. Almost, but not quite. And in fact NATO would have lost as much through the exclusion of the neutral countries from Atlantic economic co-operation as Sweden, Switzerland and Austria themselves. In fact this untidy proliferation of international tissue provides a much tougher and more resilient basis for world order than an artificial symmetry.

The objection is often made that co-operation between governments cannot provide an absolute guarantee against secession. The interests which originally stimulated co-operation may change, or governments may come to power which take a different view of those interests. At most co-operation over a period may accumulate a number of marginal disincentives against a breakaway. Only statesmanship and good fortune can ensure that the group is not subjected to strains powerful enough to overcome such disincentives.

All this is true enough. Yet on balance it constitutes yet another argument in favour of the intergovernmental approach. Even supranational institutions allow the possibility of secession in practice though they deny it in theory. They simply ensure that if secession takes place, it inflicts far more damage on other members of the group. And by enforcing uniformity in fields where those concerned might well differ without harming the common interests of the group, they narrow the field within which statesmanship can avoid dangerous strains.

In fact the intergovernmental approach is far better suited to allow the adjustments which a changing situation makes desirable. And since this is above all an age of change, flexibility is an essential element in any international organization. Any approach to world order must allow the possibility of peaceful change – what Jaspers has called the possibility of continuous self-rectification through the voluntary renunciation of power – both by members of the group and by the group as a whole. This is indeed one aspect of the eternal conflict between freedom and authority. And it is a powerful argument against the juridical approach to international organization. A social order must reflect the existing pattern of power relations among its component parts; but it must also be capable of adaptation to any change in that pattern. A closed supranational grouping carries real dangers in this respect. Besides setting rigid limits to the freedom of its members to associate with others outside the group, its juridical constitution is bound to reflect too faithfully the relations between its members at the moment of its foundation. For example EDC was originally conceived by France as a means of controlling Germany's revival. But in the interval between its conception in 1949 and its completion in 1952, Western Germany had already recovered so much strength that EDC was more likely to be dominated by Germany than to control Germany. And after its rejection by France in 1954, Germany herself had developed so many interests outside Europe that she had become reluctant to confine herself too narrowly inside a single continent.

Today the major unsolved problem in Europe is that of German reunification. A supranational link between the Federal Republic and her western neighbours would create so direct and obvious a conflict between German reunification and European union that Bonn's co-operation with the West would be subjected to dangerous strains. The present system by which Bonn is associated with NATO leaves a latitude for negotiation with Russia which is essential whether or not German unity can ultimately be achieved.

In the world as a whole the major problem is to construct a system which will permit the Asian and African peoples to carry through their double revolution against poverty and white control without coming into conflict with the richer white nations. Here the danger of too rigid a pattern of association between Asia and the West is more obvious still. Only the loosest framework of relations is likely to survive the gigantic political, social, and economic changes through which Asia is passing. It is essential to avoid pressing diplomacy into a rigid mould which later developments are bound to crack.

It may be dangerous to snatch temporary opportunities for tying Asian countries into military alliances with the West if the general trend of their development is in a contrary direction. In the economic field, some well-meaning Western proposals assume a willingness in the Asian countries to accept a type of external direction and control which is bound in time to appear as imperialism in a new dress. And in general, the sense of a common Asian unity *vis à vis* the white countries is so important a factor that the advantages the West might gain through special associations with particular Asian countries must be weighed against the possible damage to a wider *entente* with Asia as a whole, if such associations are resented outside the countries concerned.

In fact the transition from a polity of power to a polity of consent based on international order poses difficult problems of judgement at every stage. The dynamics of power politics continue to function during the evolution of a system which is intended ultimately to transcend them. Just as in the mixed economy typical of a democratic transition to socialism the laws of capitalist development continue to apply so far as the profit motive influences economic behaviour, so, even while governments are trying to construct a new international polity by collective action, their behaviour remains governed to a large extent by their conception of their national interests and by the physical power which they can mobilize to secure those interests. Different states, or different parties within each state, may legitimately differ in their analysis of a situation, in the priority they give to the national and international strands in their policy, in preferring a larger community at the expense of closer integration, or vice versa. Often the most difficult choice of all is between the use of power and the pursuit of consent when the ultimate aims of the other party are uncertain – British Guiana and the Suez base provide interesting examples.

There are grounds for believing that circumstances may melt the present rigidity of Communist international doctrine, and undermine Russia's present confidence. Already the existence of independent Communist parties in China and Yugoslavia has compelled Khrushchev to surrender the total authority which Stalin once exercised within the Communist world. Sooner or later the latent conflicts between rival Communist Parties may erupt as conflicts between the states they rule.

But the only sure basis for long-term optimism depends on the success of the non-Communist countries in mastering the conflicts among themselves. For if we refuse to verify Communist predictions of our disintegration, we shall not only be immune to further Communist pressure, we shall also shake the doctrinal certainty which Communist experience in the first forty years since the October Revolution has done more to confirm than to weaken. Only then will the Communists have any real incentive to modify their opinions and their policies.

For the time being the Communist bloc provides the rest of the world with just one more argument for transcending its own international anarchy. In fact, this may prove the strongest argument of all. Fear is unfortunately still the most potent stimulus to international action, and a visible danger inspires a livelier reaction than a theoretical argument. In the days when herrings were carried back alive to harbour from the fishing grounds, nearly a third were liable to die on the long journey. Finally the fishermen solved the problem by putting a dogfish in the herring hold. Though it might eat hundreds, it saved the lives of thousands more by keeping them on the move. Professor Toynbee may well be right in predicting that future historians will see Communism as playing an indispensable role in the twentieth century – as the dogfish in the tank of herring.

NATIONALISM AND LIBERTY

Privately Circulated, 1956

Under the liberal theories current before the Second World War, the right to national self-determination was regarded as one of the most basic human liberties – as an essential part of the right to democratic self-government. Nationalism has grown up together with democracy in most parts of the world, since it is above all a popular force; Liberals could scarcely avoid assuming that the democratic nation state was the highest form of social organization, and that lasting peace could best be secured through the free co-operation of nation states under the rule of law. With characteristic optimism they believed that the interests of nation states were not only compatible but also mutually supporting, so the difficulties encountered by earlier forms of state in the anarchy of power politics would disappear through the acceptance by these new 'natural' societies of a code of conduct designed to express their enlightened self-interest.

The Liberals' optimism about the natural community of national interests in world politics has proved no more justified than their optimism about the natural community of individual interests in a market economy. Bitter experience since Versailles has shown that the principle of national self-determination is often inoperable in practice, and when operable, often incompatible with the economic interests of the people concerned. Worse still, the association of nationalism with democracy has made the traditional international polity almost impossible to work. The diplomatic reconciliation of conflicting state interests was a comparatively simple task in the eighteenth century. In those days state power was vested exclusively in a narrow ruling class whose culture was often international rather than national, and whose interests were not deeply engaged in relations between their state and others. Diplomatists of goodwill had usually both the time and the authority to compose differences between their governments.

Universal suffrage and the industrial revolution have transformed this situation. Modern diplomatists have to deal with the immediate and vital interests of whole peoples. They have to work under the fitful and excited stare of a public opinion which is rarely well-informed. They scarcely ever have time for that delicate manipulation of the balance of power which the eighteenth century is said to have brought to a fine art. It is precisely because nationalism is a popular force that the nation state cannot survive as the ultimate level of social organization.

The case for some larger entity than the nation state is rarely disputed nowadays. But though nationalism no longer has the same moral cachet as it had a generation ago, it remains the strongest single force in world affairs. All other claimants for popular support fail when they dare to match themselves against nationalism. Neither religious faiths of long standing nor the more recent doctrine of class war have managed to triumph except when they could make nationalism, if not an ally, at least a neutral. In the age of nationalism Khrushchev journeys to Belgrade instead of Henry to Canossa.

A frontal attack on nationalism has no chance of succeeding. The problem is to persuade nation states to consent to limitations on their freedom of action sufficient to secure the fundamental interests of their members. Unless the case for larger international communities can be argued in terms of hard national interest, it is likely to fall when the moment of decision arrives – as, for example, did the European Defence Community. Fortunately the political, economic, and strategic cases for transcending nationalism are much more widely understood today than they were even when the Second World War came to an end.

The political case against a world anarchy of nation states rests on three simple facts. First, the shrinking of the globe under the advance of science, and the disappearance of unclaimed territory for national expansion has brought states so much closer together in time and space that the methods of the Old Diplomacy can no longer adjust state relations in time to meet rapid changes. The tragic predicaments in international politics grow ever more frequent and more hopeless. Second, the staggering increase in the power available to nation states means that their conflicts have become increasingly catastrophic. We have reached a situation in which even a small industrial state could develop the power of destroying human life on the planet. Third, popular interest in the processes of diplomacy has introduced an irrational element into international negotiation which robs governments of the power to compromise as needed. For these three reasons the hopes of eighteenth-century rationalism have no relevance to the world today.

The strategic case against the primacy of the nation state is no less conclusive. Modern warfare requires that defence be organized in depth on an intercontinental scale. Protection against an atomic blitzkrieg depends on having so many bases so widely scattered over so vast an area that the aggressor could never be sure of destroying his victim's power to retaliate in kind. In practice there is no state in the world, not even the USA or the Soviet Union, which could organize the requisite dispersal of bases exclusively on its own territory. For the smaller states between the two colossi the case for allies is stronger still. And a modern alliance will work in war only if it has made all the complicated preparations required in peacetime. Moreover, the cost of modern weapons is so high that no small state can afford to produce a sufficiency for itself out of its own resources.

At the moment Conservatism is fighting a rearguard action against these conclusions by arguing that the threat of thermonuclear retaliation would be sufficient to deter any sort of aggression. This argument is used to discourage too intimate an interdependence in the strategic field in two ways. On the one hand a state with the power to produce its own thermonuclear striking force is tempted to believe that it could possess therein a deterrent capable of guaranteeing absolute national security almost independent of allies. On the other hand a state incapable of mounting its own thermonuclear deterrent is tempted to believe that a promise by the great powers to meet any aggression with thermonuclear retaliation would relieve it of the need to take any steps in its own defence. So nationalism is reviving in the Third Force concept for great powers, and in the form of neutralism for small powers – neutralism is simply nationalism with an inferiority complex.

This sort of confidence in the thermonuclear deterrent is dangerous wishful thinking. For the growing impossibility of a defence against thermonuclear bombardment means that no power will invite thermonuclear destruction by dropping the first H-bomb on an enemy with the power to retaliate, except perhaps in the very last extremity of its own national survival. Once 'atomic saturation' arrives, as is expected within the next ten years, the thermonuclear deterrent will lose most of its effect against local aggression with conventional forces. The case for an international defence community to provide for adequate local defence against major 'conventional' aggression – though tactical atomic weapons would have to be used against military targets – will be immeasurably reinforced by the atomic stalemate.

The economic case against an exclusive nationalism has different force for different states. Any country which depends much on foreign trade, like Britain or most of the continental European countries, has a powerful interest in organizing trade and payments communities at least with its main markets and suppliers of raw materials. And for the smaller countries which have no adequate internal market and lack the resources required to support heavy industry there is a strong case for much closer international co-operation still. Here the main obstacle to progress is not so much conservative reaction as the liberal illusion that the removal of national barriers to the flow of trade will in itself produce better distribution of manpower and resources. But the democratic right of the people to organize its own protection against the mechanical operation of the market has produced national barriers to trade: it is only by planning their adjustment so as to avoid painful dislocations that progress can be made against economic nationalism.

The force of the political, strategic, and economic cases against nationalism is much increased by the Cold War. Indeed perhaps the Cold War can best be seen as a struggle between two approaches towards an international community. The Communists believe that national conflict is inevitable in any form of society except their own – that the disruptive effects of power politics can be overcome only if political and economic power is concentrated at a single centre – the Praesidium of the Communist Party of the Soviet Union. Lasting peace can thus be secured only by the progressive extension of their system until it covers the whole world. It is therefore impossible to distinguish the extension of Communism as a system from the extension of the Soviet Union as a state.

It would be a mistake to write off this approach simply as a cover for Soviet imperialism. The failure of the Second International to maintain its solidarity in face of the First World War led many sincere Socialists to accept the rigid discipline of the Third International when the war ended. In the same way, to the extent that the non-Communist world fails to reconcile its own internal differences, many sincere people who put peace first may be tempted to take the Communist road towards an international society, however high the price in terms of freedom.

In fact, however, the Soviet claim to have ended national conflicts within its own camp is very far from the truth. It is true that under a totalitarian dictatorship national tensions rarely have the opportunity of rupturing the social fabric – the long procession of nationalist Communist Party leaders who have been sent from the constituent republics to the forced labour camps has seen to that. None the less, when the German armies reached the non-Russian parts of the Soviet Union the desertion to their side was astonishing. In 1948 the autonomous republics of the Crimean Tarters and the Chechen-Ingush in the Caucasus were both abolished and their peoples deported on the grounds that they had fought *en masse* with the Germans during the war. It was only the pathological brutality of German occupation policy which saved Stalin from an even larger defection in the Ukraine.

Moreover, the reliance on force to suppress national feeling in the Soviet empire leaves the Russians at a loss once force proves insufficient. The secession of Yugoslavia from the Cominform has proved final and absolute. And the most interesting case is of course Russia's quandary in relation to Communist China. The autonomy of the Chinese Communist Party has been an anomaly in the Soviet system for over twenty years. Now that the Chinese Communist Party controls the destiny of 600 million people on Russia's eastern flank, the problem of how to conduct relations with it is bound to obsess the Soviet leaders. There is already evidence that the Chinese are demanding a very high price in economic aid and territorial concessions in return for adjusting their foreign policies to meet the needs of Soviet strategy. And it is not inconceivable that the experience of genuine negotiation with an independent Communist Party in their own camp may influence the Russians' attitude towards some of the Communist satellites in Eastern Europe. The cold douche received by Khrushchev in Belgrade may shift Soviet policy in either direction. But it is at least safe to say that nationalism is presenting the Soviet leaders with problems no less perplexing than those which face their rivals in the West.

If the Russian attitude towards nationalism is that of the engineer, that of the Western governments fluctuates between that of the lawyer and that of the gardener. Liberal rationalism dies hard, particularly in some parts of Europe, and there is still a widespread belief in the possibility of changing the behaviour of nations for good by juridical formulas. The collapse of EDC and the fading of grandiose plans for a European political community should have taught all but the fanatical enthusiasts that though constitutions can express or confirm a change in the social facts, they cannot in themselves change the facts. There is not at present even among the six continental members of Little Europe sufficient common social tissue to support a formal surrender of national sovereignty by legal statute.

Unfortunately the collapse of hopes for a European federation has induced excessive pessimism on both sides of the Atlantic about the prospects for any form of international community in the West. Yet if progress since the war is measured against the basic needs of the period there is room for satisfaction, though not complacency. Enough has at least been done to protect the democratic world against the sort of breakdowns which might have been expected. Through NATO and the nascent Western European Union an international defence community has been established, and what is more, has been adapted so as to include a formidable recent enemy. Economic co-operation between Europe, North America, and the Commonwealth has saved Europe from the disaster she suffered after the First World War, in spite of much greater damage to her productive apparatus. Western imperialism has in the main adapted itself to the revolt in Asia against poverty and white control. And even in areas where the democratic world has accepted no formal commitments to reconcile its policies a remarkable degree of agreement has in fact been reached. Even in the western Pacific America, Europe and southern Asia no longer argue so fiercely with one another about the principles of policy, however much they still disagree about its practice.

But it would be idle to deny that much of this progress would have been unlikely without the spur of indiscriminate hostility from the Soviet camp. The best proof of progress has been the recent shift in Communist strategy. And the question now arises whether the nature of international co-operation in the democratic world has yet produced enough social tissue to withstand the centrifugal pressure of reviving nationalism when the external counterpressure no longer exists.

In democratic Asia the problem is perhaps less serious than in Europe, since in Asia nation states in the European sense do not yet exist. The Asian revolt against white imperialism like that today in Africa is not primarily a national revolt – it involves broader concepts of race, colour, and religion. And in spite of the prophets of *schadenfreude*, the new Asian states have shown a remarkable capacity for co-operation with one another. Moreover there is still an expanding internal frontier in most of the new Asian states which makes them demand little more of the outside world than the chance to solve their internal problems in peace. Though most of them would be prepared to resist Communist aggression and to seek Western help in so doing, they feel satisfied that such aggression is unlikely unless it can appear to be provoked by Western blunders. Given the West's unwillingness to offer military help in the only form which would be useful – i.e. conventional forces – one can scarcely complain at neutralism in Asia.

The major threat to democratic solidarity comes in the white countries on both sides of the Atlantic which are the home of nationalism. There is a double problem. On the one hand they must create a type of interdependence which will keep them united even if the external threat seems to have disappeared. On the other hand they must ensure that the machinery they create does not prevent rapid adjustments to changes both inside and outside their community.

The double problem arises most acutely over Western Germany. Without Western Germany the defence of the Atlantic community through NATO would become impossible. Moreover, if France thought there was any danger of Germany doing a deal with Russia she would be tempted to bolt the Western camp so as to get to Moscow first. NATO and the Paris Treaties are designed to keep Western Germany in the democratic community. But in accepting Western Germany as an ally the other members of NATO accept a commitment to realize the first aim of German national policy – reunification. Since the atomic stalemate rules out all roads to liberation except diplomacy, Germany can only recover the Soviet Zone by negotiation with Russia – and Russia is most unlikely to surrender her zone if this means advancing NATO frontiers to Poland and Czechoslovakia. Thus Western Germany's commitment to NATO can easily be made to seem a decisive obstacle to the recovery of the Soviet Zone. If this idea became implanted in German minds through undue rigidity in talks with Russia it would plant a time bomb at the heart of the NATO framework.

The danger in any sort of political order is that it tends to reinforce the *status quo* in such a way as to drive all who are dissatisfied with the *status quo* into total opposition. Since this is above all an age of revolutionary change, not only in the political sphere, but also in the techniques of peace and war, the need for flexibility in order is peculiarly great. That is why what Mr George Kennan has called the gardener's approach to international co-operation is so much better than either the engineer's approach of the Communists or the lawyer's approach of the rationalists. Through consultation on all matters of common concern, to co-operation in specified fields of common interest, the democratic nation states are moving towards integration in an organic international community different in kind both from the old-fashioned military alliance and from the old-fashioned political federation. It is true that this type of community contains no guarantees against secession, but the experience of working together so intimately over a period creates new habits of mind, new vested interests in solidarity, which may amount to formidable disincentives against a breakaway.

Nationalism remains the strongest single force, at least in the politics of the Western world. But it need no longer be in the vital issues a destructive force so long as governments take care not to commit their peoples to courses which deny their vital national interests.

CHAPTER TWO

Communism and Social Democracy

As INTERNATIONAL SECRETARY of the Labour Party after the war I was responsible for restoring contact with the Socialist parties in Europe and helping to reorganize the Socialist International. My most urgent task was to help the East European parties to withstand the overwhelming pressure imposed on them by the Soviet Union to merge with the local Communist Parties. In spite of my efforts, one by one they all succumbed: the Red Army was always available to intervene if the Communist secret police proved insufficient.

On the other hand, countries such as Yugoslavia and Albania, which had no Soviet troops on their soil, were able to break away from Soviet control. That is why I later supported military disengagement in Central Europe. We have recently seen that once Gorbachev renounced military intervention, no Communist regime in Eastern Europe was able to survive.

My visits in 1947 to Hungary, Czechoslovakia and Poland taught me the horror of totalitarianism at first hand and gave me an abiding hatred of Stalinism. They also gave me a love and understanding of the East European peoples and of their contribution to European culture. As a result I have always felt that the reunification of Eastern and Western Europe was at least as important as the integration of Western Europe, and that the latter should never be allowed to become an obstacle to the former.

My familiarity with the 'salami tactics', as Rakosi described them, through which the Communist Parties established total control of Eastern Europe, enabled me to recognize the techniques used by Communists and Trotskyites to penetrate the labour movements in the West. I now watch for signs of similar tactics being used against the democratic revolutions which have taken place in Eastern Europe itself.

In 1951 I edited *The Curtain Falls*, in which three East European Socialist leaders who had escaped into exile told how their parties had been destroyed; it carried an enthusiastic foreword from Aneurin Bevan. My own introductory chapter, entitled 'The New Russian Empire', may provide a useful background to the news from Eastern Europe today. I pointed out that in Eastern Europe 'nationalism has been a disruptive force, even when unity was required against a common enemy . . . Almost every country in Eastern Europe contains national minorities from other countries within its frontiers.' That is why Balkanization is so real a threat to the new democracies at present.

My essay on 'Socialism' was one of a series of talks on the European Service of the BBC in 1953 about 'The Unity of European Culture'; T. S. Eliot contributed the talk on 'Literature'. Its main purpose was to stress the essential unity of Eastern and Western Europe. I hope its message may serve as a corrective to the view so widely propagated today that the recent democratic revolution in Eastern Europe is at bottom a triumph for free market capitalism in its assumed guise as the fundamental tradition of the Western world.

'The last time Eastern Europe fought an alien tyranny,' I wrote, 'the danger came from the West and not from the East. . . . Hitler and Mussolini are as much a part of West European history as Bevin and Blum. . . . That is why it is so wrong to make culture the tool of a regional chauvinism. The pharisees of Western culture forget that they owe their political values to a country of south-east Europe and their religious values to a country of the Middle East.'

The national differences and divisions which hampered the East European Socialists in their struggle against Stalinism were equally evident in Western Europe. I tried to describe the problem in an article for the American *New Leader* in 1957. My description of 'European Socialism Today' admits that 'socialism is often as various, confused, and ambiguous as democracy itself. . . . As an international movement it is a community but not an organization, still less a machine. . . . Its only rigid principles are moral imperatives, not political programmes.'

It was still possible at that time to boast that 'the British Labour Party has come to occupy the position in the international socialist movement once held by the German Social Democrats' and to attribute this to its pragmatism and Christian traditions; I had earlier written that the Labour Party owed more to Methodism than to Marxism. Yet in fact the Labour Party has wasted two whole decades since the Second World War in a sectarian civil war, first over Bevanism, then over Bennery. As a result the

German Social Democrats, who settled this argument for themselves by abandoning Marxism at their Bad Godesberg Conference in 1959, have now recovered their leading role not only in both parts of Europe, but even in Latin America too. It is only since Neil Kinnock became its leader in 1983 that the Labour Party has once again taken its international responsibilities seriously.

My confidence in Britain's national homogeneity has since suffered rude shocks from events in Scotland and Northern Ireland. Similarly my praise for the two-party system, as against a multi-party system which leads to the compromises of coalition, would be qualified today by the experience of a decade of Thatcherism, as well as by the spectacle of successful coalitions led by the SPD in Germany.

None the less I showed some prescience in my concluding words. European economic integration has indeed provided 'the external impetus for countries like France and Italy to lay the foundations on which socialism can build.' The Common Market has forced Britain and Denmark to throw in their lot with the Continent. The decomposition of Communism as an international movement has led the French and Italian Communist Parties to break their ties with Moscow. And, more important still, great power diplomacy has led to 'a settlement which reunites Eastern Europe with the West, with profound yet unpredictable consequences on the internal situation of both sides.'

I hope my concluding sentence may prove equally true: 'If European socialism is seen in its historical context, its present state may appear not as old age, but as adolescence.'

THE NEW RUSSIAN EMPIRE

(from *The Curtain Falls*, Lincolns Prager, 1951)

The other day I came across an interesting article on Russian expansionism in the eastern Mediterranean. It was in an American newspaper. The writer was warning Britain that unless she intervened to support Turkey in resisting Russia's demands, the whole of Eastern Europe might be lost to the Russian dictators. He wrote:

> The broken and undulating western frontier of the [Russian] empire, ill-defined in respect of natural boundaries, would call for rectification, and it

would appear that the natural frontier of Russia lies from Danzig or perhaps Stettin to Trieste. And as sure as conquest follows conquest and annexation follows annexation, so sure would the conquest of Turkey by Russia be only the prelude for the annexation of Hungary, Prussia, Galicia, and for the ultimate realization of the Slavonic Empire which certain fanatical Pan-Slavistic philosophers have dreamed of.

These words appeared in the *New York Tribune* on 12 April 1853. The writer was Karl Marx.

Nearly a hundred years later Marx's prophecy has come true. It is ironic that the Russian dictatorship which finally justified his fears claimed Marx himself as its source of inspiration.

THE PEOPLES OF EASTERN EUROPE

By seizing Eastern Europe after the Second World War the rulers of Russia have immeasurably increased their resources. To the 200 million people living within the boundaries of the Soviet Union they have added a further 100 million, most of whom are more advanced in civilization than the Russians themselves. The oil of Romania and Galicia, the great coal and iron basin of Silesia, the industries of Czechoslovakia, Poland and Hungary; these are an invaluable prize for a regime which is particularly backward in industrial development. By pushing forward to the Stettin–Trieste line the Russians have obtained a strategic position which students of geo-politics have always considered the key to the control of all Europe.

This book is not primarily concerned with the international implications of Russia's advance into Europe or with the economic changes which were one of its results. It deals mainly with the political struggle in Eastern Europe as it has affected the Socialist parties. As such it presents a case-history which socialists all over the world should examine without prejudice. But before the drama is unfolded the stage must be set by a short description of Eastern Europe in general and of the techniques by which the Soviet rulers added it to their empire.

Eastern Europe as a whole presents some striking contrasts with its Western neighbours. It is mainly inhabited by Slav nations from the same stock as the Russians. But between the Poles, Czechs and Slovaks to the north and the Slovenes, Croats, Serbs and Bulgarians to the south live two non-Slav peoples – the Hungarians and Romanians.

The vast majority of the East European peoples live and work on the land. Industry developed late, becoming important only in Czechoslovakia,

Poland and Hungary. Except in these three countries there scarcely exists a middle class or working class of the Western type. In this social and economic setting it is not surprising that democracy had a slow and uncertain growth. Before the Second World War Czechoslovakia was the only country in Eastern Europe which recognized Western ideals of Parliamentary democracy. The other countries were all dictatorships to a greater or lesser degree. In some cases the tiny ruling clique drew its strength from a land-owning aristocracy exercising feudal power. In others the army was the decisive political factor. But in all cases political oppression and social injustice were the rule. The prewar regimes maintained their position by a brutality which was often barbaric. Many of them were disfigured by an anti-Semitism as bestial as Hitler's, if less thoroughgoing.

Though the countries of Eastern Europe can be considered together as a whole in contrast to Western Europe, they differ greatly among themselves in national character, social development and political outlook. It has always been the tragedy of Eastern Europe that nationalism has been a disruptive force, even when unity was required against a common enemy. The Czechs will not easily forget that in 1938, after Munich, Poland took advantage of their extremity to seize Teschen. Almost every country in Eastern Europe contains national minorities from other countries within its frontiers. Indeed nationalities are so mixed up that it is impossible to draw frontiers so as to include a homogeneous population. In Poland and Czechoslovakia minority problems often hampered the work of the Socialist parties. When I attended a conference of East European Socialists at Budapest in 1947 I found that even under the Russian occupation conflicting national interests prevented the Socialists from framing a common economic policy.

National differences also affect the attitude of the East European countries towards the Russians. The Poles, for example, have seen Russia invade and mutilate their country so often that they tend to hate the Russians whatever their views on Communism. The Bulgarians, on the other hand, have always felt towards the Russians as a small boy towards his big brother.

THE COMMUNISTS CAPTURE POWER

Everything that happened in Eastern Europe after the war was conditioned by the presence of the Red Army. It was, of course, inevitable that the Red Army should advance far into Europe in its victorious campaign against Germany. A series of Big Power conferences during the war fixed the boundaries of Russian occupation in great detail so as to include all the countries of Eastern Europe except Greece. Indeed, in some cases the Western armies deliberately refrained from advancing so that the Russians could take up the positions which had been allotted to them. This had particularly bad results in Czechoslovakia. American troops could in fact have liberated Prague some days before the Russians, but they were held back so that the Red Army could enter the Czech capital instead. To many Czechs this seemed as much a betrayal of their country by the West as the Munich Agreement of 1938. It was in any case a clear sign that Czech democrats could expect very little aid from Western countries in the years which followed.

On the other hand, in return for the right to occupy Eastern Europe as a zone of Russian influence, the Soviet rulers undertook to establish democracy throughout the area by free elections as soon as possible after the fighting ceased. There is no doubt that the Russians never intended to keep this promise. Indeed there is some evidence to suggest that they did not fully realize that the Western powers were sincere in demanding free elections.

The Communist rulers of Russia do not believe in the possibility of lasting co-operation between Communist regimes and regimes of any other type. Thus every attempt by the East European democrats to prove their desire for friendship with Russia was wasted. The Russians could be satisfied with nothing less than total surrender. They wanted to control every East European country through a Communist dictatorship whose leaders they could choose themselves.

On the other hand there could be no question in 1945 of imposing Communist dictatorships on Eastern Europe by violent revolution or by Russian force.

In most of these countries the Communist Parties were tiny minorities. Administrative breakdown would have deprived Russia of badly needed reparations. Open civil war would have invited intervention by the Western armies from nearby Germany and Austria. In any case Russia could not afford to tie down her own troops indefinitely simply to suppress disorder inside her security zone. Somehow she had to produce speedily but without undue disturbance a series of Communist regimes which would be strong and stable enough to continue without direct Russian support in future. In this sense at least the Molotov Plan for Eastern Europe was like the Marshall Plan for Western Europe – standing on its head.

There was thus little in common between the Communist seizure of power in Eastern Europe and the revolution in Russia nearly thirty years before. The Russian revolution was a revolution of the traditional type – the state apparatus was overthrown by the armed uprising of oppressed classes. It is doubtful whether such a revolution is still possible in any modern state. On the one hand the social and economic functions of the state machine have become immensely complex and far-reaching. If the revolution wrecks this machine the winner will face insoluble problems. On the other hand the techniques of oppression available to those who control the state machine are exceptionally efficient. A direct assault on the power of the state has not much chance of success.

The Russian revolution is the exception which proves this rule. It took the Bolshevik Party five years in Russia to establish itself securely in power after the First World War. During this period it deliberately shattered the whole fabric of the Tsarist state and tried to build up a new state on the ruins. But the whole operation was attended by terrifying difficulties and dangers. Administrative collapse brought starvation to millions. There was widespread and bloody civil war, with armed intervention by foreign powers. The revolution survived mainly because Russia was geographically so remote. Attempts to produce communism by similar methods in Europe failed catastrophically.

During the quarter of a century after 1917, Communists saw the problem increasingly as one of capturing the bourgeois state machine rather than destroying it. So they studied intensively the anatomy of power in a democracy. They mapped the location of the strong points – not only in the state institutions themselves, like the armed forces, police and civil service, but also in the whole economic and social structure, particularly the trade unions and professional organizations. They explored the techniques by which public opinion could be roused and exploited. They grew expert in mobilizing support for their aims through organizations in which they played no obvious part themselves. And they insinuated their agents secretly into the civil service and the other political parties.

By the end of the Second World War the Russians had digested all this experience and had developed an entirely new pattern for revolution – the so-called Popular Democracy. There is no basic difference of aim or function between Popular Democracy and the Soviet system which emerged from the Russian civil war. This has been made clear repeatedly by Communist leaders. Georgi Dimitrov, former general secretary of the Comintern and premier of Bulgaria from 1946 to 1949 declared on 25 December 1948:

> The Soviet regime and the Popular Democratic regime are two forms of one and the same system of government. Both are based on the dictatorship of the

proletariat. Soviet experience is the only and the best pattern for the building of socialism in our own country as well as in other countries.

Mathias Rakosi, leader of the Hungarian Communists, who had himself experienced the failure of a Soviet revolution in Hungary after the First World War, described Popular Democracy in his Party paper as 'a dictatorship of the proletariat without the Soviet form'.

Revolution by Popular Democracy was engineered as follows in Eastern Europe. In most of the countries concerned, Russia encouraged the construction of a state mainly on the bourgeois and democratic model; these states were controlled by coalition governments in which the Communist Parties did not appear to exercise an exclusive or even a predominating influence. But the Communist Parties did invariably take over the Ministry of the Interior or National Security. So they controlled the direct apparatus of state power, and particularly the police force. In the countries which had fought against Germany – ex-enemy countries were not allowed armed forces – the Communists also secured control of the army, either directly or through ostensibly non-Party ministers of defence. Finally the Communists took the Ministries of Information wherever possible, with control of all state propaganda. These Communist-controlled departments were immediately consolidated as separate satrapies, and all non-Communist officials in them were purged.

The Communist Parties themselves were rapidly expanded from small groups of devoted revolutionaries into great mass organizations numbering millions of members. Readiness to accept Party discipline was the only condition of entry, but the incentives to join were various. There was, for instance, genuine enthusiasm for a Party which showed courage, initiative, experience and purpose, and which gave scope for such qualities in new members. Then the Communist Party offered a sanctuary for individuals with a guilty past – collaboration with the enemy or membership of organizations now considered criminal. Furthermore, the Party, alike in its policy and propaganda, exploited every current in popular feeling, including nationalism, religion and even the property instinct. There was the intimidation and victimization of non-Communists – sometimes the use of force but more often the withholding of necessary privileges, the right to furniture dockets, a new flat, or the right to work; for instance, intransigent individuals would be removed from their home and families to a post far away in the provinces. And there was the usual instinct to jump on the bandwagon. So the Communist Parties grew. But inside these swollen mass armies the old Communist élite remained as a general staff.

Outside the Party proper the Communists tried to get control of all existing social organizations. They got a footing even in other political parties. Blackmail has rarely been used so extensively as a political weapon. The minister of the interior, with his unrivalled opportunities for uncovering guilty personal or political secrets, often preferred to use his knowledge to secure a docile tool rather than a new tenant for the overcrowded prisons. And of course the Communists paid special attention to the trade unions; in most of these countries the trade unions expanded as fast as the Communist Parties themselves, and under the same direction. Through them the Communists obtained effective power over the whole industrial machine; and in them they acquired a useful instrument for special pressure; a newspaper could be suppressed as easily by a strike of printing workers as by a decree of the minister of the interior.

By using these methods the Communists managed to obtain decisive influence inside every East European country within a few months of the German withdrawal. But their final capture of power depended in every case on direct intervention by Russia as the occupying power. And, of course, it was only in virtue of the Red Army occupation that the Communists were able to begin the process at the outset.

POLAND

For various reasons Russian intervention was more open in Poland than anywhere else, and in Poland the Communists violated democratic forms far more flagrantly. The Polish Resistance Movement, which had inflicted more damage on the Germans than any other resistance movement in Europe, was completely independent of the Communists. Even before the war was over, the Russians crippled its chances of taking over the country when the Germans left. Through refusing to support the Warsaw rising the Red Army connived at the annihilation of the Polish Home Army by the Nazis. After this the Russians tricked the Resistance leaders into visiting Moscow where they were all arrested and tried. Finally the Russians forced Poland and the Western Allies to include members of the so-called Lublin Committee in the provisional government of Poland, though these were almost without exception agents or puppets of the Soviet Union and the tiny Polish Communist Party.

Small groups of guerrillas continued to fight the imposed authorities in Poland for at least two years after the Russians arrived. But in the absence of an authentic socialist party, the focus of legal opposition to the new regime was the newly formed Polish People's Party (PSL) under

Mikolajczyk, a peasant leader who had served during the war in the Polish government in London. In 1945 the PSL was nominally part of the Polish government, but with the approach of elections it was treated by the Communists as beyond the law. Its members were regularly beaten up by the police. When in March 1946 a Peasant Co-operative Congress was being held in Warsaw 1,200 of the 2,000 delegates were arrested on the way. Every type of fraud and intimidation was used to reduce PSL polling strength. A new electoral law gave disproportionate representation to the western territories which were under total Communist control. Political trials were held in an attempt to implicate Mikolajczyk in plotting against the state. Bogus anti-Communist parties were created outside the government bloc so as to split the PSL vote. The sponsors of PSL candidates were arrested and tortured in large numbers. In districts which contained a quarter of the country's population, PSL election lists were disqualified. In many other districts the voters were forced to march to the polls and to cast their votes in public under police supervision. When the elections took place in January 1947 the government bloc received 394 seats and the PSL only 28.

Persecution of the PSL continued throughout the year and Mikolajczyk, warned that he would shortly be arrested and condemned to death, decided to flee the country. He left Poland secretly at the end of October 1947. From now onwards the only obstacle to Communist control was the legal Polish Socialist Party, or PPS.

HUNGARY

In Hungary the Communists played a weak hand with great skill and finesse. Apart from the indirect influence of the Russian Army, the elections held in November 1945 were free. The Communist Party found itself a minority of 17 per cent in a coalition government dominated by the Smallholders, who had an absolute majority over all others. The Smallholders' Party was a conglomeration of diverse elements. It claimed to represent the small farmer, but, as the only non-Marxist party, it was supported by every type of anti-Communist in the population. So the first aim of the Communists was to disintegrate the Smallholders' Party by isolating and detaching each group of its supporters in turn. The Communists obtained Social-Democratic support in this by playing on ideological sympathies and fears of a new white terror.

In January 1947 the Communist minister of the interior announced discovery of a plot against the regime, in which many Smallholders were said to be involved. For a time the Smallholders showed fight; they used their majority in Parliament to save their General Secretary, Bela Kovacs, from trial. But at the height of the argument about his Parliamentary immunity the Russian Army police arrested Kovacs for military espionage. He has never since been seen. This Russian intervention broke the back of Smallholder resistance; in June the same year the Smallholder prime minister was frightened into leaving the country and offering his resignation. When new elections were held in August all the real leaders of the Smallholders' Party had been replaced by Communist stooges – and the Party's support dwindled to 16 per cent.

The second general election was a masterpiece of political expertise. This time anti-Communist feeling was diverted into new mushroom parties; with 40 per cent of the total vote, these formed the legal opposition. The Communists used just sufficient fraud to ensure themselves a dominant position inside the government coalition. Here the only group with any independence left was the Social Democrats; but their loyalty had been severely tested by the election frauds, of which they were the main victims. So they now received the same treatment as the Smallholders; those of their leaders who retained the confidence of the working class were forced to resign. A fake party congress agreed to merge the Social Democrats finally in a single party with the Communists. Thus, though it had only 25 per cent of the Parliamentary seats, the Communist Party became the only organized political force in Hungary.

CZECHOSLOVAKIA

In Czechoslovakia, on the other hand, both the problem and its solution were significantly different. The Czech nation was conceived and reared in the ideals of Western democracy. But, like the Russians, they are Slavs; they had fought as allies with the Soviet Union against Hitler. And the prearranged liberation of Czechoslovakia by the Red Army strengthened the popular belief, born of the Munich Agreement, that Czechoslovakia's only dependable ally against Germany was Russia. Moreover, even before the war, the only strong Communist Party in Eastern Europe had been in Czechoslovakia. So the elections in May 1946 were completely free, and the Communists emerged as by far the strongest single party, though without an absolute majority. A coalition government, the so-called National Front, was formed under a Communist premier, Gottwald. As always, the Communists held the ministry of the interior. But all parties in the front were united in treating the Czech-Soviet alliance as the basis of their foreign policy, and in carrying out a radical programme of socialist reform.

Co-operation between the parties ran smoothly until summer 1947. In July the Soviet Union forced the Czech government to reverse its unanimous decision to join the Marshall Plan talks in Paris. In the autumn the Communists strained the unity of the National Front by a series of provocative and unacceptable demands – on economic issues, and in connection with the alleged discovery of a plot in Slovakia. Simultaneously they opened a campaign of terrorism against non-Communist workers in the factories. They made great efforts to obtain an alliance with the Social-Democratic Party, with whose support they would have had an absolute majority in the government. But when Fierlinger, then the Social-Democratic leader, tried to force such an alliance on his party, the resulting fury of the rank and file swept him from office at the party congress in November. The Social Democrats' refusal to break the unity of the National Front increased their own party's popularity at the expense of the Communists, who now felt certain of defeat if free elections were held, as planned, the next April. In December, Drtina, the Socialist minister of justice, produced evidence that Communists were responsible for an attempt to assassinate President Benes. Tension grew, but the firmness and competence of the non-Communist leaders, confident that they represented the vast majority of a democratic people, made a repetition of the Hungarian débâcle seem unlikely. Then in one week the whole structure of postwar Czech politics was shattered; a single-party dictatorship was imposed without serious opposition.

In spite of occasional obscurities, the main features of the technique are clear. The resistance of the non-Communist elements was broken by two facts which immediately emerged with startling clarity. Firstly, the state machine was already so far penetrated by the Communists that resistance might wreck the whole structure. And in addition, the Communists had sufficient organized strength outside the machine itself to challenge even the authority of the state. Secondly, the Communists were fully prepared to meet resistance with civil war, and were confident of direct Russian support if civil war was necessary.

The police acted throughout as a private instrument of the Communist Party – for example, they occupied the offices of rival parties and replaced their officials by Communist stooges. The press, wireless and all means of publicity and propaganda were controlled by the Communist minister of information. Meanwhile Communist-controlled action committees mobilized extra-constitutional power and in some areas took over the functions of government. The trade unions threatened a general strike. The armed mass demonstration in Prague on 21 February performed the same function as Mussolini's march on Rome. On the other hand, the possibility of Soviet intervention was impressed first on the party leaders by the presence of the Russian deputy foreign minister, who arrived when the crisis broke on 17 February and did not leave until it was over. And the possibility was also held continuously before public opinion by Communist statements that the Soviet Union was interested in the victory of the so-called democratic forces. Indeed, the Russian consul-general in Bratislava broadcast a statement that the Soviet people, 200 million strong, stood ready to support the struggle of their Czech brothers. Under the pressure of these two facts, every organized opposition to the Communists crumbled.

A superficial study of Communist successes in Eastern Europe might well make a Western observer think the Communists have almost superhuman intelligence and political skill. But closer examination shows that throughout Eastern Europe the Communists obtained power only because they had Soviet assistance and because national politics were overcast by the shadow of a Red Army occupation. This point has been made many times by the Communists themselves. The leading Hungarian Communist, Revai, wrote in the *Sociological Review* of Budapest in April 1949:

> In the beginning we were a minority. Nevertheless we had a decisive influence in the armed forces. Our strength was increased by the existence of the Soviet Union and the presence of the Soviet Army, on whose support we could always rely.

The Central Committee of the Communist Party of the Soviet Union itself declared on 4 May 1948:

> The Soviet Army came to the aid of the Yugoslav people and in this way created the conditions which were necessary for the Communist Party of Yugoslavia to achieve power. Unfortunately the Soviet did not and could not render such assistance to the French and Italian Parties.

Ironically enough, Yugoslavia was the one country in Eastern Europe where the Communists obtained power with little help from the Russians.

RUSSIA TAKES ECONOMIC CONTROL

By the end of 1947 the Communist Parties had won effective control of the state machine in every East European country, though in some cases the formal liquidation of the Socialists by fusion remained to be accomplished. The next stage was the assimilation of the whole region into the Soviet empire and the elimination of nationalist elements inside the Communist Parties themselves.

Soviet Russia began to obtain economic control of Eastern Europe the moment the Red Army arrived. She used three separate methods. Against the ex-enemy countries like Hungary and Romania she used the right of conquest to acquire direct influence inside the national economy. In every country she used her military and political predominance to enforce commercial agreements on terms excessively favourable to herself. And, most important of all, as one by one the local Communist Parties captured control of all spheres of government, Russia made these Communist Parties administer the national economies in her own interest, according to a plan made in Moscow.

Of course, in some countries Russia used all three techniques at once. But in general she avoided direct pressure on countries with wholly Communist governments. For example, Bulgaria was an ex-enemy country, but the Communists had won power there immediately after liberation. So Russia did not exert the right of conquest so ruthlessly against her. On the other hand, where Russia saw great possibilities of plunder, as in Hungary and Romania, she deliberately kept the local Communists in the background, so that the non-Communist parties bore the main odium of accepting her terms. Perhaps, too, Russia's racial prejudice partly explains the difference between her favourable treatment of Bulgaria, the little Slav brother, and her harshness to the non-Slav peoples of Hungary and Romania.

In Hungary and Romania Russia acquired direct influence through the armistice agreements and later the peace treaties. There were three main economic conditions: each country was compelled, firstly, to pay the expenses of the Russian occupation armies; secondly, to surrender all German property to Russia; and, thirdly, to pay $300 million worth of reparations – though a third of Hungary's reparations went to Yugoslavia and Czechoslovakia instead of Russia.

The Red Army's occupation expenses were, of course, fixed by the Russians themselves. Every township from Vienna to the Black Sea knows how closely the Russian commanders always calculated their pound of flesh, and how widely the Red Army interpreted its rights under this section of the treaty. In the twelve months from August 1946 Hungary spent 13 per cent of her budget purely on Red Army maintenance.

By taking over German assets, Russia inherited Nazi Germany's economic stranglehold over Eastern Europe – for German capital had deeply penetrated most East European countries before the war. Russia's gains by this transfer were particularly immoral. Many of the so-called German assets were property which the Nazis had confiscated from local Jews and anti-Nazis. But despite the rights of the original owners they passed straight from German to Russian hands. In Hungary alone Russia took over 300 different firms. And in effect Russia often doubled the value of these assets. She formed companies jointly with the Hungarian or Romanian state, and contributed German assets as her own share towards their capital. In Romania these joint companies monopolized the steel and timber industries, in Hungary the bauxite industry, and in both countries the whole of air and river transport, most of the oil and much of the banking. Though in these companies the interests of Russia and Hungary or Romania were supposed to be equal, it is known that Russia often failed to contribute her full share of the capital. But she invariably claimed more than half the key posts and most of the profits. For example, in the Soviet-Romanian Oil Company, Russia contributed only her German assets. But she claimed a 70 per cent interest, and demanded moreover that her lion's share of the profits should be remittable in dollars. When I was in Budapest in 1947 there was a popular saying that the Soviet-Hungarian Shipping Company was divided half and half – Russia took the big ships that sailed up and down the Danube, while Hungary took the little boats which went from side to side.

These Russian-controlled companies, owning key industries in Hungary and Romania, were the most visible sign of direct Soviet influence. But reparations were an even more important factor in the period following the war. Though the value of each country's reparations was fixed at $300 million, 1938 prices were taken as the basis of assessment. So the present-day value of these reparations was more like $700 million in each case. Moreover, Hungary had to pay a penalty of 5 per cent per month for delayed delivery. In 1946 reparations took up a quarter of Hungary's national budget, and almost the whole output of her metal and engineering industries. The proportion of the total national budget taken by reparations was of special importance. Russia had the right to choose the goods in which the reparations were to be paid. Consequently she was able to play a decisive part in drawing up the whole production plans of Romania and Hungary.

One more point is needed to complete this picture of how Russia exercised the right of conquest for her economic gain. Quite apart from individual looting by Red Army soldiers, the Russians steadily dismantled machinery and equipment from Hungary and Romania, and transferred them to the Soviet Union. No precise figures of this war booty are available, but Russia had probably taken goods exceeding the value of her reparations long before payment of reparations was officially under way. And it is estimated that the total value of goods directly acquired by Russia through the conquest of Romania and Hungary is more than $4,000 million – quite a tidy sum for an anti-imperialist power to extract from two People's Democracies.

These methods were used by Russia mainly against Hungary and Romania. The next method was used indiscriminately against all the East European countries. Russia exploited their needs and weakness to obtain trade agreements on unfair terms. It is more difficult to cite exact figures here. Russia made a series of trade agreements with all the East European countries after the war. But in nearly all cases she refused to publish details of the values and quantities of the commodities concerned. In some cases political conditions were written into the trade agreements, but these have not always come to light.

But two main points are fairly certain. In the months following liberation, Russia supplied to many of the East European countries goods without which their recovery would have been much slower. In return the East European countries had to supply Russia with goods at a much lower price than they would have fetched elsewhere. In particular Russia exported raw materials like cotton, wool, iron ore and copper, and the East European countries paid with goods manufactured out of these raw materials – like textiles, steel and machinery. In such cases the prices were often so unequal that the East Europeans themselves would privately describe the transaction as 'reparations from current production'. In 1947 the Bulgarian minister of trade, a Communist, resigned because he would not stomach the terms proposed by Russia for her trade treaty with Bulgaria.

Poland suffered particularly, because she had to send Russia coal which she could otherwise have sold in Western Europe for higher prices in hard currency. The Soviet-Polish trade agreement of January 1948 contained an interesting condition: Russia gave Poland credit to buy capital goods on condition that Russia, not Poland, should draw up the plans for steel, chemical, cement and light-metal plants to be set up with Soviet aid in Poland. Moreover, Poland had to surrender to Russia some of her reparations claims to dismantled German machinery.

Such trade agreements in themselves did much to give Russia economic control over Eastern Europe. As Yugoslavia has learnt to her cost, a pattern of trade, once established, is not easily changed without great inconvenience to the weaker partner. Before the war the Soviet Union took scarcely one-hundredth of Eastern Europe's trade. In 1946 she took nearly half. This proportion declined in 1947 as the volume of East European production leaped ahead, though the quantity of exports to Russia increased. In 1948 Russia took about a third of Eastern Europe's trade.

The economic influence thus exercised by Russia over Eastern Europe does not differ essentially from the influence any powerful and rapacious state may exert over its weaker neighbours – over allies weakened by war or enemies prostrate in defeat. It makes a striking contrast with the scrupulous generosity shown by America to Western Europe in a similar situation. But it does recall a striking parallel – the economic influence of Germany over Eastern Europe in the years before the war. In some respects the parallel is so close as to be misleading – particularly since Russia has directly inherited Germany's capital investments. But in fact there is a difference as important as the similarity. Russia possesses a form of political control over every East European country which Germany could never have hoped to equal. By the end of 1948 the Communists were the only real political party in every state from Poland to Albania. Each of these Communist Parties – with one significant exception – was controlled by Soviet agents. Each accepted the authority of Soviet Russia as decisive in any question of domestic or foreign policy. What are the aims of Russia's economic control in Eastern Europe?

Soviet Economic Aims

Russia wants to integrate the East European countries completely into the Soviet economy. And since she herself produces all the food she wants, she is mainly interested in developing their industrial potential – in shifting the emphasis of their economy from agriculture to industry.

In principle this should be entirely to their advantage. Before the war Eastern Europe's trade was based mainly on exporting agricultural products to Germany. Farming methods were primitive, the land was overpopulated, and Germany ruthlessly exploited her position as the chief market. So standards of living were much lower in these countries than elsewhere in Europe. The obvious cure for this poverty is more industrialization. Agriculture must be mechanized, and the surplus rural population employed in the towns.

But, unfortunately for the East European countries, Russia herself cannot provide the capital goods required for their industrial development. And she does not need the agricultural products which they can most easily supply. The obvious solution would be for the countries of Eastern Europe to plan their development in conjunction with the countries of Western Europe, which can provide them with machinery and take their foodstuffs in return. That is how Australia and New Zealand, for example, became industrialized. And it is worth stressing that industrialization need not bring a fall in agricultural production. Take the United States – she produces both more manufactures and more grain than any other country in the world.

But this solution was excluded by Russia's veto on the Marshall Plan in 1947. Russia wants to integrate her satellites into her own economic system. She does not want trade with Western Europe to play more than a marginal part in their economic planning. So Russia is forcing them to industrialize themselves largely out of their own resources. This is probably the most tragic consequence of the Iron Curtain. The process of self-industrialization – what Marxists call the primary accumulation of capital – cannot help being immensely painful to the peoples of Eastern Europe. It must cause human suffering on the same scale as the Industrial Revolution in England 150 years ago. In order to reach the required level of capital investment, the East Europeans will have to forgo indefinitely any improvement in their own standard of living. In the age of nineteenth-century Liberalism, the social strains arising from such a process inspired Marx and Engels to make their critique of capitalist economy; in fact they gave birth to socialism and the trade union movement. In Eastern Europe today, where the Communists wield absolute power, the same strains can only increase the rigour of the police state. For the people's misery can be kept from exploding only by the monstrous apparatus of totalitarianism. In Soviet Russia the same economic policy killed off millions of people and helped Stalin to consolidate his dictatorship.

In 1947 I visited Eastern Europe several times. Everywhere I found the Socialists, then still in the governments, pressing the Communists in vain to reduce the merciless rate of capital investment. For democracy cannot survive the inhumanity of Communist economic theory. Moreover, the workers and peasants alike find it impossible to achieve the targets of production set. A vicious circle begins to operate. The freedom of the workers is progressively limited, efficiency falls. Managers are imprisoned as saboteurs and replaced by ignorant opportunists. A growing percentage of the population finds its way either into concentration camps or into the organizations of state oppression.

The whole situation is made worse in Eastern Europe by constant Russian intervention. First of all, Russia insists that all her satellites adopt

Soviet economic techniques – however unsuitable they are to local circumstances. Everywhere the present drive for collective farms is causing sullen resistance among the peasants and a fall in agricultural production. But, especially after Tito's quarrel with the Cominform, none of the governments dares to change a policy prescribed by Stalin.

Any East European country is bound to suffer by economic integration with the Soviet Union. As the Red Army soldiers demonstrated everywhere in person, the Russian people's standard of living is well below the average in Eastern Europe. So economic integration can only be at the expense of the East European peoples. It is inconceivable that the men in the Kremlin would allow living standards to rise faster among their satellites than in their native land.

And integration carries a much more unpleasant menace. The rulers of Soviet Russia never hesitate to transfer whole populations over great distances whenever it suits their political or economic purpose. For example, many millions of men, women and children from the Baltic states and the Ukraine have been forcibly uprooted from their homes and deported to Central Asia and other remote parts of the Soviet empire. Apart from such mass transfers of population the Soviet secret police (or MVD) runs forced-labour camps containing between 5 and 15 million prisoners; their main function is to supply slaves for great development projects under conditions which no free man will tolerate. Though Eastern Europe suffers at the present time from a shortage of labour, it is much more densely populated than the Soviet Union. So there is a real danger that the Russians will use it as a reservoir of manpower for their own purposes. Forced-labour camps have already been set up in Czechoslovakia and elsewhere.

Integration and industrialization are the aims of Soviet policy in Eastern Europe. What degree of success has it achieved so far? It is not easy to be certain – Communist statistics are always incomplete and often deliberately misleading. But a good deal of incidental information can be obtained from newspapers published in Eastern Europe.

Integration has already gone a long way. The main flow of East European trade has been diverted from Western Europe to Russia. Quite apart from the disappearance of the German market the East European countries have not been able to supply Western Europe with prewar quantities of foodstuffs or timber. Agricultural production has fallen for various reasons – the war, drought, Communist incompetence and peasant resistance. But in any case the Communist governments are paying less attention to agriculture. Moreover, their agricultural policy concentrates more on livestock, dairy produce and industrial crops like sugar beet, than on the cereals which Western Europe needs. From 1945 to 1949 the value of Western Europe's exports to the East far exceeded the value of Eastern exports to the West. Quite apart from strategic considerations, Western Europe could not have carried such an export surplus indefinitely, but Eastern Europe did not seem eager to produce more of the things which Western Europe needed and could afford.

Apart from foreign trade it is difficult to unearth specific proofs of economic integration. We know that the East European countries provide cheap factory labour for processing Soviet raw materials. The degree to which Russia can call on her satellites' resources is shown by the fact that Romania supplied much of the coarse grain which Russia sent to Britain under the 1947 Anglo-Soviet trade agreement. All the East European countries have made Two- Three- or Five-Year Plans which are adjusted to meet overall Soviet requirements. Czechoslovakia has suffered greatly through supplying heavy industrial equipment to Russia and the other satellites without receiving a fair return.

But the industrial development of Eastern Europe is now facing great difficulties. By replacing experienced technicians with safe Party men, the Communists have caused a catastrophic decline in many industries. Before the war the Romanian oil-wells produced 8,700,000 tons of oil a year. In 1946 they produced 4,800,000 tons. The yield fell a million tons in 1947.

The fall in production is caused above all by resistance inside the working class. The workers are naturally unwilling to work hard for little reward. They now get much less protection from the trade unions than they obtained even under the prewar regimes. Passive resistance by the workers has been most marked in Czechoslovakia where the government has introduced a six-day working week. The new Czech regime has dealt out merciless sentences for what it calls economic sabotage. Two workmen were sentenced to death at Brno in 1948 for stealing food cards. There is similar trouble in Hungary. The secretary-general of the Hungarian trade unions told his congress in October 1947 that discipline among the workers was slack, and poor quality goods were often produced. He said the future function of the trade unions in Hungary would be to explain government policy to the workers and tighten the state's control over them; so, for example, works committees now include persons who have no connection with the factories concerned, so that the regime can supervise their activity.

Of course the most striking setback Russia has received is in Yugoslavia. When Tito refused to let the Russians decide every detail of his policy for him, he struck a shattering blow at the foundations of Soviet power. For two years Russia has imposed an economic blockade to bring Tito to his knees; this has wrecked the whole structure of Tito's economic planning. He has complained that the Cominform is treating him worse than any capitalist country. All this shows two things very clearly. Russia can manipulate as she wishes the economic policy of any East European country, provided its rulers are loyal to Stalin. But equally, even if one of her satellites chooses to break away from Russian control, it will find it has become dependent on trade with the Soviet area.

MILITARY INTEGRATION

Parallel with Russia's capture of the East European economies has been the strategic integration of Eastern Europe into the Russian military machine. In the two years after Hitler's defeat, Russia made new military alliances with all the East European countries which had been on the Allied side during the war – Poland, Czechoslovakia and Yugoslavia. As soon as she had won political control in the defeated countries she made alliances with them too – Hungary, Romania and Bulgaria. Most of the East European countries have also made military alliances with one another, so that the whole area is now covered with a thick network of pacts, all centring on Moscow.

In Poland, where the Russians had most reason to suspect the allegiance of the population, they actually imposed one of their own Red Army marshals, Rokossovsky, as minister of defence and member of the Political Bureau of the Polish Communist Party. Most armies in Eastern Europe swear allegiance not only to their own government but also to the Soviet Union.

Everywhere the military strength of Eastern Europe is being increased. It is estimated that the satellite armies now number 1,500,000 men – more than half the size of the Red Army itself. These armies have together more than 2,000 tanks. Apart from the armies themselves, in most countries the youth are given military training, particularly shooting, gliding and parachuting. The Soviet Zone of Germany has embarked on a programme for training thousands of young Communists as glider pilots. Yet after the defeat of Hitler, Russia joined Britain, France and the United States in a decree outlawing German gliding. This was doubtless prompted by the recollection that many Luftwaffe officers had obtained their initial training as glider pilots during the interwar years when Germany was technically 'disarmed'. In Poland, a Russian-sponsored Aviation League, with 500,000 members, is training pilots for gliders and aircraft. Physical training is everywhere linked up with military training.

The Russians have, of course, found it very difficult to reconcile the encouragement they give to militarism in Eastern Europe with support of the so-called Peace Campaign. The Hungarian minister of defence, Farkas, in a leading article in *Szabad Nep* of 12 April 1949, wrote:

> A certain pacifism has appeared within the ranks of our party, particularly of late. Slogans like 'We want no more wars!' are very significant of this pacifism. First of all, therefore, we have to overcome this feeling in order to suppress it in the masses.

Small wonder that when Moscow radio reported the Communist May Day demonstrations in 1950, it said: 'The name of Stalin sounded like a war-cry at the demonstrations in Prague, Budapest, Peking, Warsaw, and Paris.'

THE 'NATIONAL COMMUNISTS' ARE LIQUIDATED

The final stage in imposing Soviet control on Eastern Europe was the purging of the Communist Parties themselves. As already described, most of the East European Communist Parties were tiny minorities rapidly inflated into mass organizations, and their leaders made little discrimination among the flood of ex-fascists, careerists and opportunists who applied for membership. Once the Communist Parties had achieved supreme power in the state, however, they began to purge themselves of unreliable elements. The first to go were ex-Socialists who had been absorbed into the Communist Party when their parties were destroyed by fusion. The leadership began to pay more attention to the social origin of their followers, so as to maintain a large proportion of industrial workers. In Hungary, 17 per cent of the Party membership was removed by the great purge of 1948. In Czechoslovakia, over 100,000 persons were expelled from the Party and 500,000 more reduced to probationary status. But the most important of all were the purges of the so-called national deviationists, which began in 1948 and are still going on.

When the Red Army reached Eastern Europe in 1944 and 1945, it brought in its wake small groups of Communist leaders of East European origin who had spent the previous ten or twenty years in Moscow – sometimes working in the various Comintern organizations, sometimes simply drumming their heels in obscure hotels. Such 'Muscovites' immediately assumed leading positions in the national Communist Parties of

Eastern Europe. Friction naturally developed between them and the small number of their colleagues who had spent the difficult years fighting Fascism and the Germans on the spot. Whereas the Muscovite Communists acted simply as Soviet agents, the national Communists often fought against Soviet attempts to subordinate their own countries to Russian interests. The most famous case of such resistance is of course the Yugoslav Communist Party in its break with the Cominform in 1948.

Even before the breach between Tito and the Cominform, the prominent Romanian Communist, Patrascanu, had been purged for nationalism. He had often been imprisoned by the prewar reactionary regimes, but he had never been in exile in Moscow.

After Tito's defection the Russians became terrified of similar defections in other countries. The only Polish Communist with any national standing, Gomulka, was repeatedly attacked for failing to appreciate the role of the USSR and ignoring the struggle against nationalism. In 1948 he was deprived of his position as general secretary of the Party and later expelled completely from the government. On the other hand, he does not yet appear to have suffered severe punishment like national Communists in the other countries, no doubt because of his strong following inside the Polish Communist Party.

In Bulgaria, on the other hand, the former secretary of the underground Central Committee of the Bulgarian Communist Party, Traycho Kostov, was put on trial for 'nationalist demagogy' and 'left-wing sectarianism'. It appeared that he had failed to inform the Russians of Bulgaria's trade relations with other countries and had kept certain state secrets from the knowledge of the USSR. He was accused of being a British agent. But to the fury of his judges he refused to confess these crimes, when put on public trial. Nevertheless, he was condemned and executed. Kostov was one of the outstanding martyrs of East European Communism. During the struggle against the prewar regime he had thrown himself out of the window of police headquarters in Sofia, lest further torture should force him to reveal the names of his comrades. Both his legs were broken, but he served his prison sentence, returned to the underground, was again arrested, maltreated, and imprisoned. When he was tried for treason in December 1949, Communist journalists mocked him because he was a hunchback. His back had been crippled by torture in prewar prisons.

The most important Communist trial so far in Eastern Europe has been that of the leading Hungarian Communist, Rajk, formerly minister of the interior. At the trial, which took place in September 1949, he confessed to all the charges of acting for the American secret service and working as an agent of Horthy's political police, though at times he stumbled in giving evidence and had to be prompted by the presiding judge. He was condemned to death and hanged. It is interesting to note that Rajk, like Tito and Patrascanu, had served in the Spanish Civil War, a distinction which is now dangerous in Eastern Europe.

After the break between Tito and Stalin it is unwise to exclude any possibility. But it seems almost certain that the Russians have by now liquidated every potential nucleus of national resistance inside the Communist Parties themselves. The only probable exception is Poland, where the Russians seem to have considered the Polish Communists too unreliable to trust with the vital keys to policy, and where a Soviet marshal, Rokossovsky, wields direct power.

The Fate of the Workers

In the last year there has been a good deal of evidence, most of it from Communist sources, to show that all over Eastern Europe the Communist regimes are running into heavy trouble with the workers. Day after day the government newspapers in Poland, Czechoslovakia, Hungary and Romania carry stories of slacking, absenteeism, and even sabotage in the factories. It seems that the workers are organizing go-slow movements, are refusing to work overtime, are combining to practise wage-frauds, and are trying to 'terrorize the management'. The Communists say it is all a conspiracy by those well-known agents of Anglo-American imperialism, the old Socialist trade union leaders. So they have arrested all the prominent Socialists still at liberty and given them heavy prison sentences. They are purging known Socialists from the trade unions and factory committees. But the trouble is still going on. At the end of July 1950 the Politburo of the Hungarian Communist Party published a severe attack on its own nominees in the trade union leadership. It said they were lazy bureaucratic opportunists – and so playing the socialist game.

It is a tragic irony that a system which claims the description of 'socialist' and appeals above all to the working class for support should arouse such opposition among the workers themselves. But the reason is not far to seek. Many of the worst features of Russian Communism developed because Lenin and Stalin were trying to produce in ten years a process which took over a century in the rest of Europe. The East European satellites are being forced to compress the same process even further into two or three years.

The trade unions are a case in point. It was not until 1928 – eleven years after the Revolution – that the Soviet Union began its first Five-Year Plan and the destruction of Russian trade unionism entered its final stage. And even then it was nearly ten years before the trade unions in Russia achieved that perfection of rigid automatism which characterizes all modern Soviet institutions – except perhaps the Red Army. The only function of Soviet trade unions today is to act as 'the transmission belt from the Party to the masses' i.e. as a machine for administering the government's economic policy. Of course in Russia the government is the only employer of labour. So in fact Soviet trade unions represent the employer rather than the workers. They are what the Western labour movement would call 'yellow' or 'company' unions. Indeed, by Western standards they are not trade unions at all. They are denied the right to strike, and they play no part in deciding wage policy. So they are not capable of protecting their members' basic interests. The only functions they have which are comparable with those of a Western trade union are to administer the social insurance and welfare schemes and to act as a sort of factory inspectorate. The result is that the workers have no means of protection against exploitation by the management and the regime.

This is the model which the Communists have been trying to imitate in Eastern Europe. They had no difficulty in capturing the trade union organizations at the centre by physical force. But it was not so easy to destroy the traditions built up in the union branches through years of struggle against earlier regimes. In Poland, Hungary and Romania, for instance, the trade unions have generations of experience in dealing with agents-provocateurs and police spies. And the economic policy the Communists are forcing the unions to carry out is detested by all the workers alike.

Eastern Europe plays a vital part in the economic plans of the Soviet Union and fills some important gaps in its war machine. So the Russians want more production whatever the cost. The job of the trade unions under Communist control is to sacrifice everything for higher output and to tighten discipline so that it stands up to the consequent strain. Everywhere possible the Communists have introduced piece-work. They are trying out the Russian system of Stakhanovism – that is, they build up an exceptional worker as the model for the average, and so keep forcing up the rate of production. Unfortunately in Poland the first of these 'Labour Heroes', a miner called Pstrowski, died of overstrain, and the Polish workers invented the slogan 'Work like Pstrowski and prepare to meet your Maker!'

Another job for these 'yellow' trade unions is asking the government to cut holidays and increase working hours. In Czechoslovakia they demanded a six-day week – and got it. The Communist prime minister, Zapotocky, admitted that 'the appeal to work the six-day week was often not readily accepted and even criticized'. This is a mild way of describing what really happened. In many places the workers chased their trade union secretaries out of the factories.

The fact is that all over Eastern Europe the workers have reacted to this new form of exploitation by going slow and absenteeism and by combining secretly to cheat the management. That, in turn, led the regimes into passing the most oppressive labour legislation – again on the Soviet model.

In June 1940 – long before Russia entered the war – the Soviet Union decreed new punishments for labour offences – for instance, a year's imprisonment for any worker who changed his job without permission, and six months' forced labour for being more than twenty minutes late for work. Eastern Europe has followed suit. Last year ordinary negligence got a Polish weaver three years in prison for producing faulty cloth. And in general, any labour offence is liable to be treated as sabotage and thus as a crime against the state. More than half the people tried for anti-state activities in Czechoslovakia in 1948 were ordinary manual workers. The pattern is familiar to anyone who knows the struggle of trade unionism in the Western world fifty and a hundred years ago when all militant workers were victimized, and misrepresented as agents of a foreign conspiracy. The fact is that in this respect, Eastern Europe is moving rapidly backwards.

Even worse than the suppression of free trade unionism is the existence of slave-labour on a large scale in the Soviet Union and all the other Cominform countries. This is the final sanction behind all Communist labour legislation – a nightmare which haunts every man and woman.

In Czechoslovakia the Five-Year Plan demands an increase of $18\frac{1}{2}$ per cent in the industrial labour force. Much of this increase can only be met from forced labour. The Communists set up forced-labour camps for their opponents as soon as they had taken power. This year they have budgeted to spend nearly £700,000 in keeping them going. About 40,000 Czech and foreign prisoners are serving forced-labour sentences in the uranium mines alone.

THE SOCIALIST PARTIES IN EASTERN EUROPE

Nothing in the postwar history of Eastern Europe is more tragic than the history of its Socialist parties. The attitude of the East European Socialists towards the situation created by Red Army occupation was not everywhere the same. Their reaction differed from country to country and even from man to man. There was in most countries a group of Socialist leaders who genuinely believed that they now at last had a chance to transform the social and economic system according to the principles of democratic socialism. Many of the early economic changes – land reform, nationalization, and so on – received their full support. But it soon became clear that the purposes underlying Russian and Communist policy had nothing whatever in common with socialist principles. From that moment on Socialist resistance to totalitarian methods grew ever stronger and more unanimous.

('The Curtain Falls' continued with accounts of the postwar history of the Polish, Czech and Hungarian Socialist parties.)

SOCIALISM

(From *The Unity of European Culture*, BBC, 1953)

I often think it is a mistake to talk, as we so often do over here, of the struggle between Western democracy and Eastern totalitarianism. Inevitably, this presentation of the Cold War, as a conflict between two political ideals which have precise geographical locations, encourages the tendency to write off everything east of the Iron Curtain as somehow belonging to totalitarianism by birth. So the agony of Eastern Europe is taken for granted as the natural fate of peoples who have never known freedom and therefore cannot feel its loss. I imagine this attempt to rationalize another's suffering conceals a profound sense of guilt. In any case it has received a rude shock in the last few months when from all over Eastern Europe news has come in of men and women fighting for their liberty.

It is true of course, that among the peoples now behind the Iron Curtain parliamentary democracy has had a shorter and less happy life than in most of Western Europe. But for that very reason these peoples prize the ideals of liberty and justice more deeply than men who cannot remember what life was like without them. This struck me very forcibly when, in the years after the Second World War, I used to visit Eastern Europe myself as international secretary of the British Labour Party. For the socialism of Eastern Europe is more deeply rooted in the hunger for liberty than even the socialism of some Western countries. There were, of course, opportunists in the East European Socialist parties who compromised with tyranny for personal gain. There were others who had convinced themselves sincerely that liberty was a luxury too expensive for the harsh years after the war. Such have their counterparts in Western Europe too. But in Eastern Europe they were everywhere a tiny minority. Nowhere could they win control of their parties without the most flagrant trickery, supported by an open intervention from the Russian occupation armies. Men like Cyrankiewicz, Fierlinger, and Szakasits were no more representative of the parties they claimed to lead than their miserable fellows in France and Belgium who had collaborated with the Nazis. The true spirit of East European socialism was demonstrated again and again by the martyrs like Zulawski, Dundr, and Anna Kethly who preferred prison or death to betraying their ideals. It is demonstrated anew each day by the countless anonymous workers who brave forced-labour camps and Russian tanks to fight for bread and freedom.

The history of European socialism has never known an Iron Curtain. There were often fierce disagreements in the formative years of the nineteenth century. But they never followed regional lines. Marx himself was a Rhinelander who lived much of his life in England. The first great libertarian challenge to his authority in the international socialist movement came from the Russian anarchist Bakunin. And it was another Russian, Lenin, who presented the first real challenge from totalitarianism. Lenin drew on the techniques of terrorism and conspiracy developed by the Narodniki in his own country, techniques which had no relation whatever with the policies or ideals of socialism. So one of the most effective opponents Lenin had to meet in his own camp of revolutionary Marxism was the Polish Jewess, Rosa Luxemburg. And when the deadly efficiency of Lenin's revolutionary techniques had been tested in the laboratory of Russia, the only big Socialist parties to succumb to their attractions and join the Communist International intact were both of Western Europe – the Norwegian and Italian – though neither stayed there long.

If there is any general difference between socialism in Eastern and in Western Europe it lies, not in their degrees of devotion to democracy, but in the importance which they attach to the nation. Before the First World War most East European countries were under either Austrian or Russian rule. So their struggle for socialism was allied with the struggle for national independence – as it is nowadays in Asia. This naturally brought them into conflict with the internationalism of the Marxists, which was in any case a national interest of the German and Austrian Socialists. But the sharpness of these divisions was reduced when the great French Socialist Jaurès revised Marxism so as to make it more compatible with the realities of national feeling, and when the First World War presented issues which could no longer be evaded by general slogans. A few years later Lenin offered the movement a new form of internationalism which meant automatic subservience to the dictates of the Soviet state. But then as earlier the Socialists of Eastern Europe continued to fight for the independence of their parties and their nations. They are still the backbone of national resistance to Russian colonialism today.

We have seen recently in Czechoslovakia, in Poland, in Eastern Germany, in Hungary, in Romania, and in Bulgaria that the Russians still consider the Socialists their most deadly enemies, for the Socialists still command the united allegiance of the working class. To the workers freedom is not an abstract word. It means the right to choose the men to represent them in the factory every day, the right to have those representatives protect their interests without fear of victimization – and, failing that, the right to strike. In most of Eastern Europe, even where the state itself was unresponsive to the worker's needs, a century of struggle and self-sacrifice had established free trade unions which could at least help to satisfy the worker's minimum demands at factory or pit. By destroying these trade unions, worse still, by perverting them into something like the Nazi Arbeitsfront, the Communists have outraged the workers' deepest feelings and robbed them of their dearest possession. The right to elect a member of Parliament is a remote privilege compared with the right to elect a shop steward in your own workshop or a branch secretary for your own trade union. By turning factory elections into a terroristic ritual, by replacing the workers' choice by a creature of the secret police, the Communist regimes have earned the undying hatred of the labour movement throughout Eastern Europe. No one knows better than the Communists how deadly the hostility of the workers can become. It survived all the persecution of the Tsars and the Hapsburgs. And it came triumphantly through the long agony of the Nazi occupation. Indeed nothing proved the unity of European socialism better than the common struggle fought by the workers of every European country during the Second World War. That was indeed socialist internationalism at its highest point, when workers of France, Germany, Austria, Poland and so many other countries fought together against the enemies of freedom. But that struggle taught another lesson. It should not be forgotten that the last time Eastern Europe fought an alien tyranny the danger came from the West and not from the East. There is indeed a division in European culture, but it is a spiritual, not a geographical, one. Hitler and Mussolini are as much part of Western European history as Bevin and Blum. Pastukov and Petrescu share the East European stage with Pavelic and Horthy. That is why it is so wrong to make culture the tool of a regional chauvinism. The pharisees of Western culture forget that they owe their political values to a country of south-east Europe and their religious values to a country of the Middle East. The values for which democrats and socialists have fought throughout the centuries have been better expressed in Europe than in other continents – and they have been worse betrayed in Europe than elsewhere. They are values common to humanity. In the field of social and political action, the unity of European culture is asserted by the international socialist movement – but it is a unity which does not stop even at the boundaries of the European continent. It is a unity which knows no boundaries at all, for it is based on the brotherhood of all men on this earth. That is why we socialists of Western Europe feel that you of Eastern Europe are fighting our fight – a fight for a Europe and a world united in freedom and social justice.

EUROPEAN SOCIALISM TODAY

(from the *New Leader*, 16 September 1957)

As a political movement, socialism is barely a century old: the First International was formed in 1864. Yet it has already established itself as a dominant political ideal in most parts of the world. Indeed, its appeal for the masses is such that a bewildering variety of systems has claimed some part in its heritage. Among the dictators, Stalin, Hitler, Perón and Nasser have all described themselves as socialists. At the other extreme, there are not only the official Labour and Social Democratic movements of modern Europe; there are the French Radical Socialists, and the Belgian Social Christians. And in Britain the architect of postwar Conservatism, 'Rab' Butler, has boasted: 'We are all social democrats now.'

It is obvious that socialism meets a fundamental need of modern man, or its attraction would not be so widely felt. Indeed, the human need it satisfies is so fundamental that it is impossible to give socialism any political definition which can be applied equally in all countries at all times. As a respose to the social environment, it must change with every change in its political or economic context. In this sense 'revisionism' – a cardinal sin in the Soviet doxology – is an indispensable element in socialist development. Each generation of socialists in every country has the right and the duty to reinterpret its principles in the light of the situation in which it finds itself.

Socialism first developed in nineteenth-century Europe as a reaction of intellectuals to the moral degradation and material suffering imposed on the new working class by the Industrial Revolution. Never since the days of slavery had the economic exploitation of man by man assumed so dreadful a form. Yet, few of the early socialists had a clear idea of what precisely needed changing in the existing system, or of the general shape which a socialist society should assume. Marx and Engels remedied this deficiency. In an intellectual achievement which has few parallels in history, they described contemporary society as a war between classes whose characteristics were determined by their place in the process of production. The Marxist method undoubtedly provided better tools for understanding industrial Europe in the nineteenth century than reformers or revolutionaries had ever had before. Yet, despite Marx's claim that his task was not to understand the world but to change it, Marxist groups made little real impact on the system they analysed so cleverly. The big social, political and economic changes took place under other auspices. Marx and Engels could only explain how they had happened after the event.

Meanwhile, all over Europe, ignorant of Marx's ideas and without his advice, the working class was beginning to organize in trade unions for its own protection. The trade unions were particularly militant and successful in Britain and America – indeed it was the American unions which established May Day as the workers' annual festival. It is interesting to read the comments of Marx and Engels on the Anglo-Saxon labour movement – particularly in the Sorge correspondence. They saw clearly enough that the future of socialism in these countries lay with the organized trade unionists rather than the cliques of 'Marxist' intellectuals.

As the trade unions grew in strength, the more intelligent members of the ruling class had the sense to meet their demands half way. In Germany, Bismarck laid the foundations of the welfare state. In Britain, Disraeli and Shaftesbury began to mitigate the worst evils of industrialism. In fact, wherever democracy gave the workers the opportunity of political influence, they were able to obtain improvements in the existing capitalist system which little by little changed its very nature. Thus the generalizations which Marx made about capitalism a century ago no longer conform to the reality in Europe or North America – indeed, in some cases they apply better to the system in Soviet Russia, where in the absence of democracy the primary accumulation of capital continues, albeit under a different system of ownership, at the same pace and with the same ruthlessness as in Western Europe during the worst period of the Industrial Revolution. It is no accident that the cultural and artistic standards of the Soviet ruling class resemble so closely those of the nineteenth-century bourgeoisie.

By the beginning of the First World War, the socialist intellectuals had achieved some sort of alliance with the working-class trade unionists in most European countries. On the Continent, the bulk of these intellectuals were Marxist – though the process of revising early Marxism had already gone some way, particularly in Germany. In Britain, the socialist intellectuals tended rather to be Christian idealists or Fabians. At this time, the German Social Democrats were the dominant influence in the Second International.

The war itself brought the total disintegration of the International and the disintegration of many member parties, as the working class chose to fight for King or Kaiser. But four years of slaughter and privation produced a great revulsion against the existing order. And when peace came, nearly all the European Socialist parties made great gains. During the next twenty years, socialism was to get its first chance for office at the national level.

At this time, all the Socialist parties were committed to the same general view of their role. Having won power, they were to exercise the major economic functions on behalf of the people through the state machine; this would require that much, if not all, of the national capital should be transferred from private to public ownership. The British Labour Party, reputed the least doctrinaire of all, had bound itself in its written constitution to seek the public ownership of the means of production, distribution and exchange.

Experience in the interwar years profoundly modified these ambitions. The Great Depression revealed that socialist economics, as it then existed, was no better able than Conservative economics to overcome the contradictions of contemporary capitalism. In Britain, the Labour government collapsed after only two years in office because its leaders had not the slightest idea of how to use their power. Ironically enough, it was Franklin D. Roosevelt in the United States who first used state intervention effectively to deal with the consequences of the slump. But he took his advice from John Maynard Keynes, not Marx. Only in Sweden did a

Socialist government use scientific economic techniques to control the crisis, simultaneously producing the most advanced social services in the world.

Meanwhile, the Bolshevik Revolution in Russia had produced a great schism in the international socialist movement just at the moment when the auspices were most favourable for it. By using a rigid distortion of Marxism as the ideological cement for his revolutionary machine, Lenin associated the socialist ideal with conspiratorial terrorism. Tsarism had so long been a symbol of the sort of tyranny which Socialists hated most that the October Revolution was greeted all over the world as a triumph for socialism, although in fact it was the defeat of the Liberals and Socialists who had overthrown the Tsar by a dictatorial minority of terrorists. When the Bolsheviks tried to get control of the international socialist movement by the same methods, they were at first met with open arms in many countries. The Italian and Norwegian Socialist parties joined the Comintern *en bloc*. And though experience soon brought wisdom, every Socialist party in the world finally split into a democratic and a Communist group.

The Russian Communists used their dictatorial power to enforce economic planning and control by the state machine – indeed, they are largely responsible for the popularity of the concept of national planning which has played so central a part in economic development throughout the world in the last generation. But though they eliminated some of the economic disturbances which result from private capitalism, they showed that state capitalism is subject to contradictions which are no less damaging. Immune from the world crisis because they had no foreign trade, they nevertheless condemned millions of peasants to death by starvation. And their enormities compelled the Socialists to examine the central problem which Marx and the Fabians alike had failed to recognize: How is it possible to combine democratic control at both the national and local level with effective central planning? Or, in other words, how can Socialists realize the assumption which is basic to all their economic thinking, that the state should represent the people?

Communism and the economic crisis between them helped to produce the third catastrophe which dominated the interwar years – the rise of Fascism. Though many Socialists in every country tried to see Hitler as just another Kaiser playing his part in a game of bourgeois power politics which was no concern of the working class, the rise of Fascism contributed a great deal toward educating the European Socialists in the realities of international affairs. Until then, there had been a tendency to imagine that war was exclusively a phenomenon of capitalism and that conflicts between nations would disappear automatically as Socialist parties took power. They had yet to face the unhappy paradox that, to the extent that Socialist governments democratically represent the whole of a nation, they are responsible for protecting its interests even against other nations. There is a danger that the socialization of the nation will lead to the nationalization of socialism!

When Europe emerged in 1945 from the Second World War, the prospects for socialism were much brighter than in 1918, and the Socialist parties were infinitely more mature. In nearly every country, they formed at least a third of the government. In Britain and Scandinavia, they won absolute majorities. It was customary in those years to look upon Europe as a socialist continent midway ideologically as well as geographically between capitalist America and Communist Russia. Since then, the European Socialists have everywhere lost ground. And though the socialist ideal is spreading like a flame through Asia and Africa, the European Socialists have so far failed to develop the influence and prestige in these new continents which the Russian and Chinese Communists exert among their co-religionists. It is absurd to talk of the decline of democratic socialism – the movement as a whole is more powerful than ever before, and everywhere the Socialist parties are much stronger than before the Second World War. The real disappointment is among those – not all of them Socialists – who hope to see democratic socialism present itself all over the world as a clear and simple alternative to Communism, and who now find that socialism is often as various, confused and ambiguous as democracy itself.

Communism is essentially a conspiratorial technique for winning and maintaining power, concerning itself with means alone, not ends. As such, it can be applied with only minor modifications in every country alike. The structure of a communist party, like its jargon, differs little from Moscow to Rome or Jakarta. Socialism is a social response by human beings to their economic and political environment. It must differ from place to place and time to time. As an international movement it is a community but not an organization, still less a machine. As an intellectual system it is an art, not a science. Its only rigid principles are moral imperatives, not political programmes.

For this reason, it may have been a mistake for the new Socialist International to have attempted to formulate general policies on either domestic or world problems. By doing so, it has created an unnecessary rift between the European and Asian Socialist parties. And it is doubtful whether, on the occasions when it has forced a single European party into isolated opposition, the movement as a whole has gained thereby more than it has lost. For even in Europe there are national differences so radical as to defy any useful generalization.

In the last twelve years, the British Labour Party has come to occupy the position in the international socialist movement once held by the German Social Democrats. It started by inheriting the immense national prestige of Churchill's wartime Britain. After winning a crushing election victory, it organized Britain's postwar recovery so successfully that Britain was the first European country to dispense with Marshall Aid. Simultaneously, it established Britain as the most advanced welfare state in the world and nationalized basic industries covering 20 per cent of the British economy. Abroad it gave freedom to most of the British Empire, including the whole of the Indian subcontinent, and helped organize the Atlantic community as a working partnership of Western Europe, the United States of America, and the British Commonwealth.

It was a remarkable list of achievements which inevitably gave the Labour Party a predominant position in the Socialist International. The domestic programme was carried out by a system of economic planning and control more sophisticated than any other country has yet developed. In Scandinavia, majority socialist governments achieved similar results by much the same methods. Why, then, did the Continental socialists fail where their northern comrades succeeded? Not because they refused to adopt the Labour Party's techniques of organization and government.

In the first place, British socialism depends on a degree of civic responsibility and administrative efficiency which does not yet exist in southern Europe – indeed, it did not exist in Britain until the siege economy of wartime forced its growth. In the second place, few continental countries enjoy the national homogeneity which centuries of isolation have produced in Britain. The British two-party system, which gives such exceptional authority to the government in power, could not work in countries which are bitterly divided by religious, communal and historic feuds. It is interesting that constitutional monarchy has almost everywhere gone hand in hand with socialist government of the British type: both depend on a rare degree of national unity and toleration.

A socialist party in a multi-party state, however, can rarely hope for office except in coalition with another party which does not share its views. Coalition government has a dual disadvantage in that it forces compromises on socialist leaders without enabling the rank and file to learn the lessons of government experience. A dangerous split is liable to develop between socialist ministers and those they purport to represent, which can sometimes be overcome only by undemocratic control of the party machine. In such countries, the weakness of socialism and the strength of communism are only a symptom of the weakness of democracy itself. A socialist leader often faces the choice between trying to strengthen democracy at the expense of his party or vice versa. This is essentially a question of judgement, though it is easily represented as one of principle. And it has been particularly agonizing in the last twelve years when Soviet support for foreign Communist Parties has meant that democracy and national independence stand or fall together.

There is, in fact, only one lesson which the less successful Socialist parties can learn from their more fortunate northern comrades – the habit of pragmatism itself, the determination to relate programmes to the concrete problems of the nation, and to test the prescriptions of doctrine or tradition at all times by the welfare of the human beings concerned. Pragmatism, of course, is not enough by itself, as Pierre Mendès-France has discovered in France. But unless socialism is related to the realities and possibilities of specific situations, it is liable to degenerate into a hypocritical jargon for disguising casuistry.

What, then, are the prospects for European socialism at present? It is likely that the northern parties will continue to develop along their present lines as governments or potential governments. The German Social Democrats have already revised their programme and doctrine pragmatically, and are likely to win power at least in the next ten years. The major problem is in France and Italy, where the Social Democrats are ground between the millstones of a clerical Right and a Communist Party with considerable working-class support. The French Socialist Party now faces the choice between ossifying into a historical curiosity, like the Radical Socialists, or leading the fight to turn France into a modern democracy when the final débâcle in Algeria brings the long-awaited *crise de régime*. But even if the official French Socialist Party fails to fulfil its destiny, there are many ardent spirits in France who will be able to take up the torch it drops.

In Italy, too, the fate of democracy depends most of all on the capacity of the Socialists to lead the national revival. As in France, there are millions of people, at present uncommitted to any party, who long to see the Socialists provide a democratic alternative to Communism and who see the reunification of the two existing parties as the first step to this end. The difficulties of restoring genuine democracy inside Pietro Nenni's PSI machine are well known. But even if the organizational problems of reunification can be overcome, the Italian Socialists will still have to formulate a realistic programme of legislation which can provide a basis for economic and social advance without demanding that Italians turn into Englishmen or Swedes.

It could be that European economic integration may provide the external impetus for countries like France and Italy to lay the foundations on which socialism can build. Significantly, this was the first major issue on which the Nenni Socialist party split with the Communists. And though there have always been good reasons why the healthy and prosperous social democracies of Britain and Scandinavia have hesitated to throw in their lot with the Continent, the Common Market is likely to force them to overcome their reluctance – with consequences from which socialism in southern Europe is bound to benefit.

Finally, the advance of European socialism is certain to be assisted by the evident decomposition of Communism as an international movement. Within a generation at most, the French and Italian Communist parties will either break their ties with Moscow or shrivel into insignificance. More important still, great-power diplomacy may lead to a settlement which reunites Eastern Europe with the West, with profound yet unpredictable consequences on the internal situation of both sides. Indeed, if European socialism is seen in its historical context, its present state may appear not as old age but as adolescence.

CHAPTER THREE

European Unity

IN 1947 I WROTE THE Labour Party's statement on the European Recovery Programme, which Washington had made a condition of providing aid under the Marshall Plan. So I was deeply involved in winning the support of the other European Socialist parties for this united approach to European reconstruction. In 1948, however, a division opened up over the route which Western Europe should follow towards greater unity. Jean Monnet organized a movement which argued for the creation of supranational economic institutions as the foundation for a merger of sovereignties in a federal union of Western Europe. The Schuman Plan for a European Coal and Steel Community and the proposals for a European Economic Community, or Common Market, were explicitly based on this approach. The schism they created persists to this day.

In September 1948 the Labour Party published my pamphlet, 'Feet on the Ground', which developed the argument for functional co-operation between governments rather than the supranational route to federal union. I still hold the opinions I expressed in the extract below. But I chose not to describe some of the other factors which led the Attlee government to reject the first steps towards the Common Market. At that time Britain still saw itself as a world power, and was arrogant enough to describe London as the centre of three concentric circles – the Commonwealth, the Atlantic community, and Western Europe. But the government was desperately conscious of how Britain had been weakened by six years of war: it sought new sources of power, not new sources of responsibility. The United States was, of course, the only possible source of power; but Britain was deeply suspicious of Washington's demands that London should lead Western Europe into a federation, seeing this as a design enabling the United States to withdraw from its entangling alliance with

Europe as soon as possible. Churchill and Eden were as strongly opposed to the supranational approach as Attlee and Bevin. In those years, British leaders of all parties also saw the Commonwealth as far more important than it later proved to be, an illusion which Hugh Gaitskell and Harold Wilson were to share: Conservative faith in the Commonwealth, however, suffered a mortal blow in 1956 at Suez.

Looking back on those days after forty years, I tried to explain Britain's position frankly to an audience which included many of my old sparring partners, like George Ball and Lincoln Gordon. My speech, on 'European Political Co-operation and the Marshall Plan' was given to a seminar at the Johns Hopkins University in Bologna, a few weeks after the Black Monday of October 1987 had rocked the stock markets all over the non-Communist world.

Two years later the whole framework within which these arguments had been conducted since the war was dissolving under the impact of Gorbachev on the Soviet bloc. I spoke to a seminar organized by the *Financial Times* in Stockholm on 'Europe and the Nordic Countries' in October 1989, a few weeks before the Berlin Wall was breached and Europe was plunged into a maelstrom of change.

The process of creating a single market in the European Community by 1992 was already bogging down. But the prospect that it might succeed had led to a massive invasion of the Community by American and Japanese capital, to make sure that if 1992 produced a European fortress, the Trojan horses would already be inside. Swedish industry had followed suit, and was pressing the Swedish government to join the Common Market, whatever the consequences for Sweden's neutrality.

The main point of my talk on whether the European Community was capable of further enlargement was that Brussels should not make the impossible best the enemy of the possible good. There was in fact no chance of developing the Community into a political union. Major disagreements between France, Germany, and Britain on defence policy had ruled that out for many years. German reunification was no longer a distant dream. If Western Germany alone could dominate the Community already, closer integration would not enable the Community to control a united Germany; the opposite was more likely to be the case.

On the other hand the Community, which already included a neutral Ireland, had no right to refuse the application for membership of a neutral Austria. Honecker's East Germany had been given country membership of the Community years earlier; if a democratic Poland or Hungary wished to join, they should not be excluded either.

I had always believed that if the reunification of Eastern and Western Europe ever became possible, it should take priority, if necessary, over the closer integration of the existing Community. In any case, a Community which included Germany's northern and eastern neighbours as well would provide a far more comfortable framework for a united Germany. And a new security system which included all the signatories of the Helsinki Agreement would have far more chance of surviving than some botched-up arrangement between a NATO which had lost its function and a Warsaw Pact which no longer had any military reality or political support.

I have returned regularly to these themes as the revolution in Eastern Europe and the Soviet Union developed.

FEET ON THE GROUND

Labour Party, 1948

The difficulties and dangers inherent in the creation of a Western union have led many people to argue that the obstacles will be insurmountable unless all the countries begin by limiting their national sovereignty within a federal union. The federalists claim that the overriding necessity for co-operation is never sufficiently obvious when all the detailed problems involved are dealt with separately, but that nations which strain at a million gnats may swallow one camel.

Many of the classical arguments for federation are inapplicable in the modern world. Most of the present-day federal states were founded in new continents by small immigrant populations. As they grew in power and complexity their economic and social systems adapted themselves to the existing federal framework. It is infinitely more difficult for Europe to federate today than it was for America in 1789 or Australia in 1901. But the main argument against approaching Western union through federation – rather than completing Western union by federation – is that in itself federation would not solve the immediate problems of Western Europe, while the attempt to achieve it would exaggerate the differences between the West European states instead of exploiting their common interests.

Federation depends on a division of powers between the central federal authority and the participating states. When the existing federations like the USA were formed, the federal government was given mainly the right to decide foreign policy and defence arrangements for the group. Apart from the abolition of internal tariffs, the separate states decided their economic and social policies as before.

But today a nation's economic activities are so complicated and interwoven, and the part played in them by the government so greatly increased, that any attempt to disentangle separate spheres of competence for federal and state governments would involve serious dislocations in the economic and political life of the states concerned; modern defence involves almost every part of a nation's economy. Indeed, even in the USA, Australia, and Canada the adequacy of federalism for a modern industrial society is increasingly questioned. Moreover, the European countries differ greatly among themselves about the way in which a state's economic life should be organized; each country would do its best to ensure that the federal government had as little power as possible to interfere in its domestic policies; certainly socialists, at present a minority of about one third in Western Europe as a whole, would insist on the right to organize socialism in countries where they were a majority, as in Britain and Scandinavia.

Thus an attempt to federate now would exaggerate divisions, excite mutual fear, distrust, contempt, and jealousy and greatly favour centrifugal tendencies. If it succeeded, the federal government would find itself hedged in at every turn by immovable constitutional obstructions, and special opportunities for united action would constantly have to be forgone for fear of creating a general precedent. The European countries differ much more widely in race, language, temperament, political institutions and economic organization than states in any existing federation, and those differences are rooted in centuries of usage. Even if agreement could be reached on a means of electing a federal parliament, of reconciling multi-party proportional representation with the British two-party system, republic with monarchy, there is no reason to think that a parliament so heterogeneous would be wiser or more united in judging the complicated practical issues of co-operation than committees of national experts and Cabinet ministers, like the OEEC or Brussels Treaty organs.

Finally Europe's history of separate national existence has produced clearly defined interest groups. When such groups do exist no written constitution can by itself compel them to act against their imagined interests. More than most federal governments, a European federation would require forcible sanctions against secession. The prolonged and bloody American Civil War is not an encouraging precedent.

These arguments against federation carry special weight at the present time, when the urgent need is for immediate common action to solve critical problems. Any attempt to create a federation now would raise innumerable general issues unconnected with those problems. Precious years would be wasted in wrangles which created disunity and contributed nothing to solving our difficulties. There is a further danger in any approach which depends on changing the whole basis of the existing system. In both the economic and strategic fields, many of the European countries are operating on the edge of danger with no margin for error. At all costs these countries must preserve their ability to react quickly and vigorously to crises. An attempt to consolidate Europe now by federation, even if it progressed favourably, might find these countries in a crisis having lost their capacity to react effectively as individuals without having developed the ability to meet the situation as a collective unit.

THE ALTERNATIVE

The federal idea comes to us from an age when the only alternative to federation was a pattern of treaties in which states promised to act together if certain emergencies arose, and whose value depended solely on the will of each state to honour them when the point came. Certainly a common organ of government and common armed services provide a more dependable bond of union than unsupported promises.

But the type of economic co-operation which is possible today can create a vested interest in union fully as binding as a federal government, without any constitutional changes in the countries concerned. Moreover in such functional co-operation the countries can choose those issues in which their common interest is agreed. Success in joint action on concrete economic and political problems will greatly weaken the force of sectional interests, creating such interdependence and mutual confidence that federation may finally become possible. Failure to solve these problems will make federation futile in any case. But it is possible that even a fully developed Western union will prefer an undefined and flexible association, like that of the Commonwealth, to a rigid written constitution. As Ernest Bevin told the House of Commons:

> ... I think that adopting the principle of an unwritten constitution, and the process of constant association step by step, by treaty and agreement and by taking on certain things collectively instead of by ourselves, is the right way to approach this Western union problem. When we have settled the matter of defence, economic co-operation and the necessary political developments

which must follow, it may be possible, and I think it will be, to establish among us some kind of assembly to deal with the practical things we have accomplished as governments, but I do not think it will work if we try to put the roof on before we have built the building.

Public Opinion

Federation can however provide one advantage which the functional approach may easily forfeit: it enables issues to be debated in democratic discussion under the guiding influence of public opinion. Of course public debate can often make agreement more difficult, as we know to our cost from diplomatic history since 1945. Above all, the problems of Europe today demand swift and vigorous action. But there is a danger that if Western union is organized exclusively inside expert committees far removed from the public gaze, vested interests and bureaucratic inertia may slow down progress below the critical speed, and bad decisions may be reached under pressures which public opinion would not tolerate. Moreover at some points national groups may be faced with sacrifices which are unacceptable if people are indifferent to the issues involved and ignorant of the problems.

If is therefore vital that the work of organizing a Western union shall be made much more accessible to democratic interest than it is at present, and that the governments concerned should individually and collectively do their utmost to see that public opinion is informed of the problems and mobilized to support their solution. Moreover the campaign for Western union can help to restore confidence and hope to millions of Europeans who feel helpless between the Russian and American colossi. The immense psychological value of this united attack on common problems will be lost unless victories are dramatized and public opinion is aroused to watch the progress of the battle.

Finally, the functional approach depends on creating as many international ties as possible across the frontiers to supplement and correct the influence of the existing national vested interests. For this reason the movement for Western union must not be restricted to government officials and ministers. Once the broad outlines of a plan for Europe have been reached by the governments in council, private and public bodies in every country should be encouraged to co-operate in solving the detailed problems. The trade unions and Socialist parties have already taken the lead in this field by establishing their own standing organizations to study the issues of European co-operation.

CONCLUSION

This brief survey of the main problems involved in creating a Western union may seem discouraging to those who think that international action is a magic wand before which difficulties vanish. The problems facing a Western union are little less formidable than those facing the nations separately. In some ways they are even more complicated. Moreover for some of the European countries co-operation means an additional burden. But the decision to press onward in spite of all these difficulties is the best evidence of what all countries stand to gain by success – or lose by failure.

Others may feel that the spreading network of international activity outlined here, however profitable its results, does not deserve to be called a Western union – to earn that title the European countries must agree to merge their national sovereignties in a central supranational authority. It is possible that a growth of mutual confidence due to successful co-operation on all the major issues may persuade the countries to submit to such an authority. But it is certain that few, if any, would wish to do so now. Any attempt to limit national sovereignty by constitutional changes would quickly disintegrate what common organizations do exist. But national sovereignty is an academic concept for philosophers. The type of co-operation now under way in the OEEC and Brussels Treaty organs is steadily making the European countries more and more dependent on one another. The abstract freedom of each country to decide its own policies is already limited in a thousand ways. By constant teamwork in planning and action the nations of Western Europe are slowly growing together. And whether they ultimately express it by a political fusion or not, their union will only be effective in common action.

Little has been said about the relation between a Western union and socialism. But the facts are clear. Western Europe will not survive either as a union or as a collection of separate states unless the governments responsible for its future face their economic problems with the courage and foresight shown by Labour Britain. It is equally clear that economic measures alone will not suffice; the degree of austerity which governments must impose will be unacceptable without social justice and equality of sacrifice. All over Europe the history of the last few years bears witness to these facts. Attempts to impose the burden of adjustment unfairly on the working class have invariably resulted only in a growth of Communism.

We as socialists believe that the type of economic planning and social reform required is incompatible with the survival of competitive capitalism. But so long as other countries adopt the policies which are necessary for recovery, it is not for us to insist that they call these measures socialism. And in Europe recognition of immediate economic and social necessities is not confined to those who describe themselves as social democrats. Labour Britain has no more right than America or Russia to force others to accept her chosen way of life. But she has the right to make her co-operation depend on a realistic approach to the economic and political problems which face Western Europe. If others can meet these problems with measures which are not socialism then Britain can have no complaint. We in England can justly feel proud of our own progress since the war and of the contribution we have already made towards the recovery of Europe. We must also learn the humility needed to appreciate the achievement of those with different problems and unfamiliar traditions.

Finally it must be stressed that the success of international co-operation depends on the same factors as the success of each national effort – on the hard work and social responsibility of the ordinary man and woman, on the leadership and intelligence of those in authority. In itself the establishment of an international committee will not produce more of the right goods at the right prices. It is not too much to say that the future of civilization may well depend on the success of the great enterprise to which we have pledged ourselves. The issues are too tremendous for us to indulge in illusions of an easy success. We must keep our feet firmly on the ground and resist all the tempting mirages which seem to offer a short cut to our goal. If we do so the coming years will see a dramatic transformation in the whole world situation, and the nightmare which has haunted mankind since the defeat of Hitler will be forgotten in the dawning of a brighter day.

BRITAIN AND EUROPE

(from lecture at the Bologna Center of the Johns Hopkins University,
10 November 1987)

Britain's whole postwar history has largely been an attempt to bring our commitments in the world into line with our diminished resources. When I was defence secretary, my most difficult job was to liquidate our commitments east of Suez and to accommodate a major nuclear role, which promises to be increasingly expensive in the coming years. The essence of the postwar Labour government's approach to the world was the continual search for new sources of power rather than new sources of responsibility. So we tried to involve the USA long term in the economic support of and military protection of Western Europe. We saw NATO and the Marshall Plan as two halves of the same walnut, as was said at the time. Because we wanted America involved long term, we were much more interested in trying to develop some sort of Atlantic community than in just European unity. Moreover, some of the Europeans, like Jean Monnet, who at first were primarily concerned with European unity, later came to feel it would work only if America itself could be more deeply and permanently involved.

But there was a contradiction in the British position of which I was not aware at the time: we wanted to remain a world power; we wanted to be equal with the USA, but we were quite prepared to try to build up the rest of Western Europe to be equal with us and with the USA. William Clayton at the time warned us that attempting to equal the USA in the postwar world would be playing Yugoslavia to America's Soviet Union. There was a horrid truth in that remark, although I think our experience and our friendships with key Americans at the time gave us an influence which was out of proportion to our material strength. Nevertheless, for the first time in Britain's history, a British government was prepared to work for a united Europe, seeing that as the only way in which Western Europe could survive in the long run as a narrow fringe on the west of the great Communist empire of Eurasia. Nevertheless, we were never fully prepared to join in this European unity because we wanted to remain a world power. Our prime concern was to commit the Americans to Western Europe, and we had a nasty feeling that if we went off into Europe and left the Americans outside, they would reduce their own commitment.

Indeed, there were some influential Americans, like Ben Moore in the State Department, who did see the main case for European unity as creating a cordon sanitaire against the Soviet Union behind which the USA could retreat into a less exposed position – do not forget that America had committed itself by Act of Congress ten years earlier to permanent neutrality in world affairs. The postwar shift in America's position was quite as dramatic as the shift in Britain's position. The dominant American view at the time was that Britain could not play a full role in Europe without actually being inside it, and many Americans saw the federal model of the USA as what Western Europe should aim at.

But America's pressure on Europe to adopt that model was unconvincing to us in Britain and to many Europeans, not least because the USA was not prepared to envisage any diminution in its own constitutional sovereignty. At that time Washington was causing great difficulties about bringing Hawaii and Alaska into its own federation because it would have made a difference of two votes in the Senate, and possibly one in the House, if they joined. We also could not ignore the fact that America's federal constitution had been imposed by the victors on the vanquished after a bloody civil war in which the USA lost more men than in all the wars that followed put together, including Vietnam. Even today, we cannot help noticing that many of America's problems in the modern world have arisen from its constitution, particularly the division of powers between the executive and legislative branch. Most people who have had to work in Washington have often felt that policy-making in Washington is like a standing conference of great powers trying to reach agreement on one policy after another: the White House, the Pentagon, the State Department, and both houses of Congress. Moreover, there is usually a great variety of views inside each of these great powers. I cannot remember any time when the State Department itself has been united on what should be done. In sum, the USA's federal model is not too convincing as an example for Europe to follow.

Confederation might be another matter, but that depends on how it is defined in a specific constitution. We are all looking for something which recognizes certain permanent derogations of sovereignty without compelling countries to work together in areas where they really have little common interest in co-operation. Oddly enough, the constitutional lawyers have given very little thought to models which might be appropriate for co-operation between democratic industrial states in the modern world.

Some of the pressure exerted by American administrations on European governments and legislatures turned out to be counterproductive. That was particularly true of the pressure on the French Parliament to ratify the EDC; in the end it was the French Parliament which rejected it although it was a French government which had proposed it. Yet every now and then America returned to its federalistic ideas, notably what we used to call Ball's 'Last Stand' – the Multilateral Force, a device for artificial dissemination which in the end died the death.

The British approach to European unity has not changed a great deal since those days, although I think in some respects that approach is outmoded, particularly the attempt to remain a world power. We had a very able scientist called Sir Henry Tizard who was the scientific adviser to the British government after the war. When the government was discussing whether to develop British nuclear weapons, he said, 'I warn

you, if you try to remain a great power you will cease to be a great nation.'
I think there was something in what he said.

Now we will take a look at continental Europe in those days. The
dominant politicians in the continental European response to the Marshall
Plan tended to be Christian Democrats, largely because they happened to
be in power: Alcide de Gasperi in Italy, Adenauer in Germany, and
Robert Schuman in France. They always favoured a supranational or
federal model in principle, though in practice even the institutions they
succeeded in setting up did not really work supranationally. The Schuman
Plan for coal and steel now operates by fairly effective bargaining between
states, although it has had terrible difficulties in recent years because of
the world surplus in steel. The only supranational element in the Common
Market is the Common Agricultural Policy, which seemed to be modelled
on the worst excesses of Hitler's finance minister, Hjalmar Schacht. It has
succeeded in producing a European surplus of food, in which there is
already a world surplus, and threatens to suffocate the Common Market
under its burden. Since it began, the Common Agricultural Policy has
been a major irritant in Western Europe's relations with both the USA
and the Third World. In any case the supranational model for the
Common Market was doomed to failure once it was clear that it was going
to include the southern European states. Italy was in from the beginning;
since then Greece, Spain and Portugal have come in. It has always seemed
to me, with respect to my Italian friends, that the 'olive line' is as
important as the Iron Curtain in dividing Europe, because south of the
olive line people do not pay their taxes, they do not respect their government, indeed they get on very well without governments altogether. To
expect a Sicilian landowner to pay taxes as honestly as a Dutch manufac-
turer, even in these days, is expecting a bit much.

Many of us hoped that we could develop greater political co-operation
inside Western Europe; but the dominant approach at the time was to try
to create institutions whose duty would be to produce political agreement;
that was doomed to failure for the reasons I have explained. I myself have
found, as a minister, that the only way to get political co-operation is to
talk to European colleagues and identify an area where there is a strong
common interest *vis-à-vis* the USA or the Soviet Union. In this way we
got the Nuclear Planning Group set up in NATO to permit the
Europeans to contribute to alliance nuclear planning, which had previously
been the sole prerogative of the USA – even the British were not much
involved. We also set up the Eurogroup to try to get closer co-operation in
arms procurement, and that worked quite well as long as ministers were

prepared to put some weight behind it. And when I was chancellor I did manage to organize a European lobby against the American proposal for an OECD support fund, and in favour instead of the second Witteveen oil facility.[1]

My own experience has been that if the Europeans can put a rational collective case on an issue in Washington it will always find sufficient supporters in the Washington great power conference to have a chance of getting it through. The one exception is the Middle East. The basic problem in the Middle East is that only the US administration can put effective pressure on the Israeli government, and no American administration since Eisenhower has been prepared to do that, although there was a limited attempt by Cyrus Vance in the last years of the Carter administration, which was scuppered by the Russian invasion of Afghanistan.

Now let us look at the lessons we can derive forty years later from all this experience. Those forty years have seen enormous changes in the world, some of which have been brought about by the success of the Marshall Plan and of NATO, as George Ball indicated in his introduction. First of all, if you take Western Europe as a whole, particularly if you add in the Scandinavian countries, which are not at the moment in the Common Market, it is potentially by far the strongest single group of countries in the world – even stronger economically than the USA, more populous than the Soviet Union. But it has not achieved a corporate identity. That is the great tragedy of Europe. It is still hugging its American nuclear chains in the field of defence and it is terrified to think independently about any defence problem because it is so much more comfortable to rely on the Americans. Political co-operation is rightly described by my Italian friends in the acronym POCO. It has produced very, very little indeed and has mainly concentrated on trying to develop Middle East policy, which is the only part of the world where the Europeans have very little scope for useful intervention unless they can persuade America to change its position on Israel. And it is divided even on many of the major economic issues. So it is a very ineffective unit, although in terms of economic strength and military potential it could be at least as influential as the USA or the Soviet Union.

Britain's role in Europe is the key to its future. The illusion that the Commonwealth would form a power base for postwar British influence in

---

[1] Measures of 1975 organized through the International Monetary Fund (Managing Director Dr Johannes Witteveen), aimed at dealing with the monetary consequences of the four-fold increase in oil prices in 1973–4.

the world is now completely dead – it really died at Suez. But we are still fighting to remain a world power by depending on the USA for nuclear weapons. There is an obvious contradiction here which is going to become very acute as the Americans move towards agreement with Russia on a 50 per cent cut in strategic nuclear forces. For example, will America agree to limit the number of submarine-launched warheads to 2000-a-side and simultaneously agree to give Britain missiles which have the capability of carrying 900 nuclear warheads? And will the Soviet Union agree to such a deal, even if the Americans wish to?

There has been a striking change in the pattern of our economic interest. Even in the mid 1950s, by the time the Marshall Plan's major effects had taken place, Britain's trade with Europe was only a quarter of its total world trade; yet last year for the first time it surpassed 50 per cent. So our economic and commercial interest at the moment is overwhelming in our trade with Europe. Our political influence – to the extent that we want to play a major role in the world, and I hope we shall, will depend primarily on mobilizing European unity to exert influence in Washington rather than Moscow, because we shall have less chance of influence in Moscow. At present, we are having serious difficulties about that: Mrs Thatcher tends to be rather Gaullist in her approach to these questions. Gaullism still dominates French foreign as well as defence policy. Germany, I think, is increasingly attracted by the perspectives opened by Ostpolitik. This is not an issue which divides the parties; Mr Strauss is now as keen on the Ostpolitik as Chancellor Helmut Kohl, and both are practically as keen as the opposition Social Democrats who launched the Ostpolitik. I am not over-optimistic about the chances of immediate progress in these areas.

However, the biggest changes which have taken place in the world since the Marshall Plan was launched have been changes outside Europe – changes in the positions of the superpowers and even more important changes in various parts of the Third World.

Perhaps before I get on to that I should just make one more remark about defence. In Europe at the present time there is increasing impatience and frustration at what is seen as a lack of wisdom and consistency in American leadership of NATO, and a yearning to create what is again being called a European pillar for the Alliance. But if you look at the defence issues immediately coming up for decision, Europe is deeply divided. The Germans want to get rid of all tactical nuclear weapons because they would kill only Germans. Britain and France want to keep them because they are frightened that their own strategic nuclear weapons will be next in the firing line if there is a reduction in Europe's tactical nuclear forces. But there is a very big difference between Britain and France. France is building her own nuclear weapons and can afford to ignore American pressure. Britain will be totally dependent on the USA for servicing, testing, and replacing its D-5 nuclear missiles and therefore will tend always to give in when it is under pressure from the USA. There is no doubt that in recent weeks the French particularly were deeply disappointed that we did not stick to our guns in putting what is really the Anglo-French position on the INF agreement and what will follow it.

Let us look at the changes outside Europe. If one tries to look at the world with the perspective of postwar history, one sees that today both the Soviet Union and the USA are feeling very over-extended and would like to find a way of cutting their foreign commitments – just like Britain after the war. Moreover, I think the wiser Americans and Russians realize that the time when America and Russia can jointly decide what happens in the rest of the world if they can agree, is disappearing very fast. So those Americans who would like to substitute an American-Soviet duopoly in the world for the American monopoly in the West have very little time in which to achieve it, even if the Russians stick to their present desire to move in that direction.

America's output is now 20 per cent of world GDP: it was 40 per cent after the war. But America is spending twice as much as Europe on defence; it has over a million men under arms, half of whom are outside the USA in foreign countries or at sea.

America is also beginning to discover that its expenditure on modern weapons is damaging its ability to compete with Japan and Germany in high technology. In the last decade the American surplus in high technology trade turned into a deficit for the first time, and in the last eight years the American government, as George Ball suggested, has financed a big defence build-up only by borrowing money from Japan and Germany. But how long Japan and Germany will be prepared to go on funding the American deficit if the value of the dollars they buy or borrow is falling as fast as it has been falling is an open question.

A hard landing for the dollar, caused by a withdrawal or reduction of Japanese or German financing of American deficits, could lead to a world slump, a trade war, and very substantial cuts in American defence spending abroad. Meanwhile, the main opposition to that trend in the USA is coming not from the Atlanticists so much as from the global unilateralists. Since President Reagan came to power the idea of global unilateralism has been winning out over the idea of Atlantic unity, and there has been less and less consultation with the allies about major issues of mutual concern.

In the last fifteen or twenty years political power in the USA has followed economic power to the southern and western states; these states are more concerned with what happens in Central and Latin America and the Pacific area than with what happens in Europe. With the massive immigration of Hispanics into California and Texas and Asians into California, the population balance in the USA is swinging in a direction which is less favourable to Europe's interests than the balance was forty years ago, when the Marshall Plan was launched.

The Soviet Union seems to me to be facing very similar problems. Very high defence spending is reducing its ability to introduce new technologies into its industrial processes and indeed into its service industries. It certainly needs to cut defence to carry out economic perestroika. Gorbachev has consistently noted that the economic imperative must determine Soviet foreign policy. Meanwhile the Soviet Union is facing serious political problems, not only in Eastern Europe but also in the Asian and Baltic republics. Muslim fundamentalism is beginning to spread in Central Asia and today the Russians are probably a minority people inside the Soviet Union. So they have enormous internal problems to deal with, and an arthritic and corrupt state and party bureaucracy which needs complete renewal if they are to be able to succeed.

Gobachev has been talking recently about our common European home. That may seem an irrelevance to many people in the USA. It does not seem irrelevant to people who live in Western Germany, or to countries which have very long historic links with some of the peoples in Eastern Europe. But it must sound odd to the Soviet peoples of Asia.

Now let us take a quick look at the Third World, which is no longer a Third World. It is at least a third, fourth, fifth, and sixth world. On the one hand, you have the countries of Africa and the Middle East which are disaster areas for various reasons. Then you have the Latin American countries which are well advanced in the industrial revolution, but at the moment, because of the way the debt problem has developed, are actually exporting capital to the richest country in the world, the USA. The countries of the subcontinent are also developing but are divided by national tensions which could prove explosive. Finally, you have the countries on the western Pacific rim which are moving ahead of the USA and Western Europe in many areas of industry, particularly in the new technologies. Japan is the most striking, but by no means the only, example. It is easy to forget that when the Bandung Conference met as the first great postwar assembly of the Third World (1955), Japan was a member, and now Japan is regarded throughout the world as economically almost as strong as the USA and a good deal stronger than any individual country in Western Europe. The Japanese have shown a staggering ability to adapt their society and their economy rationally to external shocks. I believe that we can all learn a lot from the way in which they are able to create internal consensus in order to achieve a united approach to necessary change. China is the mystery wrapped in an enigma these days. We know and understand Russia fairly well. We do not really understand China, how far Deng Xiao Ping will succeed, and what he will really want to do. It is much too early to say, but many of us who have been even a little bit in China feel that the Chinese tend to lurch regularly from one extreme to another, and if their present course runs into difficulties they could well lurch back in another direction.

There are three other developments which deserve study. First of all, many aspects of the world economy are already supranational. Most attention has been devoted over the years to the growth of the multinational companies, of which Italy has some important examples, and which owe no allegiance to any government anywhere in the world. Even more important is the revolution in the international financial system which has taken place under the triple blow of globalization – because of the new information technologies – deregulation – because all governments decided they did not want to control the markets, and innovation, the invention of new financial instruments for hedging risk – which means that now nobody knows where the risk lies if anything goes wrong. If we do have another world recession, the fragility of the new international financial system is such that it could collapse under the weight. If you talk privately to commercial bankers and central bankers, they all appear very doubtful the new system could survive a prolonged bear market.

Then there is the enormous change created by nuclear weapons. My political life has been dominated by nuclear weapons. When I was a soldier in Italy and I heard that atom bombs had been dropped in Japan, my immediate feeling, like that of all American and Allied soldiers in Italy, was immense relief that at least we would not have to go out and fight the Japanese as well. When we started looking more closely at the problem, my wartime brigadier – we were specialists in combined operations – said the only importance of nuclear weapons as far as he could see was that we would not be able to carry out opposed landings like we did on D-Day!

Now we understand much more about nuclear weapons. I think it is agreed in NATO that you cannot control a nuclear conflict; certainly cannot rely on controlling one – for all sorts of reasons: the fog of war; Sod's Law; but also unpredictable electromagnetic pulses; finally, we have the horror of the nuclear winter, which could be even more horrible than the damage we have long known could be created by nuclear blast and fire.

The lesson which people have already drawn is that nuclear war is out. No country is going to expose itself deliberately to nuclear war. Moreover, conventional war between nuclear powers is probably out as well, because it might turn into nuclear war. That may be a comforting conclusion for us to draw in the West. But it ignores the problems that would arise if Khomeini or Gaddafi developed their own nuclear weapons. It also assumes a degree of rationality which anyone engaged in politics has known to be unreliable. Nevertheless, it has given us a weather window for a more constructive approach to the problems.

If you look at the way the world has changed since the Marshall Plan, and if you accept some of the caricatures of the changes which I have described, the need for the type of energy and vision which was shown by those who devised the Marshall Plan is overwhelming. It is easy now to identify the major areas where we need that type of inter-national co-operation. In the economic field, Europe and Japan must spend more and import more. The USA must save more and export more. But the scale of the adjustment needed to deal with the massive debt which America has accumulated could be extremely painful, not only for the Americans but also for the countries to which they would have to export the goods. We also need an answer to the problem of the Third World debtors, which could become explosive in even months from now if the present turmoil on the stock exchanges were to continue or to be repeated. And we need some new programme for a long term transfer of resources from the richer countries to the poorer countries, such as Paul Hoffmann, another figure in the great postwar renaissance of constructive imagination, put forward forty years ago.

ENLARGING THE EUROPEAN COMMUNITY

(from 'Europe and the Nordic Countries', *Financial Times* Conference at
Stockholm, October 1989)

The question I was asked to discuss was, is the European Community
capable of further enlargement? The anwer of course is obviously, yes.
The European Community started as a group of six countries and is now
twelve. Britain and two other EFTA countries joined, then Spain and
Greece and the Republic of Eire, which is a neutral country. The real
question is what is the attitude of the present members of the Community
to its possible enlargement in certain directions, and what is the attitude of
potential members of the Community to membership? The answer to
these questions is different according to the person you talk to in each of
the countries concerned.

Just a short glance back at history. De Gaulle strongly opposed Britain's application for membership of the Community because he saw
Britain as the Trojan horse of the United States. Other members of the
Community at that time supported our application because they saw
Britain as a counterweight to possible domination of the Community by
the close alliance between France and Germany, then represented by de
Gaulle and Adenauer. In fact Britain's entry became possible only when
de Gaulle had gone and when Willy Brandt was Chancellor of Germany.

When Portugal, Spain and Greece applied, their application was spon-
sored in a sense by the other southern members of the Community,
France and Italy: but the whole of the Community thought it was their duty
to accept into membership democratic regimes in European countries
which had until just then been dictatorships: Portugal under Salazar,
Spain under Franco, Greece under the Colonels. Eire was accepted
although it was a neutral country because it was democratic, and I
suspect perhaps because it was so small that people felt that any precedent
they set by accepting a neutral Eire would not count very much for
the future.

Talking today in 1989, enlargement of the Community is conceivable to
the north to the Nordic countries, to the east to the Eastern European
countries and to the south to some of the so-called orphans in the
Mediterranean area, and even to some countries on the south coast of the
Mediterranean, particularly Morocco. I know friends in Italy, for example,

who feel that it is very important to bring some of the countries of the Maghreb into some direct relationship with the Community.

Now, as a very broad generalization at the present time, those who believe that it is possible to develop the Community into a political entity – into what we call in England a polity – tend to oppose enlargement in any of these directions because they think it would dilute the Community. There is no question whatever that by bringing in the Mediterranean countries the Monnet dream in its original form went out the window, because you cannot expect Sicilian landowners to pay taxes as honestly as Dutch or even Swedish bankers. Those who oppose the Monnet conception of a European political union tend to support additional members for exactly the same reason and that I think to some extent is true of the present British government.

There are divisions on this in all countries and if you listen to a description of the present state of negotiations between the Community and the EFTA study groups you will recognize the truth of the conclusion I reached when I was British chancellor and chairman of the IMF Interim Committee – international economic diplomacy is rather like rowing a boat through cold treacle: it is very difficult indeed to make any progress at all.

The real question is how much further will the 1992 process proceed. I must say I have never met anyone who thinks that the European single market will be achieved by 1992. The question is how far the process will have gone by then and will it ever be completed? It is possible to have different views on those questions.

So far the most difficult questions have not been approached – the question of tax harmonization which would create such enormous difficulties, not only for Denmark, but certainly for Britain, and the question of local content, particularly for motorcars. Anybody who thinks Gianni Agnelli will agree to more than 3,000 Japanese cars entering Italy every year obviously believes that Italy will undergo a revolution within the next three years.

The problem of border controls raises great difficulties for many members of the Community. Above all there is the question of government procurement which is 15 per cent of GDP in the Community as a whole and raises appallingly difficult questions about telecommunications, for example, and about national airlines.

Moreover, so far only half of the issues have been resolved and of the 68 directives which embody many of the solutions reached, only seven have yet been passed into national law in all the countries concerned.

They only apply to the countries that have passed them into national law.

On European Monetary Union, it is difficult to know how far that will go. At the moment, Mr Delors has organized an unofficial group which put some proposals forward, but they were not binding on any of the individuals who participated in their official capacity, for example, the Governor of the Bank of England. There is total opposition to the Delors proposals, not only from Mrs Thatcher, but also from Karl Otto Poehl, the Chairman of the Bundesbank. In fact the Poehl/Thatcher alliance is sometimes described in Britain as twinset and Poehl.

Then there is the example of the five members of the Community – Germany, France and the Low Countries, which agreed to get rid of all internal barriers between one another, particularly frontier controls, some years ago, but they have made very little progress so far, certainly within the timetable which they set themselves.

Many of us believe that the Social Charter is absolutely indispensable if the 1992 process is to be completed, because countries will not accept the disruptions caused unless there is some machinery for compensating and helping people affected by the disruptions. That is strongly opposed by Mrs Thatcher who now is assuming a new disguise as the Honnecker of the West.

It is possible to take the view that the main effect of the 1992 process has been to stimulate an enormous amount of inward investment into the Community from outside, from the United States, from Japan and indeed from some of the Scandinavian countries, notably, Sweden.

The fear of exclusion has been a very powerful factor in leading companies to set up shop inside the Community: but although the Japanese and the Americans can afford to invest in the Community without damaging the prospects of their own economies, the fact that Swedish businessmen and bankers can vote with their feet against staying out must cause serious problems for the political authorities in some of the EFTA countries.

Let us have a quick look at the attitudes inside the other countries. The opposition of Sweden, Finland and Switzerland to joining the Community seems to me to be rooted essentially in the argument that it would jeopardize their neutrality. Their neutrality is a matter of choice. Austria already has applied to join, although its neutrality is imposed by a treaty signed by the western powers with the Soviet Union. Although the Soviet Union has said that it is hostile to the Austrian application, that has not so far deterred the Austrians from continuing to pursue it.

Norway does not face the neutrality problem, but it is very jealous of its sovereignty. I recall 1956 when the East European joke during the Hungarian rising was that the Hungarians behaved like Poles, the Poles behaved like Czechs and the Czechs behaved like pigs: Art Buchwald produced a variation on the old story of the books written on the elephant, *L'éléphant et L'amour* was the French one and *Prolegomenon to a Future Metaphysics of Elephants* was the German one, but the Finnish one was *Our Debt to the Elephant*, the Swedish one was *What Sweden did for the Elephant in the Second World War* and the Norwegian one was, of course, *Norway and Norwegians*.

I tend to feel that when the incoming coalition in Norway collapses it is very likely that the succeeding government, which will be dominated by the Labour Party will be tempted to apply for membership unless there are signs that the Nordic countries as a group are likely to reach a much closer relationship within the foreseeable future.

Nevertheless, the feeling among the Community members that if they allow in neutrals they will rule out political and strategic unity is operating as a deterrent to accepting them. My own feeling is that the Community should not make the best the enemy of the good, especially when the best is impossible. I see no prospect whatever of the Community becoming a defence Community, because the British, the French and the Germans have been deeply divided on strategic questions for many years and that division is likely to increase as a result of developments in Eastern Europe which I shall come to in a moment. They are also deeply divided on the priority they give to links with the United States: France gives them much lower priority than Germany, and Germany now than Britain.

I think the key question will be, how are the EFTA countries and how is the Community going to react to the changes which are taking place now in Eastern Europe. Developments in Eastern Europe in the coming years may hold the key to whether or not it is possible to achieve the reunification of Europe as a whole, and if that does appear to be possible then many of the detailed rules and regulations over which the Community and EFTA now are haggling will appear as very small beer indeed.

Let us have a quick glance at the possibilities in Eastern Europe. If, as seems very likely, Hungary and Poland shake off the dictatorships under which they have been obliged to suffer over the last forty-five years, there is no more case for rejecting an application from them to join the Community than there was for rejecting an application from Greece and Spain and Portugal after they shook off their dictatorships.

One of the ironies at the present time is that the East German Republic now is already a country member of the European Community although it is the most dictatorial and Stalinist of all the East European regimes, with the possible exception of Romania, which has produced a Stalinoid family dictatorship.

I believe that if East European countries want to join the Community, the Community should not reject their application and it would be unwise to say that we will not look at any new applications until after 1992, especially if the 1992 process is unlikely to move very much further than it has already. I think we must kiss the joy as it flies in this case and start seeing if we can bind these countries into a relationship with us.

What is happening in Eastern Europe raises very much bigger issues than those I have mentioned now. Glasnost and Demokratsia have released national feelings which were suppressed during the Cold War and they have put in question not only the settlements after the Second World War, at Yalta, and Potsdam, but also many of the settlements after the First World War. Yugoslavia is in danger of breaking up as the state which was created after the First World War. Greece and Turkey would be fighting one another now if they both were not members of NATO: so incidentally would Hungary and Romania over Transylvania if they were not both members of the Warsaw Pact.

The danger of Balkanization in Eastern Europe as this process develops is a very real one and would pose serious threats to the stability of the whole of Europe, if not to world peace, unless sensible ways can be found of allowing these new national entities to be managed in some sort of political framework. One of the odd things about the situation is that what is happening in Eastern Europe and the Soviet Union now is reviving all sorts of ancient patterns. Mittel Europa now is talked about openly by people in Austria, South Germany, Czechoslovakia and in Hungary.

When I last went to Budapest I had the feeling that Maria Theresa was back on the throne. You will recall that recently one of the deputies at the European Parliament who happens to be called Otto von Hapsburg, when he was asked if he was going to the Austria/Hungary football match said: 'And who are we playing?' I must confess being back in lovely Stockholm, one can see the Swedish empire reviving. If the Baltic states really become independent, not to speak of Poland, I suspect the only ex-Swedish colony that would stick out against incorporation is Norway.

Talking seriously, I think that the flux, to use my favourite phrase, in relations between the Soviet Union and Europe is bound to become more turbulent for some years yet. The most worrying thing and yet the most hopeful thing in some ways, is the likely disintegration of the Russian empire. The Russian empire is the only great nineteenth-century empire which has survived through almost to the end of the twentieth century, but it is quite apparent that with the liberation of national feelings – in the Baltic states, in the Ukraine, in Georgia and in the Central Asian republics – the Russian empire in the form it has persisted in under the Tsars and since Lenin is unlikely to survive very much longer. I suspect the biggest problem facing Gorbachev at the moment is whether he can go far enough to meet national aspirations inside the Soviet Union to avoid a civil war.

I remember Arbatov, whom many of you will know, saying recently in Harvard, when asked what would be Gorbachev's attitude if they go beyond asking for national autonomy, and they demand to secede, said he thought Gorbachev probably would take very much the same line as Abraham Lincoln did in the United States in the last century. It is worth recalling that the American Civil War, which was an attempt by the North to prevent the Southern states from seceding, caused more deaths in the United States than all the wars that have followed – two world wars, Korea and Vietnam – and at that time the United States had only one third of the population it has today.

I hope nothing like that happens because the Soviet Union is not an island and on its southern frontiers you have very unstable countries, which in some cases share the same language and religious views as some of the national republics in the south of the Soviet Union. They not only share their views but now they have long-range missiles and are capable of developing chemical weapons, if not nuclear ones. So we face a very very difficult and dangerous situation and for us in Europe I think the most important aspect of this new development is the possibility that Germany will become reunited simply through the disintegration of the East German regime.

Looking back on the period since the war, it is worth recalling that Eastern Germany now has only a quarter the population of Western Germany because nearly half its population has walked into Western Germany during the great migration of 1945 and the years that have followed and that is happening as I speak to you now. I think there is no doubt that if that extra sixteen million join the sixty million in West Germany it would alarm many people – in my view, quite unnecessarily. In my experience the West Germans are the least nationalistic people in the whole of Europe in the present time: they have turned into Belgians.

Nevertheless, if these changes are going to take place, it is very important to the whole of the world that there should be a new security framework for the whole of Europe which minimizes the risk that they could lead to unnecessary confrontation between the Warsaw powers and NATO.

This is why I believe there is an urgent need for a new security system covering the whole of Europe which is based on co-operation between the Warsaw Pact and NATO in very large arms cuts. General Goodpaster, who was Eisenhower's chief of staff and later Saceur, suggested a reduction to half the present NATO level – a reduction of half also in America's troops in Western Europe and then the restructuring of forces so that they become incapable of surprise attack, something which Gorbachev has started unilaterally on the Soviet side.

The one certain thing, however, is no such system is conceivable unless it includes both the United States and the Soviet Union. I do not think it is possible for Western Europe and Eastern Europe by themselves to come together in the short run in this particular way. But if in fact you do have this type of co-operation between the blocks in the military field, then I think what Gorbachev described as our common European house actually would become possible. Then all the worries about whether you can abandon neutrality, which are inhibiting some EFTA countries from seeking a much closer relationship with the Community, if not member-ship, would become meaningless.

One of the Russian republic's delegates at the last meeting of the new parliamentary assembly in Moscow, after he had listened to many fiery speeches from Baltic representatives and representatives from Georgia, said: if it goes on like this I think Russia may have to secede from the Soviet Union.

To conclude. I believe very much in the wisdom of Heraclitus, panta rhei, everything is in flux. In the short run until we have a little clearer view how things will pan out, I think it makes a great deal of sense for EFTA to shadow the Community as Community co-operation develops during the continuation of the 1992 process, rather as the pound has shadowed the Deutschmark without actually joining the exchange rate mechanism of the EMS.

We learned last week that shadowing the Deutschmark meant accepting Karl Otto Poehl as Europe's central bankers and whether you are all prepared to accept the implications of shadowing the Community to that degree I think remains to be seen.

I think it is possible, but too early to say, that if the EFTA really works at the problem it might conceivably be a bridge between Eastern Europe and the Community. Perhaps some of the East European countries might prove to be a bridge between EFTA and the Community instead, particularly if Hungary and Austria actually join the Community as I think is not impossible.

We are holding this seminar at a time when the uncertainties about the framework within which EFTA has to decide its relations with the Community are quite enormous. I cannot remember a time since the war when there has been so much uncertainty. Enormous changes, however, are under way and I think we would be wise to accept the wisdom of a conservative French politician in the nineteenth century: 'We cannot see clearly to the other side of the river, but the darkness does not destroy what it conceals.'

CHAPTER FOUR

Dilemmas of the Cold War

IN MAY 1947 THE LABOUR PARTY published my pamphlet, 'Cards on the Table', setting out what I took to be Ernest Bevin's foreign policy – both he and his officials were reluctant to describe it in public for themselves. 'Cards on the Table' was intended in part to rebut a pamphlet just published by the self-styled 'Keep Left' group which attacked Bevin for being too anti-Russian and pro-American, and argued that Britain should organize a European Third Force to mediate between Moscow and Washington. The signatories of 'Keep Left' included Woodrow Wyatt as well as more familiar radicals such as Dick Crossman, Michael Foot, and Ian Mikardo.

Ironically enough, as Gladwyn Jebb told Bevin at the time, the Foreign Office itself would have regarded 'Keep Left' as sensible even eighteen months earlier. It was only Soviet hostility which had compelled Bevin to seek help from a reluctant United States. And 'Cards on the Table' rejected a permanent British alliance with America against the Soviet Union. As Alan Bullock points out in his magisterial work on Bevin as foreign secretary, even at the height of the Cold War Bevin continued to hope, in my pamphlet's words, 'that sooner or later the Russians will realize that the policy they have pursued since 1945 is both impracticable and unnecessary'.

In fact, however, the Leninist doctrine of the 'two camps', which I described in 'Cards on the Table', continued to determine Soviet foreign policy for another forty years, until Gorbachev finally renounced it at the United Nations. Nevertheless, the West probably exaggerated the danger of a Soviet invasion of Western Europe. Like all other Western experts at the time, I grossly exaggerated Russia's capacity for aggression, since Stalin deliberately concealed the scale of Soviet losses in the war. Her dead were then estimated at seven million; they are now known to have numbered twenty-seven million. In addition Stalinism itself had cost the Soviet Union forty million lives.

When Russia refused to join the Marshall Plan and prevented her satellites from joining too, Washington realized that it had no hope of co-operating with Stalin. A year later the Soviet blockade of Berlin brought the world to the brink of war, and led to the formation of NATO in 1949. Within twelve months the Korean War convinced NATO that it must build up its armed forces, starting an arms race which is only now coming to an end. Some European countries refused to join NATO because they had a long tradition of neutrality, like Sweden and Switzerland. But the increase in tension caused by the arms race, and the fear that it would end in a nuclear war, produced a new phenomenon inside the NATO countries themselves and among the non-committed countries of the Third World – neutralism.

I saw neutralism as a decision in principle to opt out of the struggle to build a better world, as distinct from a decision to protect a national interest by adopting neutrality in a particular conflict. In the Labour Party it was often a lethal mixture of anti-Americanism and unilateralism, inspired by nostalgia for a world in which Britain could take all the decisions for itself alone; so I used to describe neutralism as 'nationalism with an inferiority complex'. In 1955 I wrote a booklet on 'Neutralism' in a series called Bellman Books, published by Ampersand.

I tried to disentangle the complicated root structure of this new phenomenon. A well-justified horror of nuclear war had led many to adopt the slogan 'Better Red than Dead', without realizing that if their neutralism made war more likely by upsetting the balance of power, they might finish up both red and dead. For others, neutralism was based on the belief that there was nothing morally or politically to choose between the Soviet Union and the United States; it was not difficult to prove them wrong. In the Third World, neutralism rested on the view that European and Soviet imperialism were identical; so I spend some pages comparing the postwar record of Britain and France in Asia and Africa with that of the Soviet Union in its non-Russian republics. Here again, we have had to wait until Gorbachev to see the end of Soviet imperialism – though its death-throes may be as bloody as those of British imperialism in India or French imperialism in Algeria.

Meanwhile NATO's reliance on the American nuclear deterrent was beginning to impose severe strains on the unity of the alliance. Washington refused absolutely to give its allies any say in the use of its strategic nuclear forces. While it distributed some shorter-range nuclear weapons to its allies, they remained under American ownership and control; the allies had the right, in theory, to veto their use, but not to order their use if Washington disagreed.

Britain retained total control over its own nuclear forces, as France was to do when it produced them. Since Germany was forbidden by treaty to produce or possess nuclear weapons, this discrimination began to create difficulties when the Federal Republic joined NATO in 1954. Germany insisted on the forward defence of its territory, which meant in practice that the United States was committed to drop nuclear weapons on the Soviet Union once NATO's weak conventional forces along the Iron Curtain were overrun. When the Soviet Union acquired the ability to retaliate in kind against the United States, forward defence meant America's readiness to commit suicide if there was even a small Soviet incursion into Western Germany.

So the stage was set for the so-called 'transatlantic bargain', which was renewed every year and never completed. The Europeans would be asked regularly to provide more conventional forces so as to reduce America's nuclear liabilities; in return the United States would reaffirm its nuclear commitment. Yet so long as Germany insisted on forward defence, it was impossible to hold up a Soviet attack for more than a few days, or even hours; in any case the Germans were unwilling to contemplate prolonged fighting on their own territory.

Both as a young MP in opposition, and later as defence secretary, I spent many exhausting weeks every year exploring the arcane theology of nuclear strategy with American and German experts, compelled to use an artificial vocabulary which was hopelessly inadequate to encompass the political dimensions of the problems we faced. Every year new and more frightful weapons were being produced on both sides. But the essential insolubility of the problems remained absolute.

In 1956 the British and French governments conspired with Israel to invade Egypt without informing the United States – in the middle of a presidential election. This subjected the alliance to its greatest strain so far. But when Khrushchev threatened to attack Britain and France with nuclear weapons unless they stopped the invasion, Eisenhower immediately announced that America would in that case bomb the Soviet Union. However, the aggressors did cease military operations immediately, and then Eisenhower used economic sanctions to force them to withdraw from the territory they had occupied.

The Suez affair produced a wave of anti-American feeling in London and Paris; both governments felt they had been humiliated and betrayed by their closest ally. One result was Macmillan's decision to abolish conscription and to use the resources thus released to produce his own strategic nuclear missiles. It was in this situation that I attended a seminar at Princeton in January 1959 on NATO and American security. I was the only European present; the other main speakers included the leading American theorists on nuclear strategy, while key figures in the government defence establishment, such as Bob Komer and Herman Kahn also took part.

My own contribution, on 'Britain and NATO' attempted to bring some political realism to the proceedings, by explaining how America's allies saw the problems. I concluded by arguing that by far the best answer to NATO's strategic dilemmas would be disengagement in Central Europe. Since I saw the removal of Soviet troops as the precondition for the liberation of Eastern Europe, I had been promoting disengagement ever since the suppression of the Hungarian rising in 1956. The Hungarian tragedy was all the more agonizing for me because the Suez affair distracted NATO at the critical moment from attempting to dissuade Khrushchev from sending the Red Army into Budapest.

As I pointed out in Princeton, Western governments had not seemed wholly averse to the idea of disengagement: 'As of January 1959 [their] official proposals for a German settlement conceded the military feasibility of disengagement in principle by offering to keep NATO forces out of the present Soviet Zone when German reunification has taken place and the Red Army has withdrawn to Poland or points east.' It has taken them thirty years to get back to the same starting point.

CARDS ON THE TABLE

(Labour Party, 1947)

INTRODUCTION

It is now nearly two years since the British people put the Labour Party in charge of its foreign policy. Ernest Bevin, at the Bournemouth Conference in 1946, emphasized the difficulty of judging a foreign minister's achievements fairly over a short period: '. . . Any step you take now does not only determine what is going to happen to the people in this hall, but what is going to happen to the generations unborn; the effects of your work either for peace or war will reveal themselves in twenty, thirty, forty, probably fifty years' time . . .'. Nevertheless, the last twenty-two months have already provided ample evidence of the success of Labour's foreign policy, and of the approval it has won both at home and abroad.

It is clear, however, that a minority of Labour's own supporters are sincerely disturbed about the government's activities abroad. Apart from disagreement on particular issues like Palestine, Greece or Spain (which are not discussed in this pamphlet), some loyal members of the Party are genuinely concerned about the general line of Labour's foreign policy – because it is held to take sides with a capitalist America against a socialist Russia, or to entail a diversion of men and money from home production which this country cannot afford. It is mainly to answer these general criticisms that this pamphlet is directed.

Much of the anxiety is due in the last analysis to misunderstanding of the conditions under which foreign policy is always carried out, and to ignorance of the special difficulties facing Britain at the present time. No Labour man blames Aneurin Bevan for the housing shortage, but many seem to think that Ernest Bevin is personally responsible for the apparent deterioration in relations between the Big Three since 1945. We often forget that the world's affairs are not settled by the British government alone, but by all the governments working together or in conflict, subject continually to the necessity of compromising to avoid a breakdown.

The Importance of British Power
Until international relations can be conducted entirely under a guaranteed rule of law, the effectiveness of Britain's part in this international activity depends on her power, whether her policy is capitalist, socialist, communist or fascist. As socialists, we of the Labour Party want in all spheres a policy which will promote the spread of democracy and social progress. In domestic policy, our government can count on an intelligent and mature understanding by the people of the techniques for achieving those aims; such an understanding is often lacking from the consideration of foreign policy. We all fully realize that socialism can only be achieved at home if the Labour Party stays in office and if the country's economy is put on its feet as a going concern. It is easy to forget that a socialist foreign policy equally depends on the continued support of the British electorate and on the stability and strength of Britain as a world power. Slogans alone cannot prevent wars, or win them.

The maintenance of Britain as a world power is, however, more than the precondition of a socialist foreign policy. At the present time, when the world is torn between the economic attractions of capitalist America and the ideological appeal of Soviet Russia, democratic socialism will only survive as an alternative to these extremes if Labour Britain survives as a world power. Socialists and small nations the world over, whatever their public quarrels with aspects of British policy, pray above all that Labour's experiment shall succeed and that Britain shall continue to take an effective interest in their national problems.

Now, of course, Britain's power does not consist simply in her economic, strategic and military resources (even including her moral prestige; for this last is effective only on countries with an informed public opinion which can act through democratic institutions). It depends even more on Britain's position in the game; even small forces can be tremendously effective given the right opening, in politics as in football or chess. Much of the last two years has been spent in preserving Britain's power of initiative and in manoeuvring for a favourable opening. In fact, our foreign policy, like our home policy, has been dominated by the limitations of scarcity.

It is difficult for the average Englishman to adjust himself to the change in Britain's world position; many of us expect Britain to act as if she were still, as in the nineteenth century, the only world power in existence, a mighty empire unchallenged either in the military or economic spheres. Even more seem to imagine that in 1945 the Labour government could survey the world scene free from any immediate problems or commitments, and choose among infinite possibilities the precise policy best calculated to achieve a world socialist millennium.

THE BACKGROUND IN 1945

What in reality was the world background when Labour took office in 1945? The whole of Europe was in a state of moral, social and economic collapse. The physical destruction alone was immense – cities laid waste, ports destroyed, railways and bridges shattered, harvests ruined. In addition the wreckage of the Fascist new order was not yet replaced by stable democratic governments; the black market was rampant, violence and fraud were taken for granted. Vast armies of occupation were scattered far from their own homes. Twelve million displaced persons presented an urgent human and economic problem. In the absence of peace treaties frontier questions threatened new outbreaks of war in a dozen places. Europe trembled at the approach of famine and disease.

*

The Strategic Revolution

Moreover, the end of the Second World War established a strategic revolution whose consequences we are still unable fully to foresee. The elimination of Germany, Japan and Italy, the weakening of France and China, had reduced the number of effective world powers to three – Soviet Russia, the USA and Britain. Yet the absolute power of each of these was increased by new technical developments to such an extent that any one, in the absence of the others, might have controlled the world. The victorious powers were like three elephants in a boat.

A dangerous aspect of this elimination of secondary powers was that the world was strategically saturated. The frontiers of territorial influence of the Big Three ran everywhere together, so that no power could increase its security without directly weakening the security of another great power. New weapons of mass destruction like the atom bomb and biological warfare, together with new long-range carrying agents like the rocket and the jet-propelled aircraft, threatened to make any one part of the globe vulnerable from any other part; thus no power could feel really secure if there were a potential enemy on any part of the earth's surface. Unilateral security on the old pattern, a peace guaranteed by national power, could only be obtained by world conquest.

Today, each great power takes a direct interest in any new development in any part of the world, in case it alters the existing balance in Big Three relations. The Austrians, for example, used to notice how the slightest change in the Persian situation was reflected in the behaviour of the Big Three representatives on the Control Council in Vienna; America closely inspects the Swedish negotiations for a trade agreement with Russia; Russian policy in Korea may be modified to meet a new situation in Poland. This makes it extremely difficult to treat any issue on its merits and may make nonsense of attempts to explain the policy of a great power in one particular country without introducing the world situation as a whole.

Finally, the development of total warfare as the organized activity of the whole state, and the need for adapting industry in advance to meet the claims of a war-machine, since an armaments programme now requires years for fulfilment, conferred an absolute advantage on the aggressor. The possibility of winning a war by a single unexpected knock-out blow, delivered when the aggressor was at the peak of his military-economic efficiency, weighed the scales heavily in favour of a nation which could plan such a crime without interference from public opinion or democratic control.

The unhappy consequence of this revolution in military science was that universal fear has been a major factor in world politics since 1945, and that the moral distinction between defensive and offensive action is growing increasingly obscure.

It is worth emphasizing here that the part played by the atom bomb in nourishing this fear, though considerable, is less important than generally believed – there are too many other factors. The really striking feature of world politics today is not that Russia is frightened of America, but that America, with undisputed control of half the earth and all the oceans, is frightened of Russia. If we aim to prevent war simply by reducing each nation's capacity to inspire fear, item by item, we may be engaged in an endless task and engender more fear than we remove.

Britain After the War

The effects of the war on Britain are familiar to all of us. But some of their implications are still only partially understood.

For the first time we were unable to produce a coal surplus for export. We were seriously short of manpower. Our economic system, distorted and exhausted by the war effort, critically weak in some sectors through generations of Tory neglect, needed reconversion and re-equipment. Our foreign investments were largely sold during the war, much of our merchant fleet was sunk, so that our ability to pay for imports was gravely reduced, and we had to concentrate on bridging the dangerous gap in our balance of payments by increasing our exports. Our moral responsibility as socialists to convert our imperial subjects into friends and equals was made urgent by the great surge of independence movements which the war had stimulated. The economic character of our relations with the Dominions had changed, too; having developed their own industries for war purposes they were no longer to be regarded simply as sources of raw materials for manufacture in the mother country. Only thirty years since the 'two power naval standard' was a cardinal principle of our foreign policy, we found our American ally with a navy six times the size of ours and a merchant fleet more than three times as large.

It was obvious that we must face the necessity of reducing our foreign commitments as much and as fast as possible consistent with our security, and seek to adjust our policy to our diminished resources. Yet this reduction must be carried out in an orderly way so that at no point would we lose our power of initiative and our ability to control the process. Above all, we must avoid creating by our withdrawal vacuums into which the other great powers might surge in irresistible and world-shattering conflict.

Most important of all, we could have no illusion of guaranteeing our security entirely by our own resources. With our dense urban population, our key industries concentrated in known locations, we were exceptionally vulnerable to attack by the new weapons. Collective security is now the overriding condition of Britain's survival. It is indeed fortunate for Britain that the party which took office in 1945 has always, in foreign as in domestic affairs, insisted as a moral principle on policies which have now become a national necessity.

THE CONSTRUCTIVE ACHIEVEMENTS

The constructive achievements of Labour's foreign policy are already impressive – particularly since they can be contrasted so clearly with the aims which a Conservative government would have pursued.

International Relief Work
At all points we have promoted and supported international action to clear away the debris of war. Labour Britain alone has spent £750 million on world reconstruction. Of the twelve million displaced persons there now remain only a million, whose fate we are trying to make an international responsibility; so far only the Labour governments of Britain and New Zealand have paid their contributions to the International Refugee Organization. Over £1,000 million has been spent through UNRRA in preventing famine and disease – 100,000 lorries have been sent to Europe. It is easy to underestimate the success of such preventive action; for, in spite of destruction infinitely worse than in 1918, there have been no epidemics and no widespread famine in Europe – in 1918 thirteen million people died of influenza, and in Russia alone thirty million died of typhus. Britain's contribution to these achievements has been continually criticized by the Tories: Englishmen of all opinions must have been shocked by Winston Churchill's cynical selfishness in the debate of 12 March 1947, when he blamed the government for forgoing improvements in the British standard in order to save millions of Europeans from starvation and disease.

Abolishing Imperialism
In two years we have gone far to abolish the old type of imperialism; Transjordan is already independent, India and Burma are in the final stages of their transition to freedom, constitutional advance is seen in

British colonies all over the world from Ceylon to the West Indies. Our attempt to withdraw from Egypt is held up only by a threat to the liberty of the Sudanese, and we have made an important contribution to Indonesia's fight for freedom. An ironic comment on the ignorance and malicious criticism of Britain's support for Indonesian independence was provided by the final words of the native socialist premier of Indonesia, Sjahrir, to the departing British troops '. . . fate brought you here together with the beginning of a great upheaval in the movement of emancipation of our nation. Coming to aid and to bring relief, you suddenly found yourselves plunged into a very awkward and ungrateful position. Under all circumstances we learned to appreciate and admire traits of Western culture our people have rarely seen before from white people they know. I mean your politeness, your kindness and your dignified self-restraint.'

A tremendous impetus has been given to social and economic progress in the colonies. We are spending £120 million on development and welfare in ten years, in addition to special schemes like the farsighted plan for producing groundnuts in Tanganyika, in which we shall spend £40 million and bring health, education and prosperity to thousands of Africans, as well as additional essential foodstuffs to the people of Britain.

By continuous argument and pressure we have succeeded in getting peace treaties signed with all the satellite powers – Bulgaria, Romania, Hungary, Finland and Italy – so that the peoples of Europe can direct their energies at last to constructive programmes, free from the unsettling influence of national disputes.

The United Nations

Support of the United Nations organization has been the key to Britain's action in all these spheres – in converting mandates into trusteeships, in fighting for international responsibility and guidance on every problem, economic and political alike. British pertinacity was mainly responsible for obtaining a World Food Organization against American reluctance and Russian indifference, and more recently for setting up an Economic Commission for Europe. For as socialists we recognize the economic interdependence of all nations; Ernest Bevin has continually stressed the fact that inequalities between the standards of living of nations in any area are a menace to world peace.

We have fought, and are still fighting, for an effective disarmament plan, and even under the greatest provocation we have preferred international arbitration to direct action. Any previous British government would have responded to the mining of British destroyers by Albania with a summary bombardment. We took the case to the Security Council, and when, as so often before, the verdict favourable to us was vetoed by Russia, we still sought an international solution and transferred the case to the International Court. For we believe that, whatever the suspicions and fears which still bedevil world politics, the experience of co-operation for practical purposes inside international institutions will teach the powers to grow together in peace.

THE BIG THREE

The Meaning of the Veto

But here we come to the crux of the problem. The United Nations organization is by its very constitution formally prevented from dealing with disagreements between the Big Three; and any chance that it might have developed into an instrument for such purposes was destroyed by the use made of the veto by Soviet Russia. Consequently, so long as disagreements between the Big Three are a major factor in world politics, the ability of any power to conduct its foreign policy exclusively through the United Nations is gravely weakened.

How is this so? It is continually reaffirmed by spokesmen of Britain, America and Russia alike that the United Nations will work only so long as the Big Three are united; so the United Nations can no more deal with problems which menace Big Three unity than a man can lift himself by his own bootstraps. The Soviet Union was not the only power responsible for drafting the veto proposals; but the crippling practical consequences of this theoretical weakness in the constitution of the Security Council, which were never envisaged when the veto clause was originally tabled, are incontestably the responsibility of Russia. She has used the veto not only to prevent action, as in the case of atomic control – but sometimes even to prevent the recording of a decision with which she did not agree – as in the cases of Greece, Syria and Albania – on any matter which bears even remotely on a conflict of interest between herself and another great power.

So long as Russia so rigidly asserts this right, the progress of the United Nations in dealing with many fundamental problems like disarmament or the control of atomic energy will be slow, and confined to registering agreements which are reached by other methods than public argument in an international assembly. So though it would be wrong to attack the veto in principle, since it merely represents a political reality, the Labour government has fought continuously for some code of conduct which will resist its damaging effects. However, the veto power does in fact commit the Big Three to appeasement of one another so long as action is confined to UN – a situation which puts a premium on aggressive action. Let us consider now the effects of the war on the other two great powers, America and Russia.

The United States of America

The United States ended the war with prodigious assets; unchallengeable control of all the oceans, a great long-range bomber force, sole possession of the atom bomb, 70 per cent of the world's productive capacity, great surpluses of all products in a world of scarcity. But she was both unwilling and unable to shoulder the responsibility of this immense power. Her central government was weakened by a complicated series of constitutional checks and balances. The public opinion to which it was responsible was opposed to 'entangling alliances' and foreign commitments: there was a widespread feeling that Europe was a breeding ground of universal wars, that America lay safe in geographical isolation behind her stupendous power – a Maginot complex. Britain was felt by many to be a worn out imperialist power scheming to trick America into protecting her rebellious possessions against a Russian expansion which was historically inevitable. Indeed at the wartime conferences from Teheran to Potsdam agreements between America and Russia were often at Britain's expense. Above all, American public opinion was deeply opposed to any policy which might conceivably lead to war. The most damaging epithet employed against Roosevelt was 'warmonger', and in spite of the clearest warnings, the American people would not accept war against the Axis until Pearl Harbor; even then some critics accused Roosevelt of arranging Pearl Harbor himself in order to make war possible. The extraordinary propaganda build-up for Truman's declaration on the loan to Greece and Turkey is worth studying in the light of such factors.

The Soviet Union

Soviet Russia ended the war 'dizzy with success', to use Lenin's phrase. The magnificent record of her armies gave her immense prestige and popularity in all countries; for the first time since the revolution she was everywhere accepted as a major world power whose agreement was indispensable to the settlement of any world problem. Few people outside Russia realized the cost of her victory, and the Russians themselves preferred to minimize their crippling losses. But in fact the development of the Soviet Union had been set back ten years. Her dead were estimated at seven million, her homeless at thirty million. The destruction of a third of European Russia and the dislocation of Soviet industry were made worse by a serious weakening of Communist discipline. The collective farm system was menaced not only by individualistic peasants but by the illegal encroachment of public organizations. Contact with European civilization had disturbed the army. The war had disclosed serious minority problems; two autonomous republics – in the Crimea and the Caucasus – were degraded in status, their populations deported, for fighting with the Nazis. New forms of nationalism, stimulated by the war, threatened Bolshevik ideology.

While foreigners were dazzled by what they saw as the miracle of Russian resistance, the Russians knew how near defeat they had once been, and their traditional feeling of insecurity was reinforced by this evidence of its justice. The famous Russian spaces, which had defeated Napoleon and helped to defeat Hitler, were a wasting asset against attack by modern weapons, especially if it should have to be met on more than a European front. In particular Russia's lack of warm-water ports put her at a great disadvantage against ocean powers which controlled the entrances to the inland seas; for the Baltic and Black seas are immovable salients into the heart of western Russia.

But with all her weaknesses, Russia had one great strength in world politics compared with America. The Soviet system concentrates the whole of Russian power in a few little-known men who, far from being responsible to public opinion are capable of making it. This freedom to fit policy closely to the scientific calculation of a fluctuating national interest was demonstrated by the volte-face of August 1939, and gives the Soviet government an inestimable advantage. If we are to understand and predict Russian foreign policy, we must put ourselves in the position of the men who control the Soviet state.

The Principles of Russian Policy
The collapse of Litvinov's policy when the Western democracies betrayed the League, may be responsible for the lack of faith shown so far by Russian leaders in the establishment of an international rule of law. They have used international institutions only to secure an immediate national advantage, or as a convenient mechanism by which the moral principles of others are exploited to prevent or inhibit effective resistance to their own unilateral policies. Russia has yet to join UNESCO, the Food and Agriculture Organization, the International Trade Organization, the International Bank, the International Refugee Organization, and the International Civil Aviation Organization.

Stalinist theory in 1945 must have made an ultimate conflict between America and the USSR seem inevitable. For the time being America was prevented from using her strength aggressively by public opinion and constitutional obstacles; but the Russians expected an inevitable economic crisis to bring Fascism to the USA, a Fascism which for innumerable economic reasons would be openly imperialistic in its foreign policy, aiming at world conquest. The most that Russia could hope for was to exploit the immediate American reluctance to accept foreign commitments, in order to expand her defences as far and as fast as possible.

Just as between 1939 and 1941 Russia used the breathing space offered by her non-aggression pact with Hitler in order to cushion herself against the inevitable clash, so she sought at Yalta and Potsdam, by limiting her claims to compete with America in the Far East, to free her hands for expansion in Europe and the Middle East.

Russia and Britain

In Europe and the Middle East, however, an expansion of the Russian security system meant an equal contraction in the British security system. In theory Russia could have chosen in 1945 between a close alliance with Britain to replace the necessity for expansion, or the elimination of Britain as a European and Middle Eastern power. In fact she chose the latter without considering the first. It is a major tragedy of socialist history that the advent to power of a pro-Soviet Labour government in Britain coincided with the opening of a sustained and violent offensive against Britain by her Russian ally.

It is unnecessary to believe that this was a typical ideological or religious war of communist against social democrat. Any nation prefers to guarantee its security by its own power if possible rather than to rely on the promises of potential enemies. And for a Russia which foresaw a struggle with America, Britain was not a possible ally; for Britain could not under any circumstances adopt a policy which might lead her to war against America. Apart from all other considerations, Britain depends entirely on supplies imported by sea, and could be starved to defeat in a few weeks by the American fleet.

But in addition, as Communists, the Soviet rulers had no faith that the Labour leaders they had described as 'social-democratic lickspittles' as recently as 1941 would not be replaced by a Churchill government within a few months. They knew moreover that Britain needed economic help which only America could supply. They thought they could see the British empire crumbling, and that expansion to fill Britain's place in Europe and the Middle East would be easy and inexpensive.

Nor is it necessary to believe that Russian policy was determined by economic or imperialist motives. No doubt Russia needs material help, but that alone is not sufficient to explain her recent policies. In the modern world, fear for security is a sufficient motive to cause war: in 1939–1941 Russian attacks on Finland, Poland, the Baltic states and Romania were caused by fear of war. It is all too easy to justify such attacks, particularly as for many people 'non-Communist' means 'capitalist' and 'capitalist' means 'Fascist', but no Englishman with a faith in democratic socialism could contemplate the elimination of Labour Britain in order to strengthen Soviet Russia against a conflict with the USA. And the Labour government does not propose to take sides in a line-up for the next world war; as Clem Attlee stated, we do not believe in the forming of groups.

The attempt to destroy Britain's freedom of initiative was double-edged. On the one hand Russia opened a series of propaganda attacks through UN and the international Communist machine, which aimed at isolating Britain morally as a decadent reactionary power. British policy in Greece, Syria, Indonesia, Spain and Palestine was a special target, and though in every case submitted to the United Nations for judgement, Britain was wholly cleared of all accusations, much of the mud stuck, and in some cases Russia vetoed the recording of the verdict. It is difficult to forgive, from a recent ally, such attacks as the following, broadcast to Norway by Moscow radio on 8 June 1946: 'This little country [England] went to war because it and its Fascist reactionary leaders love war and thrive on war. The attack on Hitlerite Germany was purely incidental.' Moreover, the damage done to British prestige abroad by such lies should not be ignored. British relations with France will remain complicated for some time by the falsehoods spread by the French Communist party concerning British exploitation of the Ruhr.

On the other hand, there was an attempt to tip the scales against Britain in important strategic areas, by diplomacy or direct action – in Trieste, northern Persia, the Dardanelles, Greece, Turkey and Eastern Europe.

But the Soviet policy proved worse than a total failure, for two reasons. The Labour government of Britain stood patiently firm against Russian encroachment, and where necessary answered Russian accusations with the facts. Secondly, the immoderate ineptitude with which the programme was pursued swung American public opinion into support of Britain. The first clear sign of the change occurred during the Peace Conference in August 1946, when Yugoslav guns shot down an American aeroplane. The most dramatic example so far was the Truman declaration on Greece and Turkey in March 1947.

The world situation is now clarified and the cards are clearly on the table. Moreover, if, as it appears, the USA is about to take the weight of Russian expansion off British shoulders, Britain will be freer to pursue a constructive initiative for improving Big Three relations. American policy is still capable of much vacillation, however, and it is too early to feel certain that the 'Truman doctrine' will remain a guiding factor in American foreign policy.

THE OUTLOOK TODAY

Bevin and Churchill

The foregoing analysis of Britain's reaction to Russian policy since 1945 may seem to justify the critics who say Bevin has been pursuing the Fulton policy, and is in this respect indistinguishable from Churchill. But here again there is a decisive difference.

The policy of the Conservative Party, if Winston Churchill can be said to represent it, is to seek an exclusive Anglo-American alliance expressly directed against Soviet Russia. The policy of the Labour government, however, is to judge all questions on their merits, to seek or accept common action with the United States only where there is a clear common interest, but in no case to be drawn into commitments which exclude the possibility of similar collaboration with Russia. Churchill wants a permanent alliance with America against what he sees as a permanent political danger. Bevin wants as close an association with Russia as we now have with America, based on the recognition of the economic and political interdependence of all nations. For example, we accepted the economic fusion of the British and American Zones of Germany to save our zone from bankruptcy only when we had failed to persuade Russia and France to join us; and at every opportunity we continue to press Russia to join the union on exactly the same conditions as ourselves and the United States.

Moreover, we have resisted every temptation to regard Russian policy as final. In particular, where the Tories have continually pressed us to recognize the permanent incompatibility of the communist and democratic systems, to make a final decision about the frontiers of each, and to build up an entirely independent Western bloc, we have fought doggedly to prevent the crystallization of zones of influence behind rigid ideological barriers. In fact, many Labour people feel that the division of Europe into zones of influence which Churchill promoted during the war with a brutal disregard of human factors, is responsible for many of the heaviest problems the Labour government now has to face.

America and Britain

For many reasons, an exclusive line-up with America would be as danger-ous and undesirable as its opposite, and there is no harm in emphasizing the fact. But many common criticisms of our present relations with the United States are wholly mistaken.

It is said that our dependence on American supplies amounts to econ-omic serfdom. But no one has tried harder than the government to reduce our dependence on American imports; the stark fact is that no country except America was capable of satisfying our economic needs. Wherever possible we are finding other sources of supply, whether or not the Americans object, as over the wheat agreements with Canada and the Argentine in 1946. The conditions on which we obtained the loan were hard and in many ways embarrassing, but we had no alternative, and we insist on dismantling our economic defences only in proportion as America dismantles hers. As the war-damaged countries of Europe recover we are working to conclude trade agreements with them. But so far it remains broadly true that America gives us more than we can immediately repay, while we give the other countries more than they can immediately repay.

The idea that we are somehow bound politically to follow American policy is equally false. We fought the Americans bitterly to obtain a world food organization. Bevin did not mince his words over American interfer-ence in Palestine. Most striking of all, we opposed the American proposals for taking over the Japanese mandated islands in the Pacific, when Russia had already declared her intention of supporting them. The fact is that we have found ourselves voting on the same side as the Americans against Russia on many occasions because on those occasions we considered that the Russians were wrong!

It should be said here, too, that much of the facile talk about American reaction and dollar imperialism is not justified by the facts. America provided 72 per cent of UNRRA's budget without any political control over its spending; and there is no evidence that America is prepared to fight to protect her foreign investments. On the contrary, when in 1936 Mexico confiscated foreign oil holdings, America took no action whatso-ever, while Britain broke off diplomatic relations and threatened worse. The absence of a political Labour party in the USA can mislead Europeans; for in spite of this, the fifteen million organized workers have decided the result of every American election since 1932, and if, as we must hope, the cautious negotiations for a merger of the AFL and CIO succeed, an anti-Labour government in the United States may become virtually impossible. The 1931 slump produced a New Deal government;

there is no reason to be certain that a future slump will have the opposite result.

There has been much muddled criticism of some military aspects of our common interests with America today. During the last few months the American government has come to realize that the preservation of Britain's security is of vital importance to America herself. In consequence, the United States has made certain contributions towards lightening the burden which falls directly on Britain; and these contributions have been fiercely criticized by Americans both of Right and Left who think that their government has been tricked into pulling British chestnuts out of the fire. In fact, of course, such American co-operation has been given purely in the interests of American defence; there is no case therefore where Britain has been required in return to assist in protecting anything which is primarily an American interest. Indeed we refused pointblank even to retain our troops a day longer in Greece because of the proposed American loan to the Greek government. But we can only be grateful if America is prepared in any way to make it easier for us to defend our security. So the gibe that America provides the money while we provide the men is simply answered – for that suits us better than providing both the men and the money!

Some critics gloomily prognosticate a third world war in which a shattered Europe is liberated by America only after years of Russian occupation; and that our relation with America is the same as France's was with Britain; but a relationship is not less necessary because it is imperfect. An alliance with Britain is a permanent necessity for France so long as the danger comes from Germany.

Britain between Russia and America

But the aim of an Anglo-American understanding is to prevent war by proving to Russia that an aggressive anti-British policy is doomed to frustration. Every historical precedent suggests that no government will continue to pursue a policy whose failure is known to be certain; the danger is always lest a world war develops out of a local aggression which would not have been committed if the aggressor had realized that his ultimate enemies were determined to resist it.

Our hope is that sooner or later the Russians will realize that the policy they have pursued since 1945 is both impracticable and unnecessary; and that the existence of Labour Britain as a stable world power is a protection to Russian security and a guarantee against anti-Soviet aggression. For so long as Britain plays a decisive part in the defence of American security, it is impossible for America to adopt a policy of world aggression without British agreement. The nature of the military co-operation between America and Britain makes it impossible for either to fight if the other remains neutral.

There have been signs for some time that Russia is coming to recognize these facts, though her opposition in Moscow to a four-power pact against German aggression was disappointing, and it is possible that she will continue a little longer attempting by some means or other to make a separate bargain with Britain or America at the other's expense.

A British trade delegation left for Moscow in April, and at this moment Ernest Bevin is seeking to obtain an alliance with Stalin which will associate Britain as closely with Russia as with the United States. But the condition of such an alliance is that it should not aim at isolating America. Moreover, we cannot accept as part of an alliance with Russia the censoring of all British press and radio comment which the Soviet leaders might consider unfriendly – even our own government does not enjoy such immunity in Britain. Labour's policy for Big Three unity requires infinite tact and patience, and a resolute firmness on all crucial issues. But its success is the only condition on which the United Nations can operate as the guardian of world order; and the replacement of power politics by an international rule of law is the only condition on which Britain can survive indefinitely. Bevin is indeed right when he aims at producing results which will remain effective for generations to come.

Britain and Europe
A number of critics would agree broadly with this interpretation of events since 1945, but they would maintain that instead of associating herself with America, Britain should have aimed at a policy completely independent of both Russia and the USA as the leader of a European bloc. However attractive at first sight, this policy is both undesirable and impractical.

In 1945 Europe was a power vacuum; there was no nation strong enough to count as an economic or political factor in world politics. Moreover, the reconstruction of Europe depended on large-scale American assistance. Britain herself was too weak to cut herself off from American aid, and as such she could offer little to attract any European country away from the rival appeals of American money and Russian military power.

Much of Europe was not free to choose British leadership. The foreign policy of every East European state was controlled by Russia. Germany, the economic key to European unity, was prostrate under four-power occupation. In most of the countries which were free to choose their foreign policy, government was shared between Communist parties with Russian affiliations and right-wing parties which looked to the USA, while the Socialist parties lay uneasily between them; wherever possible we have tried to help these Socialist parties.

We have put the attainment of a united independent Europe in the forefront of our aims. Above all, we have fought steadily to prevent the wartime division of Europe into spheres of influence from crystallizing into a permanent thing. The last nine months have seen British loans to Czechoslovakia and Hungary, trade agreements with Poland and Czechoslovakia, and gifts of food and medical supplies to relieve famine in Romania. The slow progress previously of these relations was due to the inability of the East European governments to offer much in return, not in any way to political prejudice.

In Western Europe we continue to strengthen our ties. The keystone was laid in the alliance with France in March. A generous financial agreement with Italy was signed in April. And we hope the UN Economic Commission for Europe, whose secretary, Gunnar Myrdal, is a Swedish Socialist, will open a new era in continental history. But a detailed policy for Europe cannot be framed while Germany remains the object of a violent struggle between the world powers. And our progress is limited by the fact that we cannot afford to give economic loans on a large scale for purely political purposes. A few million tons of coal for export would change the face of our European policy in a night. So while we shall do everything possible to restore Europe as a vital and independent factor in world politics, we cannot base our foreign policy on the assumption that this aim is already achieved. Furthermore, our dependence on overseas trade makes us a world power by necessity, and we will remain as much part of the Atlantic as of the European community. Our interests are too widespread, as our principles are too international, for us to restrict ourselves to the idea of regional blocs, however constructed.

The idea that we should have extricated ourselves from the quarrel between Russia and the USA does not make sense; during the period under review, Britain was the main target of Russian hostility, while until a few months ago America was an undecided spectator.

Can We Afford the Cost?
Finally the objection remains that our foreign policy entails a diversion of resources and manpower from home production which this country cannot afford. But our foreign policy costs much less than another war would cost

us, even if by a miracle we should survive it. So long as Russian hostility persists, the burden will only be lightened in proportion as it is assumed by the United States in our stead. A nation which puts domestic comfort before its own security and independence is condemned to a foreign policy of appeasement leading inevitably to capitulation or to war under unfavourable circumstances. It is wrong to condemn the expenditure entailed by Labour's foreign policy since 1945 unless an alternative is suggested which would preserve British security at less cost.

There is in fact only one such alternative, and it has been steadfastly pursued by our government – that all countries should scale down their armed forces by multilateral agreement under the guarantee of international inspection. We are continuously pressing for the conditions under which this may be possible, on the Military Staff Committee, and in the General Disarmament and Atomic Energy Commissions of the United Nations. Mr Gromyko's refusal to allow inspection on the ground that this would violate national sovereignty was, however, a bitter blow.

CONCLUSION

So what are the achievements to date? Two years is not a satisfactory period over which to judge a policy which aims at achieving peace and security for generations to come. Many urgent and complicated problems remain, above all in Germany and the Middle East. But under disadvantages which have hampered no other British foreign minister since the days of Napoleon, Ernest Bevin has played a major part in saving Europe from division and collapse, in establishing the United Nations as the basis of world relations, and in preventing a final rift between the Big Three. Due to British pertinacity, America has come to realize the responsibilities of her power before it was too late to assert those responsibilities except in war. In the field where Britain is free to choose her policy, we have seen the liquidation of Tory imperialism, and an immense impetus to economic and political development in the colonies. And at all these points the contrast with what a Conservative government would have attempted is sharp and clear.

Many years of patient and determined effort lie before us. Diversions and setbacks may abound before a genuine and permanent understanding between the great powers clears the road for the United Nations, and we can look forward with realistic hope towards a parliament of man. But under the broad and generous statesmanship of a Labour government, Britain can be sure of making a major contribution to the achievement of that future.

NEUTRALISM

(from *Neutralism*, Ampersand, 1955)

The concept of neutrality is, of course, as old as history itself. Whenever two states have come into conflict there have been other states which saw no interest in committing themselves to one side or the other. In some cases their neutrality not only served their own interests but also helped to effect a reconciliation between the combatants. So long as world affairs consisted of struggles between states in an anarchy of power politics, neutrality was a policy which could be held not only to have benefited the states pursuing it – providing they were strong enough to defend their neutrality by force of arms – but also to have served humanity by limiting the damage caused by war.

With the first attempts to transcend power politics by establishing an international community, neutrality lost some of the moral superiority it had hitherto enjoyed. By joining in the effort to impose the rule of law, a state, like an individual, loses the right to abstain from action against the breaker of the law. And though the legal obligation is binding only on those states which commit themselves formally to uphold the framework of world order, the moral obligation falls also on every state which benefits by world order, whether it accepts the legal obligation or not.

Thus Switzerland, which is constitutionally committed to neutrality as a principle in world affairs, has refused to join the United Nations, and accepts a responsibility to moderate the evils of international conflict only when she feels this compatible with her neutrality. By contrast, Sweden, though she pursues neutrality as a national interest in the given situation, is, nonetheless, a member of the United Nations; and therefore feels so doubtful of the moral implications of neutrality that she prefers to describe herself as 'alliance free'.

There can indeed be no argument that neutrality is incompatible with the spirit of the United Nations Charter. For the charter assumes that in any case of war there will be an aggressor who must be confronted with the united strength of all its signatories: no nation can contrive to avoid the responsibility of helping to name and restrain the breaker of the law.

This is a hard truth. And ever since the League of Nations made the first attempt to transcend power politics, some historians, philosophers and politicians have argued that such a price for world order was too high to pay. If the attempt to establish the rule of law meant turning every local conflict into a world war, they said, mankind would do better to stick to classical power politics, which at least offered the opportunity of achieving temporary peace through the construction of a balance of power.

Those who framed the United Nations Charter admitted that this argument has some force. The purpose and effect of the great power veto in the Security Council was to ensure at least that the great powers would not be involved in war with one another through the automatic operation of the rules.

The postwar history of the United Nations has raised further objections in many minds to the charter's implicit ban on neutrality. World politics in the last nine years have been dominated by the Cold War. And many people feel that the Cold War is essentially a typical struggle between rival imperialisms, between two power blocs, one dominated by the Soviet Union, the other by the USA. Circumstances, they say, have enabled the USA to conduct its policy through the United Nations, where its wealth and power can always command a majority of votes; against this automatic majority the only defence of the Soviet bloc is the veto. Little therefore remains, in practice, of the United Nations as the framework of a new world order. In this situation these critics believe that moral and legalistic arguments based on the charter no longer weigh against pragmatic arguments for neutrality.

The validity of the United Nations suffers a more fundamental assault from another quarter. The Cold War, runs this argument, is essentially a struggle not between two groups of states, but between two social ideals which run across national boundaries. Some see it as a struggle between Communism and capitalism, some as a struggle between dictatorship and democracy. But though they may differ on how to describe the competing systems, these critics all agree that the United Nations is by its very nature, irrelevant to the real problem. Men, they say, must make up their minds by comparing the two systems whether to support one or the other, or to remain neutral.

Finally, there looms behind all these calculations the shadow of the hydrogen bomb. As knowledge of atomic weapons becomes more wide-spread, many people are beginning to wonder whether any policy which envisages war even as a possibility can be accepted. Could anything be worse than atomic world war and the mockery of peace which would follow it? Would it not be better somehow to contract out of the whole miserable game of world politics and accept whatever follows as at least better than universal suicide?

*

This complex of reactions to the postwar crises has produced a new political attitude – neutralism. Neutralism differs from neutrality since it is primarily an attitude of individuals rather than a policy of states. And it is a reaction to a phenomenon which did not, and could not, exist before recent increases in the range and weight of political power. The Cold War differs from all earlier international conflicts in that it is conducted in peacetime between antagonists who are able to exert their power simultaneously in all parts of the world. Every state and every individual is asked to declare his allegiance in the struggle. The neutralist refuses to declare an allegiance to one side or the other, and justifies his refusal not only as expedient but also as moral.

At one extreme neutralism is the sort of social nihilism which appeared in postwar Germany under the slogan 'Ohne mich'. But it was first established as a rational and moral attitude in the French newspaper, *Le Monde*, by the respected Catholic philosopher, Etienne Gilson, and in various forms it has found supporters among serious-minded and responsible persons all over the world. Though in one form it asks little more than a defeatist passivity, in another it is expressed by demands for the creation of an active third force.

Neutralism as a moral attitude rests on an interpretation of the so-called Cold War either as a struggle between rival power blocs or as a struggle between opposing social ideals. Both these interpretations are dangerously inadequate. And as a practical policy neutralism is vitiated by its failure to meet the need for an international order sufficient to prevent a third world war.

There are defects in American democracy, as in all other democracies, notably the treatment of Negroes and a tendency to intolerance of dissent which is the price paid for welding so many different streams of immigrants into a single nation. But here, too, democracy is promoting progress. Though much remains to be done before coloured citizens enjoy full rights and status, particularly in the South, there has been a steady and continuous advance since the Civil War. The recent decision against segregation in the public schools was a signal victory.

Indeed this type of neutralism depends essentially on the argument that there is nothing to choose between a little of a bad thing and a great deal of a bad thing: and it ignores the fact that in a democracy there is a chance of removing such evils as do exist, while in a totalitarian state one is committed to endure all evils without any hope of relief.

*

In Asia and Africa neutralism often springs from a similar false equation. It is granted that the Soviet Union is a dictatorship, and seeks to extend its dictatorship to other lands; but, it is argued, the Western regimes opposing Soviet advance are also dictatorships so far as Asia and Africa are concerned. Moreover, though Communist dictatorship may be in some ways more rigid than Western colonialism, at least it is exercised by nationals of the country concerned, and local nationalism is given full expression in the Soviet Union.

Although the writings of the early Bolsheviks might give this impression the facts today completely contradict it. By the constitution of the Soviet Union adopted in 1936 the so-called Union republics have no autonomy in any important field of government. Article 14 reserves to the central government in Moscow matters of war and peace, diplomatic relations, defence, foreign trade, state security, economic planning, credit and currency, education, criminal and civil codes, and many other matters. The natural resources of the Union republics, like coal, oil, copper, and agricultural land, are by law the property of the USSR as a whole. Moreover, the central prosecutor of the USSR has the power to order the annulment of any local laws and decrees.

The powers of the so-called autonomous republics are even more limited. For example, *Izvestiya* and *Pravda* of 18 June 1950 show that new water pipes and drains and a new trolley bus line at Nalchik in the Kabardine ASSR and the building of a bridge in autonomous Bashkiria required Moscow's permission.

To this constitutional control over the republics must be added the even more important party control through the centralization of power in the Soviet Communist Party. The Party plays the decisive role in the government of every republic, and all Party organizations in the republics are strictly subordinated to the Party Central Committee in Moscow.

This type of centralization might be less open to criticism if all the nationalities in the Soviet Union were proportionately represented in the central organs of the Communist Party. In fact, of the thirty-six members and candidate members of the 1952 Praesidium of the Communist Party of the Soviet Union, thirty are Slavs – the majority of them Russians. None is of Muslim or Turkic origin. Moreover the Russians have taken over the most important posts even in the local Communist Parties. In 1949, 55 per cent of the leading Party workers in Kirghizia were Russians. Even in district and town Party Committees, 40 per cent were Russians.

The same is true of government officials throughout Central Asia. All the general prosecutors are Russians. In 1948 the Soviet press stated that the percentage of local nationals holding posts in Kazakh ministries varied from 14 per cent in the Ministry of Meat and Dairy Industry to 2 per cent in the Ministry of Local Industry. The fact is that since 1917, under the Communist regime, Russia has been systematically colonizing Central Asia. In Kazakhstan, by 1939, Kazakhs formed less than half the population of the republic. The proportion of Kirghizs in the Kirghiz Republic dropped from two thirds to a half between 1926 and 1939.

Moreover, even in the cultural and social field Moscow allows little freedom for national tradition. Muslims and Buddhists are persecuted like members of all other religions. For example, in the Tajik Republic, Friday, the traditional Muslim day of prayer, has been abolished as a day of rest; on 9 August 1949, the Supreme Soviet of Tajik SSR decreed: 'To meet the numerous requests of the workers, the weekly day of rest throughout the whole of the territory of the Tajik SSR is transferred from Friday to Sunday.' Anti-religious organizations have been set up since the war in Tashkent, Bukhara, and Samarkand, and Article 156 of the Uzbek Criminal Code provides the death penalty for 'the use of religious prejudices for counter-revolutionary purposes'.

Attempts to preserve national cultures are stigmatized as 'bourgeois'. For example, in 1950 a campaign was organized to depose Shamil, the nineteenth-century Muslim leader of the Caucasian mountaineers, from the position he had previously held in local tradition, on the grounds that he 'sowed distrust and held up economic and cultural unification'. In 1948 Kazakh writers were told to show the 'positive influence of Russian and Soviet culture' and were warned against 'the counter-revolutionary and anti-Soviet trend of pan-Islamism'. In 1935 textbooks were standardized throughout the Soviet Union. In 1936 all university education and advanced training were put directly under a Moscow ministry. The Russian language is obligatory in all national schools, and by 1939 throughout the Muslim regions the Russian had become the only legal alphabet.

This rigid subordination of Soviet Asia to Russian control in both government and culture is enforced by all the machinery of a police state. But on at least three occasions local unrest grew so dangerous that Moscow decided on the total destruction of the nationality concerned. In 1943 the Kalmyk Autonomous Soviet Socialist Republic was liquidated by a decree of the Supreme Soviet, and the whole people was deported to Siberia. This ancient Buddhist people of Mongolian origin had suffered continual persecution in the years following the Bolshevik Revolution, but many of its soldiers were decorated for bravery against the Germans in 1942. Today the nation as such no longer exists. The capital of the

Kalmyk Republic has been renamed, and none of the postwar Soviet reference books available to the outside world even mentions the Kalmyks.

In 1944, as already mentioned, the Muslim nationalities of the Chechen-Ingush and Crimean Autonomous Republics suffered the same fate. Their crime was that some had fought for national liberation on the German side against the Russians. Today these nationalities, of ancient history and culture, have disappeared from the face of the map. There is no reference to them in the *Large Soviet Encyclopaedia*, and the towns they inhabited only ten years ago have been given Russian names. It is interesting to compare the indiscriminate mass punishment of these peoples with the treatment by Britain of Burmese and Indians who fought for national liberation with Japan.

This is the reality behind Communist propaganda about Soviet nationality policy. There is nothing evil in the history of Western imperialism which cannot be paralleled inside the boundaries of the Soviet Union since 1917.

Conversely, the history of Western imperialism contains pages quite as dark as anything from Soviet Central Asia – pages for which all the material benefits which colonialism may have brought cannot compensate. Even so, there is a difference of decisive importance. Since the Western imperialist powers are all democracies at home, enlightened opinion has exerted continuous pressure on their colonial policy. In many cases this pressure, and the influence of humane administrators, has pushed imperialism into liquidating itself. Moreover, once the period of conquest was over, Western imperialism even in its worst periods never centralized power so completely as Communist Russia. There is not a single Western colony which suffers so total a loss of administrative autonomy and popular representation as each of the Soviet Asian Republics.

The British Empire has, of course, undergone the most striking transformation of all. In the last few years India, Pakistan, Ceylon, and Burma have become sovereign states, and all but Burma have voluntarily chosen to become equal partners within the Commonwealth. The West Indies, Nigeria and the Gold Coast have reached the last stage before full self-government – for example the Gold Coast government can now prevent Englishmen from taking residence in its territory. There is not one of the more than forty territories for which Britain is responsible which has not made important progress in this direction since the Second World War. And throughout the colonies local cultures and religions are not only permitted but encouraged.

No doubt much of such progress in liquidating imperialism in the

Western world is due as much to the pressure exerted by local nationalism as to idealism in the mother country. But democracy at home helps to ensure that nationalist pressures in the empire overseas are met by reform rather than suppression. Even in countries which so far have not learnt wisdom in dealing with their colonial problems, democracy at least provides a point of appeal for the nationalist movements which does not exist at all in the Soviet Union. The Russian people themselves have suffered almost as much from the Soviet regime as their 'colonies' in Asia. And their fellow-Europeans in Latvia, Estonia, and Lithuania, not to speak of the Volga Germans, have endured a fate scarcely less terrible than that of the Chechens and the Kalmyks.

It has been said that what matters is not where a man comes from but where he is going. By this test Western imperialism emerges far better than Communist imperialism. For everywhere Western imperialism is transforming itself either by its own choice or under pressure. Soviet imperialism on the other hand has grown ever more rigid and oppressive since the Revolution, offering no prospect of advance whatever for its colonial subjects. The final cause of the break between Yugoslavia and the Kremlin was Tito's discovery that there is no dominion status in the Soviet empire.

There remains neutralism in the most absolute form of all, as it has been expressed in England by the Methodist Church leader, Dr Donald Soper. Better Soviet occupation than a third world war, it runs. So let us contract out of the whole miserable mess of power politics and accept Communism as at least a lesser evil than atomic annihilation.

Even if one accepts the premise that such a choice lies before us, it can well be argued that even physical annihilation is preferable to spiritual annihilation. But the real choice is not as this type of neutralist presents it. If all the peoples of Europe and Asia surrendered forthwith to Communism, this would make atomic world war not less, but more likely. For so long as the Communist bloc is weaker than all its potential opponents, it is unlikely deliberately to initiate a world war. Once, however, its war potential were decisively greater than that of the non-Communist camp, this restraint would not operate any more than it did in Finland in 1939. For this reason superhuman restraint would be required on the non-Communist side not to intervene with force at some stage to prevent the surrender of what remains in Europe and Asia to Communism. The choice in fact is between an alliance to stop both war and Communism, or a surrender to Communism which would make war inevitable.

Often the assumption underlying this absolute neutralism is that passive resistance could transform the Soviet regime as it has already transformed the British regime in India. But in India, passive resistance was used against an occupying power which at home permits conscientious objection to military service and has for years subjected its use of power abroad to some moral restraint. The Soviet regime permits no conscientious objection to military or any other form of service to the state and recognizes no moral laws except the interests of the regime itself.

There is thus a strong case against neutralism in all its forms. But what does the rejection of neutralism imply in terms of a positive policy or attitude? Does it commit one to accept without demur all the vagaries of Western policy in the Cold War? Does it mean passive submission to American leadership? Does it mean subordinating all other moral and political ends to the struggle against Communism? Does it indeed mean a fight to a finish with the Communist camp, and a refusal to negotiate or compromise with Communist governments?

These questions cannot be answered without a more general analysis of present world problems than non-Communists will usually attempt. Indeed, part of the attraction of Communist theory is that it does provide an analysis of the international scene which, by fitting all particular events into general categories of interpretation, offers an intellectual guide through chaos which the West does not provide. Moreover, many of its categories correspond sufficiently closely to reality to make possible a remarkable accuracy in prediction. Above all, in describing the so-called contradictions to which the non-Communist camp is prey, and to which Soviet policy is so carefully adjusted, Communist theory touches on some important aspects of the truth. Where Communist analysis goes wrong, is in emphasizing the element of economic determinism to the exclusion of all political factors arising from the human will to power.

Developments in the atomic age must lead one beyond the economic categories which provided Marx with such powerful new tools of analysis in the nineteenth century. It is now clear that the fundamental political problem is the distribution and control of power in all its forms, and that economic power is only one element in the problem. Today the tools of power available are infinitely more effective than ever in the past. Even the stupendous increase in economic productivity achieved by modern industry is less important than the increased power of military destruction produced by modern physical science and the increased power of political control developed by totalitarianism.

Though the light thrown by Marx and his followers on the anatomy of economic power was particularly valuable to an age trying to adjust itself to the Industrial Revolution, it is now clear that in analysing the contradictions of capitalism Marx was simply illustrating a special aspect of power politics. Marxism belongs to a general trend in political theory which runs back through writers like Hobbes and Machiavelli to Plato.

The basic problem of the modern world springs from the fact that recent increases in the amount of economic, military and political power available to man have reached a point where if the nation state remains the highest political organism and power politics is allowed to continue unrestrained, the conflicts of interest inherent in an anarchy of nation states may destroy civilization and even life itself on this planet. To this problem totalitarianism and democracy offer different answers.

The totalitarian answer of the Communists requires that all power in the world be concentrated at a single centre – the Praesidium of the Communist Party of the Soviet Union. This must be achieved by the steady expansion of the Communist camp through the conquest or subversion of all states at present outside its boundaries, till the whole world is one enormous prison administered from Moscow. It requires the deliberate aggravation of all the inherent contradictions in the non-Communist camp, so that the victims may be isolated and reduced one by one, through what Rakosi has called 'salami tactics'.

The democratic answer requires the progressive subordination of the power of nation states to collective control in a democratic international society. Since this progress can only develop with the consent of the states concerned it is bound to be slow and uneven. It demands that governments concentrate on working together on the issues where they can recognize a clear common interest, in the hope that thus they may gradually expand the area of co-operation. Where the interests of states diverge they must try to reconcile their conflicting interests at least sufficiently to clear the way for positive co-operation on common interests. In this slow progress from consultation through co-operation to integration it is difficult to decide at what point national sovereignty will give way to supranational authority, and independence become interdependence, particularly since the states concerned are unlikely, at least in the early stages, to commit themselves formally to a merging of sovereignty in general fields of government.

Is there then any common interest which may serve as a starting point for such co-operation? When the United Nations Charter was drafted in 1944 it was assumed that all states in the world had at least one major interest in common – the prevention of a third world war. The charter envisaged co-operation for this purpose through the Security Council and its subordinate committees on atomic weapons, conventional armaments, and collective police action (the Military Staffs Committee). It soon became apparent that Russia was not prepared to co-operate in the United Nations even to pursue this basic interest of all states. And when Prague, Berlin, and Korea revealed that Russia had an alternative solution to the world problem, the countries immediately threatened joined together in the North Atlantic Treaty Organization so as to effect the co-operation which Russian sabotage prevented them from achieving in the United Nations.

Some have argued that since Soviet policy prevents the United Nations from operating as the charter implies it should, the Communist states should be expelled and the veto abolished. Quite apart from the fact that all the non-Communist great powers would wish to keep the veto even if Russia were not a member, the expulsion of the Communist states would rob the United Nations of its immense value as the one universal world organization, and would in present circumstances lead to the withdrawal of many other states. Moreover, Communist co-operation will ultimately be obtained more easily and quickly within the United Nations if the necessary conditions for this are created by action outside its institutions – though, of course, within the limits laid down by the charter.

Besides the universal common interest of avoiding a third world war, the non-Communist states now have another common interest, the containment of Communist expansion. These two aims have become the lowest common factor promoting progress in the non-Communist world towards the goal of a democratic international society of states. But the nature of Soviet strategy imposes co-operation in many fields. For the non-Communist states must try to eliminate the existing conflicts of interest among themselves from which the Communist camp might hope to profit. Besides the power political collisions of national interest, which Communist theory describes as the inter-imperialist conflict, these include the divergence between the rich white peoples of the Atlantic basin and the poor coloured peoples of Africa and Asia which Communists call the colonial conflict, and the social tensions which Communists describe generally as the class war. As Professor Toynbee has suggested, the non-Communist world has good reason to be grateful to the Soviet Union for giving it a special incentive for uniting to remove these conflicts, which in modern conditions might well lead to war whether or not the Communists are present to exploit them.

This indeed is the crux of the case against neutralism. Refusal to commit oneself in the struggle against Communist expansion in fact means an abdication of responsibility to play an active role in progressing beyond power politics towards an international society. If international co-operation is to be limited to what the Communist states will participate in, it cannot go far enough to solve the problems of power politics. But the neutralist is not prepared to co-operate fully in any activity with the states which have already taken their position against Communist expansion unless the Communist states are also involved. Positive neutralism, by attempting to form a third force, is even more damaging to the movement towards a democratic world society, since it depends on dividing the non-Communist camp so as to create a new balance of power.

The need to build an international society by consent through exploiting a minimal nucleus of common interests helps to answer some other questions which neutralists may put. How can democratic states compromise their ideals by co-operation with undemocratic regimes, like those of Spain, Yugoslavia, South Korea, etc.? Do not the alliances formed for the struggle against Communism destroy the moral reason for carrying on the struggle?

The answer is, of course, that the overriding international interest in avoiding world war and halting the expansion of totalitarianism not only excuses but even demands common action by all states which are prepared to work together for these minimum aims. The United Nations Charter does not exclude undemocratic states from membership, providing they are prepared to abide by the rules and obligations of the organization. If a greater degree of international unity can be built through common action for these limited aims, it may later be possible by consent to extend the scope of international obligation, just as in a national society once the rule of law has been established, the range of the law can be extended.

Now that atomic weapons have so greatly increased the destructiveness of war, aggression must be made the one unforgivable international crime. The only demand which should be made of any state before it joins in the movement to build a world society is whether it will forswear aggression itself and join in the common effort to deter or halt it in others. It was by refusing to accept this fundamental obligation that the Soviet Union compelled the non-Communist countries to act independently of the United Nations, though still within its framework. The operation in which they are now engaged is not a crusade against Communism or any other type of society. It is an attempt to establish the minimum basis of international co-operation required to prevent war and halt the forcible expansion of the Communist camp – an attempt which became necessary in its present form only when Soviet policy had frustrated intentions to pursue the same aim through the United Nations.

This raises the second question which worries many neutralists. Does a commitment to join in this common effort exclude the possibility of compromise with the Communist states? Must the Cold War last for ever, or worse still, be fought to a finish with the unconditional surrender of one side or the other?

The answer to these questions depends primarily on the Communist camp, for it takes two to make a compromise. But the history of Soviet foreign policy confirms the implications of Communist doctrine. The Communist states are likely to avoid steps which might lead to world war so long as the unity and strength of their prospective victims renders Communist victory in such a war unlikely. In other words, if the non-Communist states can master their own internal conflicts, it is probable that the period of co-existence in Soviet foreign policy can be prolonged indefinitely. Moreover, if the non-Communist states can achieve lasting unity, they will thereby falsify the doctrinal basis of Communist foreign policy, creating the conditions in which a fundamental change in the Communist attitude to the outside world will at least be possible.

By contradicting the predictions of Lenin and Stalin about the inevitable decomposition of 'capitalism' under the stress of its inherent contradictions, the non-Communist world may in fact turn co-existence into co-operation. And this process may be helped by developments inside the Communist camp itself.

Soviet Communist theory has never admitted the possibility of contradictions inside the Communist camp. It has always assumed that, however far Communism expands, it will remain a monolithic bloc in its relations with the non-Communist world. And it has taken for granted that the centre of power in the Communist camp will always lie in Moscow. This assumption was justified so long as Communist parties won their victories under Soviet direction and with Soviet help, as was the case throughout Eastern Europe except in Yugoslavia. Russia tried to bring Yugoslavia into line by capturing the Yugoslav Communist Party. The attempt failed, with results which are common knowledge.

Since then a far more formidable exception has appeared in Asia. The Chinese Communist Party won its victory against Soviet advice and without Soviet help. Its theory of revolution differs in many ways from Soviet orthodoxy. It is less penetrated by Soviet agents than any other

Communist Party in the world. And though circumstances have impelled Communist China into a close working alliance with the Soviet Union, there are many obvious national and party issues which divide the two Communist states.

So far as outsiders can tell, the decisive bond between China and Russia is that at present they believe they have the same enemies. But there have been signs that they may disagree about the appropriate strategy for dealing with these enemies. Whereas in the West the North Atlantic Treaty Organization has produced a shift in Russian policy towards co-existence, the absence of countervailing power in the Far East may have persuaded China that she will benefit more by continuing an aggressive policy while the going is good. In other words, even though the two great Communist states share the same hostility towards the outside world, and base their foreign policy on the same general theories, the fact that their political power is not concentrated in the same centre means that differences in their regional situation may impose great strains on their alliance.

The moral for the non-Communist world is clear enough. The intransigence of Communist China can only be modified if in Asia, as in Europe, the prospective victims combine to defend themselves. But if such action can impose a shift towards co-existence in Chinese policy too – and the Indo-China settlement suggests this may be the case – the consequent relaxation of tension between the two camps will enable the other strains between the two leading powers of the Communist camp to exert a greater pressure on its unity. So the doctrine of the two camps will be falsified at yet another point. The non-Communist world will prove capable of unity while the Communist camp is torn apart by its own contradictions.

Such a situation would destroy the dogmatic element behind present Communist policy which makes it so difficult to hope for the sincere co-operation of Communist states in building an international society. But it is only whole-hearted co-operation by the whole of the non-Communist world to moderate its own internal contradictions and thus present a barrier to the further expansion of Communism by force which can create the conditions for such a change.

The last question which the neutralist may ask about the consequences of committing himself to the non-Communist world is whether his commitment involves accepting the leadership of a single power, like America, and closing his eyes to all the evils which exist on this side of the Iron Curtain. The answer should be clear after what has already been said.

The immediate aims of the non-Communist world are limited to its overriding common interest in preventing war and Communist expansion. Providing these aims are accepted, there is no necessary commitment beyond them. Each country and each individual is free to act as he pleases, so long as his action does not jeopardize the main aims of the community. The policy adopted by the non-Communist community to achieve its ends must be formed by compromise depending on the consent of all concerned. It may well be that on some occasions an agreed policy does not emerge even after the most patient consultations. When this is the case, members of the community remain free to travel their separate paths without ceasing to watch for opportunities of reconciling their policies at a later stage.

Examples of this are already numerous inside the Western coalition, and are bound to multiply as public opinion in the countries concerned faces the need to adjust itself to the new polity that is emerging. In 1954 the European crisis over German rearmament and the Asian crisis over Indo-China illustrate the problem.

But though states will normally be satisfied with the minimum co-operation required to meet immediate problems, the real abandonment of neutralism must give individuals a far less limited purpose. Indeed it will be seen that to secure even the minimum aims of the non-Communist world far-reaching changes will ultimately be needed. Every source of conflict outside the Iron Curtain presents Communism with opportunities to exploit, just as every evil reduces that moral distinction between Communism and freedom which justifies the will to resist.

It has been shown already that neutralism breeds essentially on those aspects of the non-Communist world which most closely resemble Communism. If America abuses her power to dominate the non-Communist camp, the argument for resisting Russian domination is to that extent weakened. Social injustice or economic exploitation in the West undermine the case for opposing the same evils in a Communist regime. Racial discrimination and political intolerance again blur the distinction between democracy and totalitarianism.

Thus the abandonment of neutralism does not by any means imply a complacent acceptance of the existing situation outside the Communist empire. On the contrary it calls for a vigorous struggle against all the evils and weaknesses which might undermine the moral and material strength of resistance. When a state abandons neutrality it can limit the nature of its new commitments so as to satisfy its minimum national demands. When an individual abandons neutralism he thereby takes on an unlimited liability to fight for good against evil wherever it may be.

BRITAIN AND NATO

(from 'NATO and American Security', Princeton, 1959)

For the first ten years after the Second World War, Britain's thinking about military problems was completely overshadowed by the prior need to construct a political framework of alliances within which her defence efforts might have a meaning. The year 1945 found Britain, relatively much weaker than before the war, facing much greater demands on her limited resources. What remained of the system by which she used to protect her world interests was scattered throughout the power vacuum between America and Russia, under heavy pressure not only from Soviet imperialism but also from local nationalism. During the whole period that the Labour government was in office, its foreign policy was dominated by the need to find new sources of power and to liquidate any inherited responsibilities which were not essential to national survival. In practice this meant transferring authority in the Empire wherever possible to the local inhabitants and implicating the United States in the protection of Europe and the Middle East. The United States was the only potential ally with which association would not mean a net drain on Britain's power.

In 1946 American support for the ultimatum which led to Russia's evacuation of northern Persia gave at least a temporary security to the Middle East. In 1947 Britain's withdrawal from Greece jostled the United States into accepting responsibility for the security of the Eastern Mediterranean. It was a longer and more difficult process to commit America to the defence of Western Europe. In 1948 the Marshall Plan gave America a stake in the economic survival of the area; her military undertaking required not only the demonstration of Soviet hostility at Prague and Berlin but also some evidence of Britain's readiness to lead the defence of Europe, as provided in the treaties of Dunkirk and Brussels.

The Dunkirk and Brussels Treaties had little military significance. Their essential function was to attract an American commitment with real meaning. Lord Montgomery tells in his memoirs how he found it impossible as CIGS to persuade the British government to make the treaties a military reality by stationing more forces on the Continent. The fact is that there was at this time no prospect of organizing any effective defence for Western Europe without American support; and after her experience in 1940 Britain was determined never again to risk losing the bulk of her army at the outset of war by making unsound military dispositions for purely political reasons.

Even when America finally did make her own commitment in April 1949, most Englishmen in authority felt that NATO's main value was as a political instrument which put Western Europe under America's atomic umbrella. The caution shown by both sides during the Berlin blockade made it seem fairly certain that neither Russia nor America would risk a world war. And military planning went forward inside NATO for the first twelve months without any real sense of urgency.

In Britain itself the military were working on the official assumption that no major war was likely for ten years, and were concerned mainly to digest the lessons of the Second World War for their own particular service. No clear strategic concept had yet emerged for the defence of Europe in global war. In any case, each of the services already had immediate practical tasks to perform in the overseas territories for which Britain was still responsible.

With the outbreak of the Korean War, the whole picture changed completely. It was almost universally assumed that Korea exemplified a new Soviet technique of war by proxy which might be applied at any moment somewhere in Europe. Thus the purely political guarantee of American involvement contained in the North Atlantic Treaty was no longer considered sufficient to deter aggression.

Scarcely anyone noticed that in Korea America had withdrawn her political commitment together with her troops, and that it might have been the formal disavowals of strategic interest made by Secretary Acheson and General MacArthur rather than the evacuation of American forces which invited the aggression. On the other hand, it was quite reasonable to believe that the Korean War itself, even if no other local aggression were committed, might spread into global war irrespective of the wishes of either side. In any case, the British chiefs of staff now adopted the assumption that major war was possible within three years, and for the first time began to plan seriously for that contingency.

Again, the essential precondition of effective military action was full-scale American co-operation from the outset. The Labour government, now clinging precariously to office with a majority of only six, introduced a rearmament programme which involved spending £4,700 million in three years. The economic and social sacrifices it entailed led to a major split in the Labour Party itself and contributed to Labour's defeat in the general election of October 1951. There is no doubt that the main reason why the Labour cabinet consciously assumed the political handicap of so daunting an arms programme was not so much the belief in its military necessity as such, but the feeling that unless Britain gave a dramatic and unequivocal pledge of her readiness to lead Europe in building a serious military force on the Continent, the United States might not be prepared to make her indispensable contribution. The first aim of British military policy was still to strengthen the deterrent by increasing the probability of America's atomic response to aggression in Europe. The essential conditions to achieving this aim were to obtain General Eisenhower as supreme commander of the allied forces and to station American troops in force along the threatened frontier.

Nonetheless, with the prospect of general war now seriously envisaged for the first time, Britain was also concerned to develop a practical strategy for NATO in case the deterrent failed.

Military thinking in Britain at this time was in many ways similar to Soviet military thinking today, if the picture presented by Raymond L. Garthoff[1] is to be trusted. Though it was agreed that nuclear weapons had great value as a deterrent, they were not considered as necessarily decisive in actual warfare against the Soviet Union. But British planners were obsessed by two implications of Russia's nuclear armament – she had exploded her first atomic bomb in 1949. In a future war, if Russia was able to drop atomic bombs on the Channel ports and beaches, it would be impossible for Britain either to evacuate large forces from the Continent as at Dunkirk or to carry out another 'Overlord' for their return. On the other hand, Britain would be unable to survive Soviet atomic bombardment if the Russians possessed airfields and launching sites on the continental coast of the Channel. London's ordeal during the days of the V1 and V2 was still fresh in Britain's memory.

Thus, if war came, Britain must keep the Red Army as far east as possible, even if this meant tying up the bulk of her armed forces permanently on the Continent in peacetime. This was a complete reversal of the thinking which had dominated Whitehall a year or two before. But there were good grounds for it. Russia's acquisition of atomic weapons had made it necessary, and America's commitments under NATO had made it feasible.

There was at this time little prospect of a serious conflict between Britain and the United States on the need for a forward strategy in NATO. Though America had her advocates of a peripheral strategy, particularly in SAC (Supreme Allied Command), she still depended on medium-range aircraft to deliver her atomic weapons, and therefore needed foreign bases even for a peripheral strategy. No European country was

[1] In *Soviet Strategy in the Nuclear Age*, New York, 1958.

prepared to accept American bomber bases without obtaining an American commitment to help in its defence. Under the conditions of 1950, America had no alternative to the forward strategy which Europe itself desired.

On the other hand, once NATO had accepted the concept of a forward strategy, America was in a strong position to impose her own terms for making the contribution without which such a strategy would be impossible. She did so by obtaining Europe's reluctant agreement in principle to a defence contribution from Germany as well. The British government considered the demand for a German contribution as premature in both the political and the military sense. It foresaw the political difficulties in both Germany and France which did delay agreement in practice for almost another five years. And while it was possible to plan for the defence of France and the Low Countries even without German troops, the addition of German troops would involve extending the defence commitment up to the Iron Curtain itself, thus increasing NATO's responsibilities together with its capacity. But though Britain argued strongly that the German contribution should be limited for the time being to an increase in size and armament of the Federal police forces, she had to bow, like the other European powers, to the American ultimatum.

France achieved more to delay German rearmament by refusing to permit it except in the framework of a federal European Defence Community. But when after four years' negotiations France herself rejected the EDC Treaty, Britain's alarm at the possible consequences led her to make a pledge to the continental powers which apparently involved a break with her basic principle of avoiding military commitments in Europe unless they were shared by the United States. In fact, Eden's promise to keep the equivalent of four British divisions in Western Germany until the end of the century was so hedged about with qualifications that Britain has already been able to reduce her land contribution to NATO by almost half without violating the words of her pledge. But by violating its spirit, she has cast a doubt on the sincerity of her concern with European defence which has infected all recent discussions of NATO strategy.

All this, however, was far from the mind of the British government when NATO began seriously to discuss a European strategy in 1950. The general trend of informed opinion in Britain in the months following the outbreak of the Korean War is well represented by the contemporary report of a Chatham House Study Group.[2] This put the target for an Atlantic force to hold a front in Europe at 50–55 divisions (at least one

[2]Royal Institute of International Affairs, *Defence in the Cold War*, London, 1950.

third of them armoured), a tactical air force of 5,000 jet fighters, and 1,000 tactical bombers. It went on: 'Generally speaking, the American and British task for a period of three to five years appears to be this: to furnish the hard core of élite divisions and air squadrons under one command and stationed in and close to Germany, for the defence of western Europe, while France and other members of the Atlantic Council build up around it an integrated European force. . . . In time it should be possible – if the German contribution is made available – for the United States and Britain to hope for a lightening of the burden. But until that prospect is far clearer than it is now, it is they who must take the strain. And even that can only be done if the American readiness to send arms and war supplies is matched by an equal readiness to station more ground forces in Europe.'[3]

This was the sort of thinking which led the Labour government to condemn itself to electoral defeat in 1951 by undertaking to spend on defence an average of 10 per cent of the national income over the next three years, and to seek a German military contribution.

The Conservative government which succeeded it held views which were different in some important respects, although at the Lisbon Conference in February 1952 it accepted military targets for NATO which corresponded closely to those quoted above from the unofficial Chatham House Report. However, from the moment it took power, the Conservative government held that its predecessor's programme could not be carried out in as little as three years, and that to attempt such a task would inflict irreparable damage on the British economy. In its second White Paper on Defence, in 1953, it decided not only to spread the programme over a longer period, but also to hold it to a lower peak. Electoral considerations probably played some part in this decision. In more than one country, those parties which are pledged primarily to cut government expenditures nowadays find little scope for this activity except in the field of defence, which commands less organized support among the voters than other fields. But there were also more relevant grounds for this shift in British defence policy.

It soon became apparent that the Lisbon targets were practically unattainable, and that only Britain and America were making a serious effort to achieve them. Yet the danger of war did not appear to be growing. The course of the Korean fighting in 1951 showed what care both sides could take to prevent the dangerous extension of a local war. Moreover, Russia made no attempt elsewhere to repeat the Korean experiment of aggression

[3] *Ibid.*, p. 73.

by proxy. One of the chronic difficulties in obtaining support for NATO's military demands is that NATO's supporters claim that it has achieved its political aim of preventing Soviet aggression in Europe while simultaneously admitting that it has failed to achieve its military targets. After ten years of reiteration, this is bound to weaken public confidence in the will and the ability of the military to limit their demands to what is necessary.

Even during the first critical months of the Korean campaign the Conservatives had been less disposed than the Labour government to fear general war, although they shared its desire to see America committed as fully as possible to the defence of Western Europe. Once the American commitment had become a fact, with the appointment of General Eisenhower and the dispatch of more American formations to Germany, the new British government was satisfied so long as it could ensure the continuation of this commitment, framing its policy inside NATO to achieve this political end rather than to implement a purely military strategy. Churchill himself had always believed that Western Europe's immunity depended on the American atomic umbrella. More than the Labour leaders, he saw NATO as a political instrument for tying SAC to automatic retaliation if Europe were attacked, rather than as a military instrument for the defence of Europe if the deterrent failed.

On the other hand, he recognized that America would not keep troops in Europe unless some attempt was made to find a strategic role for them in war, and unless America's European allies showed themselves ready to co-operate in fulfilling this role. Thus when the RAF argued that NATO should formally admit that Western Europe's security depended upon the deterrent of air-atomic retaliation, and should trim its ground forces accordingly, Churchill rejected its advice for political reasons, and continued to support the concept of forward defence. Moreover, the continental governments knew that their peoples would not support NATO unless they could be persuaded that its aim was to defend them from occupation by the Red Army. One experience of 'liberation', even in the pre-atomic age, had been enough. On the other hand, the continental countries showed no readiness to make the sacrifices required to implement a forward strategy. The proportion of their defence expenditure to national income, like their period of military service, remained constantly below that of the peripheral powers, Britain and the USA.

This failure of the continental allies to make sacrifices equal to Britain caused more and more irritation in London as the postwar seller's market began to disappear, and Britain faced more serious commercial competition from European countries which carried a lighter military burden. Britain has always depended heavily on the exports of her engineering industry, which was particularly hard hit by rearmament. This problem assumed increasing prominence in each successive White Paper on Defence after 1952. Britain particularly resented competition from Western Germany, which, though it made some financial contribution to Western defence even before its own rearmament got under way in 1955, was able to devote its engineering industry wholly to investment and foreign trade.

Meanwhile Britain was waking up to the strategic revolution wrought by the staggering advances in military technology. The problem first presented itself in the appallingly rapid rate of obsolescence which stultified much of Britain's defence expenditure. Despite a level of military spending which imposed crippling burdens on the British economy, the British services never seemed to have enough up-to-date equipment in operational use. The history of military aircraft production, particularly fighters, became a major political scandal. It was the need to rationalize defence production which first compelled the British government to re-examine its strategic assumptions and to seek a unified defence policy to cover all three services. This was a slow and spasmodic process, made no easier by continued changes in the political control of the services – there were seven different ministers of defence between October 1951 and January 1957.

The first public product of the strategic reappraisal came in the Defence White Paper of 1954,[4] for which Churchill himself was believed to have a large personal responsibility. Naturally enough, at this stage in the discussion, the 1954 White Paper was an uneasy compromise between the traditions and vested interests of the individual services and the demands of new weapons which were only just coming into operational use in Britain. It was revealed that 'atomic weapons are in production in this country and delivery to the forces has begun. . . . An air-to-air [guided missile] weapon will be the first to come into service and surface-to-air weapons will follow. . . . Clearly, within a limited defence budget we may not be able to afford both new weapons and conventional forces of the present size. But the balance between the two can only be decided in the light of the situation as it develops over the years ahead. The new weapons can in any event only be introduced gradually as they become available.'[5]

The division of opinion about NATO strategy was reflected in the

[4] Cmd. 9075.
[5] *Ibid.*, pp. 5–6.

passage: 'The Government will continue to regard it as a defence measure of the first importance to maintain the strength and efficiency of the British forces on the Continent assigned to the supreme allied commander Europe. The primary deterrent, however, remains the atomic bomb and the ability of the highly organized and trained United States strategic air power to use it.'[6]

However, Britain herself intended to build her own atomic striking force to ensure the destruction of Soviet targets which directly threatened her and might not have a high priority for SAC. This must, for economic reasons, be accompanied by a reduction in Britain's land forces. The reduction would fall not in the NATO area, but overseas, entailing the replacement of foreign garrisons by a central strategic reserve. Such a shift would be possible because, 'as the [atomic] deterrent continues to grow, it should have an increasing effect upon the Cold War by making less likely such adventures on the part of the Communist world as their aggression in Korea. This should be of benefit to us by enabling us to reduce the great dispersal of effort which the existing international tension has hitherto imposed on us.'[7]

The practical implications for British defence policy of these general propositions might have been considerable. However, they were almost nullified by another passage which gave the individual services an opportunity for maintaining all their traditional demands. If the deterrent failed and global war were forced upon us, it was likely that 'such a war would begin with a period of intense atomic attacks lasting a relatively short time but inflicting great destruction and damage. . . .'[8] But this phase might be followed by a period of 'broken-backed warfare during which the opposing sides would seek to recover their strength, carrying on the struggle in the meantime as best they might.'[9] Therefore, besides active forces able to withstand the initial shock, Britain must have reserve forces capable of rapid mobilization behind the shield.

It was still assumed without argument at this period that the West could 'keep the lead we now hold in technical development on which we must rely to offset the preponderance of the Communist states in manpower.'[10] The few voices, like that of Professor P. M. S. Blackett, which warned that

[6] *Ibid.*, p. 4.
[7] *Ibid.*, p. 5.
[8] *Ibid.*
[9] *Ibid.*
[10] *Ibid.*

the West could not rely on maintaining such a lead were treated as defeatist, if not fellow-travelling. But a little later America's belated publication of the effects of the explosion of the thermonuclear bomb had a tremendous impact on the British government, which was then still led by Winston Churchill. It removed most of the remaining doubts about the atomic revolution in warfare, and started in Britain the debate about the diplomatic and strategic consequences of nuclear weapons which is now shaking NATO to its core.

The British White Paper on Defence in 1955[11] was devoted almost entirely to examining the impact of the thermonuclear bomb. It recognized at the outset that a much smaller number of H-bombs less accurately delivered would provide a much more efficient deterrent than the very large number of accurate fission bombs till then believed essential for deterrence. For this reason it would be worth Britain's while to provide herself with an independent thermonuclear striking force. But the Russians, too, were 'clearly following the same policy; though we cannot tell when they will have thermonuclear weapons available for operational use.'[12] In other words, the availability of the thermonuclear weapon would allow a larger number of powers to contemplate the independent development of their own deterrent, and also reduce the time required to produce it.

So far as Europe was concerned, Britain was more certain than ever that the threat of nuclear retaliation would be an effective deterrent. 'The knowledge that aggression will be met by overwhelming nuclear retaliation is the surest guarantee that it will not take place.'[13] For understandable reasons, government spokesmen refused even to discuss the possibility that Russia's growing power to respond in kind to nuclear retaliation by America might make America more reluctant to commit herself to such retaliation on behalf of her allies. But in fact most of the strategic debate in Britain since 1955 has taken this possibility as its starting point. The real argument between the government and its critics has been about the best way of coping with America's reluctance to remain tied to a NATO strategy of massive thermonuclear retaliation.

The government has on the whole taken the view that America's reluctance to initiate strategic nuclear warfare could be overcome if NATO adapted its local strategy so as to commit the United States

[11]Cmd. 9391.
[12]*Ibid.*, p. 3.
[13]*Ibid.*, p. 6.

automatically to some form of nuclear warfare in the European theatre itself. NATO did in fact take a decision in this sense as far back as December 1954. But the decision had only limited political meaning so long as there were hardly any nuclear weapons available to the NATO commander himself and their use was subject to a veto from Washington. The NATO Council decision in December 1957 that strategic as well as tactical nuclear weapons should be widely distributed among the European allies which desired them was partly designed to make an all-out nuclear response to Soviet aggression more probable, though the fact that the warheads remain under American control still limits its effectiveness in this respect. However, under this theory, the essential function of NATO's nuclear weapons remains deterrence, not defence. Now that Russia is as well prepared for tactical nuclear warfare as the West, the role of atomic weapons in Europe is primarily to 'raise the stakes' and so increase the NATO deterrent, as explained by Mr Dulles,[14] rather than to provide the possibility of effective local defence. The early hope that battlefield nuclear weapons might give special advantages to the defending side seems to be weakened by recent exercises. Certainly the British government's main aim in NATO has been to counter America's reluctance to make a total response to aggression in Europe by making her physical commitment in the danger area more complete and inextricable.

The government's critics, including not only the official Labour opposition but also some prominent Conservatives – notably former Defence Minister Anthony Head – have argued, however, that America's reluctance to be committed to total war on behalf of her allies must be met by providing an effective response to aggression in Europe which is short of total war. They argue, on the one hand, that if a local aggression takes place and the only alternative to appeasement is total war, the Americans, and the British too, for that matter, might choose appeasement. And, on the other hand, they have been impressed, particularly since the Hungarian rising, by the possibility that fighting might break out on the frontier even though the Russians did not intend it; in such a case, a deterrent strategy is irrelevant and it is vital to have military forces which are capable of smothering the outbreak without risk of total war.

The debate on this issue, however, which is now raging in all the NATO countries, has been distorted in Britain by considerations not directly relevant to the technical problems of European strategy.

[14]John Foster Dulles, 'Challenge and Response in United States Policy', *Foreign Affairs*, XXXVI, No. 1 (October 1957), pp. 25–43.

The first factor is the long-standing determination of the British Army, now supported by the government, to end compulsory national service as soon as possible. While the Navy scarcely takes any conscripts at all, and the Air Force relies on them for a little over a third of its strength, and that entirely in non-combatant roles, nearly half of the Army's manpower has been conscripted for the last ten years. Moreover, the Army has had to use conscripts on a large scale as fighting troops and junior officers. Conscription is a particularly wasteful way of providing the British Army with operational manpower, since nearly three quarters of the conscripts are always undergoing training, making great demands on the regular army for instructors. Moreover, much of the six to twelve months of a conscript's operational life is spent travelling to and from stations like Hong Kong or Malaya which may be many weeks away by sea.

Even when the conscript is actually available for operations, he tends to be inferior in both training and morale to the regular soldier. As warfare becomes more complicated, the inferiority of the conscript becomes ever more marked. And so long as a large part of every army unit consists of conscripts who have just arrived or are just about to leave, enthusiasm for joining the regular army is lower than it could be. The disadvantages of conscription have been aggravated in Britain by the refusal of both the political parties to consider selective service. As a result, the government has always called up more conscripts than are actually needed, and a proportion of these have inevitably wasted their time.

The first move towards abolishing conscription came in 1955 when knowledge of the effects of thermonuclear bombing persuaded the government that conscription was no longer required as a means of producing large numbers of trained reserves for total war. A White Paper on National Service then stated: 'In a nuclear age the conception of reserve forces waiting to take part in large-scale conventional war is out of date. In the initial stages of such a war the reserve manpower of the services will, in the main, be required to help to maintain the life of the nation and to deal with raids and sabotage.'[15] Now that conscription was required primarily to provide troops for immediate military commitments, the government decided to reduce the annual intake by calling men up more slowly. Two years later a new defence minister decided to cut the Gordian knot outright.

In his famous Defence White Paper of 1957,[16] Duncan Sandys decided

[15]Cmd. 9608, p. 5.
[16]Cmd. 124.

to go all out for the total abolition of conscription by 1962, the last conscript being called up in 1960. This assumed that by 1962 Britain could make do with an army of only 165,000 men – a figure which some informed persons claim was reached, not by making an honest estimate of Britain's military commitments in 1962, but by making the most optimistic possible guess at the potential increase in regular recruiting during the intervening years. So far as regular recruiting is concerned, there has been so great an increase in the last twelve months that the government claims to be confident of reaching its target. On the other hand, the Report of the Advisory Committee on Recruiting in October 1958,[17] which was endorsed by the government, argued that the target could not be achieved unless during 1958–1962 one in three of all available young men volunteered for regular service on reaching the age of eighteen. No one believes that so high a recruiting rate is possible; but many argue that the committee was far too pessimistic in assuming that 64 per cent of Britain's young men would not be available for recruiting either because of their profession or because they were medically or otherwise unfit.

Though the government has undertaken to introduce some form of compulsory service if voluntary recruiting fails to meet the target, there is a widespread belief that, if the shortfall is a small one, it will lower its target instead. And since Britain's overseas commitments are exclusively national and cannot be transferred to others, the reduction is most likely to come in her contribution to NATO in Europe. Indeed, Britain's desire to end conscription has already led to a greater reduction in her NATO forces than her allies believe justified. And it may also have influenced her views on the strategic concept which NATO should follow.

The other external factor which has exerted a major influence on British views about NATO has been the development of Britain's military commitments overseas and the failure of her allies to support them. The major part of Britain's land forces have been serving outside Europe ever since the end of the Second World War, either as garrisons in the long chain of imperial bases from Gibraltar to Hong Kong or in active operations against large-scale terrorism in Malaya and Cyprus. For many years there were also substantial British forces carrying out occupation duties in Austria and Trieste or supporting the United Nations campaign in Korea. Apart from adopting the appropriate political measures – which ultimately succeeded in Malaya – there are obvious limits on Britain's ability to reduce her military commitments in the colonies. She therefore sought

[17]Cmd. 545.

and obtained formal permission to reduce her NATO contribution in case of emergency in her overseas territories.

A much more serious problem arose over Britain's interests in the Middle East. Besides sharing with the rest of Western Europe a vital economic interest in access to Middle Eastern oil on reasonable terms, Britain also has a unique financial interest in the existing system by which Middle Eastern oil is produced and marketed. This special national interest is most dramatically illustrated by the stupendous contribution made by Kuwait to the dollar reserves of the sterling area and to the investment funds of the London capital market. For many Englishmen, particularly if they are Conservatives, even more important than Britain's material interests in the Middle East is the symbolic value of Britain's semi-imperial position in the area.

Most Conservatives felt that ever since the war Britain had been unnecessarily abdicating from her imperial heritage through weakness of character, a misplaced sense of guilt, socialist heresy, and pressure from American vested interests masquerading as anti-colonialism. After the Persian oil dispute, this feeling acquired pathological violence. When Colonel Nasser nationalized the Suez Canal Company, many people in Britain positively welcomed his act as providing an opportunity for that display of military force in the area which they considered an indispensable precondition for restoring British influence. America's refusal to countenance such a display without better legal grounds led to the Anglo-French conspiracy on the ill-conceived and worse-executed Suez campaign. The isolation of Britain and France inside NATO over Suez led to a frightening explosion of anger in Britain against the alliance as a whole and the United States in particular. Besides the Conservative politicians, at least one senior civil servant in a key position began talking as if America's 'betrayal' must mean the end of NATO.

In this atmosphere the acquisition of an independent thermonuclear striking force became an absolute priority for the British government, while for a large section of the British people the H-bomb became the indispensable symbol of national greatness. Randolph Churchill spoke for this section when he told the American Chamber of Commerce in London: 'Britain can knock down twelve cities in the region of Stalingrad and Moscow from bases in Britain and another dozen in the Crimea from bases in Cyprus. We did not have that power at the time of Suez. We are a major power again.'[18]

[18] *The Times*, 14 November 1958.

The impact on NATO of Sandys' 1957 White Paper was to some extent distorted because he and other government spokesmen deliberately presented it so as to excite this element in British opinion. In fact it represented no dramatic shift in the current of British defence policy as it had been developing since 1952. Indeed, its novelty consisted in the fact that for the first time the British government was drawing the practical conclusions for defence organization from the strategic assumptions which it had stated quite unequivocally in 1955. Because it was impossible to defend the British people against thermonuclear attack, British policy on global war must consist entirely in deterrence. The considerations which had led the Labour government in 1950 to aim at holding the Russians in Europe as far as possible to the east were no longer relevant, given the present capabilities of Russian air power.

Thus Britain was no longer prepared to make major economic sacrifices for a NATO strategy of forward defence whose only purpose was to encourage the continental countries in clinging to illusions which had been out-of-date for years. In the discussions which followed inside NATO about the projected British troop reductions in Germany, however, Britain does not seem to have pressed this strategic argument, for fear of raising unnecessary opposition. Instead she concentrated on the economic argument that she was making a disproportionate sacrifice and overstraining her balance of payments. But statements made by leading British figures – notably Lord Montgomery, even before he retired as deputy supreme allied commander – show clearly enough that the troop reductions were felt to be justified in any case because Western atomic striking power has ruled out any possibility of a major Soviet attack on Western Europe for at least ten years.

In fact, NATO itself has dropped the idea of forward defence as it was conceived by the Lisbon Conference. Apart from their function in triggering off massive retaliation, the task of the ground forces is now seen not as to hold the whole front against a major Soviet attack, which would in any case involve full-scale thermonuclear retaliation, but as to smother frontier incidents and to block any limited and local aggression whose success might prove fatal to the morale of Europe as a whole. The British government would argue that the task of smothering frontier incidents does not require the thirty divisions SHAPE demands, while the second task assumes a Soviet readiness to risk global war which does not now exist, but which might be encouraged if NATO too obviously prepares to limit its liabilities. In any case, experience has shown that the use or threat of armed force by the Soviet Union on local issues is more likely to drive the West together on a massive arms programme than to demoralize and disintegrate the alliance.

The Labour opposition, and an important section of Conservative backbenchers, are less sanguine about Soviet intentions, and less ready to be tied to a suicidal strategy if any fighting develops in Central Europe which it is beyond the very limited capacity of the present NATO forces to contain with conventional weapons alone. They doubt whether it would be possible to prevent limited atomic war in Central Europe from spreading rapidly to all-out thermonuclear world war. So while recognizing that the distribution of 'tactical' atomic weapons to the NATO forces will strengthen the deterrent against a major Soviet attack, they fear that it might also weaken the Western will to offer effective resistance to a military challenge which is presented ambiguously – for example, one which arises out of frontier fighting for which the initial responsibility is unclear. Thus they have tended to support NATO criticism of recent British troop reductions in Western Germany.

Up to this point, both sides to the argument about NATO strategy assume that the alliance remains united in its reaction to attack on any one of its members. But, in the long run, a much more serious challenge to NATO is presented by the line of reasoning which lay behind Britain's decision to build a thermonuclear striking force, which, like the American SAC, lies wholly outside NATO. The main argument publicly used by the government to justify this decision has been that the British H-bomb would 'strengthen' the allied deterrent, though how and to what extent it would do so have never been explained in detail. The secondary argument implicit in much of the government propaganda for the H-bomb is that it would enable Britain to use military force for pursuing her special interests outside the NATO area, without having to rely on United States support if she were again threatened, as at Suez, with thermonuclear attack by Russia – *v.* the quotation above from Randolph Churchill.

But a much more important reason for Britain's decision than either of these is the belief, once incautiously expressed in Parliament by Duncan Sandys himself, that as America comes to rely less on overseas bases for her own atomic striking force, her strategic interest in defending Western Europe may decline so dramatically as to threaten her support for NATO. Indeed, even before America acquires a fully intercontinental striking force, Russia's ability to inflict intolerable damage on the United States itself may make automatic nuclear retaliation by SAC a far less credible deterrent than it was a few years ago.

British strategic thinking now is much concerned with the distinction between 'active' and 'passive' deterrence. Active deterrence is defined as the threat to initiate global thermonuclear war in response to an aggression which is limited, in the sense that it does not put the survival of the deterrent's possessor directly at stake. The doctrine of 'massive retaliation' was an example of such active deterrence. Passive deterrence is defined as the use of thermonuclear striking power to deter a direct all-out attack on one's national existence by displaying the capacity to inflict intolerable damage on the aggressor's homeland even after he has struck the first thermonuclear blow at one's own. A country which aims at active deterrence against, say, the Soviet Union must have a thermonuclear striking force hundreds of times larger than one which aims only at passive deterrence. For, since it plans to strike the first thermonuclear blow, it must aim primarily at ensuring its own survival by destroying the enemy's power to retaliate in kind. In fact, most experts believe that in a few years' time such an aim will become unattainable even for the richest and most advanced country in the world. Apart from the difficulty of locating the tiny targets presented by underground and undersea missile bases, the weight of nuclear explosive required to destroy them might threaten the survival of the human race itself.

Passive deterrence, on the other hand, requires only sufficient thermonuclear striking power to inflict damage on the aggressor which is out of proportion to what he would gain by defeating the country concerned. Since it assumes that the enemy has already struck the first thermonuclear blow, it can ignore his military bases and concentrate on major population centres and agglomerations of economic power. Even a small country could contrive sufficient dispersal of its striking force to have a good chance of keeping some retaliatory power intact. And if it were close to the Soviet Union, it might find a relatively unsophisticated delivery system sufficient for its purpose. Sweden, for example, might well feel itself immune from Soviet attack if it was thought to have the capacity for dropping one H-bomb on Leningrad. However, if Soviet interception techniques improve, the number of weapons required to saturate Russia's defences could rise beyond the capacity of a small country.

On the other hand, the value of a small but independent thermonuclear striking force in passive deterrence is reinforced by the possibility that a single H-bomb exploded in Russia, whatever its country of origin, might trigger off a general thermonuclear exchange between Russia and the West. So far as the potential aggressor is concerned, this possibility adds a small and variable risk of massive retaliation to the more calculable probability of losing a few cities. And so far as the United States is concerned, an independent H-bomb may give any of her allies a degree of influence over her use of SAC more certain than could be secured by any purely institutional arrangement.

There is little doubt that the main aim of the British thermonuclear striking force is to provide passive deterrence for Britain in case America drops her present policy of active deterrence for NATO as a whole. Though some Englishmen believe that the political likelihood of Russia presenting Britain with the sort of threat to which passive deterrence would be relevant is too small to be worth preparing against, the majority, including the leaders of both the political parties, feel that the additional expenditure required to mount a passive deterrent on the basis of Britain's existing atomic resources and delivery system is small enough to be worth making. This majority might dwindle dramatically if its assumptions about the low cost of a passive deterrent prove to be mistaken.

What is more controversial is the British government's attempt to carry out a policy of active deterrence with a capacity which is adequate only for passive deterrence. The 1958 White Paper on Defence, for example, included the passage: 'But it must be well understood that, if Russia were to launch a major attack on them [the Western powers], even with conventional forces only, they would have to hit back with strategic nuclear weapons.'[19] And there has been much talk in government circles about the possibility that when America loses her strategic interest in Europe, Britain will be able to step into her shoes by providing the necessary atomic umbrella for the Continent. Moreover, there is some evidence that the government may be spending more on its thermonuclear striking force than would be required for strictly passive deterrence, though nothing like enough to make a strategy of active deterrence credible. This line of criticism, which is broadly supported by the Labour Party, was well summarized in two articles by the *Times* defence correspondent on 15 and 16 October 1958, which concluded:

'If we believe that America will not defend us because of her vulnerability, we cannot credibly pretend that we, with our much greater vulnerability, will risk our extinction for NATO. The possession of an independent deterrent cannot therefore be used as a substitute for limited war forces.

'We must also recognize that the threat of Russian nuclear blackmail which gives us a military justification for having our own deterrent is the least likely of the various Communist threats that face us. We should give

[19]Cmd. 363, p. 2.

first priority in our defence preparations to the Cold War, which is with us all the time; second priority to limited war, which the deterrent can no longer be relied on to deter, because of the nuclear stalemate; and last priority to global war preparations.'

Of course the government has not been so single-minded in the pursuit of the Sandys policy as both its friends and opponents sometimes suggest. Ever since the publication of the 1957 White Paper, the individual services have been fighting a rearguard action – and not without success – against its implications for them. As in the United States, a conflict of vested interests between the services is apt to produce a mixture of incompatible strategies. On the other hand, some of the inconsistencies in the government's words and deeds are due to its legitimate desire not to hasten the reduction of America's strategic interest in Europe, to which it is trying to adapt its defence policy in time. One of the major problems facing the democracies in framing their defence policies arises from the difficulty of maintaining public support for existing strategies while simultaneously explaining the need to adapt strategy and weapons to the changes which may be expected over the next ten years – a difficulty which has troubled Secretary McElroy in the United States just as much as Duncan Sandys in the United Kingdom.

Thus, as the implications of the thermonuclear stand-off sink in on both sides of the Atlantic, military staffs and political leaders are more and more exercised by the problems of limited war as the only sort of war which the West can afford in the future. But official discussion of limited war, in Britain as elsewhere, is inevitably confused by a natural wish not to weaken the deterrent by casting doubt on the certainty of retaliation by SAC to any attack on Western Europe. In discussing the Central European problem in particular, the confusion has been confounded by the fact that some parties to the argument see limited warfare in the area – particularly limited atomic warfare – as a means of strengthening the trip wire which leads to massive thermonuclear retaliation; while others see it as a means of replacing massive retaliation by a less suicidal and more credible strategy. Still others believe that it can fill both roles at once.

Thus, when Britain first agreed to the use of nuclear weapons by SHAPE in 1954, she did so wholly as a means of reinforcing the American deterrent. It was not until 1956 that the government half-heartedly hinted at the possibility of limited atomic war as something which might happen in reality without leading to global war. The 1956 White Paper included the passage: '. . . we have to be prepared for the outbreak of localized conflicts on a scale short of global war. In such limited wars the possible use of nuclear weapons cannot be excluded.'[20] On the other hand, one of the government spokesmen in the debate on this White Paper defined a limited war as one in which nuclear weapons were not used.

The debate on the 1958 White Paper was only a little less confused on this issue, though the minister for war, Christopher Soames, made a statement which was at once precise and discreet: 'The real danger,' he said, 'lies in the fact that an unscrupulous nation playing upon the natural abhorrence and reluctance of the Western world to launch into a mutually devastating nuclear exchange might indulge in military adventures, or encourage other countries to do so whilst giving them thinly-veiled support. This is a field in which no government can say in advance to what weapons they would need to have recourse in any of the possible different sets of circumstances. . . . [We] would use the doctrine of minimum force. We would not deploy more forces, nor would we have recourse to bigger explosive power, than what was absolutely necessary to protect our interests. What is important here is that the Western world, and we in particular, should devote a sufficiently high expenditure to conventional weapons, so that we will not be in a position of having to resort to undue force.'[21] Unfortunately this admirable statement was a *cri du coeur* from the minister responsible for an army which is being starved of the weapons it would require to implement such a policy, for the sake of providing the air force with weapons it could not afford to use except in the most unlikely contingency of all – a direct nuclear attack on Britain herself.

Not surprisingly, most of the public discussion of limited war has been confined to politicians in opposition and to experts of no party at all. The Labour leaders have recently committed themselves to a fairly comprehensive doctrine on the subject which may be summarized as follows: if ever Britain finds herself engaged in fighting, she should use the minimum force required to bring the fighting to a halt – but not to 'win the war'. They recognize that the essential condition for limited war is limited war aims and that the old slogan, 'There is no substitute for victory,' must be replaced by the slogan, 'There is no substitute for survival.' Most interested opinion in Britain would agree that so far as the limitation of warfare itself is concerned, limiting the theatre of war has been proved possible in Korea and elsewhere, while limiting targets within the theatre is perfectly feasible. There is still, however, a widespread feeling that, though a clear distinction

[20]Cmd. 9691, p. 4.
[21]Hansard, 27 February 1958.

between conventional and nuclear weapons is easy to maintain, it would be well-nigh impossible in actual warfare to maintain a distinction between the various types of nuclear weapons, and that the employment even of small-yield nuclear weapons would make the limitation of targets and even of theatre much more difficult to maintain.

However, most of this discussion must remain largely theoretical. For the fact remains that Britain by herself cannot afford to produce a wide enough spectrum of options to permit her to apply the doctrine of limited force, particularly while she is diverting so much effort to the maintenance of her thermonuclear capacity on a scale which is probably larger than required for passive deterrence. The obvious answer is to seek within NATO that specialization of function and production which was en-visaged when the concept of balanced collective forces was first launched. The slogan of 'interdependence' has indeed been heard increasingly over the last twelve months on the Prime Minister's lips. But so far it has been applied in practice only to relations between Britain and the United States, from which Britain can hope to be the net gainer, and hardly at all to relations between Britain and the Continent, which is still seen as a net drain on Britain's scarce resources.

Moreover, it is difficult to see how Europe and the United States could ever afford to commit themselves in the long run to genuine interdepend-ence in the military field unless each member of the system thus created felt confident of its ability to commit the rest to its defence in an emergency, and was itself prepared to be so committed when another was under attack. This was possible – indeed, was a reality – in the days when America had a direct strategic interest in the defence of Western Europe and ran only a marginal risk in committing herself to retaliation on its behalf. The situation is so different today that it is difficult to see how the mutual confidence required for strategic interdependence could be created by anything less than full political federation. There was a time during the Anglo-American honeymoon from 1946 to 1950 when there seemed to be the possibility of a slow development in this direction. But apart from Norway and Holland, the rest of Europe has always been indifferent or hostile to the concept of an Atlantic community, and enthusiasm in Britain and the United States seemed to dwindle rapidly, particularly after 1952.

The existing divergence between the strategic situation and interests of America and her European allies is well illustrated by the course of the current argument about NATO strategy. America seeks a strategy of limited war on the Continent which would relieve her of the commitment to automatic thermonuclear retaliation. But any strategy for limited war in

Europe not only weakens what is left of the great deterrent, but may imply suffering for the continental countries which is for practical purposes indistinguishable from that involved in global atomic war. This is particularly true of a strategy which involves the use of nuclear weapons on the battlefield. A strategy for purely conventional defence, on the other hand, besides being politically unacceptable to the Continent in practice, however attractive it might be in theory, could always be outflanked if the Russians themselves chose to introduce the tactical use of atomic weapons, facing America once more with the choice between suicide and abandoning her allies.

It seems probable that in this situation most of the continental countries in NATO will follow the British lead in trying to build a passive deterrent for themselves as soon as they are physically capable of doing so. It is true that a passive deterrent is a sure protection only against direct all-out attack on the nation possessing it. But most of the continental countries have no immediate strategic interests outside their national frontiers in any case. There remains the theoretical possibility of nuclear blackmail or limited aggression, but a country which had the power to destroy a few Soviet cities would feel fairly secure against this risk. The declared interest of Sweden and Switzerland in acquiring nuclear weapons is an obvious pointer for countries at present in NATO.

The cost of producing nuclear weapons, and even more of constructing the delivery system required to make them effective, is likely to compel countries which begin building their own deterrent to reduce their contribution to whatever collective forces NATO then maintains. Moreover, as the power to initiate thermonuclear war spreads to more and more governments in NATO, membership in the alliance may seem to confer more risks than security. If every country with atomic weapons could be relied on to use them rationally – that is, exclusively as a passive deterrent – there would be little to fear. But experience suggests that a country which has just acquired atomic weapons may suffer from a rush of blood to the head and be tempted to use them for diplomatic purposes which involve great risks, even if not for actual warfare. German defence minister Strauss, for example, has said that when his country has atomic weapons, she will be able to compel both East and West to take the problem of German reunification more seriously. Statements in Paris about the French H-bomb have been much more extravagant. There can be no guarantee that this type of thinking will not prevail when the problem is faced in practice.

Once a country comes to feel that it can guarantee its own security against Soviet attack, it may well begin to consider using its nuclear forces to pursue exclusively national interests outside the alliance itself. Yet the risks it runs in such adventures are bound to threaten other members of the alliance. European anxiety about Chiang Kai-shek's behaviour during the Quemoy crisis imposed real strains on NATO, even though Taiwan is not directly allied with America's Atlantic partners. Such anxieties would have been enormously multiplied if Chiang had had nuclear weapons under his own control. Or, to take another example, if nuclear weapons had been given to Turkey or Greece, they would have been just as likely to have increased the division between these countries over the Cyprus issue as to have strengthened their unity against possible Soviet attack.

The spread of thermonuclear weapons does not threaten only the internal stability of the Western alliance. It also threatens the precarious stability created in the world as a whole by the fact that at present major atomic striking power is confined to two countries which, though hostile, are widely separated from one another in space and – by comparison with some other countries – are fundamentally satisfied with the *status quo*. The interest shared by Russia and America in preventing any extension in the possession of atomic weapons, except under their control, is suggested by the extent of their agreement on the need to end nuclear tests. For the greatest importance of a nuclear test ban would be in impeding the spread of nuclear weapons. No new country can build its own nuclear weapons system unless it is allowed to test its products. And since the main value of nuclear weapons is in deterrence, it is essential that a new country should be able to prove that it actually does possess these weapons by successfully exploding them.

Some of the dangers attendant on the spread of atomic weapons could be reduced if it were possible to devise an acceptable system for the supranational control of atomic weapons within the Western alliance. A recent American study[22] discounts the possibility of America herself joining such a system, but argues that she should persuade or compel her European allies to create one for their own weapons. But in practice this means pooling the decision to make peace or war, when war means total destruction. America has so far confined herself to establishing common control of atomic weapons in NATO only in the negative sense, by keeping the warhead in her own hands while entrusting the means of delivery to those of another, thus giving each the power of veto. But this is no precedent for a purely European system of control, since it has been

[22]Ben T. Moore, *NATO and the Future of Europe*, New York, 1958.

possible only because America retains the major part of her atomic striking power outside the system. In fact, she has lost nothing by accepting such a control system, because her allies would not allow her to station the weapons in their territory at all unless they had the power of veto over their use. And her allies lose nothing by accepting it, since they cannot now have atomic weapons at all unless they give America the same power of veto. The situation would be entirely different if a system were required to provide total control over the use of atomic weapons produced by individual countries inside Europe. It is difficult to conceive of France, particularly under its present leader, agreeing to give each of her allies the right of vetoing the use of the weapons she plans to start producing next year, and through which she hopes to recover status as a great power. The problem is even more difficult if it is desired to produce a system which allows positive control – that is, which would ensure that the weapons were used by the community as a whole whenever one of its members so desired.

Yet only a system of positive control would meet Europe's strategic need if America's atomic umbrella were withdrawn. As in the case of military interdependence in general, interdependence in atomic weapons is difficult to conceive under any circumstances short of the complete fusion of national sovereignties in a political federation. And though six of the continental countries have committed themselves to move over seventeen years toward political federation through economic union, the difficulties of establishing collective control of their atomic weapons are more likely to prove an obstacle than an incentive to this end. In practice, collective influence over the use of nuclear weapons is most likely to be achieved by distributing some of the weapons themselves so as to give individual members of the alliance a chance – which will vary according to the politico-military circumstances of a given crisis – of triggering off the whole of the alliance's atomic power.

At the moment it looks as if technological and economic difficulties may ensure that France is the only new Western country to produce its own atomic weapons within the next five years, though it would be unwise to rule out the possibility of a scientific breakthrough which could make atomic weapons much cheaper and easier to produce. But this is a field in which coming events cast their shadow long before. Even though the United States and Britain may wish to discourage their partners from following their example, it is quite impossible for those members of NATO which are farthest from the danger zone to deny a more exposed ally the weapons which their enemies already possess and which they themselves consider vital for their own defence. There is obvious scope for bargaining in which an ally will demand access to America's nuclear armoury against making a more effective contribution to the collective forces. General de Gaulle's *démarche* about the missile bases in France suggests a general trend. Experience with the Tripartite Agreement on rationing the supply of arms in the Middle East shows that it may be impossible for one side in the Cold War to operate a system of arms control in its own camp without the co-operation of the other side in the Cold War.

For this reason, a problem steadily assuming greater prominence in Britain is whether it is possible to reverse the whole trend of the last thirteen years and to base the security of Western Europe on some form of co-operation with the Soviet bloc in the regional limitation and control of weapons and forces. It is recognized by both sides in this debate that such co-operation with the Soviet Union would be possible only on the basis of unity and strength inside the Western alliance. And the main disagreement is not so much about the desirability of such a security system in principle, as about whether the West is yet sufficiently strong and united to undertake negotiations to this end. The Labour Party, which has now officially committed itself to aim at a form of disengagement in Central Europe, believes that NATO's bargaining position is likely to get weaker rather than stronger as time passes and that the Russian leaders may become less willing to negotiate a settlement than they appear at present. The Conservative government, on the other hand, is disinclined to weaken still further its declining popularity inside NATO by pressing issues which neither the American nor the German government is yet ready to discuss.

However, neither side believes that there is any immediate prospect of disengagement in Central Europe in its full sense, meaning the physical evacuation of the area by both the Soviet and NATO forces and the political neutralization of the countries thus exposed. The most the Labour Party hopes for as a first step in this direction is an agreement on the limitation and control of armaments on both sides of the Iron Curtain in Central Europe, leaving the existing alliances untouched and the American and Russian troops confronting one another along the Iron Curtain as at present – though in smaller numbers. It believes that the latest revision of the Rapacki Plan provides a good basis for negotiations to this end. The Conservative government in fact put forward similar proposals with American agreement in 1955 – indeed, it was only the accident of convenience in conference tactics which led to these proposals being called the Eden Plan rather than the Dulles Plan.

Hugh Gaitskell, the Labour Party leader, has repeatedly stressed that his proposals for disengagement in Central Europe should be seen not as a diplomatic alternative to NATO but as a strategic alternative for NATO. For whatever agreement were reached with Russia on the precise military and diplomatic status of Central Europe, a strong Western alliance would be required to provide sanctions against its violation. That is why the Labour Party has always refused to consider any form of disengagement which would mean the total evacuation of the Anglo-Saxon forces from the Continent. Its own proposals envisage merely the relocation of the American and British troops in the Low Countries and northern France. Perhaps it is worth pointing out that as of January 1959 the Western governments' official proposals for a German settlement concede the military feasibility of disengagement in principle by offering to keep NATO forces out of the present Soviet Zone when German reunification has taken place and the Red Army has withdrawn to Poland or points east.

I believe myself that as the implications of the thermonuclear stand-off come to be recognized more fully, it will be seen that the problems of protecting the *status quo* under the Labour Party plan for disengagement would resemble in principle but be simpler in practice than those of protecting the present *status quo*. For fighting would begin, if it began at all, on the eastern frontier of Poland rather than in the centre of Germany. And the existence of a strong buffer of conventional troops between the atomic forces of both sides would reduce the risk that a frontier incident or local explosion might lead to an unnecessary thermonuclear holocaust.

This of course assumes that Russia would not attempt a massive military invasion of the whole of Europe after disengagement had taken place. But Russia could hardly hope to gain more by such an invasion than she holds at present by the peaceful occupation of Eastern Europe, while the risks of thermonuclear destruction she would run would be out of all proportion to the gain. If Russia were really prepared to run such risks, she would not agree to disengage in the first place, since she is in a stronger position to exert military pressure on Western Europe from where she stands today than she would be if she withdrew to her own territory.

Here again, there is less disagreement than appears between the two sides to the debate on disengagement in Britain. Both of them believe that, with all its obvious imperfections and dwindling credibility, the thermonuclear deterrent is likely to retain its efficiency for some time in preventing Russia from deliberately initiating global war. And they both feel that the difficulty of keeping a war limited in Central Europe will deter Russia from pursuing her aims there by piecemeal local aggression. But while the supporters of disengagement fear that the continued division of Germany may produce an explosion in the Soviet Zone which could drag the great powers into nuclear war against their will, its opponents believe that the danger of such an explosion would be greater if the Red Army were known to be on its way out of Eastern Europe. The other disagreements expressed by the two sides are probably due more to the difference between the inhibitions of office and the licence of opposition than to genuine conflicts of judgement on the issues themselves. An opposition party can afford to look further ahead and to speculate more freely about the future than any government.

It is perhaps worth making a final point about the difference of political climate in Britain and the United States concerning strategic problems in general. It seems to an outsider that the American people, who came face to face with their vulnerability in total war only a year ago with the launching of the Soviet Sputnik, still believe it is possible to find a military policy which would restore their nation's historic immunity by guaranteeing absolute security against all possible threats. The British, on the other hand, have come to accept the fact that armaments can offer only a precarious and relative security. Having already suffered much destruction in the Second World War, they have now grown accustomed to the idea that they cannot survive in total war, and they believe that the Soviet leaders are realistic enough to know that Russia too is indefensible against thermonuclear attack. And they feel that knowledge of her vulnerability in total war will discourage Russia from using her superiority in conventional forces to attempt limited local advances against Western Europe – although this danger is not wholly insignificant.

Thus the fundamental argument in Britain is shifting from purely military issues to the political assumptions on which defence is based. It is between those who believe that the stability now offered by a bi-polar balance of terror may be shattered so soon that it is urgently necessary to probe Soviet readiness to co-operate in measures of arms control, and those who feel that there is plenty of time before this problem need take first place in British and Western thinking. The division emerges most clearly in the debate about Britain's H-bomb. Some of the former group, who are by no means confined to one party, would like Britain to declare now that she would stop producing her own nuclear weapons in return for a sure guarantee that no countries other than the United States and the USSR would produce them in the future. Some of the latter group would like to increase the number and variety of Britain's nuclear weapons considerably before negotiation on the major problems begins in earnest.

No one doubts that there is bound to be an increase in the number of countries with their own atomic weapons unless there is agreement either inside NATO on the positive centralized control of these weapons or between NATO and the Soviet Union on measures of disarmament which would reduce the desire and ability of other nations to acquire them. Both of these alternatives to thermonuclear anarchy require a degree of international confidence and co-operation which seems unlikely at present. Even among those in Britain who regard the spread of atomic weapons as the most urgent problem facing mankind, there are some who are reconciled to the possibility that it may be some years before either solution emerges clearly as a practical choice. In the meantime, British thinking about NATO strategy is likely to remain, like that of other powers, an uneasy compromise between the inheritance of the past, the realities of the present, and fears or hopes which can only be confirmed in the future.

CHAPTER FIVE

Searching for Solutions

I T WAS ABOVE ALL the Hungarian tragedy, and the possibility that Britain shared in responsibility for it, which directed my attention to disengagement as a means of giving the East European countries a chance for freedom. For several years I argued the case for disengagement. By drafting Hugh Gaitskell's Godkin lecture on the subject for Harvard I became the author of the Gaitskell Plan. I debated disengagement, mainly with James King, an old friend from prewar Balliol, in the American *New Republic*, and with Geoffrey Hudson in *The Scotsman*. The best statement of my case, however, was the first, in a Fabian lecture on 30 October 1957. Many of my arguments have a special resonance today, with the popular revolutions in Eastern Europe and the imminence of German reunification.

I saw Hungary as the first of a series of possible risings in Eastern Europe which might conceivably involve the two alliances in direct conflict with one another, and to which the nuclear deterrent of NATO would be quite irrelevant. At the same time Russia's launch of her first Sputnik demonstrated that Washington's strategy of massive retaliation would lose credibility as Moscow increased its ability to retaliate in kind. Eisenhower and Dulles were already feeling their way towards alternatives. But their preferred option of limited nuclear war on European soil would be quite unacceptable to their allies; it would be less effective as a deterrent and no less destructive for them than massive retaliation.

On the other hand, it would be impossible for NATO to adopt a strategy of purely conventional defence against a conventional attack so long as its American and British forces were trained and equipped to fight only with nuclear weapons. In fact Britain was moving under Macmillan towards a strategy of massive retaliation at the same time as America was moving against it.

So the only way of making certain that a political explosion in Eastern Europe would not involve nuclear war between the two alliances was to create a physical space between them. But I thought that Russia would not withdraw its troops eastwards unless America and Britain withdrew westwards. The Communist regimes in Eastern Europe were increasingly demanding independence from Soviet control. Gomulka had actually threatened Khrushchev with war if he tried to impose Soviet policy on Poland. The Hungarian rising had been led by Communists – like the Prague Spring twelve years later.

Direct control of Eastern Europe by the Red Army was proving more expensive both economically, politically, and militarily every year. This was one reason why in the end Gorbachev decided to make unilateral reductions in Soviet forces in Eastern Europe. Indeed he went even further by announcing that he would not intervene militarily to prevent political change in the satellite countries – even if NATO forces stayed put in Western Europe. But by the time he renounced the Brezhnev doctrine there was no longer local support for Communism in any form. So the central problem now is the one I described in my pamphlet over thirty years ago. What sort of military structure can be devised to ensure that the inclusion of Eastern Europe in Western political and economic structures does not threaten the security of the Soviet Union? Unless some new security structure can be devised for this purpose, 'both sides are likely to feel that the new situation would be less stable and less secure than the old one'.

My arguments against trying to neutralize Germany alone still hold good: 'if you try to neutralize Germany alone, you put Germany in the one situation in which she could exploit her bargaining power to upset whatever *status quo* is agreed.' For this reason not only Khrushchev, but Air Marshal Sir John Slessor and George Kennan had suggested the complete withdrawal of British and American forces from Western Europe in return for the complete withdrawal of the Red Army from Eastern Europe. I was less ambitious, aiming to construct a neutral belt which included only both parts of Germany, with Poland, Hungary and Czechoslovakia.

I was, however, hopelessly mistaken in suggesting that a neutral belt could have its neutrality protected by 'the disincentive of punishment in limited atomic war'. This version of what later became known as the NATO strategy of 'flexible response' obviously makes no sense when there is no guarantee that a limited nuclear war will not rapidly escalate into an all-out thermonuclear holocaust. I have been looking for more acceptable alternatives ever since.

However, there were no takers for disengagement among Western governments in the later fifties, although several had played with the idea a few years earlier. In the United States my only prominent supporters were George Kennan, who put forward similar ideas in his Reith lectures, and a pale young Pole called Zbigniew Brzezinski, who later became President Carter's national security adviser. In the Soviet bloc the Polish foreign minister, Adam Rapacki, made proposals for disengagement, but when I discussed them with him it was clear that he had no guarantee of support from Khrushchev.

NATO had only just managed to get Western Germany into its ranks, and did not want to see everything in the melting pot again. Before long Khrushchev embarked on his hair-raising Cuban adventure, and was replaced. Once Brezhnev was in power, the Cold War in Europe went into the deep freeze. Washington and Moscow concentrated on trying to manage their mutual nuclear relationship. *Détente* between the super-powers seemed to imply immobility in Europe. Even Brezhnev's brutal suppression of the Prague Spring produced no reaction from the West. Both alliances seemed to prefer the stability of a divided Europe to any possible change.

I had to concentrate on the strategic problems of NATO during my six years as defence secretary from 1964, and was then plunged into the unfamiliar jungle of economic policy as shadow chancellor and chancellor of the exchequer. It was not until I became shadow foreign secretary in the early eighties that I returned to the central problems of East–West relations.

Reagan had adopted a posture of extreme belligerence towards the Soviet Union as 'the focus of evil in the modern world'. I was deeply disturbed by the ignorant irresponsibility with which he was treating the problems of nuclear war. So I spent most of the eighties wrestling again with the anfractuosities of NATO strategy, as the arms race propelled humanity ever closer to the brink of self-destruction.

Little had changed since I had last been directly involved as defence secretary. NATO was still committed to the ambiguities of 'flexible response' which I had helped to devise in the mid sixties as an un-satisfactory compromise between the American desire to be rid of its nuclear responsibility for Germany and the German desire for massive retaliation. I myself, like my one-time colleague in Washington, Bob McNamara, and my best military adviser at the Ministry of Defence, Field Marshal Lord Carver, now believed that NATO must move towards a strategy of 'No First Use' of nuclear weapons, while retaining the American nuclear umbrella as a deterrent against a Soviet nuclear attack.

Meanwhile the Labour Party had turned unilateralist. I was increasingly impatient of its tendency to treat these problems of life and death as a Punch and Judy show between an absolute unilateralism and an equally absolute multilateralism. It became more and more difficult for me to express the whole of my real thinking without breaking ranks with my colleagues. Nevertheless I succeeded in clearing with Neil Kinnock the text of my article in the New York journal *Foreign Affairs* just before the 1987 general election. It was described, on occasion, as 'probably the most revisionist interpretation of the rationale and timetable of the party's policy' at that time. Those days have gone, I hope for ever.

The best statement of my current views on NATO strategy appeared in a Fabian tract entitled 'Labour and a World Society' based on a lecture I gave in 1984, shortly before Gorbachev took over in the Soviet Union. I compared the situation we then faced in trying to build a world society with that I had described a third of a century earlier, in my essay on 'Power Politics and the Labour Party' with which this selection of my writings begins.

Both the United States and the Soviet Union were increasingly distracted from the problems of Europe. America's growing tendency to global unilateralism was fed by the dangers it saw beyond its southern and western frontiers, and by the linked domestic problems of crime, drugs, and race, now exacerbated by Hispanic and Asian immigration. Russia faced daunting challenges from a collapsing economy and the growth of nationalism in its peripheral republics. Meanwhile the stability of the nuclear balance between them was threatened by new twists in the arms race – including Reagan's 'Star Wars' initiative – which might offer one side or the other the incentive or possibility to carry out a first strike.

I argued strongly against the unilateralist approach towards NATO's existing strategy, believing that if the European allies could be persuaded to agree to a non-nuclear strategy, it would not be difficult to persuade the United States to follow. Moreover the time had come 'to seek common security through multilateral agreements between the superpowers and their allies'. The possibility of a nuclear winter had destroyed the main argument for neutralism. There would be no survivors in the northern hemisphere if the superpowers exchanged blows. However, the danger of Soviet aggression in Europe was at its lowest since the war. Instability in the Third World was now the major threat to world peace.

Since then, the force of all these arguments has been much increased by the policies of Mikhail Gorbachev and the new instabilities created by the revolutions in Eastern Europe.

A NEUTRAL BELT IN EUROPE?

(Fabian lecture, October 1957)

THE CASE FOR DISENGAGEMENT

In my opinion the next phase in world politics will be dominated by the impact of three new factors. First of all, the development of long-range nuclear weapons and their distribution over an increasing number of nation states. Secondly, the decay of international Communism as an instrument of Russian foreign policy – not necessarily decay as such, but its decay as a tool of Russian policy. And thirdly, the appearance of new centres of power and political initiative outside Washington and Moscow.

What I want to do tonight is to examine the impact of these three fundamental changes on the European situation, and to suggest how the West should adapt its policy in order to take account of them. Twelve months ago, a great variety of people felt that the existing *status quo* in Europe was likely to be permanent, and that on the whole it was fairly acceptable. The fact that Europe was divided into two camps and that the dividing line ran through the centre of Germany was welcomed by many people, including even some Germans, on the grounds that the division of Germany between two power blocs was the best guarantee that Germany would never again disturb the peace of Europe. And the confrontation of American and Soviet troops on the dividing line was also welcomed by many people because it was generally held that world peace depended on a balance of mutual terror, that the threat of massive retaliation was the most effective deterrent against aggression, and that this threat would only be convincing if the powers which had the capacity for massive retaliation were certain to be immediately and directly involved by any violation of the *status quo*. So that you had this double situation: on the one hand, Germany apparently divided for ever, and therefore no longer a dangerous factor in European politics; on the other hand, through the confrontation of American and Russian troops, the certainty that any aggression in central Europe would lead to massive retaliation; and therefore no aggression would take place.

The Lessons of Hungary

In my opinion, events in the last twelve months have thrown doubt on whether the existing European settlement is likely to be lasting and also on whether it is a desirable settlement even if it does last.

Two tremendous things have happened in the last twelve months – the decay of Communism in Europe, and the development of the Soviet Union of long-range thermonuclear striking power, or, to use a word to symbolize each change, Hungary and the Sputnik.

The Hungarian revolution and its suppression by the Red Army twelve months ago wakened the moral conscience of the West, and made many decent people wonder whether a European settlement could be a desirable one if it was based on the suppression of freedom-loving peoples by a hated army. But the Hungarian revolution also revealed that if the peoples of Eastern Europe were ever to achieve their freedom, they could only do so by peaceful means. The thermonuclear stalemate has closed all roads to liberation except diplomacy.

Hungary also, I think, gave us a warning. It showed that war might start in Europe, not as a result of a decision by a great power to commit aggression, but by a process of what you might call spontaneous combustion through a local explosion which involved a great power against its will, and then perhaps involved other great powers. In the case of Hungary there was never, I think, any possibility that the West was likely to intervene by force to help the Hungarians, and so find itself directly fighting Soviet troops. But people have come to realize that a situation would easily develop in the future in Eastern Europe which might involve the West as well as the Soviet Union in fighting, whether the West wishes it or not.

Precarious Peace

The most obvious case, which has been much discussed by governments in the last twelve months, would be a rising in Eastern Germany, suppressed by the Red Army, at a time when the West German forces were fully mobilized along the Iron Curtain and perhaps possessed tactical atomic weapons. Nobody can confidently say that if thousands of defeated East Germans were driven by the Red Army up against the Iron Curtain their West German brothers would not come physically to their assistance.

And there are other possibilities of war arising out of the present situation. When Tito dies, as he will some day, there might be the possibility of civil war inside Yugoslavia and of outside intervention. And it would be unwise to rule out the possibility that at some stage in the next few years Polish relations with the Soviet Union might become so strained that the Soviet Union might make a threat of force against Poland in order to get her way, and Poland might appeal for military help to the United Nations – help which she has every right to receive under the charter.

In other words, so long as the Red Army is occupying the whole of Eastern Europe, there is a time bomb at the very core of the existing European settlement. The most important factor about this situation is that a military strategy of deterrence is completely irrelevant to it. It is possible to deter a rational and self-controlled government from taking action which is certain to be disastrous to it; but it is not possible to deter ordinary men and women who are subjected to intolerable economic and political strains from rebelling against these strains and using force to get their way. That essentially is the problem and the threat presented not only to the Russians but also to the West and to world peace as a whole by the Red Army's occupation of Eastern Europe. It is a danger to which, as I say, the Western strategy of deterrence is totally irrelevant. Not only that, but if in fact fighting does break out, a strategy of massive retaliation, which we all know to be suicidal, is totally inappropriate for dealing with it. And that leads to the second big change in the world situation during the last twelve months.

The Lessons of the Sputnik

This change is that the United States and her European allies have become conscious that it is impossible to unleash thermonuclear retaliation against the Soviet Union without suffering crippling destruction in return. The Sputnik has simply underlined this lesson. It has not really changed the situation, because the Russians have been capable of dropping megaton bombs on the United States for over a year; but it has brought this fact home to American opinion. Indeed the situation is even a little worse than that, because not only has the Soviet Union the power to inflict thermonuclear counter-retaliation on the United States; her sea power also gives her the capacity for separating Europe, with all the NATO forces including the American troops, from their essential bases of supply on the other side of the Atlantic.

As a result the American government in the last month or so has taken the initiative in asking the whole of the Western alliance to consider alternatives to massive thermonuclear retaliation. Mr Dulles' article in the October number of *Foreign Affairs* suggests as an alternative the local defence of territory by limited atomic warfare, rather than all-out thermonuclear warfare to destroy the Soviet Union itself.

The Western governments are still discussing whether there is an alternative to massive retaliation in the NATO area, and if so what it is.

I have a feeling that this is one of the topics on which Mr Macmillan and Mr Dulles disagreed in their recent talks in Washington. Because, oddly enough, the British government has picked up the slogan of massive retaliation just at the moment when the American government has thrown it away.

Limited Atomic War

And, of course, from the point of view of the European members of NATO, there are very strong arguments against the strategy of defence by limited atomic war. The only limited atomic wars which have been fought in exercises so far – Exercise *Carte Blanche* in Germany and Exercise *Sage Brush* in Louisiana – involved the total destruction of life in the areas concerned. A strategy which necessarily involves the atomic annihilation of the country which is attacked, and which the alliance exists to defend, is not an attractive policy to the countries in the front line, however attractive it may be to those in the rear.

So inevitably the Europeans are beginning to demand a purely conventional defence as an alternative to limited atomic warfare. The European countries are feeling their way towards an increase in the number of conventional forces on the frontier, so that they are capable of dispensing wholly with atomic weapons in dealing with any minor war which may arise either through a deliberate Communist incursion or through a spontaneous explosion of the type to which I referred earlier.

But that, too, raises great problems. The British and American governments have already decided that they are going to reorganize and re-equip all their NATO forces so that they can only fight with atomic weapons. And it is very difficult to see how you can have, side by side on the same front, forces which can only fight with atomic weapons and forces which can only fight without them. It seems to me that Western defence planning has, in consequence, fallen into a state of almost total paralysis. Uncertainty about the strategy which the alliance possesses for the defence of its members is now corroding the alliance at its very heart.

The Idea of Disengagement

What is the conclusion to be drawn from the impact of these two factors – the Hungarian revolution and the Soviet Union's development of thermonuclear striking power? It is, first, that the existing *status quo* in Europe is inherently unstable, and, secondly, that if this instability leads to an armed conflict, there is at present no obvious military means of preventing this from leading to total global war. And the question to which we must all address ourselves is this: is there any practicable alternative to the existing *status quo* in Europe which gives a prospect of greater stability and of less disastrous consequences if the stability breaks down?

Because the main cause of instability of the existing situation arises from the hostility of the peoples of Eastern Europe to occupation by the Red Army and to all that this involves in Soviet control of their policies, I think you can only get greater stability if you can get the Red Army withdrawn, so that Germany can be reunited, and the satellite countries to the east of Germany can achieve greater national independence.

On the other hand, as we have already seen, you can only produce any change in the *status quo* by agreement with the Russians. Any agreement with the Russians has got to involve concessions by the West parallel to those made by the Soviet Union. Consequently the answer must involve a reciprocal withdrawal of Western forces and Soviet forces from the existing Iron Curtain with mutual control of the area thus exposed; in other words the neutralization of at least Central Europe. That is what it involves in practice, no matter what words we use.

The idea of disengagement in Central Europe as an alternative to the Iron Curtain is almost as old as the Iron Curtain itself. The last time it was seriously advanced by a Western government was when Sir Anthony Eden put it forward at the Geneva Conference in 1955. He suggested it might be possible to agree on an area with no armaments at all right in the middle of Europe, and on either side of that a zone of limited armaments under inspection and control by both sides. But the suggestion he made at the Geneva Conference two years ago was conditional. The conditions were that there should first be free elections in the whole of Germany and that the resulting all-German government should decide what course it should take in foreign policy – though it is obvious that the second condition was implicitly nullified by the idea that a united Germany should fall into this area of limited armaments.

It is easy enough to see why two years ago Sir Anthony made free elections a pre-condition of disengagement. At that time, it was generally believed in the West that all the Communist Parties in Eastern Europe were absolutely subservient to the Soviet Union, and that therefore withdrawal of the Red Army would mean nothing so long as the Communist regimes survived; the places left vacant by the Red Army would soon be filled by local troops which were under Soviet orders through the Communist Party network – Marshal Rokossovsky's position as the Polish minister of defence appeared to prove this assumption.

Consequently, ever since Potsdam the West has made free elections in

Eastern Europe the first condition of any agreement with the Soviet Union. But I believe that the events last year have shown that this is no longer a necessary condition. What happened in Hungary, and what happened in Poland, showed beyond any doubt that if the Red Army is removed from Eastern Europe, the Communist Parties there will no longer be simply passive instruments of Soviet policy.

The Decay of Centralized Communism

And here we come to the second great factor I mentioned right at the beginning, which is going increasingly to influence world affairs in the years to come: the decay of international Communism as a centralized system primarily devoted to pursuing the interests of the Soviet state. This decay, of course, began with Yugoslavia's secession from the Cominform in 1948, and was carried further by the victory of the Chinese Communist Party on the Chinese mainland in 1949. But I think what has happened since Stalin's death has carried the process very much further still. In the first place, an essential element in Soviet control of foreign Communist Parties was the local secret police, which was under direct physical control by the Soviet secret police. When Khrushchev liquidated Beria he also dismantled Beria's international police empire. You will remember how in consequence many Soviet secret police agents defected to the West. Thus the main physical instrument by which the Soviet Union controlled foreign Communist Parties has disappeared.

Second to the physical instrument – indeed, perhaps more important still to Soviet control of foreign Communist Parties – is the religious loyalty of Communists to what I hope I can call without offence a Vatican in Moscow. That type of centralized clerical control demands an absolute acceptance of the infallibility of the central authority. Once doubt is cast on that infallibility, the whole structure begins to disintegrate. At the twentieth Congress of the Soviet Communist Party in February 1956, Khrushchev did a thing which has never happened in any other similar clerical system – as the reigning pope he made an *ex cathedra* denunciation of papal infallibility. Once you have done that, nothing in the world can re-establish the doctrine. The very fact that he made this statement, whether right or wrong, proves that the pope is not infallible. In my opinion, Khrushchev's speech at the twentieth Congress has knocked the linch-pin out of international Communism as an instrument of Soviet policy. We have seen the consequences all over the Communist world in the last twelve months.

And the third factor, which is speeding this process up, is that there are now alternatives to Moscow as centres for Communist loyalty. There is Peking – China has already tried to establish some ideological authority even in Eastern Europe. And inside Eastern Europe, there are the independent national Communist systems of Yugoslavia and Poland, both of which exercise some attraction on Communists outside their frontiers. For these reasons I think it can be taken for granted that if you could get the Red Army out of Eastern Europe and convince the people of Eastern Europe that it would not come back – this, of course, is equally important – then the Eastern European countries would cease to be under direct Soviet control, although for various reasons most of them would still remain friendly to the Soviet Union and most of them would retain many of the political, economic and social characteristics of a Communist society.

The Red Army

Thus, since the events of autumn 1956, the Western powers have had a tremendous incentive to get the Red Army out of Eastern Europe and to make concessions to that end, on condition that they can make sure that it stays out. The Russians, of course, are in exactly the opposite position. They have a big incentive to keep the Red Army in Eastern Europe, unless they can ensure that the liberated zone is neutral and can be kept neutral. The Western problem, assuming that you get a disengagement and a neutral zone between the Soviet Union and the West, is essentially to protect the neutral zone from physical aggression – from a violation of its neutrality by the return of the Red Army. But the Soviet problem is to secure the neutral zone against the voluntary secession of one of its members to the West – against a violation of its neutrality by the governments of the zone itself, with the consent of the Western powers.

If you are ever going to get agreement on disengagement and a neutral zone, which, for the reasons I have already given, I think is highly desirable, you must find the answer to three questions. First of all, what will be the geographical limits of the neutral zone, what particular countries will compose it? Secondly, what limitations will you impose on its armaments, and how will you ensure that those limitations are maintained? – this is essentially a disarmament problem. Thirdly, and in the last resort most important of all, what sanctions are possible against a peaceful or forcible violation of the zone's neutrality, both sides are likely to feel that there is a practical way of intervening to prevent a violation of the zone's neutrality, both sides are likely to feel that the new situation would be less stable and less secure than the existing one.

*

A PLAN FOR DISENGAGEMENT

What I am going to do now is to put forward a model for a neutral belt in the middle of Europe. I fully admit that it is not the only model which we can construct. But I think that if you are seriously concerned to advocate a policy of disengagement you have got to work it out in some detail. It is no good saying, like the German Social Democrats, that you want a European security pact and then not being able to answer the first question about who is in it, how it operates, what military forces are involved and how they would be used in case of emergency. You have got to be able to answer these concrete questions. But, as I say, I fully admit that the model I am going to put forward is not the only possible one, and it may well be defective in certain respects.

Geographical Limits of a Neutral Belt

I do not believe it would be wise to aim at neutralizing Germany alone, as has been suggested by many in the past, including Sir Winston Churchill in his speech at Aachen.

In the first place this would mean much greater concessions by the West than by the Soviet Union. The Federal Republic is nearly three times larger and more populous than the Soviet Zone of Germany – and many times more wealthy. The manpower and territory of the Federal Republic are at the moment vital to NATO's strategy, whereas East German territory and resources are only marginal to Soviet strategy.

In my opinion the political case against neutralizing Germany alone is even stronger than the purely military one. If you had a neutral Germany which was actually next door to the Soviet Union – which had a Soviet power, the Soviet policy, the Soviet empire, immediately on its eastern flank – then I think it would be too easy for some future German government to make a deal with the Soviet Union without Western agreement and mainly, of course, at the expense of Poland. Indeed, so long as the Polish-German frontier is not settled by the free agreement of an independent Polish and an independent German government, the Soviet Union has a trump card, through her occupation of Poland, to play for the allegiance of Germany. This second reason, I think, is absolutely decisive; if you try to neutralize Germany alone, you put Germany in the one situation in which she could exploit her bargaining power to upset whatever *status quo* is agreed.

A Foothold in Europe

It is vital, I think, if you have a neutral zone which includes the whole of

Germany, that it should also include countries east of Germany, which could form both a counterweight to Germany inside the neutral area and would constitute a physical as well as a political barrier to direct contact between Germany and the Soviet Union.

So I don't think you could restrict the zone to Germany alone. A surprising number of people have suggested that you should neutralize the whole of continental Europe. Not only Mr Khrushchev, but Sir John Slessor and Mr George Kennan, have both at various times in the last few years suggested that the West could afford to accept what in effect the Russians have proposed, that is to say, the complete withdrawal of British and American forces from Western Europe in return for the complete withdrawal of the Red Army from Eastern Europe. Sir John Slessor has described this particular proposal as 'an air Locarno'. Now the weaknesses about that are two. Once again the West would be giving up far more than the Russians. Because once the British and American forces left the continent, and their bases left the continent, the British would go back across the North Sea, the Americans across the Atlantic, whereas the Russians would simply withdraw 500 miles across land to their own country. The disparity between the ease with which the Russians could return and that with which the West could return would be too great. And consequently, the only Western sanction against a Soviet violation of Europe's neutrality would be massive retaliation, because the West would not be in a physical position to do anything to counter a Soviet advance other than drop H-bombs on the Soviet Union itself.

Now, as I have already said, I do not think that a policy of massive retaliation – involving race suicide as well as the destruction of the country which initiates it – is a practical policy, quite apart from the fact that it is grossly immoral. And if a policy of massive retaliation is not a practical policy for defending an ally, it is certainly not a practical policy for defending a neutral. It seems to me that the great weakness of Sir John Slessor's proposal for an air Locarno is that it is inconceivable that Britain or the United States would expose their own territory to thermonuclear annihilation simply because there had been an infringement of the neutrality of an area in which they had no longer any direct physical involvement at all. If you are going to have an effective military sanction to protect the neutral belt, the West will have to keep a foothold on the continent of Europe from which it can exert military power short of total war.

I think the most obvious line for constructing a neutral belt would have to include the Federal Republic on the western side and Eastern Germany,

Poland, Czechoslovakia and Hungary on the Soviet side; and then, in
addition, as many other states as you could get in by bargaining. It might
be, for example, that you could bring in Denmark against Romania, and so
on. But you would have to guarantee some physical foothold on the
continent for the West as a base for military sanctions against a possible
military violation of the neutral zone by the Soviet Union.

Limitation and Control of Armaments
The second question is what arms should the countries in the neutral belt
have and how should their arms be kept within the limits agreed. I think it
is obvious that you could not afford to allow countries in the neutral zone
any atomic weapons. A country with the power for thermonuclear attack
and probably even with the power for small-scale atomic attack has total
freedom in its foreign policy. If it wants to blackmail other countries –
even large countries – it probably can. If you are going to keep the
countries in the middle neutral, it means that you cannot give them that
freedom *vis-à-vis* the guaranteeing powers outside. The Soviet Union
would insist on that, and I think we should be wise to insist on it too. On
the other hand, though these countries shouldn't have atomic weapons, I
think they would have to have quite substantial conventional forces. They
would have to have enough conventional forces to defend their frontiers
against a local infraction, an infraction which is not serious enough to call
in whatever external sanction may be envisaged to deal with a violation of
neutrality. And, very much the same as NATO today, they must have
conventional forces which are large enough to prevent a rapid *fait accompli*
by the Russians, which would face the West with the alternative between
starting up the war again or letting the thing go. In other words they
would have to be able to start the fighting and to keep it going some time if
there was a Soviet invasion. So I think you would have to have substantial
conventional forces in the neutral area.

   The question of how you control and inspect the limitations which are
agreed is a soluble one. If it isn't soluble, then of course all the discussions
that have taken place on disarmament in history are nonsense. But I
believe that you could in fact have effective inspection by the Russians and
the West of the armaments in the neutral zone by ground-control teams
along the lines that were discussed in the disarmament sub-committee last
summer. In addition to that I think you would allow the Russians to move
their radar system to the western frontier of the neutral zone, and the West
to move its radar system to the eastern frontier of the neutral zone. In
addition, if it is still relevant after the development of earth satellites, you

would have a system of aerial inspection beyond the frontiers of the neutral zone, including most of Britain and some part of European Russia. This would give you substantial protection against a surprise attack by either side. All these provisions were under serious discussion between Russia and the West this year.

Military Sanctions

The most difficult problem, it seems to me, and the one on which I confess I haven't been able to come to a conclusion which satisfies me fully, is this: assuming you have a neutral zone with limited armaments and mutual inspection, and then, in spite of that, a country on one side or the other tries to violate the neutral zone, either peacefully or by war, what physical sanctions could you impose to compel withdrawal? Alternatively, what military deterrent could you offer against an attempt at such a violation? My own opinion is that you could not really rely on the threat of massive thermonuclear retaliation to protect the neutral zone. Indeed it is doubtful if we shall be able much longer to rely on it even to protect some of our allies. This raises the whole question of the possibility of limited warfare and in particular the possibility of limited nuclear warfare.

What I think you must aim at is replacing the deterrent of thermonuclear annihilation in all-out war by what I would call the disincentive of punishment in limited atomic war. In other words instead of threatening the other side that you will blow the world up if he moves, you simply say: if you move, we will hit you so hard that it will cost you more to keep on fighting than you can possibly gain by carrying your aggression through to the end. Of course, this type of limited disincentive may not be a deterrent to all-out war; it may be that the capacity for massive retaliation is the only final deterrent to all-out war; but we assume that this capacity does remain in existence on both sides. Indeed its existence gives the best guarantee that if an armed conflict does break out, both sides will try to keep it limited.

If you want to deter limited aggression into the neutral area, then I think you must have the capacity for limited retaliation and this will involve, I am sure, the limited use of atomic weapons from air bases in Western Europe and possibly also from missile bases in Western Europe on our side, and conversely, of course, for the Russians. This is a frightfully difficult problem; it is probably the most difficult problem in the history of modern defence policy, but it is a problem that must be solved, and I think that the Western governments whatever their diplomatic policies for Europe, are going to spend most of the next five or ten years trying to solve it. The problem of limited war is just as urgent and important for NATO in the present situation as it would be for what remains of NATO under this new European settlement.

An Alternative to Massive Retaliation

Somehow or other we must find an alternative to massive retaliation which is still an effective deterrent to local aggression, and which if the deterrent fails makes it possible to smother a local war without suddenly expanding it into all-out war. It is, as I say, the essential military problem for NATO today, when Europe is divided, just as much as it would be if we had a European neutral belt.

Although the problem of finding a deterrent which is both severe and convincing, because it does not mean suicide, is the same in principle for protecting Western Europe today, in practice it is very much simpler if you have a neutral belt. The biggest problem that NATO faces today in a divided Europe is that there is just not enough room on this side of the Iron Curtain to organize any sort of defence in depth at all. The Iron Curtain is too far west. But if you had a neutral belt, the fighting, if fighting began, would begin on the Soviet frontier, and you would have a buffer of substantial conventional forces to cross before you got to the atomic forces of the West. If there is a solution to this problem, as I believe there is, it is easier to find it if you have this conventional arms buffer between the Soviet Union and the West, starting at the Soviet frontier, than it is if you have a general mingling of nuclear and conventional weapons, starting in the middle of Europe, as at the moment. Moreover, the risks of world war starting from spontaneous combustion in Central Europe are infinitely less if the whole of Central Europe is limited to conventional arms. And I think it is also worth pointing out that, as time passes, both the Soviet Union and the West will have less and less of a military incentive to violate the neutral area. In so far as they are worried about one another's aggressive intentions, they are worrying more about long-range missile attack, and of course, who occupies what part of Europe is becoming increasingly irrelevant there. If they are really worried about one another's intentions, then they won't worry so much about the middle of Europe. The real fight will be in the laboratories of their homelands, rather than in the territories between them.

The Soviet Union's Interest in Disengagement

I believe that the sort of considerations I have put forward make a very strong case for the West to take the initiative in proposing a disengagement in Central Europe along these lines. The big question is whether the Soviet Union would be prepared to negotiate seriously for such a settlement. The Soviet leaders have said they would, about once every two months, for the last two years. We have never taken up their proposals, and so we have not been able to find out whether or not they are sincere. But it is at least a starting point that they have said that they want to talk about this. In fact, on one occasion Khrushchev, who, I admit, does not always guard his words as carefully as he might, actually suggested a neutral zone along the sort of lines I have suggested. That is to say, if Western troops would only leave the Federal Republic, the Red Army would be prepared to leave the whole of Eastern Europe. Perhaps this was one of Khrushchev's *obiter dicta*; one does not know how seriously one should take it.

But I do believe that the Soviet interest in staying in Eastern Europe is dwindling all the time. In the first place, the events of autumn 1956 showed that the satellites are not a source of military strength to the Soviet Union but a source of military danger. During the Hungarian revolution, there was considerable fraternization between the Hungarian rebels and the Red Army. As you know, the Russians were unable to organize effective intervention until they had replaced almost the whole of their occupation forces by new troops, mainly from Central Asia. The satellite manpower is not a military asset to the Soviet Union. There is evidence that since last year the Russians have been systematically starving the satellite armies because they don't regard them as reliable.

Economic Factors
In the second place, the Russians know that they cannot hope to prevent another explosion in Eastern Europe unless they prevent the economic suffering of the people from becoming too great. Consequently, since the events of 1956, the Russians have probably been giving more economically to Eastern Europe than they have been getting. This is a complete reversal of the situation ever since 1944. The Soviet economic and military interest in staying in Eastern Europe is nothing like as great as it was a few years ago. For that reason they might be prepared to consider leaving Eastern Europe, providing it was within a system which gave them the sort of military safeguards which I have been describing. On the other hand, fear of change, conservatism in the Foreign Office and the Army are probably just as powerful a force in the Soviet Union as in Britain and the United States. Perhaps the situation may be a little easier now that Zhukov has gone, because what little one does know about Zhukov's personal views

suggests that he would not be prepared to withdraw the Red Army from any of its existing positions, nor would he be prepared to consider any strategy other than all-out war. But the evidence is much too poor to be conclusive.

My own opinion is that the dwindling of the Soviet Union's interest in Eastern Europe may not by itself be sufficient to induce the Russians to negotiate seriously about a neutral belt. What may finally turn the scale in favour of negotiations is the fear that unless the Soviet Union can organize a completely new sort of European settlement with Western agreement, each of the Western countries on the Soviet frontier will be equipped with atomic weapons. And I would venture to predict that within the next twelve months there will be serious public discussion about giving atomic weapons to Western Germany. And as that discussion approaches the point of decision, I think the Russians will make a really serious attempt to reach an alternative settlement of the whole European situation. It may well take the fear of a nuclear-armed Germany to force the Russians to consider so drastic a revision of their European policy as a whole. And unless the Western governments show far more imagination, I would expect to see the first real spasm of negotiations on this issue develop in one or two years' time.

A Pilot Scheme for Disarmament

I think it is worth pointing out at this stage that what we are really discussing is what is often called disarmament, but is really the limitation of armaments. It is the same sort of problem that the disarmament sub-committee has been discussing in the last few years. That is to say, a situation in which you try to reduce the level of armaments while maintaining the same balance of military power between the opposing groups. I believe some general factors will come into play to promote progress on both sides towards negotiations on disarmament. First of all, some agreement on arms limitation is immediately desirable for economic reasons. The cost of new weapons is increasing in geometric progression, on both sides. In the second place, providing that countries on both sides of the Iron Curtain adapt their strategy to meet the demands and possibilities of the new weapons, I think you can produce a situation in which war can be abolished altogether in so far as the deterrence of calculated aggression is concerned. There isn't much point in having a lot of arms if no situation is ever likely to arise in which you can use them either physically or diplomatically – by threatening to use them physically.

I think the Soviet Union and America at least, as the two countries which are most concerned with the arms race, have realized this already, and that is why they gingerly started getting to grips this year in the disarmament sub-committee for the first time. But I think what has happened in the disarmament sub-committee this year has underlined two lessons. Firstly, I don't believe the great powers will accept a disarmament agreement which involves control of their own internal system until the effectiveness of control has been proved on the little powers first. It seems to me absurd to imagine that the Soviet Union and the United States will agree to receive one another's spies in their own atomic arms installations before they have first satisfied themselves in practice that this type of control can be made to work. They can only satisfy themselves of this through a pilot scheme in other countries.

Danger on the Periphery

Secondly, I think that the dislocations and the changes in attitude involved in any effective arms inspection and control are so great that countries are not going to agree to it except in areas and on issues where there is a very great danger unless you have arms control. Nobody believes there is very much danger of either America or the Soviet Union starting an all-out thermonuclear war. In this sense people are less afraid of an H-bomb attack than ever before, because it is so obviously suicidal to the attacker as well as the attacked. Moreover, once you have got missiles you can put in submarines and hide in the ground there is no possibility of any surprise attack destroying the enemy's capacity to retaliate. What the big powers are worried about – and they are the powers, of course, which count most in disarmament negotiations, and they are the powers most engaged in the arms race – what they fear most is a war starting without their volition in a dangerous unstable peripheral area between them. Therefore the process of arms limitation and control will have to start in these peripheral areas. The two obvious areas are, of course, Central Europe, which we have been discussing, and the Middle East.

I think it is increasingly recognized by the big powers that the problem of preventing war now is essentially the problem of preventing small wars and, if small wars do break out, of preventing small wars from turning into big wars. That problem can only be solved by mutual agreement and I think that a European neutral zone along the lines I have discussed would be an admirable start, as a precedent for other such agreements.

SOME OBJECTIONS ANSWERED

I have put the case for a neutral zone. I want to end by putting the case against it and trying to answer it. I have discussed these ideas with people from many countries in the last few years. It is remarkable how uniform is the reaction of most of their opponents. They start by arguing that such a solution would be disastrous to the West, and when they have to admit the contrary, they then argue that there is no chance of the Russians agreeing, since it would be disastrous to the Soviet Union. They want to have it both ways because they are psychologically frightened to think about any change in the present situation, even though they admit the present situation is dangerous and unsatisfactory.

In fact there is only one complaint against trying to negotiate disengagement and the creation of a neutral zone which seems to me to have great force, and it is a serious one which must be answered. It is the fear that the process of negotiations itself would so weaken NATO's solidarity and undermine NATO's will to make sacrifices for defence that the Russians would be able to achieve their primary objective of weakening and dividing the West simply by dragging the negotiations out, without any intention of making compromises to reach agreement in the end. We have many examples since the end of the war of the Russians using negotiations simply to divide and confuse their opponents and to delay effective resistance. There is no doubt that this is a real danger.

Bilateral Approaches

I would reply that precisely because this danger is a real one the West must begin now to work out a collective allied approach to the problem. Otherwise the Soviet Union will choose her time to make bilateral approaches to one or the other of the Western powers, presenting whatever specific proposal for disengagement is best calculated to divide the object of its approaches from its allies. We may have seen signs of such a bilateral approach to the United States during the disarmament discussions this year, when Mr Stassen's behaviour produced howls of alarm in Europe and complaints of a new Yalta in the making. A direct Soviet approach to Western Germany is equally likely as the German disenchantment with NATO gathers strength. France is another obvious target for bilateral negotiations.

That is why I feel it is essential to start public discussion of the problem immediately inside the Western alliance. It is most important that when the bargaining begins the Western peoples should be sufficiently familiar with the issues involved to know what is negotiable and what is not. And it is highly desirable that the bargaining should begin as the result of a Western initiative so the Western proposals form the basis of negotiation.

We are continually put in an unfavourable position from the start because we wait for the Russians to take the initiative and put us on the diplomatic defensive.

The second element in my reply is that NATO is disintegrating now, in front of our very eyes. And the reason is not that we are negotiating with the Soviet Union on disengagement, but exactly the contrary. NATO remains frozen in the rigid posture it adopted in the days of Stalin. It has failed completely to adapt itself to the tremendous changes in the pattern of world politics over the last few years. Whatever governments may say, the present paralysis of NATO makes no sense at all to the peoples who must ultimately make the sacrifices required to give it meaning. Indeed the governments themselves are behaving as if they did not believe the ritual incantations they recite at the meetings of the NATO Council – they are slashing their arms programmes and allowing themselves a licence for petty quarrels with their allies which would be inconceivable if they meant what they said about the Soviet military menace and the need for allied solidarity.

The Purpose of NATO

I have always supported NATO, and I still do. But I believe it should be the framework in which the allies seek to reconcile their divergent interests and in which they adjust their policies collectively to a changing world situation. Instead of this it has become the symbol of a vanished stage in the Cold War, increasingly remote both from the facts of international life and from the aspirations of the peoples it is supposed to represent.

NATO will only survive if its members adjust themselves to the tremendous changes in the world since it was created – and for which, after all, it is partly responsible. Disarmament and disengagement should be seen, not as an alternative to NATO, as incompatible with its existence, but as an alternative policy for NATO, as the necessary condition for its survival as the core of Western solidarity. I have already tried to show that even the military problems now facing NATO are far easier to solve in the context of disengagement than in the present context of a divided Germany at the heart of a divided Europe.

On the other hand, I would not deny that if a policy of disengagement in Central Europe could be carried out and seen to work, it would be the start of a much broader process which would transform the whole nature of postwar politics. It would in fact create a precedent for similar solutions elsewhere, and for a return to the hopes of 1945, when world peace and order were rightly seen to depend on the establishment of minimum working agreements between all the great powers, including the Soviet Union.

Elimination of War

You may feel that this is starry-eyed. But I am convinced that long-range nuclear weapons are an invention which cannot be compared with earlier military innovations like gunpowder or the crossbow. They represent a change in the conditions of man's existence as fundamental as the discovery of fire. If we fail to adjust our institutions and our way of life to their implications in the next generation, I fear humanity is unlikely to survive on this planet. But if we can succeed, I think we can finally eliminate war as an instrument of policy. The absolute weapon has made war absolutely irrational and may thus prove to have eliminated the element of military power from international politics. If a violent change in the *status quo* is ruled out, some way must be found of organizing peaceful changes in a situation which is felt to be intolerable. This will involve drastic and painful dislocations for both sides, but the logic of events demands it.

I believe that the establishment of a neutral belt in Europe would be the most valuable pilot scheme for the development of a new international order. And at least those who oppose it have a duty to offer us an alternative which gives equal hope of meeting the challenge of our time.

A NON-NUCLEAR STRATEGY

(from 'Labour and a World Society', Fabian tract, 1985)

CHANGES SINCE 1951

Since I wrote my 'New Fabian Essay' important changes have taken place on both sides of the Iron Curtain, in the Third World, and in the military-economic framework of foreign affairs.

International Communism, which was already crumbling once Communists won power outside the Soviet Union, has ceased to exist as an important factor in world affairs. Once Khrushchev had denounced *ex cathedra* the doctrine of papal infallibility, the ideological cement of international Communism dissolved. China followed Yugoslavia in rejecting Soviet leadership. In Eastern Europe, Hungary, Romania and Eastern Germany have succeeded in asserting a degree of independence from the Soviet Union. Poland and Czechoslovakia are kept sullenly loyal simply by the threat of force. In Western Europe none of the Communist Parties except the French and Portuguese still avows a loyalty to Moscow.

The Soviet Union itself is a very different country from that which was led by the ageing Stalin in 1951. Russia's living standards and its military power have been enormously increased. But it faces massive domestic, economic and social problems which an arthritic and conservative bureaucracy has difficulty in handling. Nationalist resistance to control by Moscow is growing, not only in Central Asia but even in the Ukraine and White Russia. By the end of the century the Russians will be a minority in the Soviet Union. Within the next few years leadership will pass from the hands of men whose formative experience was under Stalin to a generation, on average twenty years younger, for whom even the war is only a childhood memory.

Meanwhile, however, the United States has changed beyond recognition as an actor on the world stage. It is no longer a reluctant participant in the game of nations. It is actively and enthusiastically involved in every continent. The danger today is not that the Americans will retire into pre-war normalcy, but that they will opt for a policy of global unilateralism under which they intervene all over the world without trying to win the consent or understanding of their allies or of the countries in which they operate.

This danger is increased by the fact that political power in America has followed economic power to the southern and western states where the traditional links with Europe, so important in the eastern states, are weak or non-existent. Moreover, the increasing immigration into the 'sunbelt states' of Hispanics from Latin America and of Asians from the western Pacific is bound to shift the regional balance of America's international interests. In any case, the postwar generation of American leaders who built up the Atlantic community and helped to devise the framework for world economic order which collapsed in the seventies has now passed from the scene.

The Reagan administration has been greatly influenced in its foreign and defence policies by anti-Communist ideologues who reject the postwar settlement with the Soviet Union, want to overturn the agreements made at Yalta and Potsdam and believe that America can and should build up sufficient military superiority over the Soviet Union to compel it to make concessions to American hegemony. This trend in recent American policy has shown total indifference to world opinion in areas like Central America and the Caribbean, which have been unilaterally designated as of vital strategic importance to the United States. Though Grenada is further from the frontier of the United States than London is from the frontier of the Soviet Union, it is nevertheless treated as part of America's backyard. The ideologues are as hostile to international economic co-operation as to political co-operation, regarding the International Monetary Fund and the World Bank alike with the same contemptuous distaste.

THE ARMS RACE

While these changes have been taking place on both sides, the Soviet Union and the United States have been engaged in an arms race which has led to both of them accumulating nuclear arsenals far larger than are needed for any rational purpose. The nuclear arms race has changed the whole framework of world politics. At times, one side or the other has pulled slightly ahead in one category of nuclear strength or another. But neither has at any time appeared likely to acquire the sort of superiority which would enable it to destroy its adversary's ability to inflict unacceptably high levels of retaliation. The stability of the nuclear balance has been invulnerable to quite large variations in relative capacity.

However, at present the arms race is entering a new phase which could within a decade or so seriously destabilize the nuclear balance between Russia and the United States; this could tempt the weaker to launch a preemptive strike against the stronger before the stronger was in a position to destroy its retaliatory power. Three developments are particularly dangerous at the present time.

First, both sides are deploying missiles with a very rapid flight time which would compel the adversary to launch on warning of a possible attack. For example, the Soviet SS22 missiles based in East Germany and Czechoslovakia could destroy all the Cruise missiles at Greenham Common and Molesworth some three minutes after a launch. This would mean that the decision to respond to the first sign that launch had taken place would have to be made by computers. There would be no time to consult President Reagan, still less for him to consult Mrs Thatcher. After the shooting down of the South Korean airliner, and the known examples of misinterpreted radar warnings, no one can be happy to abandon the decision between the survival and the destruction of the human race to the micro-circuits of computers.

The second dangerous development is the deployment by both sides of small but accurate weapons like the Cruise missile, which can carry either nuclear or conventional warheads. At present both the United States and Russia plan to deploy over ten thousand Cruise missiles on ground, at sea or in aircraft. In any conflict the launch of large numbers of Cruise missiles would have to be regarded by the adversary as carrying the risk of a nuclear attack and inviting a nuclear response. Besides increasing the risk of nuclear war, the deployment of these dual-capable missiles greatly increases the difficulty of verifying an arms control agreement, since they are too small to detect by satellite photography, which has been the only method of verification so far acceptable to the Soviet Union.

Thirdly, the United States is developing and hoping to deploy a system of defence against ballistic missiles which might render it invulnerable to a retaliatory attack and therefore might seem in the Soviet Union to be the prelude to an American first strike. Meanwhile, both America and Russia are developing anti-satellite weapons which, if successful, could destroy the main means on which each side depends for warning of a surprise attack.

These new and dangerous developments in the arms race are under way just at the time when scientists in the USA, Europe and the Soviet Union have concluded that if even a fraction of existing nuclear arsenals are used by either side, they might generate fires which throw up so much soot into the upper atmosphere as to blot out the sun over the northern hemisphere for a period of months. During this so-called nuclear winter, human life, and even plant life, might become impossible north of the Equator and in large areas south of the Equator. So even a successful first strike would condemn the population of the aggressor country, no less than of its enemy and of neutral countries, to a lingering death in conditions of Arctic night. There are many uncertainties about the precise number, types, and targets of nuclear explosions which would be required to produce a nuclear winter. But the general concept is now almost universally recognized as valid. This must have profound consequences for any rational government's approach to the problems of foreign policy and defence.

Most important, if the Soviet Union or the United States ever carry out a major nuclear attack, it would be impossible for any country in the northern hemisphere to escape catastrophe. General de Gaulle's main argument for creating a French national nuclear deterrent was to enable France to keep out of a nuclear war between Russia and the United States. Mrs Thatcher increasingly uses the same argument to justify a British nuclear deterrent. This argument collapses in the face of a nuclear winter.

But it would be equally impossible to opt out by renouncing nuclear weapons and declaring neutrality, because nuclear ally and non-nuclear neutral will be condemned alike to death in a nuclear winter if the Russians and Americans ever come to nuclear blows. Thus the argument that the presence of foreign nuclear bases on one's territory makes one a nuclear target loses its relevance.

I have no doubt that the strategic intelligentsia on both sides will seek to respond to the concept of nuclear winter by developing weapons and strategies which would enable them to use nuclear weapons without such consequences. The arguments for a neutron bomb may well be revived. And some will say that the case for civil defence is greatly strengthened since it is likely that a future nuclear war would involve the use of only a small number of weapons against a small number of targets on both sides.

Any normal human being, however, must feel that foreign and defence policy for any government in the world must now be to exert the maximum influence on relations between the superpowers so as to ensure that they never fight a nuclear war.

A NON-NUCLEAR STRATEGY FOR NATO

The great virtue of the new Labour Party statement on defence (*Defence & Security for Britain*, Labour Party, 1984) is that it establishes a clear framework for a rational approach to this problem. First, it argues that the Soviet Union and its allies do represent a potential military threat to Western Europe, and that their threat can be met only through deterrence by the appropriate forms of military power. Second, in the modern world the only appropriate deterrent against a major conventional attack must be a conventional deterrent.

NATO's current strategy of flexible response involves using nuclear weapons early against any conventional attack which seems likely to overrun its forces, and moving up a ladder of escalation through various levels of limited nuclear war to an all-out strategic intercontinental exchange between Russia and the United States. This is no longer feasible in practice, if it ever was. Both sides plan to attack their adversary's command and control centres at the beginning of any conflict The electro-magnetic pulses produced by the first nuclear explosion will in any case make communication between governments and their field commanders impossible. Moreover, the Soviet government has said it would observe no limitations on the use of nuclear weapons once the West had initiated nuclear war in Europe. Even if we ignore such statements, Russia has as large and varied an arsenal of nuclear weapons as NATO and could therefore win a nuclear conflict at any level if it had more numerous forces, which is the assumption on which NATO's first use of nuclear weapons depends. The central problem therefore facing NATO is to develop a non-nuclear strategy for deterring and, if necessary, frustrating a non-nuclear attack. As the Labour Party statement makes clear, the first duty of a Labour government must therefore be to shift NATO policy in this direction.

The argument about nuclear weapons will continue in Britain and elsewhere for many years. Inside the Labour Party it should now be concerned primarily with the question how best to shift NATO policy towards a conventional deterrent against conventional attack. Some conditions for success are fairly obvious. Whichever party is in office, Britain's influence inside NATO will depend partly on the strength of its arguments and partly on its military and economic power to help progress and hinder movement in the wrong direction.

My own experience under many American administrations is that Washington is exceptionally open to influence by argument from outsiders whose goodwill, experience and commonsense is accepted. The machinery for taking decisions in Washington usually involves prolonged argument between officials who favour different policies. Intelligent foreigners may often play a decisive role in such arguments.

I have also found that if Britain is able to mobilize the other European allies in support of a particular course of action the chance of its arguments carrying the day in Washington is greatly increased. This was how I persuaded NATO to set up the Nuclear Planning Group and the Euro Group when I was secretary of defence and persuaded the IMF to set up the so-called Second Oil Facility when I was Chancellor of the Exchequer.

Even under the Reagan administration there have been many officials in Washington, as well as many Congressmen, particularly in the Democratic Party, who already share our desire for a conventional defence of Europe. But we shall lose influence even with our friends in the United States if we adopt policies which they see as lacking in goodwill, experience, and common sense.

Second, if Britain wants to influence NATO towards a non-nuclear strategy, it must be able to make a major military contribution to the conventional defence of Europe. One of the virtues of the new Labour Party statement is its recognition that if we are to have the influence we need to carry out our policies, then we cannot commit ourselves to big cuts in defence expenditure in the short run.

The Role of Unilateral Action

The realities of the problem we face have too often been confused and distorted by the argument between so-called unilateralists and multilateralists. The Labour Party has never believed that it is possible to achieve its objectives by unilateral action alone, or by multilateral action alone. NATO as a whole has already committed itself to a unilateral reduction in battlefield nuclear weapons because it rightly believes this would make military sense and reduce the risk of war. The Soviet Union recently unilaterally withdrew 20,000 troops from Central Europe for much the same reasons. Similarly, unilateral actions by Britain can help to achieve our objectives providing that they do not lead to reactions by other governments inside or outside the Alliance which make the situation more dangerous.

For example, Britain must unilaterally get rid of Cruise missiles because they serve no military purpose and undermine public support for the Alliance. We must also unilaterally cancel the Trident programme because it costs far more than it is worth, diverts military spending from more desirable objectives, and increases Britain's destructive power so much as to disturb both our allies and our enemies. Trident would also make disarmament agreement more difficult, particularly if Britain, as Mrs Thatcher intends, refuses to include Britain's strategic nuclear forces in the disarmament talks with Russia. During Neil Kinnock's recent visit to Moscow, Labour's commitment to decommission the Polaris force was matched by Chernenko's commitment to match the dismantling of every British missile by the dismantling of a Soviet missile. So what was once a unilateral commitment has now become a bilateral one. This increases the security of both sides and creates a precedent well worth pursuing.

But it would be foolhardy to take other unilateral actions without first making sure that they did not provoke reactions by other members of NATO which made it more difficult to achieve the non-nuclear strategy we want. At present the balance of military forces in Europe makes it realistic to aim at a purely conventional deterrent against conventional attack. Indeed, the current gap between the NATO forces and the Warsaw Pact forces is generally recognized to be too small to give a Soviet attack an adequate chance of success.

I believe we could strengthen the defensive capability of NATO's existing forces rapidly and at a small cost by certain changes in strategy and organization so as to make a conventional deterrent totally effective. But any substantial reduction in America's conventional contribution to NATO would make a non-nuclear strategy much less feasible. If the

300,000 American troops in Europe were cut, as some senators have proposed, to a third of their present size, it would be so difficult and expensive for the European countries to make up the difference, not only in manpower but also in weapons, that most NATO governments would not even try. They would simply seek new ways of making the nuclear strategy more effective, even if this increased the risk of war.

To expel American bases from Britain without consultation in the first days of a new Labour government would create a serious danger that America would reduce her conventional contribution to NATO. It would be equally dangerous if the American response was simply to move nuclear bases from Britain to Western Germany, where they would appear very much more provocative to the Soviet Union than they are in Britain.

On the other hand, I believe that, in intelligent negotiations, we could persuade the United States to agree to some of the proposals in our document which they currently reject. For example, it should not be difficult to persuade the Americans to withdraw their nuclear bases from Britain. It is doubtful whether they will need the submarine base at Holy Loch once the Trident submarines are in service. And their F111 bombers are likely to be of little value by the time the next general election comes in Britain. If the United States regarded Britain as a valuable ally in NATO, we should be able then to persuade it to withdraw its existing nuclear bases from Britain. But if we acted in such a way as to destroy America's confidence in our loyalty as a member of the Alliance, then I think the reaction, not only in the United States but among our European allies, could be such as to destroy the possibility of achieving the non-nuclear strategy for NATO which we desire.

There is another problem to which the Labour Party has so far given little attention. It is difficult to foresee any possible government in NATO, including a Labour government, wishing America to give up all its nuclear weapons while Russia still possesses a nuclear arsenal. In my opinion, Russia is bound to maintain a nuclear capability so long as China does the same.

One of the immense changes in the world since I wrote my 'New Fabian Essay' is that China, a country of 1,000 million inhabitants on Russia's ill-defined eastern frontier, now possesses a strategic nuclear force. We are already having to face the problem of involving the Chinese government in the talks about nuclear disarmament, because the Russians have made it clear that they cannot ignore the Chinese factor in disarmament talks with the United States. For example, they reserve the right to maintain what they regarded as sufficient SS20s in Soviet Asia facing China whatever happened in negotiations in the IMF talks about Europe. So offshore American nuclear weapons will remain necessary to deter a nuclear attack on Europe even when all nuclear weapons have been withdrawn from European soil.

I know as well as anyone that in recent years membership of NATO has imposed severe strains on its left-wing supporters in Europe. It is difficult to feel confidence in an alliance if its leadership is lacking in wisdom and consistency, as has too often been the case under the last two American presidents. But it is difficult to see an alternative. For Britain in the age of nuclear winter, neutrality is not an attractive option. The nuclear winter condemns ally and neutral to the same fate if war breaks out. But a neutral Britain would have far less chance of influencing the decision between peace and war than one which accepts its obligations as a member of NATO. Neutrality would not put Britain in better company so far as human rights are concerned; there is at least as much violation of human rights in many of the non-aligned countries as anywhere in NATO.

Neutrality would not be cheaper. Yugoslavia, one of the two European neutrals which has the power independently to determine the level of its forces – Austria and Finland are restricted by treaty – is spending much more of its national wealth on defence than Britain. Sweden did so for many years and Prime Minister Olof Palme has recently seen his country's neutrality continually violated by Soviet submarines; he has had to warn his own Social Democratic Party's Congress that unilateral disarmament is just not an option for Sweden. By far the best answer, as Palme himself has argued, is to seek common security through multilateral agreements between the superpowers and their allies. This must be the overriding objective of the foreign and defence policies of a Labour Britain. We must remain in NATO, and our membership in NATO must be designed and reshaped so that we can support this objective effectively.

Instability in the Third World

Negotiations between Russia and the West on arms control are desperately urgent because of the new dangers to stability represented by the current phase in the arms race. But this is only one of the issues where co-operation between East and West is needed. I believe that we urgently need some agreement or, at least, some understanding with the Soviet Union about how to deal with political instability in the Third World. Over the last ten years the arms race has accelerated faster in the Third World than between the superpowers. Three countries in the Third

World almost certainly possess nuclear weapons already. The scale and frequency of armed conflict in the Third World is also increasing.

The great powers – not only the Soviet Union and the United States, but Britain and France among the European powers – have frequently intervened in conflicts in the Third World in the hope of national advantage. In most cases their intervention has brought them no long-term benefit. This is particularly true in the Middle East, where military intervention by Britain and France at Suez destroyed their influence for a generation. Israel's invasion of the Lebanon has done more damage to Israel's security and national unity than any other act since the creation of the state in 1947. America's attempt to determine the course of events in Lebanon was also a disastrous failure. The Soviet Union has fared no better. After a short flirtation with Moscow, Egypt has aligned herself with the Western powers.

The main danger of external intervention in the Third World is that it might embroil the superpowers in direct conflict with one another against their will. There was a real danger of this happening over the Gulf War early in 1984. Almost the only good news in world affairs during the last twelve months has been the sign of some tentative understanding between the United States and Russia on how to deal with possible contingencies arising out of the Gulf War. I believe that arguments from America's European allies helped to contribute to this understanding.

There is a strong case for trying to extend this limited understanding over the Gulf to the Middle East as a whole. Bitter experience should have taught the great powers that none of them will derive national advantage from intervention in the Middle East so long as other great powers can intervene to frustrate them. A settlement of Middle Eastern problems on American terms can be frustrated by the Soviet Union. The opposite is also true. So it would be wise for the West to treat the Soviet Union as an equal partner in the attempt to limit the consequences of instability in the Middle East. This is in any case a precondition of giving the United Nations forces a greater role in the Lebanon, which is probably a precondition of an Israeli withdrawal. But the greatest advantages for all concerned would follow the agreed limitation of arms supplies to countries in the Middle East, since the regional arms races are now an independent cause of tension in the area.

The tragedy of Ethiopia suggests that it would be sensible also to seek some understanding with the Soviet Union on keeping the Cold War out of Africa, where great power intervention has caused needless suffering to the peoples both in the Horn of Africa and among the frontline states bordering South Africa.

Recent external intervention in the civil wars of Central America has already produced an agreement among the regional powers of the Contadora group to keep the great powers out, to limit external supplies of arms, and to seek a solution of regional problems by conciliation rather than by fighting. If America's European allies give wholehearted support to the Contadora process, it may succeed in saving the United States from a type of military intervention which could be as disastrous in its consequences for America and the world as the Vietnam War itself.

European Co-operation

In a world where peace may depend on the ability of its allies to influence the policy of the United States, it is obvious that if the European allies could agree on a collective approach to Washington, their influence would be far greater than if they all act separately. Unfortunately, the European countries are deeply divided among themselves, particularly on the major problems of defence and disarmament. France still refuses to join NATO as the military organization of the Alliance, and attaches prime importance to strengthening its national nuclear forces. Germany has agreed with France to use Western European union as a forum for developing a coherent European approach to defence problems, but is not prepared to sacrifice its military relationship with the United States; on the contrary, it would like to persuade France to rejoin NATO. On the other hand, the German government would rather revert to the trip-wire strategy for massive retaliation than move forward from flexible response to an all-conventional deterrent. In particular, it opposes the preparation of anti-tank barriers in its border areas, although this would vastly increase NATO's ability to fulfil its commitment to the forward defence of German territory. The British government will soon have to decide whether to continue with its Trident programme. But even the cancellation of Trident would only delay for a year or two the more seminal choice between a maritime strategy which emphasized Britain's links with the United States and a continental strategy which emphasized its links with Europe. Nevertheless, I believe that a Labour government in Britain with a clear commitment to move NATO towards a conventional strategy would be able to organize sufficient support in Germany and France to achieve its objective. Already many influential Americans would see this as the best way out of their own strategic and political dilemmas, and there is widespread support for this approach among the NATO civil and military staffs themselves. On the major issues of Third World politics, Britain is fully committed to the Middle East policy launched by the Common Market at Venice but has been at best a very lukewarm supporter of the Community support for the Contadora approach in Central America.

CHAPTER SIX

The Economic and Financial Revolution

OVER THE LAST TWENTY YEARS an economic and financial revolution has swept over the non-Communist world, destroying the assumptions of both Keynesians and monetarists, making prediction much more difficult, rendering the Western financial systems more vulnerable to shock and recession, and widening the gap in living standards between North and South. As a result the risk of political instability has increased throughout the non-Communist world, creating a new potential threat to peace.

I became chancellor of the exchequer as the postwar economic order was breaking down, first under the so-called 'Nixon shocks', then under the impact of the sudden increase in oil prices imposed by OPEC. Because Western governments were unwilling or unable to adopt a collective approach to the resulting anarchy, we had a decade of stagflation worldwide, in which, contrary to Keynesian theories, inflation remained high despite increases in unemployment unprecedented since the war. Indeed none of the old economic rules seemed to apply any more. It was not an ideal situation in which to manage a British economy already suffering from a chronic inferiority in industrial performance and gross imbalances both at home and abroad.

Having failed to persuade my foreign colleagues to organize the official recycling of the OPEC oil surpluses, I had to join in attempts to finance the enormous deficits of the oil consumers by purely private means. The commercial banks were hungry for profit and believed that there was no way in which a borrowing government could go bankrupt, while the afflicted governments were only too glad to borrow without the sort of conditions which the IMF would have imposed. It was a recipe for disaster.

Once more in opposition after Labour lost the general election in 1979, I spent much of my time discussing the world economy with bankers, businessmen and economists in Europe, the United States, and Japan. In September 1982 I made myself unpopular by predicting that a world debt crisis would follow Mexico's inability to service its debts. That crisis has grown year by year ever since, a time bomb at the heart of the Western financial system which ticks away larger and louder every month, but has yet to explode.

At the end of 1984 I devoted the second half of my Fabian tract on 'Labour and a World Society' to the implications of the economic revolution of the seventies for the world economy and the debt problem in particular. It is reprinted below as 'The Economic Dimension'.

By that time, however, the economic revolution was being complicated by a financial revolution which is still under way. Information technology made it possible to shift billions of dollars in microseconds twenty-four hours a day from any part of the developed world to any other. This globalization of the financial markets was accompanied in many countries, particularly the United States and Britain, by the deregulation of the financial institutions. Thus building societies, insurance companies, pension funds, and large corporations were competing with one another to lend on ever-finer margins, often in areas which they did not understand.

These markets were managed by young men who treated money simply as numbers on a computer screen – as a commodity, like rice or coffee beans. As a result interest rates and exchange rates began to fluctuate violently without reference to the underlying flows of production and trade which they were supposed to reflect. This produced a third financial revolution – innovation. New financial instruments were invented to hedge against interest rate or exchange rate risks. Anything which could be given a monetary price was turned into a security which was traded on the global markets by anyone who had a computer. So there was none of the prudential supervision which was traditionally exercised by central banks over commercial banks.

Among the most notorious of these innovations were the junk bond and the leveraged buy-out, which enabled merchant banks to organize the takeover of great corporations not with money, but with the expectation of future profit which reorganization by the new owner might achieve. The bonfire of such vanities burst into flame in 1989, with the collapse of the savings and loans institutions, America's equivalent of Britain's building societies. This collapse may cost the American taxpayer hundreds of billions of dollars to put right – more than all it would require to solve the debt crisis in the Third World and to finance economic recovery in the new democracies of Eastern Europe put together. In 1990 we saw the collapse of Drexel Burnham Lambert, the leading American dealer in junk bonds. The bonfire is now crackling merrily.

The first sign that something was seriously amiss, however, was the collapse of the stock markets all over the world in what has come to be called Black October 1987. This was foreseen by no one in advance, and there is still no agreement on precisely why it happened. Everyone was wrong about its consequences, and no one knows whether or when it will occur again. I addressed a *Financial Times* conference on the matter in London in July 1988. My talk tried to answer the question: 'Is there a risk of further trouble and what might be its results?' It gave me a chance of describing my understanding of the financial revolution and speculating on some of its side-effects.

What struck me most was that the countries which had moved furthest and fastest in the financial revolution were those with the worst economic performance – the United States and Britain. Both had enormous deficits on the current account of their balance of payments and depended on inflows of capital from Japan and Germany to finance them. To attract these inflows they had to hold their interest rates far above the OECD average. In both, the supply of domestic savings was too low to finance adequate investment, still less to finance their deficits. Both had grossly excessive domestic borrowing – the United States in the public sector, Britain in the private sector; and this was a prime cause of their external deficits. Finally, both suffered from short-termism in industrial finance, partly because the threat of take-overs discouraged their businessmen from looking further ahead than next quarter's stock price.

Japan and Germany were the mirror image of the United States and Britain, with high savings ratios, large current account surpluses, high industrial output and productivity, high spending on civil research and development, and high investment. They had avoided the excesses of the financial revolution, and still allowed substantial government intervention in their economies.

However, in the last twelve months it has become clear that Japan and Germany cannot be relied on to continue financing the American and British deficits. The digestion of Eastern Germany and investment in the rest of Eastern Europe may absorb the external surpluses which Germany has recently invested elsewhere. There are growing signs that the Japanese people may prefer to raise their own standard of living rather than to finance Anglo-Saxon profligacy. If America and Britain have to finance their own deficits, besides imposing a substantial cut in their living standards, the necessary fall in their consumption may produce a world-wide recession.

In February 1990 Alexandre Lamfalussy, the general manager of the Bank for International Settlements – the central bankers' central bank – warned the world that the current long-term interest rates 'gave rise to questions of outright concern'. Economic growth might slow down or come to a halt and it was difficult to see how the current investment boom would hold up. With high debt levels of many companies and households, a downturn 'could reveal a degree of fragility in both the real and the financial sectors that has remained effectively hidden by the long cyclical upswing. It also means higher debt burdens for lesser-developed and East European countries.' The remedy, Lamfalussy suggested 'can only lie in the combination of changes in taxation, social security systems and the sheer volume of public spending'.

Which is where we came in.

THE ECONOMIC DIMENSION

(from 'Labour and a World Society', Fabian tract, 1985)

Now let me turn to the economic dimension of international affairs, where changes since I wrote my 'New Fabian Essay' have been, if anything, even more dramatic.

The men who established the postwar framework for economic order in the world were, in the main, British, American and French officials for whom the great slump of the thirties was a formative experience, who had seen the Second World War as an inevitable consequence of the great slumps, had worked together in Washington to win the war, and were determined to build a postwar system which would not repeat the errors of the past. The framework they devised included the Bretton Woods Agreement to keep exchange rates fixed in relation to one another, with only infrequent adjustments, the General Agreement on Tariffs and Trade (GATT), which made free trade in manufactured goods obligatory, and two international institutions – the International Monetary Fund (IMF), which was supposed to finance balance of payments deficits on conditions which guaranteed ultimate adjustment by the debtor country, and the International Bank for Reconstruction and Development, or World Bank, which provided help for development in the Third World.

This framework for international economic order had some obvious defects; in particular, it was unable to impose obligations on the strong countries comparable with those it imposed on the weak. Nevertheless, it helped to produce a quarter of a century of high growth and low inflation in the industrial world, together with a transfer of resources from the rich countries of the northern hemisphere to the poorer countries in the South, as a result of which the economic gap between North and South slowly but steadily grew smaller.

The Collapse of Economic Order

This golden age of high growth and low inflation came to an end in the late sixties, partly because the United States was unable and unwilling to accept the unique responsibilities it imposed. The Bretton Woods Agreement was replaced by a regime of floating currencies, the GATT was rejected by one major industrial country after another in favour of import controls, and the richer countries became increasingly reluctant to give the IMF and the World Bank the resources they required to carry out their responsibilities. This process was aggravated by the massive increase in oil prices imposed by the OPEC countries in 1973, and the unwise policies adopted by most industrial countries to cope with the consequences of the OPEC increase in oil prices.

In consequence, the 1970s were a decade of 'stagflation' – a combination of high inflation with stagnant or even negative growth rates which conventional economics had taught to be impossible. During the seventies, as a result of this new phenomenon, economic behaviour began to change at every level from the housewife to the treasurer of a great multinational corporation. We do not yet quite understand exactly how and why the economic rules have changed. But they have changed fundamentally in many respects.

For example, all forecasts about the behaviour of the American economy from 1982 to 1984 turned out to be grossly in error. American growth was twice as high as predicted, for at least twice as long, while inflation in America increased only two thirds as fast as the forecasters assumed. The

American dollar rose steadily through most of this period, although America was acquiring the biggest balance of payments deficit in its history. President Reagan won re-election in the autumn of 1984 because in the previous two years the American economy had produced seven million more full-time jobs while inflation had fallen to 4 per cent from 14 per cent in 1980. On the other hand, in Europe unemployment has been rising steadily for several years, economic recovery is feeble and very dependent on the unique combination of high American economic growth and a high dollar. Meanwhile, economic statistics have become exceptionally unreliable. The latest GATT statistics of world trade show a gap of $100 billion between the aggregate trade surpluses and the aggregate deficits, although these should be equal.

Yet politicians and economists continue to base policy on economic rules of thumb which have no foundation in reality. Most European economists argue that the high American internal deficit is responsible for high interest rates in the United States. Yet in 1984 the deficit for the Netherlands was estimated by its government to be $10\frac{1}{2}$ per cent of GDP – twice the relative size of the American deficit – while inflation in Holland was lower than anywhere else in Europe and interest rates were among the lowest too. On the other hand, the large Dutch deficit was accompanied by a level of unemployment higher than in any other European country. So both the monetarists and the Keynesians were contradicted by the experience of the Netherlands.

It is too early to be certain exactly how economic behaviour has changed in the last ten years, and what are the new rules which describe the current performance of national economies. But it is possible to point to some elements in this revolution.

Some Features of the New Economic Anarchy
First, most industrial countries lost confidence in Keynesian demand-management during the seventies, and adopted instead a policy of sado-monetarism, based on three propositions, each of which is easily shown to be untrue: that the only economic variable which can be influenced by government policy is inflation, that inflation can be influenced only by controlling the growth of money supply, and the growth of money supply can be influenced only by the price of money i.e. by changes in interest rates. Sado-monetarism has given the industrial world the biggest recession since the thirties, combined with real interest rates higher than they have ever been since the usury of the Middle Ages – over twice as high as was normal in similar periods of recovery.

Secondly, doubts about the future behaviour of the economy have made everyone reluctant to commit funds to long-term fixed investment. Governments and private firms have accumulated an unprecedented volume of liquid funds. The money in the Euromarkets alone amounts to over $2,000 billion. This, with other liquid funds, is moving in microseconds all over the world for twenty-four hours a day. It is officially estimated that at present $50,000 billion cross the exchanges in search of profit every year as against only $2,000 billion which cross the exchanges to finance world trade. These capital flows have become the biggest single influence on exchange rates, and exchange rates have become a major factor in determining the prices of international traded commodities, including oil. Most of the fall in oil and commodity prices over the last twelve months has been due to the rise in the dollar. Their price in other currencies has scarcely shifted.

Meanwhile, there has been an institutional revolution in the financial markets. The barriers between the banks and other financial institutions have broken down. The banks themselves have been freed from many regulations on both sides of the Atlantic, and are now engaged in cut-throat competition for business and profits, which is pushing up interest rates. Salesmanship has replaced reliability as the test of a financial institution's success. The impact of this institutional revolution in a period when international capital movements have swamped all other elements in the financial scene has produced a steadily increasing growth in the interbank markets which the central banks and the international institutions are unable even to monitor, still less control. For example, in America and Britain the central banks under highly conservative governments decided to nationalize institutions in trouble, like Continental Illinois, and Johnson Matthey, not because they knew what would happen if they failed to nationalize them, but precisely because they had no idea what would happen.

THE DEBT CRISIS

These developments in the industrial world were mainly responsible for the debt crisis which has threatened the survival of the Western banking system since the middle of 1982. The deficits imposed on many Third World countries by the increases in the price of oil – particularly the second round of oil price increases which began in 1979 – should under the postwar rules have been financed by international institutions like the IMF and the World Bank. But Western governments were not prepared to give these official institutions the resources for financing world deficits, and insisted that they imposed conditions which many debtor countries were unwilling to accept. The private banks stepped in, in search of more business and higher profits. Even so, most of the loans made to the Third World as a result of the increase in oil prices, would have remained viable had it not been for the world recession, the increase in interest rates and the effect on exchange rates of the staggering increase in international capital movements.

Although in Latin America the debt problem was aggravated by the enormous outflows of funk money from wealthy individuals, it has been estimated that 80 per cent of the increase in Third World debt over the last ten years is the result not of mistakes by governments in the debtor countries, but of policy decisions taken by the industrial countries, or by OPEC. As a result, the magic of the market place has produced a private banking system which can survive only by lending ever more money to bad debtors, and is bullied into doing so by central banks and international institutions which were set up to guarantee its prudence, not to promote its profligacy.

The total burden of world debt is still steadily increasing. Despite continual rescheduling, at least $800 billion of private bank lending is now irrecoverable. The debtor countries are now beginning to determine the terms of their rescheduling and the banks are turning a blind eye to default. Indeed, a chain reaction of defaults is now being avoided only by semantic devices, which describe default by other words – like 'a temporary interruption of debt service'. The conditions imposed for IMF lending, which unlocked further lending by the private banks, are now being regularly ignored by the debtor countries, and often by their creditors too.

In fact, the system is still working because the creditors are determined to ignore the facts, or to redefine them by changing the meaning of words. Nevertheless, the risk of breakdown is steadily increasing because the strains are becoming intolerable at both ends of the process.

The smaller private banks have already pulled out of the rescheduling process, leaving the burden to be carried solely by the larger banks. The larger banks are trying to reduce the percentage of bad debts on their books by frantically making new loans to domestic borrowers, often with only the most cursory examination of their creditworthiness. In the United States the number of 'problem banks' has doubled in the last twelve months with an increasing number of failures expected.

In early 1984 the orthodox view was that the problem could be overcome by the end of the decade through a series of reschedulings and packages of aid which the IMF would sanctify by imposing adjustment programmes on the debtors – the 'case-by-case' or 'sticking-plaster' approach. No one believes that now. As the managing director of the IMF himself explained, the case-by-case approach required the fulfilment of four conditions of which only one has the slightest chance of being met.

The developed countries would have to achieve growth rates averaging 3–4 per cent till 1990 – their feeble recovery has fallen short of that except in the United States, and world growth is likely to decline in 1985. Interest rates would have to fall – they rose 2 per cent in early 1984, imposing an additional \$8 billion in servicing costs on the debtors. Trade restrictions would have to be reduced – they are increasing almost everywhere. And inflation would have to fall – the only assumption which has yet to be falsified. So on the basis of present trends, existing indebtedness will almost double by the end of the decade.

Moreover, there is always the risk of an unpredictable change in the situation wrecking the system. For example, if, as a result of increasing violence in the Gulf War, Western access to Middle East oil was interrupted for a period of months, the consequent increase in the price of oil would wreck any hope that the non-oil debtors would be able to get through. Equally, if Iran and Iraq made peace and the supplies of oil from the Gulf suddenly increased, the price of oil would drop so far as to destroy the ability of the oil producing debtors like Mexico, Venezuela, Indonesia, Nigeria and Argentina, to get through.

Road to Revolution

The most important change in the situation is the growing unwillingness of the debtor countries to risk revolution by making herculean efforts to improve their balance of payments when their markets in the developed world face mounting restrictions and the bulk of the money they earn goes to pay debt service at steadily mounting interest rates. The poor countries are now exporting capital to the rich.

For the Latin American countries which carry half of world debt, the debt crisis is really a growth crisis. As Tom Enders has written, 'For a generation, in one of the great upward thrusts in history, Latin America grew by almost 6 per cent a year in real terms. By 1981 the economy was three times the size it had been in 1960.' (Thomas Enders and Richard Mattione, *Latin America: The Crisis of Debt and Growth*, Brookings Institute, 1984.) The IMF adjustment programmes have compelled these countries to cut their growth so that in the five years to 1987 they can expect a 7 per cent drop in national income in the course of which many of the poor will starve and many of the middle class will be wiped out – the historical recipe for revolutions.

For at least two of these countries it may seem better to default than to be crucified upon a cross of gold. Argentina is self-sufficient in energy and food; its new democratic government feels little responsibility for the debts its military predecessors accumulated, in part to buy unnecessary armaments. Venezuela's position is not dissimilar. Both may feel that if they freed themselves from the burden of past debts they would not need to borrow new money to start growing faster. In any case, what is the point of borrowing simply to pay off foreign banks when one of the prices of borrowing is to abandon growth? But if Argentina or Venezuela were to default, most of the other Latin American governments would be compelled by public opinion to follow suit, even against their better judgement. Moreover US military intervention in Central America could trigger a wave of anti-Yankee feeling which could overturn governments or compel them to default even if Argentina had not led the way.

So in recent months we have seen a game of brinksmanship in which the weak have begun to exploit their power over the strong by dictating the terms of rescheduling and of new lending. Whether the West's 'good boys' like Mexico and Brazil have restrained the 'bad boys' like Argentina from default, or whether by agreement they are playing different roles in the same script it is difficult to say. The result is the same and the underlying political reality remains. The popular pressures to bring down the whole system are growing remorselessly.

None of the creditor governments can allow the collapse of any bank to trigger the collapse of the banking system as a whole. So they have to protect the depositors of a bank in trouble even at the cost of taking it over altogether. Political connoisseurs will long cherish the spectacle of President Reagan, the champion of small government and free enterprise, nationalizing Continental Illinois. What is more important is that his treasury secretary has promised to nationalize any major bank in trouble while allowing the smaller banks to go to the wall.

But although the FDIC, which organized the take-over, wrote off a billion dollars' worth of Continental's bad domestic debts it did not dare to do so with its bad foreign debts for fear of compelling the accountants to do what the government regulators do not dare to do – to expose the true fragility of America's private banking system.

It now seems clear that if the final catastrophe breaks and there is a chain reaction of defaults, the Western governments will save their private banks even if it means general nationalization and the abandonment of monetary stringency – for they will print the money needed to meet the banks' liabilities.

But this will not deal with the problem of the debtor nations, who by definition will in this situation have embarked on a revolutionary course, which is likely to involve tragic suffering for most of the peoples involved. Even if the Western governments think they can ignore that suffering, the United States is likely to face a generation of violent instability on its southern frontiers which could send millions of refugees flooding into California and Texas, with social and political consequences which could well destabilize American society and pre-empt the bulk of America's international energy till the end of the millennium and beyond. This would be a consequence which neither Western Europe nor Japan could contemplate with equanimity.

The stakes are huge. If things go wrong, as now seems probable, the political and economic adjustments required of the West will be stupendous and unavoidable. Is it really impossible for Western governments to make the much smaller changes in their policies which are required to prevent the catastrophe from happening at all?

The Necessary Solutions

All in fact that is required is a return to the sort of policies which gave the Western world a quarter century of unprecedented growth and low inflation after the Second World War. In domestic policy that means a pragmatic mixture of demand and monetary management with social consensus which, though at present scorned by the major Anglo-Saxon governments, is still working well in countries as diverse as Japan, Sweden, Australia, and Austria.

In international policy it means giving the World Bank and the International Monetary Fund the scale of resources which their founders envisaged, with a mandate to encourage the structural adjustments which will favour growth. Once this were done there are already scores of blueprints for the sort of techniques which would be required to restructure the existing debts of the Third World and to finance its future deficits. For although in the Pacific basin the newly industrializing countries have achieved miracles of growth through free enterprise capitalism without much foreign borrowing, for most of the Third World, which still depends on exports of commodities to finance development, as for America in the nineteenth century, external loans are likely to be essential for industrial development. There must, as the Brandt Commission proposed, be an organized transfer of resources from North to South.

Twenty years ago the policies now required would have been adopted without much argument by governments of all political complexions throughout the West. If the neanderthal economic bigotry which infected so many Western governments in the seventies is allowed to prevent their adoption today, President Reagan, Mrs Thatcher and Chancellor Kohl are likely to go down in history as the gravediggers of the very capitalism which they claim to defend.

Even today, all serious observers of the debt crisis, both in the private banks and in the central banks and governments, have come to the conclusion that a long-term solution to the debt crisis requires higher growth in the industrial world and a substantial increase in the role and resources of the international institutions like the IMF and the World Bank. But these same experts despair of governments ever having the wit or the will to shift their policies in this direction unless the crisis suddenly becomes worse. Whether a sudden worsening of the crisis would give time for these changes in government policies is obviously most uncertain.

BLACK OCTOBER

(Financial Times Conference, July 1988)

I think one can draw some conclusions from the crash of October 1987. Firstly, no one foresaw the nature and the timing of the crash. Absolutely no one. Many people did not foresee that there would be trouble at all, including some prominent people. Alan Greenspan, who had recently taken over as chairman of the Fed, appeared on the cover of *Fortune* the very day of the crash in October and said 'I can detect none of the excesses which could cause expansion to turn brittle and self-destruct. The stock market's speculative fever has cooled a bit.' It was not only the Americans: the *Financial Times*, which has organized this conference, published the same day a supplement on global equities and markets which showed a superman wearing a dollar sign revealing an equities index as marching upwards towards the stars. Even the people who thought there would be a crash got the timing and nature wrong. George Soros wrote an article in the *Financial Times* on the Friday before the crash in which he said that there would be a crash, but it would start in Japan because the price-earnings ratios were so high there and it would be more severe there than anywhere else.

So nobody foresaw it would happen when it did and how it came about.

I do not think anybody got the consequences right either. Most people forecast that there would be a fall of 1 per cent in world growth in 1988. Most of them thought there would be a fall in spending on plant and equipment throughout the Western world, and that the United States would be worse affected than the United Kingdom. Exactly the opposite, of course, has happened. Very few people forecast that interest rates would be rising as soon as they have begun to rise or that the dollar's fall would bottom out as early as it did. Nobody got it right – certainly none of the teenage scribblers of whom we read so much these days.

There are still furious arguments about the cause of the crash. Some people, especially at the beginning, blamed computerized trading. I remember reading an article that said that computerized trading produced a clash between Chicago and New York which could have destroyed the whole system if it had gone on for a few seconds longer. Most people now believe that computerized trading simply enabled the markets to get over a necessary correction rather faster than they would otherwise have done. My own feeling about the computer, as some of you will know, is that it is a useful tool for the financial markets but it has not changed their nature; a cannibal is still a cannibal if he uses a knife and fork. Some people thought there were technical features in the financial markets which were responsible. I remember reading that one reason for the crash was that in the United States the price-earnings ratio for stocks was about 20:1, whereas for bonds it was only 10:1. But in Japan, which was affected last and least, a few days after the crash they sold off NTT stock at a price-earnings ratio of 270:1.

There was quite a popular and slightly bizarre view over here that the crash was caused by the Louvre Accord on exchange rates. The argument was that by holding exchange rates fairly steady you diverted the pressures inside the system from exchange rates to interest rates and equities. Again, there may be something in that but I certainly do not think it is the whole explanation. In the United Kingdom and, indeed, generally in Europe, there was a great tendency to blame the twin American deficits – the external and internal deficits. Nigel Lawson, who started life as a teenage scribbler himself for the *Financial Times*, made a great deal of that in public, causing some irritation in Washington at the time. Very few economists now think that that was the cause of the crash, and if you take the whole of America's internal surpluses and deficits – the federal, the local and the state deficits – it amounts to about 2.6 per cent of GDP, which is a little under the OECD average. The real problem in the United States is not the size of the federal deficit, it is the very low savings ratio which makes it impossible to finance even a low deficit out of domestic savings.

I dare say that all these things had something to do with it. I think a general weakening of confidence in the United States was also an element, although the weakening of confidence was caused quite as much by the Iran-Contra affair and by other political factors as by the deficits. What I think everybody can agree, is that a major factor was that there had been a very excessive rise in share values – 40 per cent in the previous eight months – and that the speculative bubble was bound to burst at some stage because the financial markets had lost all contact with the economic realities. As Mrs Thatcher said 'It is the speculator in shares we want to get at – the person who makes a business of buying and selling shares to live on profit.' I must admit she said that in 1961 when she was something of a teenage scribbler herself. I have not heard her saying it quite so loudly in the last year or so.

Let us now look to the future. I will point to some fairly reassuring factors and some worrying factors, bearing in mind all the time that not only do we not understand quite how the economy works, but we never have fully reliable information even about what is happening now, never mind about the future. So many of the numbers I quote may turn out to be incorrect.

First of all, the reassuring factor. There was a tendency, which is still lurking around at the back of some people's minds, to say that this will be a re-run of 1929; so eighteen months after the first stock exchange crash we shall have another one which will bring the whole system down. It was indeed eighteen months after the 1929 crash that the second big crash produced the great recession, and I am told there was an eighteen months gap after the first explosion of the South Sea bubble before the market collapsed at the beginning of the eighteenth century. But the situation today is very different from that in 1929 in at least four important respects. Firstly, the effect of the stock market crash on consumer spending is now cushioned by the fact that in nearly all the developed countries there is a welfare state and people have all sorts of benefits from government which feed in the end into spending. Secondly, the big institutions whose stupidity was mainly responsible for the crash will be very slow to feel its effect – it will show up maybe in pension payments in twenty years' time. Thirdly, the central banks, which reacted to the 1929 crash by tightening the money supply, very wisely this time fed money into the system on a very large scale indeed. Finally, the crash started in the United States as it did in 1929, but the economic position in the States is very different today from what it was then. In 1929 and right through the thirties American capacity was growing much faster than demand. Now the situation is almost the opposite; demand in the United States – largely fed by easy credit – has far outstripped capacity; America is already working at 83 per cent of capacity, which most people would guess is round about its limits.

So there are these big differences between 1929 and 1987. On the other hand we cannot deny that there was a crash in the stockmarkets worldwide in 1987. So the question then is, are there any continuing factors which might play a negative role in the future and produce another crash? All I can do about that, I am afraid, is to run over some of the factors which give cause for concern and which probably contributed in some degree to the crash last year.

The first factor is the triple revolution in the financial markets – first of all the globalization of the markets which was made possible partly by information technology and party by the removal of capital controls in the major countries which play in the markets. The globalization of financial activity has made capital flows the main influence on exchange rates. I do not suppose any of us really know the total size of speculative capital flows. I was at a meeting three years ago in Aspen with Paul Volcker and other people who should know; we then guessed that there were probably about $50 trillion crossing the exchanges in search of short-term speculative profit as against $2 trillion to finance the whole of world trade in both goods and services. I would guess the amount of speculative capital flows must now be at least double what it was three years ago. These capital flows have become by far the most important influence on exchange rates; and of course exchange rates influence the flow of trade and the level of inflation, the level of interest rates and the rate of growth. The volatility of exchange rates created by the globalization of the financial markets has certainly played an important role in the uncertainty which has infected the financial markets and the main economic debtors in the world for the last ten years or so.

Secondly, you had a revolution in financial instruments, the revolution of innovation. Most of the new instruments were developed by the financial institutions as ways of hedging against the exchange rate and interest rate risk, which had increased enormously because of globalization. The most important innovation was the extent to which securitization has spread right across the world. You can now turn anything which can be given a price into a tradeable security and you do not have to be a bank to trade in securities. So you have developed a parallel financial system which is not monitored or controlled by anyone and causes great concern, I know, to the central banks in the world and to the Bank of International Settlements.

Finally, you have had, particularly in Britain and the United States, deregulation. This has led to cut-throat competition between all financial institutions – pension funds, insurance companies, building societies, multinational company treasurers, as well as banks, to lend on paper-thin margins, often in areas which they do not well understand. A friend of mine told me that when he looked into the Continental Illinois disaster because his bank was asked to take it over, he found they had been lending money on energy on the assumption that oil would reach $75 a barrel that year. When my friend told this to his shareholders, they asked 'Are you sure that is not happening in our bank?' He had to reply no, because the expansion of activity inside banks and other financial institutions has made it very difficult for even their own controllers to follow exactly what is happening all the time.

The new financial markets which have emerged from this triple revolution of globalization, innovation and deregulation, are operated by a mafia of gilded young lemmings who have square eyeballs because they never look at anything except a computer screen; they are interested only in numbers and they never relate the numbers they look at to the economic realities which lie buried somewhere at the bottom of this heap of numbers. Most economists would now agree that the effect of the financial revolution has been to produce higher interest rates than we would otherwise have had, and certainly to produce a great deal of short-termism which is greatest in the markets which are most deregulated, particularly the American and British. It does not pay an industrial company now to look further ahead than next quarter's stock price. If it does it is liable to be taken over, probably by a junk bond trader.

The effect of all this has been gravely to weaken and undermine the Western banking systems, particularly in the United States and Britain. Morgans lost their triple A rating quite recently in the United States, and two of our biggest British banks are now in the red.

The present situation should give us some cause for worry. There was a record number of bank failures in the United States last year. I was told by an expert the other day that there are now 200 savings banks which are brain-dead and which it would cost up to $70 billion to rescue. The requirement for banks to show the real value of LDC debt in their books, means that last year bank earnings were cut from $9.8 billion to $300,000 million – a fantastic fall. The return on assets in American banks last year was only 0.02 per cent – the lowest for fifty years. That, of course, is just an average figure. The troubles of the American banks are concentrated very heavily in the south-western states, and in certain areas of lending – agriculture, energy and real estate; but the problem of LDC debt is a great worry to the major money centre banks in New York and California because the twenty largest American banks hold $70 billion of this bad debt out of a total of $300 billion. Forty per cent of the banks which did the original lending have now been able to get out and the rest are under tremendous shareholder pressure not to continue throwing good money after bad by continuing to lend to the LDCs.

On the other side, the risk of default, particularly in some of the Latin American countries, is still very obviously there because the debt squads have actually cut living standards for some of the peoples of Latin America by about 8 per cent since 1982. This problem will play a part in the elections in Mexico today, and in Argentina, in Brazil and in Venezuela later this year. Although so far the Peruvian example has made people very wary about considering default, they will be pressing for a conciliatory default – trying to get some sort of default agreed by the banks. The confidence of bankers has fallen substantially. I noticed *The Economist* published the results of a recent survey of 150 senior executives in the top commercial banks all over the world and found that only one third of these banks had any sort of strategic planning. Sixty-one per cent wanted more capital but did not know how they would use it if they got it, and over 75 per cent did not think they had the right people running their bank.

Of course, a financial system which has been through these traumatic experiences is very vulnerable to shock, and the shock could come from all sorts of directions. It could be a natural shock like the drought in the United States which could have a big effect on the banking system through what happens to the farming industry in the States if it continues a little longer. It could come from a major computer disaster, but since there is a representative of the Union Bank of Switzerland here today I will not delve too heavily into that except to say that if I were a really patriotic Latin American I would be training youngsters of eighteen or nineteen to plant computer viruses in the banking systems in New York and then threaten to let them rip unless the banks made a better deal than they are prepared to so far.

There are all sorts of things which could happen which are unpredictable – a big change in the oil price, a victory either by Iraq or Iran in the Gulf War would have a catastrophic effect on major areas of the world economy and possibly world politics. There is always the possibility of war and revolution. These factors are, in the nature of things, unpredictable. But there are some factors which should give us cause for worry though their precise consequences are difficult to predict. The most important of these are in the economic field – the tremendous trade imbalances between the United States, Germany and Japan in particular. I will just look very quickly at these factors.

The United States has now more external debt than any other sovereign debtor in the world. It jumped $99 billion to $368 billion last year. Almost nothing now can prevent the United States owing more money than all the rest of sovereign debtors put together by the end of this decade. That is the external debt. The United States also has very heavy internal debt, not only government debt but debt to the banks because there has been such aggressive marketing of consumer credit in America for the last ten years and more. As you know, in order to keep the dollar fairly steady, the central banks, because commercial organizations were not prepared to finance the deficit on the same scale, put $130 billion into the United States last year. The external trade deficit is shrinking because the dollar has fallen, but the shrinking in the trade deficit is being offset by an increase in capital outflow so the overall accounts of the United States have not improved as much as they should. What is most depressing is that the fall in the American deficit has mainly been at the expense of the deficit countries in Europe rather than of the big creditor countries like Japan and Germany. Meanwhile a combination of increased external demand through the fall in the dollar and the still very high consumer credit is producing a real risk of overheating in the United States, and some of my friends think there could even be a mini crisis before the election although nearly all the authorities all over the world will try to keep the thing afloat through November.

In Europe a very interesting thing is happening. Last year Germany increased its surplus by $6 billion and the other European countries saw their deficits increase by $19½ billion. The main reason for that is that demand is rising at only 1 per cent in Germany and about 2 per cent in the other European countries. I am told it would need the deutschmark to go up 25 per cent to correct this imbalance, but it cannot because of the Exchange Rate Mechanism of the European Monetary System. If you have a mechanism like the ERM to keep exchange rates stable, but you have no mechanism to produce consistent fiscal and monetary policies in the countries concerned, you will have a very unequal distribution of the burdens and benefits in the system, an inequality which will finally become politically intolerable. What makes the mind boggle is that in this situation it was the Germans who led Europe in an increase in interest rates a week or two ago.

Now let us look at Japan, a much more cheerful picture. There has been a 90 per cent increase in the value of the yen since the Plaza agreement, and that has simply stimulated innovation in Japan. Japan has been kept up to scratch not by competition from the United States and Europe, but by competition from its Asian neighbours, or NIEs as I think we are now calling them – Newly Industrializing Economies. Domestic demand in Japan increased between 7 and 8 per cent in the second half of last year, and it is still increasing very fast. All this has led to some reductions in Japan's trade surplus but it is masked by the rise in the yen against the dollar and much of the reduction in Japan's trade surplus is due to Japan importing products produced in the United States and elsewhere by Japanese subsidiaries. The direct effect on the debtor countries in the world has been much less dramatic. Many people were arguing a year or two ago that all these factors would produce a hard landing for the dollar because the Japanese would get fed up financing the American deficit. I do not believe that is likely, because the Japanese recognize very clearly that their prosperity depends on the survival of an international economic system in which the dollar is the only reserve currency. But the Japanese will not go on financing the American deficit by buying depreciating paper. Increasingly they are going into hard assets. They have already bought Hawaii, they are now beginning to buy up California. I was told by Mr Tabuchi of Nomura the other day in Tokyo that any Japanese manufacturing firm can make a profit by producing in the United States and exporting to Japan, once the yen is at 110. At the moment many Japanese automobile firms are making very good profits with the yen significantly higher.

The real problem is that the strongest countries in the world are still capable of resisting rational pressure from the weaker ones. The rest of the world cannot get the Americans to change its behaviour, and the rest of Europe cannot get Germany to change its behaviour. So long as this is so then I think the danger of something happening in some part of the system which produces a crash is there.

A final word or two about potential answers to the problem. It is a multi-faceted problem so there is clearly no single answer. I think one or two things are worth a go. First of all, in the financial sector there is no question whatever now that we are set for re-regulation; not to restore the old system in the United States but to restructure the American banking system and remove some of the more damaging aspects of Glass-Steagal in the course of it. I think you will find increasing pressure to control and tax speculative capital movements. I was interested to see that Felix Rohatyen, who could conceivably be secretary of the treasury if Mike Dukakis wins the election, suggesting this week that there should be a 50 per cent tax on profits from securities which are held for under twelve months, and tax abatement for profits from securities which are held for over five years. Fortunately the new information technology is capable of monitoring and controlling all these movements if governments decide it should be done.

Thirdly there is a likelihood, and certainly a desperate need, to try to remove the albatross of LDC debt from the commercial banks and to shift it to the international institutions like to IMF and the World Bank. I am told that at a recent meeting in the United States of the chief executive officers of the major American banks, the youngsters now in charge, who were not responsible for the bad lending, were very anxious to get shot of the debt all together, even if it meant accepting a very large loss in order to do so.

Now let us look at the economic side. There is a good chance the Americans will move to cut their deficit after the election, and as I understand it there has been a Congressional committee working on this and I have no doubt the new president will consult it about what should be done. The problem is not as great as all that on the fiscal side because if the fiscal deficit was to be reduced at the rate of $50 billion a year you could start off by 25 cents tax on gas which would bring in $25 billion, or half of that. Anybody who has driven recently in the United States will be staggered that when there is a possibility of a world oil crisis the price of gas is so far below the price in Europe. What is desperately needed in Europe is a revaluation of currencies inside the EMS so that the deutsch-mark can go up, but that of course will be resisted to the death by the Central Bank and by German industry. We need a new long-term approach not just to Third World debt but to the problem of a transfer of resources to the Third World. Here I think Japan is likely to be able to play a key role if it regards it in its interest to do so. In the ten years before 1914 Britain exported to developing countries in Latin America and in the United States, which was still developing in those days, twice the per-centage of GDP and four times the percentage of earnings that Japan is exporting at the present time.

It is very unlikely that any of these things will happen unless there are changes of attitude in the governments concerned, and that could mean changes of government in Germany and the United States at least. In Japan political change is less important; Mr Takeshita was the only representative at the recent summit to make a constructive proposal for dealing with Third World debt, when he suggested that the debtor countries and the banks should split the discount which the banks are now making to one another on the debt.

The central problem, however, which underlies everything else, is now under discussion in the United States, and with a decent government in Washington, may appear much less formidable than it does at the moment. It has been difficult since Connally was treasury secretary for the United States to carry the full burden of underpinning the world economy with the dollar as the only reserve currency. The real question is whether it is possible to create any other reserve currency or at least to share the burden. I found when I was in Tokyo recently there was a growing interest, at least in financial circles, in giving the yen more of an international reserve status. As you know, there is a great deal of discussion as to whether the same could be done with the deutschmark perhaps disguised as an ecu or francfort. The world has enjoyed, if that is the word, a swing of the pendulum towards freedom or anarchy, and is now set for a swing of the pendulum back to order and government responsibility. I hope we shall now see governments taking these problems seriously because, I am sure you will all agree with me, banking is far too serious to be left to the bankers.

CHAPTER SEVEN

Gorbachev and After

A N INDIVIDUAL CAN PLAY a decisive role in history if he can combine the insight to recognize fundamental changes in his world, the intellectual ability to develop policies which will guide and shape these changes so as to achieve his objectives, and the leadership capacity to win support for his policies. Mikhail Gorbachev is one of the very few men to command all three of these skills. Even if in the end he fails to achieve all his objectives, he has already left an indelible stamp on his age. He has ended the Cold War and opened the way to the creation of a world society. Whether a world society is in fact established will depend largely on the ability of others to meet his challenge.

I met him first for a few days during his visit to Britain in December 1984, just before he succeeded the ailing Chernenko as leader of the Soviet Union. After brief encounters on ceremonial occasions in Moscow, I joined Lord Whitelaw and other British MPs in substantive discussions with him in the Kremlin eighteen months later. In style and personality he was quite unlike any other Soviet leader I had met. It remains a mystery to me how a man of such charm and sensitivity should have risen to the top of the system which produced Stalin and Brezhnev, still more that he should have strengthened his hold on power so rapidly in such adverse circumstances. The fact that it was Andropov, as head of the KGB, who arranged his promotion to the Politburo, only deepens the mystery.

In April 1988 I tried to explain his importance in a lecture at Princeton in honour of my old friend and sparring partner George Ball. To an audience in the United States, which had been taught for so many years that the Soviet Union was committed by its Leninist doctrine to eternal hostility, I felt it important to show how Gorbachev had changed that doctrine, first by using the Marxist dialectic to justify abandoning the dogma of the two camps, then by renouncing Russia's revolutionary duty to help the 'anti-colonial' struggle in the Third World. His formal abandonment of the doctrine by which Brezhnev justified armed intervention to support Communism in Eastern Europe, and his effective burial of Leninism itself, came later.

No less important than this replacement of ideology by pragmatism in Soviet foreign policy, was his decision to seek only 'sufficiency' in military power. He announced that the Soviet Union should cease striving for superiority, or even for equality, with the United States. No other great power has ever been so modest in relation to its rivals. Britain in its heyday insisted on having a navy stronger than the next two navies put together, while the United States after 1945 aimed at being able to fight and win one major war and two smaller wars at the same time.

These changes of doctrine were already influencing policy in practice. In the agreement on intermediate nuclear forces Gorbachev gave up far more missiles than the United States. Since then he has made unilateral cuts in his forces both in Europe and the Far East. He has abandoned military support for the freedom fighters in Angola and the African National Congress, and withdrawn from Afghanistan. A similar shift in policy now seems under way in Vietnam and Central America.

Even when I spoke in Princeton, most of the sceptics where Soviet policy was concerned had come to believe that Gorbachev was sincere. But there remained a reasonable doubt whether he would be able to survive as leader of the Soviet Union, and whether any successor would follow the same policies. I tried to meet these doubts as well. The factors which had persuaded Gorbachev to change his policies and doctrine would be no less compelling for any successor – the crying need to divert resources from defence to the domestic economy, the fact that a nuclear war, in Reagan's words 'could not be won and should never be fought', and the collapse of Soviet Communism as a model for any other party in the world to follow.

Equally important, in my opinion, were the social changes which had swept the Soviet Union – an astonishing improvement in education, easier access to Western culture, and above all the forces released by 'glasnost'. The truth not only about Soviet history, but also about the current failures of the Soviet system, has now been public knowledge throughout the Union for many years; this has led to the proliferation of bodies which are highly critical of the Communist Party itself. These changes cannot be reversed, though they might be slowed down, as Brezhnev slowed down the changes put in train by Khrushchev.

By the time I finished my memoirs, *The Time of My Life*, at Easter in 1989 I was worrying far more about the risk that the growing nationalism in Eastern Europe would produce the sort of Balkanization which bred the First World War, and that the demand for independence in the peripheral republics of the Soviet Union could lead to the disintegration of the state, creating the danger not only of a disastrous civil war, but also of armed conflicts involving some of the neighbouring countries.

In the House of Commons on 4 July I expressed my mounting despera-tion at the failure of the West in general, and of Mrs Thatcher in particular, to recognize the urgency of developing new structures, pre-ferably involving the United Nations, to meet these dangers. Even then I failed to foresee, like everyone else, the break-neck speed at which the process would accelerate once the peoples of Eastern Europe realized that Gorbachev would not allow the Red Army to save their Communist regimes.

The Berlin Wall came down on 9 November. I wrote an article for the *Observer* on the implications of this for German reunification, then flew to Berlin myself to discuss the prospects with Ted Heath for *Newsnight*, standing at midnight in an icy mist on the balcony of the Reichstag, overlooking the Brandenburg Gate. Walking round both sides of Berlin next day, I saw more happy people than I have ever seen in any other city of the world; they were laughing and crying with joy and wonder. At that time there seemed to be little demand in East Germany for reunification. Within a few weeks that too had changed, and it was obvious that if reunification did not happen soon by political decision, it would happen within months by migration. People were simply voting with their feet for a better life in the West.

I have included a few more articles on the situation as it has since developed. In some respects they have already been overtaken by events. It is impossible to see more than a few weeks ahead. So I cannot provide the sort of speculative essay I have written on other events over this astonishing half century. I have nevertheless tried to compare the sort of problems which the world faces at this moment with those which we faced when the world was moving into the Cold War. That will have to serve as an epilogue. Those who cannot learn from history are condemned to repeat it.

GORBACHEV AND SOVIET FOREIGN POLICY

(from the George W. Ball Lecture, 7 April 1988)

This is a sentimental journey for me, because it is my second visit to Princeton. My first took place nearly thirty years ago when I attended a seminar on NATO and American security under Klaus Knorr, with George Kennan, Paul Nitze, Herman Kahn and a whole slew of famous people, whose names I fear in many cases may now have been forgotten.

At that time George Kennan and I were alone in believing that Khrushchev did offer the opportunity for developing a new relationship between Russia and the West. I don't blame the majority at the meeting for feeling that we were premature. Shortly after we met we had the second Berlin crisis – the second attempt by the Soviet Union to push the West out of Berlin – and then the appalling concatenation of blunders which led to the placement of Soviet missiles in Cuba. But looking back on those years three decades later, I think one must admit that the prospects now for reaching a comprehensive agreement with the Soviet Union are in many respects more favourable today.

Let me list some of them. First of all, both the Soviet Union and the United States have come to recognize that the colossal amount of money which they've spent on the arms race has bought neither of them any additional security. But this enormous level of defence spending has imposed very severe strains not only on the Soviet economy, but on the American economy too; the United States is more fortunate than the Soviet Union because it has Japan and Germany to finance its deficits.

The central problems posed for diplomacy and strategy by nuclear weapons are as far from solution as ever. The credibility of what is called 'extended deterrence', that is to say, the ability of a country with nuclear weapons to protect a country without them, is still very uncertain. The West has long ago given up the attempt to find a formula for sharing the decision to use nuclear weapons. The last attempt really was by George Ball when he invented the multilateral force as a formula for what I used to call 'artificial dissemination' – trying to make it appear to the Europeans, as in a way I suppose the Cruise-Pershing decision was intended to do, that they could force the Americans to use nuclear weapons, even if the Americans didn't want to. And the other great problem which is as far from solution as ever is the question as to whether it is possible to use nuclear weapons at any level in any way without very rapid escalation to a total, global, thermonuclear exchange.

In fact it is much better recognized now than it was even when I was defence secretary twenty years ago that nobody can feel the slightest confidence that if nuclear weapons are used between the Soviet Union and the United States anywhere at any level it will be possible to prevent a very rapid escalation to the global holocaust. It would be quite a holocaust now, because there are 50,000 nuclear warheads between the two great powers, which are equivalent to a million Hiroshimas in destructive power. Many scientists believe that under certain conditions, although they disagree a little bit about what those conditions are, the explosion of all these weapons would produce a nuclear winter which would make human life and perhaps even plant life impossible in the northern hemisphere.

What I think people are only just coming to recognize is that a prolonged, large-scale conventional war on a world scale could have somewhat similar results – not just because of the greatly increased destructiveness of conventional weapons since the last world war, but also because there are now a lot of civilian nuclear reactors scattered around the world. Our own government in Britain in 1983 produced a report on environmental pollution which said that if the last world war had taken place when there were as many nuclear reactors in Europe as there are today, then large areas of Europe would still be uninhabitable.

These very daunting facts have caused people to think more carefully than they did thirty years ago about some of the problems which divide East and West. Some of the fears which I and others had thirty years ago have proved to be illusory. When we last met, the United States had suddenly become obsessed by what it called the 'missile gap', and the belief that the Russians might use an assumed superiority in strategic missiles to deliver a disarming first strike against the United States. Although some people with an institutional interest still maintain that a first strike is a danger to be worrying about, the fact is that the moment both sides started putting nuclear missiles on submarines the risk of a first strike practically disappeared, because there is no way of getting rid of the enormous retaliatory capability which both sides have on invulnerable boats under the surface of the ocean. The argument for a Soviet first strike has been pretty well destroyed by the split between the Soviet Union and China, because now China is a potential *tertius gaudens*; that is, if there was a war between the United States and the Soviet Union which inflicted serious damage on the victor, even though he was the victor he would be vulnerable to attack by China.

Many people, especially Paul Nitze, worried enormously at that time that as the Russians approached parity in nuclear weapons with the West they would be more disposed to take risks in conventional war. This has proved to be the opposite of the case, for reasons which I think it is easy to understand. At that time, many people believed (Roger Hilsman was one) that when both sides had intercontinental ballistic missiles, the United States would not be interested in the defence of Western Europe, partly because it would be vulnerable to Soviet ICBMs and partly because it would no longer need bases with nuclear weapons on the other side of the Atlantic – but this has not proved to be the case.

One of the most surprising things, looking back on our worries at that time, is that although it was physically possible even then for perhaps thirty other countries in the world to produce their own nuclear weapons, the proliferation of nuclear weapons has been very slow indeed. In the last thirty years, so far as we know, the only other countries besides France, Britain, the Soviet Union, and the United States which have acquired nuclear weapons are China, Israel and India. When we met here thirty years ago, Franz Josef Strauss, who was then the German defence minister, was openly asking whether Germany should acquire its own nuclear weapons. The German demand for nuclear weapons has totally disappeared. There is absolutely no sign of it whatever at the present time. And in spite of the fact that leading Americans who had government responsibility, like Henry Kissinger and Bob McNamara, have been saying publicly that they never believed that any American president would order a nuclear strike simply because an ally was attacked, the Western European countries still feel safe in basing their security policies on the American nuclear umbrella guaranteed by NATO.

On top of all this, we now have a new Soviet leader who has been in power for just three years, Mikhail Gorbachev. One can say some things about him without fear of any contradiction by anyone: his diplomacy in relations with the West has shown a subtlety, a flexibility, and a pragmatism which we have not seen in any other Soviet leader since the Revolution. One result of this is that Gorbachev is more trusted by West European opinion than the American president, according to recent opinion polls. The image of the Soviet Union in public perception in the West has changed enormously since Gorbachev took over three years ago, but all we clever people who are here this evening of course are not over impressed by image – or even by public opinion, I dare say. So the question I want to pass to now is: What actually *is* the Gorbachev phenomenon? Has anything really changed in the Soviet Union, other than the brilliance with which Gorbachev communicates his position?

I've spent quite a time with Gorbachev over the last few years – in fact, altogether twelve hours, which in the modern world is quite a time – about as long as Mrs Thatcher. But I learned a lot more from him than Mrs Thatcher did in her twelve hours, because I did occasionally allow him to get a word in, too. He is a man of immense personal charm who is genuinely attractive as a human being. But it's also the case, as Gromyko said when he proposed him as the successor to Chernenko, that although he has a nice smile he has steel teeth. He has consolidated his position as leader faster than any previous Soviet leader since Lenin. And he has made more changes at the top of the Soviet hierarchy, faster than any of his predecessors since Lenin. I think, too, that he seems to have faced the facts about the modern world and about Russia's position in it, at least as honestly as any other postwar leader of any country in the world. He has clearly recognized that Russia is no longer a political or economic model for any group of people anywhere in the world, and that although Russia remains a military giant, she is an economic and political dwarf. He accepts too that Russia will remain so unless she can make changes in her economic and social system which will depend on not being quite so much of a military giant as she is today – because Soviet defence spending is not only demanding a much higher share of the Soviet budget in general terms than Russia can afford, it is also demanding a much higher proportion of scarce technological resources, particularly of manpower, than Russia can afford if she is going to bring her industry into the second half of the twentieth century.

Gorbachev's *perestroika* – 'reconstruction', as he calls it – is bringing about changes in the doctrine and organization of the Communist church as dramatic as the changes in the Christian church brought about by the Reformation. The most obvious example of that in the external field is that Gorbachev has publicly at his own Party Congress rejected the theory about Russia's relations with the outside world which has guided Soviet foreign policy since Lenin – the theory that the world is divided into two camps – what they call the socialist and capitalist camps, or what we would call the Communist and non-Communist camps – which are historically committed to struggle with one another until one side or the other wins final victory. The only shift in Soviet policy on the two camps before Gorbachev was on whether the final victory of socialism would be achieved with a war or without a war.

Henry Kissinger, writing his memoirs in 1979, described the American perception of this position very accurately in describing Brezhnev's doctrinal approach to world politics. But the astonishing thing which

Gorbachev has done is that he has used the jargon of dialectical materi-
alism, the Communist doctrine, to abandon this central principle of
Soviet foreign policy. In his speech to the Communist Party Congress a
couple of years ago, he said that nuclear weapons require the conflict of
opposites – the struggle between the two camps – to produce a new
synthesis. And he said we have to move, I quote his words, 'groping in the
dark, as it were, towards an interdependent or even integral world'. And
here, the style he used, the words he used, are as interesting as the content.
No Soviet leader before – frankly, very few leaders in the West – have
cared to tell their own people that they were groping in the dark towards
anything. One of the new things about Gorbachev is his readiness to admit
he doesn't know quite where he's going or how he'll get there. He has said
several times in the last few years in public that he is not certain he's right
– I can't recall even my own prime minister ever using such an expression –
and he has also said that we are going to have to compromise to get where
we want to go. This is something absolutely unheard of in Soviet language
before Gorbachev.

Now, this basic shift of doctrine must be taken seriously, particularly by
people like Henry Kissinger, who has said that whatever the Russians say,
their doctrine is the same. If they change the doctrine, this is an important
fact of which we must all take note and to which we must adjust, I would
have thought. The change in doctrine on this theory of the two camps is
now moving into other areas. A fortnight ago, Mr Primakov, who is the
new head of one of the two big academic para-governmental institutes
(IMEMO), said that – horrible jargon, this, and not Gorbachev words
at all – 'the exclusion of the export of revolution is an imperative in the
nuclear world'. I used to find in my arguments with Soviet spokesmen
even five or six years ago that they would say, 'Yes, we want to get on well
with the West. Yes, we're prepared to work for *détente* and disarmament.
But we have a revolutionary duty to assist people who are fighting for
socialism in Asia and Africa.' And Primakov at least – I won't say this is
yet solid Soviet doctrine – has suggested the opposite.

On the other hand, in military doctrine the changes are unequivocal and
formal. There was a time when the Russians openly aimed at military
superiority over the West. Then in the Brezhnev years they aimed at
parity rather than superiority. But now the word which is used is 'sufficiency' – although there is still some tension between the military and the
politicians in that the military say 'defence sufficiency' and the politicians
say 'reasonable sufficiency', which is a little bit more flexible. It is this
doctrine which made it possible for Gorbachev to make an agreement on

intermediate nuclear forces the other day, in which the Soviet Union gave up twice as many missiles as the United States. And it is this doctrine which enables him to propose to the West negotiations about conventional force reductions in Europe in which the Russians as well as the West will level down in any areas of capability in which they have a superiority – and they've admitted that one of those areas is tanks.

The most important single new words which have appeared in Soviet talk about defence is that their objective now is 'stability' and 'predictability'. Their new defence minister, General Yasov, used these phrases in talking to Mr Carlucci the other day in Switzerland. And one of the most helpful things, I think, is that now an American military leader is talking to a Soviet military leader about defence doctrine and postures. For a long time the more sensible elements in the American military establishment have been saying that stability must be the major objective of policy. Brent Scowcroft did this, for example, in his report to President Reagan on strategic forces not so long ago. There is no doubt that if Gorbachev hopes to carry through the internal changes at which he aims, then he does need stability and predictability in the external environment of the Soviet Union.

If I could sum up this part of the argument I think I'd be justified in saying that although there was enormous disagreement among Western sovietologists three years ago about whether Gorbachev was sincere in what he said or whether it was just an attempt to bamboozle and divide the West, there are few experts left except perhaps Professor Pipes who think that he is not sincere. The argument now is a much more difficult one, and very important, and this is whether he will succeed in achieving his objectives. Of course, we cannot know that at this point in time. We do know that he faces appalling difficulties in domestic reconstruction. He has got an enormous bureaucracy which is corrupt and incompetent and which he has not succeeded in affecting very much through the changes at the top in the departments and the Party. And he has a people which is tremendously cynical about the ability of any Soviet leader to improve its conditions.

I have tried like all of us to consider whether he can succeed, and if not what the consequences could be, and I just put forward some considerations for you. The first point which must be made is that, contrary to the views spread by Western journalists, Gorbachev is not a new and unprecedented phenomenon in the Soviet Union. The general approach he has adopted is in a way like that of Lenin in the New Economic Policy in the twenties; it was the one promoted by Bukharin, who was shot for promoting it in the Stalin years of the thirties. As a personality he is enormously like that forgotten man, Malenkov. I was reading recently the British press reports of Malenkov's visit to Britain as deputy prime minister after he'd been deposed by Khrushchev, and the accounts were very like those in the Washington press when Gorbachev came here. He was a man of extraordinary urbanity with total self-confidence and control, witty and relaxed. Just to give you one example, if it is not sexist in the modern world to quote it, he was asked at his final press conference what he thought about British women. And he replied, 'I never make love through interpreters'. Now, that is a Gorbachev-type remark, I think you'll all agree. And Malenkov as a personality type was very similar to Gorbachev. In political terms, many of the things Gorbachev is now trying to do, Khrushchev was trying to do. When I was in Moscow in 1959 with Hugh Gaitskell and Nye Bevan and Khrushchev was in power, one could see the cultural relaxation, changes in approach to all sorts of problems – very similar to the ones which you can see in Moscow today.

The next point I would make is that the social environment in which the Gorbachev type of line may succeed is very much more favourable than it has ever been before. When the Revolution took place in 1917 in the Soviet Union, the new regime recreated a brutal, xenophobic dictatorship of very much the same type as was described by the Marquis de Custine in his travels around Tsarist Russia in the 1830s. I'm sure you all know that de Custine was a French aristocrat who thought that the Tsar might provide a model for the monarchists in France, but after going there he found it was not a good model at all, rather like Milton Friedman when he went to visit Britain and hoped to discover a model of a successful monetarist policy. The tragedy of the Soviet revolution from this point of view is that it recreated the Russia described by de Custine. De Custine described what was then called 'the tchin', which we now call the 'nomenklatura', which was the Russian establishment under the Tsar which wore uniforms. And I've been at a meeting of the tchin during the evening after the victory celebrations of the Second World War a couple of years ago, and it is very much the same now as it was then.

The Russian Revolution destroyed the liberal intelligentsia which had begun to change the Tsarist system after de Custine was there. Russia in the middle and later nineteenth century produced the three greatest novelists of the Western world in Tolstoy, Dostoyevski and Turgenyev, produced one of the two greatest dramatists since Shakespeare in Chekhov, produced political thinkers of enormous resonance and insight like Alexander Herzen, and indeed right up to and beyond the Revolution people like

Berdyaev, who had a great influence on me as a socialist. But that strain in Russian society was suppressed by the Revolution. I personally agree with the arguments which have been used in an article in a current issue of *Foreign Affairs* magazine by Jerry Hough of Duke University that what the revolutionary regime saw as its first task in 1917 was to consolidate the revolution by urbanizing the peasantry and beginning to educate them. The figures that Hough quotes are really quite startling. As late as 1939, 93 per cent of the Soviet people had had only an elementary education or less. Forty years later in 1979, 42 per cent of the Soviet people had had a high school education or more. My wife, Edna, and I were in Moscow and Leningrad in 1959, and we remember very well going to a school in Leningrad and talking to the sixth formers. It was obviously a school for the children of the nomenklatura – what we in Britain would call a 'public' school, and what you more accurately I think call a 'private' school. The children there were immensely healthy, intelligent, and really would have fitted into the pages of a novel by Tolstoy or Turgenyev. Those children and tens of thousands like them are now in their middle forties and in the middle ranks of the Soviet leadership.

Gorbachev himself is the first head of the Soviet Communist Party to have had a university education. George Kennan was telling me a couple of nights ago that Gorbachev happened to go to a law school in Moscow which was one of the very few schools that maintained the pre-revolutionary liberal tradition. I've met people from Eastern Europe who were with Gorbachev at the same school.

Secondly, the international youth culture was already spreading under Khrushchev. Indeed, a year later when I went back to Moscow I had a young guide who had been at the World Youth Congress in Moscow and had learned a lot of American from the American delegates there. Since this is a mixed audience, some of which are over the age of thirty, I can't quote the words he'd learnt, but you will find them in any novel by Elmore Leonard or George V. Higgins. When I go to Moscow nowadays, I always try to spend an hour or two in Gorky Park, which is the big park in Moscow. The changes among the youngsters there are noticeable almost from year to year. When I was there a year ago, the kids were wearing these untidy jeans and denim jackets which I've found all over Princeton in the last few days. Some of them were carrying ghetto blasters – some of them were wearing punk haircuts. When I first went to Moscow in 1959 I actually had the well-known experience of standing in Red Square and have a Russian sidle up to me and say, 'I am Rooshan. Rooshan biznismahn. I would like to buy your soot.' When I was there last year, somebody sidled up to me, but he asked me if I had a Sony Walkman or some video tapes. This is a very, very important cultural change in the Soviet Union, and it indicates a shift in perception of the outside world which is important to Soviet policy at the government level. All along the gulf of Finland now and down the Baltic coast they listen to and watch Western television from Finland or from Sweden.

These social changes mean that even if Gorbachev personally failed, it would be difficult for his successor to get back to the Brezhnev years. And some of the economic facts are equally important. Gorbachev has admitted in public that there was very little growth in the Soviet Union in the later Brezhnev years, and it's very slow in getting going even under his own reforms. The Russians cannot hope to improve their economic performance without adopting some of the Western techniques which depend on new technologies like information technology and computers, which they cannot produce for themselves so long as so much of their skill in this area is diverted to military output, and so long as they are not able to import them from the West either. And it is equally important, I think, that the moment this process begins, *that* will have social and political consequences in the Soviet Union, the extent to which it is difficult to exaggerate.

Then there is the military fact that I hope we recognize in the West – certainly President Reagan does – that to fight a nuclear war is an absolutely unacceptable option, however much the threat to fight one may be regarded as convenient for diplomatic reasons.

Finally, I think the Russians are getting very disenchanted with empire. They have occupied Eastern Europe for the last forty years, but they can only keep Eastern Europe half loyal to their system by allowing it a much higher living standard than they have themselves. This is equally true of some of their own republics, the Baltic states, Georgia and Armenia for example. In my view, all these facts are pretty well a guarantee that even if Gorbachev personally doesn't achieve his objectives, a successor leader or system will not go back to Brezhnev. What you may get is what happened under Brezhnev. Brezhnev didn't go back to Stalin, but the process which had moved fast under Khrushchev was blocked for a time and then moved ahead only very slowly. And that, of course, is certainly a possibility. On the other hand, in the field of foreign policy the arguments for Russia maintaining his broad approach would be as powerful under any successor regime, and in the foreign field, Gorbachev has made a clean sweep of the policy leadership. And in the foreign field it is a very small number of people who make policy as distinct from those who run industry. Gorbachev has already made pretty well a clean sweep of the heads of section in the

Foreign Office and the International Secretariat of the Party, and of course in very many of his embassies as well. All that is a factor for continuity in foreign policy.

I now move to a sensitive area, which I shall pass over as rapidly as I can get away with. There are some obvious parallels between the Soviet predicament today and the American one. The United States is finding the burden of defence expenditure excessively heavy. It is losing its technological lead to Japan, partly because the Japanese don't divert so much technological skill to defence as the United States. Both superpowers are increasingly conscious that their predominance is declining – and I think perhaps becoming conscious that they have a common interest in using their waning years of predominance to produce a more stable international framework which will enable them both to cut defence spending and to live in a bit more security than they live today.

So I now come to the final section of what I have to say, and that is: 'What really is the agenda if we in the West want to take advantage of the opportunities which I think Gorbachev is now offering? The first and obvious area of course is the arms race, where the first big agreement has been reached in the INF treaty. It is obviously sensible to try to cut strategic nuclear weapons as much as possible and I would hope a good deal more than 50 per cent in the not-too-distant future. Incidentally, cuts beyond 50 per cent will create serious problems with the present British and French governments and probably with the government of China, because their nuclear weapons come into the balance when you get below a certain point. On the other hand, if the Russians want to reduce the technological and spending drain, they won't do it simply by abolishing existing nuclear weapons. It may cost you more to get rid of nuclear warheads safely than you save in getting rid of the teams which are currently required to operate them. The only ways in which you can make real savings are in stopping modernization of forces, which is where the new technology goes, and that requires a comprehensive test ban treaty for a start – and secondly, in a substantial cut in the total size of the defence forces. The thing we often forget about Khrushchev is that he actually cut Soviet military manpower by half unilaterally when he was leader – by about three million it was at the time. But I don't think you can get big cuts in conventional forces either side unless you can cut in Europe. But here again we have a clear agenda which I'm sorry to say Gorbachev has set, which is to aim at asymmetrical cuts under which any side with a preponderance in one area eliminates that preponderance: the West in strike aircraft, the East in tanks, to take one example. But even more important here I think is for NATO and the Warsaw Pact to try to adjust their defence doctrines and postures towards greater predictability and stability, and I hope very much that Mr Carlucci and General Yasov have started the discussion on this when they met in Switzerland a few weeks ago.

Another proposal which attracted me very much is the one attributed to Paul Nitze in yesterday's *New York Times*, by which you get rid of all naval nuclear weapons except submarine-launched missiles, so you solve this very difficult technical problem of verifying a Cruise limitation by eliminating Cruise nuclear weapons. The main problem we all face in this area is that nuclear policy in the West has been managed for the last forty years by a tiny mafia of middle-ranking bureaucrats and staff officers who have very little contact with their own governments and none with their own peoples. To break the hold of the theologians in the high-level group, for example of NATO on strategic thinking, I think is probably going to be a pre-condition of success – although it was broken, or the INF treaty would never have been made, because all the élite experts were against it, as you well know.

The other set of problems is the regional problems. Most of the people in my generation who grew up and entered politics in the thirties have tended to see Russia in the German mould and to see the problem as one of stopping a power which is bent on military domination, of avoiding a new Munich.

But the real danger of war today lies much more in a new Sarajevo – a conflict in some other part of the world which drags in the great powers almost against their will. It's easy enough to see and list these sort of problems: in Asia you've got Afghanistan – though the Russians seem determined to leave unilaterally if they can't get agreement on how to leave; there's the Indo-Pakistan conflict, which is very serious but could be reduced if you get an Afghanistan settlement; there are the problems America faces with her bases in South Korea and the Philippines; in Africa you've got the Soviet stake in Angola and Ethiopia, though there are some signs they may be prepared at least to give it up in Angola; in Central America you've got Nicaragua, El Salvador, Guatemala, and possibly Mexico. But by far the most important area is the Middle East, because that's where the great powers are most directly involved close to one another – partly in the Gulf, partly in the western Middle East, the Levant, as we used to call it, over the Palestinian problem.

I haven't obviously time to run over what I think would be the right answers here. All I would say is that it's quite clear that Mr Shultz and Mr

Shevardnadze have already identified these as the problems. The question is whether they are yet prepared to make the concessions to one another and to stand up to the very severe pressures that one of them at least is under, to move in the right direction, so as to make the settlement possible. But there is a general point I'd like to make about that, and that's one that was raised by de Gaulle twenty years ago. You may remember, some of you, that de Gaulle worried an enormous amount about the Russians and Americans trying to establish a condominium and trying to settle the problems of the world without looking at the interests of anybody else. Certainly, they could not do that. On many of these issues the agreement of other countries is required, and I think the big question now is whether we can give more meaning to the United Nations as an organization which might create a framework for solving some of these regional problems. There seems to be half agreement in principle to this where the Israeli-Arab problem is concerned, though it was rejected by the American government so far as the Gulf is concerned. It seems to me that the place to start is the Gulf – to have a United Nations force protecting shipping which is moving up to Kuwait and Iran. Another obvious place of course would be the frontier between Honduras and Nicaragua, if the Latin American countries were prepared to accept it.

I'll just finish with a word or two about how this complex of problems and this sort of approach I recommend would affect us in Europe. What has happened in Europe in the last thirty years is that nationalism in Western Europe is at a very low ebb. The real problems in Western Europe tend to be inside countries, between the Walloons and the Flemings for example, or the Basques and the French and the Spanish. Nationalism in Eastern Europe seems to be reviving. I found when I was in Hungary last year that the hostility between Hungary and Romania over Transylvania is the sort of thing that could explode into fighting at almost any time. On the other hand, I think that contacts between Eastern Europe and Western Europe are becoming very close. Maria Theresa reigns again in Budapest: Austria and Hungary have very close relations indeed. And the relations between East and West Germany are peculiar to say the least; because of the tariff agreement, the DDR is practically part of the Common Market. I discovered when I was in Dresden last year that the East German government had had to set up a relay station for West German television in Saxony because people wouldn't go and work there unless they could watch their favourite programmes from Western Germany. These new links are extremely interesting and in many ways are taking place below the surface of what the press reports. I think myself that the West European countries can play an important role in easing the transition towards a more liberal system in Eastern Europe through bilateral contacts, and my impression is that this is the view of President Mitterand.

Looking further ahead the crystal becomes very clouded. Russia is facing terrible problems with her own nationalities. If not already, certainly within a year or two, the Europeans will be in a minority in the Soviet Union, partly because the birthrate in the Asian republics is so much higher. There is a deep resentment in Moscow that the Georgians, Armenians, and the Balts have higher living standards than the members of the Russian Republic. Now these strains – which we saw expressed in the recent troubles between Azerbaijan and Armenia – present many dangers as well as opportunities, and I don't think we in the West and perhaps the leaders in Moscow don't understand the problem very well and still less know how to control it. All I would say is that if we can establish greater predictability and stability in West-Soviet relations, we'll produce a framework which is more conducive to these problems being survived without a major risk of war.

However much as an Englishman I deplore it, the main responsibility in the West for responding to these opportunities must lie with the United States of America – partly because it's the government which the Russians are most concerned about, and partly of course because its power is still infinitely greater than that of any individual country in the West. I would like to see the European countries getting together so that they could operate more independently in the political field, but the divisions between Britain, France and Germany on defence questions alone make that seem very unlikely at the moment. But this is why we in Europe are watching your elections in the United States so closely. We all pray that your elections will produce an administration which has at least some of the breadth of vision, generosity of spirit, and constructive energy and honesty in facing reality which was shown in the golden age of American policy – in the ten years following the end of the Second World War when Truman and Acheson were in charge and George Ball was playing a major role.

BRITAIN AFTER THE COLD WAR

(House of Commons, 14 July 1989)

I hope that the hon. Member for Leominster (Mr Temple-Morris) will forgive me if I do not follow him, except to reminisce that when I first attended the Council of Europe in the early postwar years one of the French Union delegates failed to return from the summer recess because he had been eaten by his constituents. There is a risk in being a member of some parliaments that fortunately does not exist in our own.

I wish to echo the excellent speech of my hon. Friend the Member for Hamilton (Mr Robertson) and to describe both the opportunities and the dangers presented by the end of the Cold War and Britain's role in meeting that challenge. The Cold War is over. That is proved in a million ways. It is proved by the continuing talks on arms control and reduction between the Soviet Union and the United States. More importantly, and more convincingly, it is proved by the co-operation between the Soviet Union and the United States in areas of tension in many parts of the world.

In the Middle East, for example, the Soviet Union is currently trying to shift the policies of both Syria and Iraq into more constructive directions. The United States and the Soviet Union, almost single-handed but with useful assistance from the British government, produced the recent agreement on Angola. In the Far East, co-operation between the superpowers seems likely to produce a settlement of the appallingly difficult problem of Kampuchea, and even in Central America, Mr Shevardnadze recently handed President Bush a message indicating that the Soviet Union is ceasing its supply of arms to Nicaragua.

In the light of all that evidence, it is ridiculous to pretend that the situation is as it was even two or three years ago. Even more important in some ways is the fact that glasnost, which was introduced by Mr Gorbachev, has finally destroyed Communism as an international force. Now that the Russians themselves admit the appalling state of their economy, and the weaknesses in their present democracy, and now that the world has seen the response of the Chinese Communist leadership to democratic protest by the students in Tiananmen Square, it is not possible now to regard Communism as a threat to international stability. Some Communist Parties might be a threat, but the international Communist menace has gone for ever.

However, I hope that we are beginning to realize that the Cold War, by dividing the more powerful countries into two blocs under Soviet and American leadership, gave much of the world forty years of moderate stability. If the opposing alliances had not existed, it is difficult to feel confident that Turkey would not by now have been at war with Greece, and, in Eastern Europe, Hungary at war with Romania. The ending of the

Cold War has allowed the nationalisms that were suppressed in the opposing blocs to come to the surface again.

That is challenging many elements of stability in the modern world. Not only the Yalta settlement, which most of us would wish never to have been adopted, but even the settlement of Versailles is at risk in the present troubles in Yugoslavia. Concepts that were last familiar before the First World War are now re-emerging as forces in international affairs. For example, the concept of Mittel Europa is now attractive to many Germans, Austrians, Poles, Czechs and Slovenes. We now face a world that is changing fundamentally as a result of the ending of the Cold War.

Glasnost – the introduction of more openness in the Soviet Union – is now threatening the unity of the Soviet Union itself. After all, Russia is the last nineteenth-century empire to have survived until nearly the end of the twentieth century. In recent meetings of the Soviet Parliament we have seen very powerful national forces showing themselves in the Baltic states, in Georgia and in the Asian republics. All of them, to a greater or lesser degree, want something that they would call independence. How the Soviet Union comes to terms with this new wave of nationalism and what consequences it may have for stability in adjoining parts of the world is sometimes somewhat alarming to contemplate.

I noticed that, in a recent meeting of the Soviet Parliament, one Russian delegate even suggested that, if things go on like this, Russia should secede from the Union of Soviet Socialist Republics. In the Russian Republic now there is an extreme nationalist movement called Pamyat, although, fortunately, it did not win any seats in the recent elections.

One might think that, in some respects, the world is set for a return to the politics of the nineteenth century, but we cannot afford to return to the politics of the nineteenth century because the world cannot afford any more wars, even wars with conventional weapons. Science has created certain global problems that can be satisfactorily dealt with only by global solutions under the auspices of global organizations. We are all very familiar with the problems created by nuclear power, both in its civil and military forms, and we are becoming more aware of the problems created by chemical pollution which, like nuclear problems, recognizes no frontiers and can be dealt with only by international action.

As I said when I spoke in our last foreign affairs debate nearly a year ago, it is a reflection of Britain's diminished role in the world, and indeed of Britain's diminished interest in the world, that we so rarely debate foreign affairs in their broader aspects. We used to have four or five two-day foreign affairs debates every year when I first entered the House about 40 years ago.

There is an overwhelming case, as I said last time, for trying to develop the United Nations as originally intended, as the basis of a world society, with appropriate institutions to fulfil that role. For the first time since the United Nations was set up, Mr Gorbachev has created the conditions on which that might be done. For its first forty years, the United Nations could not work as the charter envisaged because the Soviet Union did not believe that a world society was desirable or possible. I am sorry to say that the only person who still holds that view is the British Prime Minister, who believes that the word society has no meaning either at home or abroad. I will discuss the implications of her position in a moment.

Action on those problems is now extremely urgent for two reasons. First, as my hon. Friend the Member for Hamilton said, we cannot be certain that Mr Gorbachev will remain leader of the Soviet Union for the rest of his natural life. There is a growing and dangerous gap between his ideas and Soviet reality. That gap is well expressed in the saying that glasnost has given the dog more freedom to bark as perestroika pushes its food bowl further away. The deterioration in the Soviet economy over the past few years is bound to create dangerous tensions in the Soviet Union, and could lead to some changes of direction in Soviet domestic policy, although not to any significant change in Soviet external policy. The facts that produced the change in Soviet foreign policy under Mr Gorbachev are facts whether or not he is there and are bound to influence his successors, if he goes, as much as they have influenced him.

There is a second reason why the problem is urgent. We have imagined far too lightly that the problems of world peace and stability are mainly for the superpowers and their allies. We now see military missile technology spreading fast all over the world. Already twenty-two Third World countries have missile programmes, and seventeen have already deployed missiles. Some of those countries either already have nuclear weapons or the capacity to acquire them quite fast. In all cases, they could use missiles to fire the poor man's nuclear weapon, chemical weapons, a problem to which my hon. Friend rightly paid attention.

Unless we can proceed much faster than governments presently seem prepared to envisage in building an international framework through the United Nations for coming to grips with some of the problems, we may find that this weather window – this moment of opportunity – is passing. The new situation creates special problems for us in Europe. I will mention a few of the more obvious.

How can we help East European peoples to return to the community of

Europe, which is not necessarily the same thing as the European Community? How can we reconcile the return of East European peoples to Europe with the desire of the European Community in its narrower sense to strengthen its internal cohesion? That problem raises some difficult questions, which, I am sorry to say, the Minister of State, Foreign and Commonwealth Office dodged when I asked her about the government's attitude to the Austrian application for membership of the European Community – an application which may be followed in the next year or two by applications from Sweden and Finland, and it is possible to envisage applications by Poland and Hungary within four or five years.

The question of how, if this development proceeds, the inevitable dilution of the European Community can be reconciled with many European countries' desire to increase the internal coherence of the existing Community will create some difficult problems for us quite soon – perhaps even in the coming months.

Another question that we must consider is whether it is possible to Finlandize Eastern Europe, which has rightly been described as a sensible objective, without Finlandizing at least parts of Western Europe. That raises some very difficult questions. When he opened the debate for the opposition my hon. Friend the Member for Hamilton rightly criticized President Bush for offering so little financial economic assistance to Poland. I do not quite understand why the European Community, which is now as wealthy as the United States, should not take the lead in offering financial and economic assistance to Eastern Europe, a lead that it would be much easier for the Soviet Union to accept than a lead by the United States. So far, however, apart from a very interesting speech this week by ex-President Giscard d'Estaing, there has rarely been even speculation about these problems by any of the Western European leaders, least of all, I fear, by our own Prime Minister.

The central question that bulked so large in the recent NATO meeting was how, in the new situation, to meet the special needs and fears of that newly created state, the Federal Republic of Germany, which is already feeling the pull of the concept of Mittel Europa that to many Germans is another word for Gross Deutschland. [HON. MEMBERS: 'Hear, hear.'] It is all right for hon. Members to say, 'Hear, hear', but these problems are with us now and underlie many of the tensions that were evident at the last summit.

With some reluctance I turn to what Britain is doing in this extremely challenging though sometimes dangerous but also hopeful new situation that has been created by the end of the Cold War. As I said earlier, one problem is that the present Prime Minister rejects the mere concept of society. She says that the word has no meaning. She rejects it – as we saw at NATO and at the recent European summit at Madrid – just as much in the international context as in the national context. She has nothing to say on these issues, except to go round the world parroting about the need to protect national sovereignty. However, by agreeing to deregulate the British financial markets and by taking the lead, as the right hon. Lady the Minister of State said, in asking for an open industrial and commercial market in Europe by 1992, she has abandoned British sovereignty. No one knows better than the Chancellor of the Exchequer that he is no longer master of his own economic and financial policies. He can be blown off course by events not only in Europe but in Latin America the United States and any other part of the world. We enter the new period in a somewhat dangerous position – very much weaker, relative to our partners, than we have ever been before.

Today's summit in Paris has exposed Britain's economic weakness. In its report the other day, the OECD pointed out that Britain has now lost fifth place among the world's largest economies to Italy. For the last two years we have been producing less than Italy. We have higher inflation now than Italy, something which would have been inconceivable to many of us a few years ago. It is obviously unfamiliar to many of the bemused faces which I have stirred out of their hebetude on the Conservative benches. I am not, of course, talking about the government representatives on the Treasury bench.

Mr Waldegrave: The Labour government managed to get United Kingdom inflation far above that of Italy.

Mr Healey: No, with respect, they did not. The interesting point about the inflation gap between Britain and her European partners is that it was much lower when we were in power because inflation generally was much higher. It was pointed out in the *Financial Times* the other day – I apologize for responding to a sedentary intervention by the minister of state – that the big difference between the time when we were in power and now is that the terms of trade deteriorated by 17 per cent in the industrial countries during the 1970s. During the eight years of this decade that deterioration has been reversed. That is the main reason why inflation has been a much less serious problem, but the gap between the British inflation rate and that of our European partners is larger now than it was. At no time when the Labour Party was in power was our inflation rate higher than that of Italy.

As my hon. Friend the Member for Hamilton pointed out, we now have higher inflation, higher interest rates and a bigger balance of payments deficit than any of our major competitors and any of our colleagues in Western Europe. That is not a good position from which a British Prime Minister can influence the policy of Britain's partners in any of the international organizations to which we belong. Unfortunately, the Prime Minister has not, like Mr Gorbachev, removed ideology from the sphere of international relations. She finds it almost impossible to make a speech these days which is not redolent with comic strip nationalist ideology – the only ideology, apart from that of the market, with which she is familiar.

During the last year the right hon. Lady has met every challenge by insulting all her allies simultaneously, which is a very odd way for the prime minister of a country that has been reduced to weakness to talk. She accused President Kohl and Mr Genscher of 'wriggling' after the last NATO summit. She insulted President Mitterrand repeatedly at some press conferences, as I see the minister of state, the hon. Member for Bristol, West (Mr Waldegrave), recalls. Although she has not yet told us so, it is quite clear that she regards President Bush as an upper-class wimp, so wet that one could shoot snipe off him. However, it has not helped Britain, or even the Prime Minister, to add the diplomacy of Alf Garnett to the economics of Arthur Daley. However, that is the twin blessing that she has showered on us in recent years.

As I pointed out in the House the other day, the Prime Minister instructed Mr Bernard Ingham to tell the *Daily Telegraph* correspondent that she was going to help Kohl to screw Genscher. Instead, Kohl helped Genscher to screw her, and he did very successfully. I apologize for the word, Mr Deputy Speaker, but it is Mr Ingham's not mine. I should have been infinitely more delicate in referring to the operation that was carried out.

The Prime Minister even rewrote the whole of British history by telling the French this week that they should not be so proud of liberty, equality and fraternity because we first introduced it in Magna Carta. I learnt some history when I was a little boy. My impression was that Magna Carta had been imposed on a wicked British king by the barons. It brought no freedom to the ordinary people of our country. If the ideals of liberty, equality and fraternity existed before the age of enlightenment in eighteenth-century France, I suppose they existed among some members of the Roundhead group in the English Civil War, notably among the Levellers.

That has not done the Prime Minister very much good, either. I read this morning, to my horror, that our Prime Minister was booed by the people of Paris when she appeared yesterday at a ceremony to commemorate the rights of man. I suggest that we all write a letter to her, offering our support, as she may find that essential. I understand that tonight the right hon. Lady will be accused by the French prime minister on Channel 4 television of what he calls her 'social cruelty' – a nice phrase that will figure more often in our debates in the future.

The Prime Minister has isolated herself in Europe, in NATO and in the Commonwealth and has done so at a time of our greatest relative economic weakness. I should like to make a timid suggestion because I want to help the Prime Minister to overcome the problems created by what my Peruvian psychiatrist friend rightly described as – what was it? I have forgotten it, but it will come back in a moment. The Prime Minister would do well to confine her rottweiler politics to her Cabinet colleagues, who are now quite used to the virago intacta and who, in any case, never feel it possible to answer back.

Better still – I am being daring in making the suggestion in the presence of the right hon. Lady's two loyal advocates on the government Front Bench – would it not be a good idea to let the foreign secretary run British foreign policy and to give the Foreign Office a look in? The Box is strangely depleted now and I suspect that that is because three of the civil servants have gone out to divide *Das Kapital* into sections and to find out which particular section justifies the Prime Minister in describing the European Community's Social Charter as a Marxist document.

What is odd and disturbing about the Prime Minister is her position on Europe and especially on the need for some institutional structure to underpin the open market which she wants and which the minister of state has told us that she is working so hard to achieve. It is not a wild idea to say that, just as the horrors in Peking, which the House debated yesterday, came about because the freeing of the market was not accompanied by the creation of democratic institutions to regulate and control it, so the freeing of the European market could lead to appalling disturbances and disruptions, unless it is accompanied by institutions capable of regulating and controlling it, of which the proposals in the social charter can undoubtedly be one.

It is now clear that, if the Prime Minister is serious about environmental problems, she must agree that the rich countries should help the poor countries to adopt techniques for, for example, freezing food, which do not involve destroying the ozone layer. If she wants to deal with the drugs problem, the rich countries will have to help the poor countries, which depend on growing crops which produce drugs, to find alternative ways of making a living. There are many such countries in Latin America and in southern Asia.

Until the Prime Minister takes off the rusting and decrepit mediaeval armour which she loves so much and returns from her time-warp to join us all in the twentieth century, Britain will remain, as she has alas become, an irritating irrelevance in world affairs whose importance does not even require a response.

REVOLUTION THAT COULD LEAD TO ANARCHY

(Observer, November 1989)

No one of my generation can watch the people's revolution in Eastern Europe without exhilaration. We spent six years of our youth fighting to prevent one form of totalitarianism from conquering the whole of Europe. Then we found another form of totalitarianism riveted on half of our continent.

To many, Communist totalitarianism seemed irreversible. New techniques of brain-washing and thought control made George Orwell's nightmare of 1984 appear a sober projection of reality. We now know from official Soviet sources that the true horror of Stalinism was even worse than we imagined. Few had the historical knowledge which enabled George Kennan to predict that containment would lead to the mellowing of the Soviet system, since its corruption and incompetence would breed the seeds of its own decay. And no one could imagine that the system would throw up a leader with the courage and imagination of Mikhail Gorbachev.

Gorbachev rightly saw that in the nuclear age the massive arsenal of Soviet military power had only limited political value, and could never be used in war. He knew he could not reconstruct his economy without cutting military spending and ending the Cold War. He rightly saw that he could not hope to generate popular support without giving the people the facts – through glasnost. But I doubt if even he foresaw the strength of the forces he was liberating by ending the Cold War and telling the truth about the Soviet Union. Nor did any government in the West.

The crumbling of the Berlin Wall marks the end of the postwar order in

Europe. It presents the West with new challenges for which it is quite unprepared. Yet for the Soviet leaders it must appear as far less threatening than the spreading disintegration of the empire which Lenin inherited from the Tsars. Georgiy Arbatov told an American audience the other day that Gorbachev would react to the secession of a Soviet republic as Lincoln had reacted to the secession of the southern states. But the Civil War cost America more lives than all its later wars put together; and America had then only a third of the population it has today. The American Civil War was not fought between different nations with different religions, a civil war in the Soviet Union would be.

The revolution in Eastern Europe, as in the Soviet Union, is in part a revolution for national independence. This new nationalism is no less powerful outside the frontiers of Soviet power; it threatens to break up Yugoslavia and set Greece and Turkey at each other's throats. Yet Europe cannot afford another series of Balkan wars. And independence is no answer to national feeling when the boundaries of potential nation states enclose powerful minorities which want independence as much as the majorities. Britain has learnt this in Northern Ireland as well as Spain in the Basque country, and Azerbaijan in Nagorno Karabakh.

The most important challenge facing mankind after the end of the Cold War is to devise new political structures which will accommodate such national feelings. These structures must also be compatible with the new international economic and financial structures created by modern technology.

The nationalist revolution and the economic revolution are marching to the sound of different drums. In Eastern Europe they are also accompanied by a political revolution which aims to sweep away all the bureaucratic structures created by the discredited Communist regimes. History can help us here. The revolutionary overthrow of all existing institutions can produce an anarchy with which liberal democracy finds it impossible to cope. France after 1789 and Russia after 1917 were thus impelled into dictatorship. Yet the waves of popular revolt which swept Europe in 1848 and again in 1968 crumbled before the forces of reaction because the liberal intelligentsia had not succeeded in destroying the power of the state – and had little idea how to use power if they won it themselves. Such lessons should serve as a warning against some of the easy optimism spread in the West by the events in the Communist world.

I myself believe that such dangers may present far more difficult problems than the reunification of Germany, which the crumbling of the Berlin Wall has suddenly made appear so imminent. Half the population of Eastern Germany has already fled to the Federal Republic since 1944. What is left would constitute only one fifth of the population of a reunited Germany and under one tenth of its economic strength. Moreover, Bonn insisted on making Honecker's DDR a country member of the European Community many years ago.

The Federal Republic is already the strongest power in Western Europe. It enjoys a vast trade surplus with its Community partners, particularly Britain. The EMS is a deutschmark zone; and the German Bundesbank already controls interest rates in Britain though we are outside the Exchange Rate Mechanism – as Nigel Lawson learnt to his cost.

In fact of all the European countries on either side of the dividing line, the Germans seem to be the least nationalistic these days. They are also the most enthusiastic for strengthening relations with the East European countries like Poland. For those who worry about German reunification the liberation of Eastern Europe offers us the opportunity of reducing Germany's present preponderance, providing we are prepared to bring its states into a close relationship with the European Community – if not full membership – as soon as they prove their democratic credentials. It is difficult to see how strengthening the cohesion of the existing Community would somehow 'control Germany' as the French seem to believe. In the new situation a West European federation or defence community is impossible, whatever the Euro-fanatics may believe. So we should not make the impossible best the enemy of the possible good.

Meanwhile there is one problem which will not wait. There is a real risk that the current revolution in Eastern Europe may produce unforeseen and uncontrollable explosions. If they are not to lead to war, we must press on with a new security system covering both halves of Europe; it must be based on co-operation between NATO and the Warsaw Pact in the reduction and control of armaments, and in restructuring their forces so that they become incapable of offensive action.

Washington and Moscow must be involved. Europe could not construct such a system without them. Fortunately they seem determined to press for an agreement in this area within twelve months at most; it is Britain and France which are dragging their feet. If the French continue to oppose such talks between the two alliances, we should proceed without them – as they would proceed without Britain towards European monetary union, if Mrs Thatcher continues to oppose it.

One thing is certain. Britain has everything to gain and nothing to lose by taking an active role in developing constructive policies both in NATO and the European Community for confronting the tremendous opportunities, and dangers, created by the revolution in Eastern Europe. History will not forgive us for hanging back.

THE RICH CAN BEAT TANKS INTO PLOUGHSHARES

(*Observer*, December 1989)

The eighties started as a decade of confrontation fuelled by ideology at home as well as abroad. The nineties should be a decade of co-operation driven by pragmatism.

It will no longer be possible for Europe to rely on Washington and Moscow, even if, as I believe, the superpowers wish to work together to produce a new framework. Both are now in decline, and increasingly preoccupied with problems inside, or just across, their own borders. They recognize that their colossal nuclear arsenals are unusable in war and even their massive conventional forces confer very limited political influence in peace.

The most urgent single challenge of the nineties is to cut defence spending drastically, and to restructure the forces which remain both in NATO and the Warsaw Pact so that they become incapable of major offensive action, but are appropriate for helping to manage the conflicts which may arise while a new political framework is developed.

This framework must satisfy the resurgent nationalisms on both sides, while remaining compatible with the internationalization of finance and industry, and with the global problems of environmental pollution.

It is no longer realistic, if it ever was, to think of the European Community as playing a military role even on its own continent. It is equally unrealistic to see it as an instrument for controlling a united Germany. West Germany will continue to dominate the Community in the coming decade, more still if, as is likely, it forms at least an economic union with East Germany.

If the two parts of Germany become one, the new state will fit more comfortably into a framework which includes also its northern and eastern neighbours; indeed the 'Common European House' might well take in the Baltic states and European Russia too.

The Community cannot afford to wait until after 1992 to consider these problems. In practice it has already achieved almost all that is likely to be achieved in the drive for a 'single European market'.

Besides the patent ambivalence of the Bonn government about any further steps which might complicate the movement towards German reunification, Italy is positioning itself to help Austria and perhaps Hungary into the Community. With the end of the Cold War and the search for a pan-European unity, the neutrality of Sweden, Switzerland, and Finland seems as archaic as that of Austria.

In any case, the countries of Western Europe have the most powerful common interest in giving the new democracies of Eastern Europe massive political, economic and technical aid. So far, Romania – where the desire for revenge comes close to the desire for freedom, and the army is playing a decisive role – is the only country where revolution stirs uneasy memories of 1789. But Poland and Hungary will have to suffer savage cuts in their living standards as part of their essential monetary and price reforms; these cuts may prove incompatible with their new-found democracy unless Western Europe is willing to cushion the shock. Only disarmament would permit an adequate transfer of resources from defence to foreign aid.

At this point, however, it is no longer possible for the West to continue ignoring the problems of the Third World as it did in the eighties. Since 1980 the gap between the rich and poor nations of the world has been widening for the first time since the end of the Second World War; 200 million more people are now living in absolute poverty. In Latin America output has been rising only 1 per cent a year, as against 10 per cent for most of the seventies. Since population has been increasing much faster, living standards have been falling heavily. Latin America's foreign debt is still rising.

To service their debts, the poorest countries in the world are now exporting $50 billion a year to the richest. Meanwhile, two of the richest, the United States and Britain, are drawing heavily on the limited pool of world savings to finance their economic profligacy; these savings must now be diverted to help the Third World.

Western selfishness may have catastrophic consequences if it continues in the nineties. Many bankers who have previously supported the current strategy for dealing with the debts of the Third World now recognize that the capacity of their victims to continue on the path to suicide is almost at an end. The risk of massive default, leading to the collapse of the Western banking system, is growing week by week.

Economic disaster will breed revolution and nationalism. Panama may prove to be the spark which starts the conflagration. American sanctions have already cut the country's output by a quarter, and the invasion has dealt the economy a body blow; by installing a rich white oligarchy in

Noriega's place President Bush may have condemned his troops to a prolonged guerrilla war which will unite the whole continent against him.

Meanwhile, there is a growing danger that desperate countries in the Third World may turn to war for a way out. Richard Cheney, America's secretary for defence, has warned that by the end of the nineties, fifteen states may have their own nuclear weapons. Twenty-seven countries in the Third World already have missiles to carry them – and the capacity to make chemical weapons too. These developments pose particular dangers in the Middle East, the Indian sub-continent, and southern Africa. Disarmament is far too urgent a problem to be confined to the superpowers and their allies while China, India, and Israel are excluded.

The decline of the superpowers, the end of the Cold War, and the insistent problems of the Third World all point in one direction. There must be a massive transfer of resources worldwide from defence to development.

The NATO and Warsaw Pact countries must cease supplying the weapons with which the Third World is fighting its wars and ruining its economies. The nineties must see the world move back to the postwar assumption that the United Nations should be the core of all foreign and economic policy.

Only Gorbachev has made this point, and he seems equally anxious to give the international economic organizations like GATT, the IMF and the World Bank a central role. So far, the West has failed to respond to his challenge, or even to test its sincerity. The United States is starving all the international agencies of the funds they need. Britain seems to see the United Nations simply as a device to assist the West in dealing with its own problems of crime, drugs, terrorism, and the environment – as a glorified instrument for riot control.

Whether the world can really move from confrontation to consensus in the nineties will depend above all on its will and ability to make the United Nations into the framework for a world society. An intelligent pragmatism will settle for nothing less.

TIME TO SHUT DOWN THE ARMS BAZAAR

(*Observer*, April 1990)

The end of the Cold War has made it possible for the Soviet Union and the West to cut their defence spending. It has done nothing to slow the arms race in the Third World. On the contrary, the arms industries in the West will now seek new markets for their wares, and Western governments are already planning to sell off, or even give away, their surplus weapons to developing countries which cannot afford to buy them as new.

Many governments in the Third World are already building up arsenals of sophisticated weapons – chemical and biological as well as nuclear – and are buying or even producing for themselves the means to deliver them hundreds or thousands of miles away. The Iraqi supergun may have been intended for this purpose; the missiles already acquired by countries outside the Eastern and Western blocs certainly are.

Besides the United States, the Soviet Union, Britain, France and China, which boast their possession of nuclear weapons, India and Israel are known to have them – the latter thanks to large-scale assistance from America. At least six other countries are believed to have military nuclear programmes.

Over the forty-five years in which the Soviet-Western confrontation maintained peace in Europe and the seas around it, nearly twenty million people may have died and many times more were rendered homeless by fighting in the Third World.

Some of this fighting involved Russia and the West, but the vast majority of these armed conflicts had wholly local causes – not least the artificial frontiers which were bequeathed to so much of the Third World by Western imperialism. Events since the end of the Cold War remind us, however, that most of the frontiers in Europe and the Soviet Union are no less artificial. In fact, it is rarely possible to draw frontiers round any nation state without including minorities of another nationality which would like a state of their own.

So the world now confronts again the problem it failed to solve after 1918 and 1945 – to create an international society which is able to solve such disputes peacefully, and which can limit and control national armaments. Though Washington and Moscow have made a useful start on controlling their own nuclear weapons, they have so far done little to reduce their total number. Their allies have yet to conclude their first agreement on the reduction of conventional forces.

If the arms race in the Third World continues along present lines, it is difficult to imagine Russia and the West continuing their mutual disarmament much further. Faced with the possible secession of its Asian republics, Moscow cannot be indifferent to the spread of sophisticated weapons beyond its southern frontiers. So long as China has nuclear weapons neither the Soviet Union nor the United States can reduce their nuclear forces below a certain level.

Inside the Third World itself, a nuclear India pushes Pakistan to seek nuclear weapons, as a nuclear Israel pushes the Arabs. If either Argentina or Brazil produces a nuclear weapon, the other is bound to follow. Yet none of the potential nuclear powers will take the Non-Proliferation Treaty seriously so long as two of its nuclear signatories, Britain and France, absolutely refuse to carry out their treaty obligation to negotiate a reduction in their nuclear forces, as Moscow and Washington have been doing for many years.

The arms race in the Third World is largely fuelled by weapons from members of Nato and the Warsaw Pact. Two-thirds of Britain's arms exports go to the Third World. In the West the United States, France and Britain are the main culprits, in the East the Soviet Union, Czechoslovakia and East Germany. It is now urgently necessary to reach agreement between at least these suppliers and China to limit such arms exports, particularly to the Middle East.

One effective instrument for limiting the arms race in the Middle East would be to refuse export credits to countries which bought arms abroad. Iraq could not have afforded to buy its supergun if Whitehall did not finance its civil purchases from Britain. Though the Government justified its pusillanimity over the murder of Farzad Bazoft by our interest in trade with Iraq, that trade is mainly financed by loans from Britain. Similarly, any scheme for large-scale debt relief to the Latin American countries should be dependent on heavy cuts in their arms spending.

There is just time to stop one major new threat to peace in the Third World, by preventing the sale or gift of weapons made surplus by disarmament agreements between Nato and the Warsaw powers. The Pentagon recently agreed to give 700 surplus M60A1 tanks to Egypt and another 110 M60s to Greece. This will lead to demands from Israel and Turkey for the remaining 120 M60s still waiting for customers. These transfers result from unilateral cuts in America's defence budget; possible arms cuts in Europe would produce far greater surpluses.

The Soviet press has reported on the illegal sale of surplus Soviet tanks to the Third World; whether there have also been legal transfers of the enormous surpluses of Soviet weapons we do not know. All the formidable modern weapons of the East German army are already surplus, since it is agreed that they can have no role after unification.

West Germany's Foreign Minister, Hans-Dietrich Genscher, so often the only Western statesman to show any imagination in confronting the world after the Cold War, has proposed that the forthcoming agreement on Conventional Forces in Europe should 'prohibit either side reducing its arsenal by selling weapon systems at discount rates to Third World states'. This is surely the minimum on which both sides should be able to agree. Another obvious step towards halting the arms race in the Third World, also proposed by Mr Genscher, would be a mandatory United Nations register of all arms deals.

Such decisions could and should be taken now. They would at least show the Third World that the West was serious about disarmament and that Mikhail Gorbachev meant what he said about the central role of the United Nations in security after the Cold War.

Other necessary steps could be more painful for some governments. It will be impossible to persuade the Third World that the West is serious about the Non-Proliferation Treaty until Britain and France start negotiating to reduce their nuclear arsenals instead of continuing to build them up. Nor is it reasonable to ask the Arab states to observe the NPT so long as Israel refuses even to sign it.

At present the West is preoccupied with the implications of German unity and the collapse of European Communism. But unless it begins to take the arms race in the Third World seriously, the problems of the new Europe may soon seem marginal in comparison.

THE CARAVAN OF HISTORY WILL LEAVE US BEHIND

(Observer, February 1990)

OBE or 'Overtaken by Events'. That is how weary diplomats describe the negotiations going on nowadays about disarmament, East-West relations and German reunification.

One glance at the political timetable for 1990 will illustrate the problem. In March the East Germans will elect their first democratic government – probably putting the Social Democrats in power – and serious negotiations on German Monetary Union will begin.

In June Bush and Gorbachev will hold a summit to sign treaties on reducing their strategic nuclear weapons, and on conventional force cuts in Europe too, if they stick to the timetable set last May.

The meeting of Germany's four postwar occupying powers to wrap up their residual responsibilities and fix the frontiers of a united Germany will follow the agreement of the governments of Eastern and Western Germany to form a single state – probably this summer. In the autumn the thirty-five members of the Helsinki Agreement will meet to discuss security and co-operation in Europe.

Meanwhile, by early July at the latest, the Congress of the Soviet Communist Party will have met to ratify the recent decisions of the Soviet Communist Party which open the way to political pluralism and a greater role for the market economy. This Congress may well have to accept the fact that the Communist Parties in many of the Soviet republics refuse to accept its central authority and are campaigning for the secession from the Soviet state itself.

The possible break-up of the Soviet Union will raise major military issues. Who will then control Soviet nuclear weapons, many of which are sited and tested in the Asian republics? Who will control Soviet conventional forces, which now rely on non-Russians for their recruits?

Against this timetable, decisions must be taken in the next few months which will decide the future of Europe, and perhaps of the whole world. Events in Eastern Germany may now force governments to telescope their decisions.

The liberal intelligentsia of the Civic Forum who organized the revolution last November did not put reunification high on their agenda, and now feel like a young virgin being forced to marry a rich and ugly millionaire, as one of them said last week. But the ordinary people of East Germany see reunification as the only escape from an economic disaster which worsens every hour.

Any setback to the prospects for early reunification could turn the stream of East Germans crossing over to the West into a tidal wave. If the price and currency reforms required as a condition of German Monetary Union throw a million East Germans out of work, that million will join the flood. East Germany might well be compelled simply to announce without notice that it is part of Western Germany, as it is empowered to do by a constitution which the Western allies agreed.

So the question of a united Germany's place in NATO could demand an answer at any moment, and with it the broader question of what role, if any, NATO has in a Europe where it is the only surviving military bloc, and its enemy has evaporated into thin air.

I find it difficult to believe that the government of a united Germany of whatever party, will want to remain part of NATO in its present form. At present there seems to be a popular majority for neutrality in both parts of Germany. Yet neutrality has no meaning, when there are no longer two blocs to be neutral between; this will prove as true of Austria, Sweden and Switzerland as of a united Germany.

Neutralism would of course be possible if that means the steadfast refusal to involve oneself in the security problems of the European continent. But it would be highly undesirable. And it would be highly undesirable for the rest of Europe to find the strongest economy freeloading for its security on the weaker ones.

The Balkanization of Eastern Europe, the disintegration of the Soviet Union in its present form, and intractable economic problems between the Elbe and the Urals will produce political instability which could lead to armed conflicts; so it is urgent to establish a new security system involving all the countries of Europe.

In its initial stages at least, such a system would require the co-operation of the Soviet Union and the United States, if only to reassure some of Germany's neighbours. That is why the Polish and Czech democrats are no longer in such a hurry to get rid of all Soviet troops.

And although the Warsaw Pact no longer presents a military threat, NATO could still play a useful role in producing a Western consensus on how to develop that new European security system which Bush and Gorbachev both agree is now desirable.

The talks about such a system, starting in June with the Bush-Gorbachev summit and continuing with the CSCE meeting in the autumn, must involve Germany's eastern neighbours no less than NATO, as the Polish prime minister rightly insisted last week. It would be wise to set up a working group now, to include all the present members of NATO and the Warsaw Pact, and to maintain contact with those other members of the Helsinki Agreement who wish to be involved, particularly Sweden.

NATO was a creation of the Cold War, and its major military function has now disappeared. But in 1967, by adopting the Harmel Report, it committed itself to achieve a just and lasting peaceful order in Europe, accompanied by appropriate security guarantees. If it is to survive in any form now that the Cold War is over, this must be its task.

But in that case it must abandon the bloc mentality altogether. It must cease using Rentathreat tactics to prolong its present military role. That role is increasingly uncongenial not only to its most important members, West Germany and the USA, but also to the vast majority of people, on both sides of the Atlantic, who are still waiting in vain to turn their tanks into tractors, as Douglas Hurd recommended.

Mrs Thatcher, however, has already rejected Hurd's approach. Congenitally incapable of accepting change, she wants to stop the world and get off. So Britain is now as isolated in NATO as in the Common Market and the Commonwealth.

Yet Britain has more to gain than any other country from the creation of a new security system, with much smaller forces restructured so that they are incapable of large-scale aggression. We still spend 50 per cent more of our wealth on defence than our European neighbours, though we are further from what Mrs Thatcher claims as a threat and desperately need to cut our defence spending not only to rebuild our social and economic infrastructure but also to help stabilize Eastern Europe and the Third World.

The Arabs have a saying: 'The dog barks, but the caravan passes.' How much longer must we continue yelping in the desert as the caravan proceeds over the horizon, carrying with it all our hopes for the future?

ASKING THE RIGHT QUESTIONS

(from a lecture at Churchill College, Cambridge, 15 May 1990)

The forty years since the defeat of Hitler were dominated by a Cold War between the Soviet Union and the West; this was reflected in an arms race on which the two sides are still, in 1990, spending about $400 billion a year, deploying about 4.5 million men on active service, and have deployed about 30,000 nuclear weapons – all this in the European area alone. On top of that the two superpowers, the United States and the Soviet Union, still deploy about 25,000 strategic nuclear weapons world-wide, whose purpose is solely to threaten one another's home territory.

Now all is changed, changed utterly, and one can say with Yeats that 'a terrible beauty is born'. Five years ago Mikhail Gorbachev took office in the Kremlin and embarked on a course which has ended the Cold War and ended the division of Europe. As a result of his decisions, Communism is now dead and gone as a factor in European affairs and will probably soon disappear in the Soviet Union itself. The spectre which Marx described in 1848, a century and a half ago, as haunting Europe, has been laid to rest. There are still a few Communist governments left in the Far East – China, North Korea, Vietnam – some revolutionary movements elsewhere in the Far East, and a few groups in Latin America which claim allegiance to

Communism. But in Europe, Communism is dead and there is no chance whatever of it returning to life.

I was lucky enough to be in Berlin that weekend last November when the Wall first crumbled, standing on the balcony of the Reichstag with Ted Heath. I spent the next day going round East Berlin, which I had previously seen on a visit three years earlier. I have never before or since been in any city anywhere in the world where there were so many happy faces. It was an extraordinary moment in history: the whole population of that great city was glowing with pleasure, laughing and crying with joy. In Wordsworth's words, 'bliss was it in that dawn to be alive, and to be young was very heaven'.

In the six months since that weekend, things have been moving so fast that it is very difficult to keep up with them. The future is now impossible to predict; in fact you can say that if you are not confused you do not know what is going on. It is like pressing the fast rewind button on a video recorder and wondering whether it will stop in 1945, 1917, 1848, 1789 or when. Certainly I think anybody with a sense of history – and this was one of Winston Churchill's greatest gifts as a politician – must reflect on two of the lessons of the past.

The first lesson is that a revolution which destroys the institutions of the existing regime tends to produce anarchy, and anarchy in turn can produce dictatorship. This happened after 1917 with Lenin and Stalin; it happened after 1789 with Napoleon. On the other hand, a revolution which does not destroy the existing institutions is liable to fail; this happened in 1848, and may be happening in Rumania and other parts of Eastern Europe at the present time.

The other lesson of history concerns what happens when a great empire disintegrates. It looks as if the end of the Soviet Empire, like the end of the Ottoman Empire and the end of the Austro-Hungarian Empire, is releasing a suppressed nationalism of frightening force all over the region it dominated, from Kosovo in Yugoslavia, right to Mongolia in the far east and even beyond, in some of the Muslim republics of China.

History can be a dangerous guide, but it is practically the only useful guide we have. It is a far better guide than ideology, on which people otherwise tend to rely in interpreting the present and guessing about the future. But if you use history as a guide you must examine the differences from the past as well as the similarities. The most important differences which affect what is going on in Europe and the world at the present time have been created by the development of science over the last half century. All these developments strengthen the case against nationalism or even regionalism as the basis for policy. Let us look at just four of these changes.

First, nuclear physics has produced atomic weapons, which have made large-scale war not a rational option, at least in the European area. Even a large-scale conventional war in Europe, as was pointed out by the Royal Commission on the Environment in 1976, given the number of nuclear power stations scattered around the continent, could make vast areas of Europe uninhabitable for a generation. Of course, nuclear weapons have not made local wars impossible, particularly between powers which do not have nuclear weapons. Twenty million people have died in the Third World since 1945 in such wars; even inside NATO we nearly had a small war between Greece and Turkey over Cyprus, in spite of the fact that both of them were in NATO at the time. But there is no doubt that the existence of nuclear weapons and the impossibility of destroying the knowledge of how to make them, is one of the major factors which led Gorbachev to abandon the doctrine of the Two Camps on which Soviet policy had been based since the time of Lenin.

The second big scientific development is in information technology; I suppose as an important international force, it is only about fifteen years old. But information technology has already produced an interdependent global financial system and has assisted the cross-border networking of industry, for example, through alliances, mergers, and acquisitions. This internationalization of finance and industry has taken place over the last fifteen years in the main without significant intervention by governments; it is controlled neither by governments nor by central banks.

The third scientific development is due to chemistry. This has produced new and unforeseen dangers to the world environment, in the ozone layer and in large-scale pollution of the land, the rivers and the sea. We are feeling the effects even in the food chain; Britain is now regarded widely as the only country in the world where the sex is safer than the food.

The fourth major development in science over the last fifty years has been in the field of television and radio. Television and radio have not only increased the ability of governments to control the opinion of their peoples, they have also reduced the ability of governments to do so. On recent visits to the Soviet Union, I was impressed by the fact that, for example, the people of Estonia every night watched television programmes from Finland and Sweden; that was true in all the Baltic states and in many parts of western Russia. The availability of foreign views and foreign news in all countries has a major impact on political developments. It is influencing how the Russians deal with the Baltic States at the present time. These new media not only make news international, they have tended to produce the internationalization of culture. I was surprised when I was in Moscow some years ago to find young people in Gorky Park with punk haircuts carrying ghetto blasters, which were playing the latest Western and Soviet pop music.

In my opinion all these scientific developments have made the creation of a world order both more necessary and more possible. Unfortunately, the international explosion of nationalism has also made it more difficult to create a world order, not only between what we call East and West but also in the Third World. My own feeling is that if we can in this new situation produce some sort of international order in the European area, that might hopefully serve as a model for some sort of wider world society through the United Nations. If we fail to take the opportunity of creating a new international order in the European area then I think we in the West no less than the ex-Communists in the East and in the Soviet Union may lose our chance for good. Nuclear weapons, chemical weapons, biological weapons and the missiles to carry them will proliferate in the Third World where nationalism is even stronger than it is in Europe and is fuelled by religious and tribal influences which are even more virulent.

I have been trying to understand world affairs ever since I left the army in 1945. As a young man I was surprised to find that nationalism was by far the most powerful single force in world politics, far stronger than ideology, class solidarity or religion. Those who think for example, that Muslim fundamentalism is more powerful than nationalism should look at what happened in the Gulf War where the Shia population of Iraq fought for the Iraqi government, for their own country, against the Shia regime in Iran. Unfortunately nationalism is essentially a product of democracy. In its modern form it hardly existed before the end of the eighteenth century. It is in fact the most important single legacy of the French Revolution, as that great political philosopher Talmon preached in his many books. Yet the nation state is a dangerous anachronism in the modern world. It is anachronistic because of the scientific developments I have described. It is dangerous because it is impossible to draw a frontier round any nationality in the world without including minorities of other nationalities which claim the same rights as the majority. We saw that problem when we tried to carve out a Protestant state in Northern Ireland which inevitably had to include a large minority of Catholics who wanted to join the South; in a united Ireland there would be a much larger Protestant minority.

In the Soviet Union the problem is perhaps more formidable than in any other country in the world. At the present time 30 per cent of all people in the Soviet Union live in republics dominated by nationalities other than their own, and 20 per cent of the Russian people, those originally from the Russian Federated Republic, now live in republics which are already demanding independence from Russian control. One of the many problems which Gorbachev faces is that if these nationalities achieve independence without consent he will face, or any Russian leader will face, the return of the 'colons'. Those of us who watched what happened in France after the colons returned from Algeria will realize how dangerous to stability that might be.

Nationalism tends to increase if an economy is failing. The economic failure of Communism is total, and as a result we see xenophobia breaking out all over what used to be the Soviet empire, including its most filthy form, anti-semitism. Unfortunately the economic failure of Communism has been made worse so far by attempts to replace it with something different. In the Soviet Union living standards have steadily fallen since Perestroika began five years ago and parts of the system are breaking down altogether. Moscow can no longer rely on oil supplies from the oil producing areas. A frightening figure was given by some Soviet economists at a meeting with CIA experts on the Soviet economy; they reported that last year only 24 million tons of the 90 million tons of potatoes produced in the Soviet Union finally reached the shops. We now hear from one of the leading Soviet officials concerned with labour that they expect unemployment to triple in the next five years. And they haven't even started to deal with the problem of realistic pricing.

In Poland, where they have in fact tried to change the economic system much more vigorously than in the Soviet Union, living standards fell by a third in the first four months of this year, for smallholders in the countryside, living standards fell by half. We are only now beginning to learn about the extent to which the Communist regimes allowed pollution to develop in their countries. Poland's biggest river, the Vistula, is undrinkable over 95 per cent of its length. Seventy-five per cent of its water cannot be used even by industry because it is too corrosive. A third of the land in south-west Poland, its most fertile area, is too contaminated to allow the cultivation of root crops. One of East Germany's nuclear power stations is as dangerous as Chernobyl and will have to be shut down. The adjustments required to correct an economic situation which has deteriorated so far are bound to be very painful; they cannot be imposed by force in a democracy where people are free to organize in protest against unpopular decisions; in Poland for example, Solidarity is already muttering about running strikes against the policy of a government which was put in power by itself.

There is no precedent for what the newly democratic countries in Eastern Europe are trying to do. At least ten thousand books have been written to tell people how to turn Capitalism into Socialism. There is not yet a single book about how to turn a command economy into a market economy. The trouble is that the old structures have now gone – the revolutions have destroyed them except in the Soviet Union. No new structures have yet been put in place to permit the market economy to work. One of the more depressing spectacles at the moment is the long procession of carpet-baggers from universities on both sides of the Atlantic, mainly I am bound to say from Cambridge Massachusetts rather than Cambridge England, who want to tell the Poles, Hungarians, the Czechs and even the Russians how to run their economies. Unfortunately when the carpet-baggers get there they find there are no reliable statistics; there are no effective communications between government and industry; there is no commercial banking system, and most worrying of all, in some of these countries the whole society seems to have lost both the desire and the capacity for working; they have lived too long in a system in which, as the old Soviet joke goes 'we pretend to work and they pretend to pay us'.

Moving from such a system to an effective market economy is very difficult. Six months after the Berlin Wall came down, I think it may be a little early to assume that Eastern Europe represents the triumph of Thatcherism. It is indeed difficult to foresee what political or economic solution will be found by these countries to the problems they now face. If we look at the countries in turn, Eastern Germany stands at one end of the spectrum, the Soviet Union at the other end.

The problems facing East Germany are the easiest to solve simply because everybody in East Germany knows it is sure to be annexed by West Germany under Article 23 of the Bonn Constitution, and then West Germany will be compelled to provide the necessary economic assistance, the necessary subsidies for the painful changes which have to be made, because if it does not do so it will be swamped by immigrants from Eastern Germany. This is the main reason why Chancellor Kohl decided to take the fast route towards unification because he is frightened that if unification is left until after the end of the year he will lose the following all-German election. It is an open question whether he can overcome the practical and constitutional obstacles so as to get East Germany to join West Germany by the end of the year, in time to replace the West German election due in December, with all-German elections. An even more difficult problem remains; can he get the Soviet Union to withdraw its troops from East Germany, and if not what will be the consequences?

Nevertheless, the problems of East Germany will be solved, and in my opinion, the digestion of East Germany by West Germany will be practically complete within five years, and totally complete within ten.

Far more difficult problems are faced by the Soviet Union itself. This is partly because Gorbachev is trying to reform the system without destroying all its institutions. He has to deal with an economy in a far worse shape than any in Eastern Europe, and he has to do it through the old bureaucracy, which is not only corrupt and inefficient but is also now deeply disaffected from the whole policy of Perestroika. Secondly, he is trying to reform the political system and introduce some form of pluralism, while maintaining personal control of how it happens. As Helmut Schmidt said in London the other day, it is as if Luther had become the Pope, and was trying to carry out his Reformation through the Vatican machine. His third great problem, which the East Europeans do not face, is to negotiate a new status for the republics which want to secede from the Soviet Union at a time when his main bargaining card has gone. He cannot credibly threaten to use force against them. When it was tried in Tblisi last year it simply exacerbated nationalism in Georgia; the same was true in Azerbaijan when it was tried in Baku. When I was in Harvard a couple of years ago, Arbatov, who is one of Gorbachev's spokesmen, was asked whether the Brezhnev doctrine still held. He said no, if an East European country wants to abandon Communism, the Soviet Union will not use force to change its position. Then he was asked what will happen if one of the Republics wants to secede? And he replied with what may have seemed a good debating point in Harvard, 'Well I guess Gorbachev would react rather as Abraham Lincoln did, in a similar situation'.

At that time I doubt whether he knew very much about the enormous casualties in the American Civil War; it took place, if you like, at the other side of the moon. It was not possible for external countries to intervene significantly. A civil war in the Soviet Union could lead to intervention along the southern frontier by some of the adjoining states, along the western frontier perhaps by some of the adjoining states as well. I don't know how he is going to solve these problems. Every politician learns that problems are often not things you solve, they are things you hope to survive. Somehow or other, I suspect, they will get through, but how, I don't know, and what it will all look like afterwards, it's difficult to say.

Now let us look at the implications of all this for the Western world. At the moment, Western governments are still stunned by the disappearance of the enemy who has given their efforts meaning for the last forty years. You will remember that poem of Kavafy about the senators who are waiting for the arrival of the barbarians in Rome and are suddenly told the barbarians have turned and gone back. It ends with the immortal couplet 'What shall we do without the barbarians? They were a sort of solution'. One can't help feeling that about the Western reaction to these stupendous changes in Eastern Europe and the Soviet Union.

The most worrying country in the West is also the most powerful – the United States – which seems to be reclining in what was recently described as a state of 'happy apathy'. Two-thirds of the Americans who are entitled to vote in an election do not bother to vote. A third do not register and half of these who register do not actually cast their vote. In fact Bush was elected by the votes of fewer than one out of five American adult citizens. The United States is now preoccupied primarily by its internal problems, which it sees as drugs and crime, both increased by the old American dilemma of how to deal with the racial problem – which is now not only black but increasingly Hispanic and Asian. The main external enemy as seen by Americans, according to the opinion polls, is not the Soviet Union but Japan. In some areas the Americans are getting quite hysterical about what they see as the Japanese threat.

Meanwhile, changes in the way the constitution works make it very difficult for an American administration to get unpopular policies through the Congress. Administrations are composed of people who serve for four, or at the most eight, years and often have no previous experience of government. Congress is composed of people, ninety per cent of whom serve for as long as they want. Once you get into the Congress it is very difficult to get you out, unless you decide voluntarily to retire. The members of Congress have no constitutional obligation to consider the national interest rather than the interests of their constituents, either in domestic affairs or in international affairs. On top of that the United States has now got a very fragile financial system. Rescuing the Savings and Loans institutions, the Thrifts as they are called, or building societies as we call them, now looks like costing up to five hundred billion dollars which as a percentage of GDP is nearly twice as much as the whole of Marshall Aid in current terms. Property losses are now threatening the banks in the north-east of the United States and there is increasing worry about highly leveraged transactions, junk bonds, and so on. Most of my American friends in financial institutions think the system would collapse if there were a recession. So far there has not been a recession because the Japanese and the Germans have been financing the enormous American fiscal and external deficits. But the German surplus is now going to be fully absorbed into paying for the digestion of Eastern Germany. Indeed

Germany is expecting to run into deficit. Bonn is planning to float German bonds to finance its deficit, a large part of which it hopes to sell to the Japanese.

Meanwhile the Japanese themselves have a shrinking trade surplus. It is now 2 per cent of GDP as against the 4 per cent when they started financing the American deficit. It could disappear because Japanese savings may soon be swallowed up by the growing number of people drawing old age pensions and by the big increases in domestic public investment which the Americans are urging on the Japanese at the moment. The Americans cannot finance their deficits themselves because they do not save enough. If they consequently have to get rid of their deficits because they cannot get someone else to finance them, they will risk generating a world recession, because a collapse in America's demand for foreign goods would reduce economic growth in all other countries in the world. This is one of many reasons why big cuts in American defence spending are now absolutely inevitable. Even the Administration is now saying it plans to cut American defence spending by a quarter over the next five years.

Now what is going to be the impact of all this on NATO and the European Community? Unless NATO makes some very fundamental changes in its role very quickly, it will be seen as a biological monstrosity, an organ without a function. Even Richard Perle, once called the Prince of Darkness, and General Powell, the chairman of the American Joint Chiefs, now agree there is no risk of a major Soviet attack on western Europe. NATO will still be required to coordinate the strategic Western response to the changes in Eastern Europe, but this is essentially a political and not a military function. Both Secretary Woerner, the Secretary-General of NATO, and a number of other Western statesmen have suggested that NATO must now find a political function rather than a military one.

The role of any security organization in Europe in the coming years will not be to deter or defeat an external attack – which has been NATO's role over the last forty years – but to police Europe's internal frontiers and to mediate in disputes which may divide the countries of Europe. This is not a function which NATO can carry out with its present membership. It would have to include the East European countries, those that used to be in the Warsaw Pact, and probably the Soviet Union as well. In my opinion NATO could perform a very useful function in helping to create a new security architecture for Europe out of the Western alliance and the relics of the Warsaw pact. But it would be fatal for NATO to try to preserve the block mentality that has kept it going over the last forty years. Having been an architect of 'flexible response' twenty-five years ago, and knowing a good deal about the contradictions in the concept of 'forward defence', my mind boggles at the current situation, in which Bonn has already agreed to pay to keep the Red Army in Eastern Germany, which according to Western policy would be part of NATO.

Even worse is the idea still fervently supported by our Prime Minister, that NATO should deploy a new type of strategic nuclear weapon, namely aircraft with medium-range missiles aboard, which could have only one military purpose – to strike targets inside the Soviet Union in a first use of nuclear weapons in a conventional war. Why new weapons are needed for this purpose God knows, because America is already deploying ships with cruise missiles all round the Soviet Union; it has an enormous force of aircraft carriers at sea, and of course has its submarine-launched missiles too. If NATO tries to turn Western Europe into a launchpad for a new means of nuclear attack on the Soviet Union, it is inconceivable that United Germany would want to join NATO, and indeed Chancellor Kohl has already made it clear that whatever the others do, he is not going to have these new TASMs on aircraft bases in Western Germany, let alone in a United Germany. The probability is that a United Germany will not want any nuclear weapons on its soil. The next stage in the disarmament process will be the so-called 'third zero' – to get rid of all landbased weapons in Europe. There is also growing doubt whether a United Germany would want any foreign troops on its soil either, because the disturbance caused now by exercising them has become extremely unpopular.

So far as I can see there is only one potential framework for a new security architecture and that is the still phantasmic structure, if we can call it that, represented by the Helsinki Conference, the ECSC framework. That has already been recommended, not only by Shevardnadze, but also by Genscher, the foreign minister of Western Germany, by the Danish foreign minister, and in part even by our own foreign secretary. Douglas Hurd suggested in the House of Commons that ECSC should be used as a forum in which to settle disputes which might arise, territorial disputes particularly, in Europe in the future. I believe we should develop ECSC into a new structure for security which would spread from Vancouver to Vladivostock including not only the European countries of the north, as well as east and west, but also the United States and Canada and the Soviet Union itself. All are now signatories of the Helsinki Treaty. NATO's main role should be to bring that about as fast as possible.

We have to see the European Community in a similar way. I believe that the European Community must be extended as fast as possible to include the rest of Europe. It cannot be done quickly, but I do not think we should make 1992 an obstacle to starting on that task now, because I do not believe that the 1992 process has got very much more life in it. I do not think there is not going to be agreement on the harmonization of taxes, on how to treat government procurement, which is 15 per cent of GDP in the Community, on how to deal with government subsidies to industry, on how to deal with technological standards. In a way 1992 has already achieved its major objective in attracting an enormous wave of investment into Europe by Japan and the United States and by European countries outside the Community, like Sweden. It has also encouraged the networking of business across national frontiers of which we see new examples every day; the French are now making a major assault on Britain in terms of alliances, acquisitions and mergers. I think all that will continue, but the community governments probably will not get very much further in removing government obstacles to trade.

We should concentrate now on bringing Northern and Eastern Europe into the Community. I suspect that Norway will apply to join as soon as the present coalition government falls. There is an increasing desire in Sweden, shared by nearly all industrialists, to join the Community. Neutrality ceases to have very much meaning when there are no blocks to be neutral between – the same applies to Finland and Switzerland. Austria, which is condemned by Treaty to non-alignment, which is a form of neutrality, has already applied to join and the Czechs, Hungarians and Poles have made it clear that they would like to join as soon as possible. I believe that the prospect of membership of the Community would be a powerful force for economic change in the East European countries.

If Europe is to become united again, and that is the great opportunity now offered to us, there will have to be a very substantial transfer of resources from Western Europe to Eastern Europe, on a scale that far dwarfs the current regional fund of the European Community with its existing membership. That again will only be possible if there are big cuts in defence spending, particularly if Western Europe is to help Eastern Europe without cutting its aid to the Third World. One of the risks in the current situation is that the Third World will suffer even worse neglect as the United States and the West European countries shift their attention to Eastern Europe.

I cannot predict now how all this will come about. But in my political experience the important thing is to set your objective clearly. Our objective today must be to take advantage of the opportunities of uniting the whole of Europe which have been created by the end of the Cold War.

If we do not set this as our objective and start working towards it quickly, I feel we may all be swept away by the bewildering speed of change. I believe this new form of European unity stretching from Brest to Brest inside a new security structure stretching from Vancouver to Vladivostock is something which could excite the imagination of both peoples and governments and particularly of the young.

When I look back on my own life – I was born in 1917 – I see governments botching the first attempt to build a world society under the League of Nations after 1918, through lack of dedication and botching the second attempt under the United Nations after 1945, mainly because the Soviet Union and its satellites refused to join in the effort. The end of the Cold War gives us a third chance. If we miss that chance I fear that anarchy in the Soviet Union and the Third World will sweep all our signposts away.

The world desperately needs at the moment the sort of vision and leadership which Winston Churchill gave us fifty years ago. The challenges we face today are physically far less formidable than those that Churchill faced in 1940. Intellectually, however, they are infinitely more formidable. However, the central problem in politics as in almost any field of effort is to start by asking the right question. The moment you have got the question rightly formulated the possibility of a solution is imminent. Our duty now is to define that question, and to start working out the answer.

CHAPTER EIGHT

Epilogue

IN 1945 THE WHOLE OF EUROPE faced the sort of economic and political collapse which Eastern Europe confronts today; Britain was the only large country to have escaped defeat and enemy occupation. The Second World War was the second European civil war this century. It brought the United States and the Soviet Union face to face across the middle of a divided continent and a divided Germany. Five centuries of European predominance in world affairs was ended.

At Yalta and Potsdam the superpowers had agreed to co-operate in building a new world society through the United Nations which would bring lasting peace and prosperity to mankind. Stalin's refusal to fulfil his part of the bargain compelled Western Europe to turn to the United States for economic and military support against a hostile power which now dominated the Eurasian land-mass from Stettin to Vladivostock.

The United States responded with astonishing generosity. For four years it gave in Marshall Aid 1 per cent of its annual output – equivalent to £200 billion today. Its leaders also showed unprecedented political creativity. They encouraged Western Europe to build a Common Market on the foundations of the European Recovery Programme. They abandoned their natural urge to return to the normalcy laid down by their prewar Neutrality Act. Instead they entered into the most 'entangling alliance' in world history, establishing NATO on the foundations laid in the Brussels Treaty and the Truman Doctrine. Western Europe, led by Britain, showed the same imagination in its response.

Although Truman and Acheson felt it necessary to exaggerate the nature of the Communist threat in order to win Congressional support, they and their successors showed remarkable flexibility in practice. Marshall himself almost succeeded in establishing good relations between America and Communist China before the Korean War destroyed that possibility for twenty years. Despite all provocations, the Western leaders displayed extraordinary patience and pragmatism in seeking constructive answers to the division of Germany.

For a few years after Stalin's death it seemed that they might succeed. But the Soviet repression of the Hungarian rising, the second Berlin crisis, and Khrushchev's Cuban adventure killed such hopes. After Brezhnev took office the superpowers concentrated on managing their bilateral relationship, while Western Europe was largely absorbed in deepening and widening the Common Market. The Vietnam War and the insoluble nuclear dilemma created strains on transatlantic relations which left both sides with little taste or energy for tackling the formidable problems of East-West relations in Europe.

One result of putting the Cold War into the deep freeze was to give the institutions which grew out of it an absolute value in the eyes of governments. NATO and the European Community became ideological centre-pieces of Western policy. Together with some of the policies on which they were founded, such as nuclear deterrence and the single market, they were elevated to a level beyond criticism. Even Mrs Thatcher signed the Single European Act.

When Gorbachev ended the Cold War and effectively dissolved the Warsaw Pact, he removed the threat NATO had been established to counter. Since the Berlin Wall crumbled and German reunification became imminent, the European Community has been confronted with the possibility of doubling its membership to include not only the countries of eastern and northern Europe, but perhaps also some of the Soviet republics and even Russia itself.

In other words the West, and Europe in particular, now faces a world as different from that of 1987 as the world of 1947 was from that of 1939. This new world presents challenges far more inspiring, and no less formidable, than those that were met successfully over forty years ago. Yet Western policy is now encrusted with ideological deposits from the im-mobilism of the last quarter of a century which seems to have rendered it incapable of responding to the new opportunities.

Despite the fact that all the countries on both sides of the north Atlantic are now enormously richer than they were after the war, they are far less ready to provide the resources needed to create stability in the world beyond their frontiers; yet they continue to spend as much money on armaments as ever. The $50 billion the United States plans to spend on 'Smart Pebbles' which are supposed to protect its citizens against missiles from Colonel Gadaffi would be enough to produce a solution for the debt crisis in the Third World. The money it once spent in Marshall Aid would be under half of what it is now spending for defence against a Soviet military threat which no longer exists.

Western Europe is no better. For all Chancellor Kohl's fine words about German reunification, he has adopted President Bush's motto – 'Watch my lips' – if it is suggested that unity with East Germany may require higher taxation in West Germany. Mrs Thatcher has already refused to contribute to Common Market funds for helping an East Germany which will soon be one of the poorest regions in the Community. Yet it is disturbingly obvious that the suffering most East European peoples will have to endure in making good the economic catastrophe of Communism will produce a dangerous political extremism, unless the world outside helps to cushion the shock. It was the Great Slump of the thirties which gave birth to Hitler.

Moreover, much of the Western advice reaching Eastern Europe at present is offered by intellectual carpet-baggers of the New Right who see the popular revolutions there as a golden opportunity for testing out theories of primitive market economics which have already failed in the West. Yet all the evidence is that, though the people there long desperately for Western living standards, they are no more attracted by unrequested capitalism than by Communism. When asked, the majority opt for the market socialism of Scandinavia or the social market of the Federal Republic.

The icy grip of Cold War ideologies still prevents the West from showing the same vision, flexibility and imagination in Europe as it displayed throughout the first two decades after the war. Too many options are ruled out automatically simply because they contradict ideological prejudices. For example, in Britain a rational discussion of the need for national nuclear forces is excluded by out-dated dogmas; yet in the fifties and early sixties it was possible for Conservative defence ministers such as Anthony Head and Peter Thorneycroft to use the same arguments as Hugh Gaitskell in opposing a British nuclear deterrent as 'no longer a wise use of our resources'. Similarly a knee-jerk commitment to NATO for its own sake may create difficulties for Germany's role in the new Europe which are quite unnecessary.

It is still possible for the popular revolutions in Eastern Europe to go terribly wrong, like so many before in history, if economic despair breeds aggressive nationalism. Yet if Europe cannot soon provide an example of international order, dealing with similar problems in the Middle East, Asia, Africa, and Latin America will become insoluble, as missiles and weapons of mass destruction proliferate. And there will be no chance of mastering the new dangers to the world environment.

I hope that, by describing how earlier leaders dealt with similar problems in the recent past, this book may teach some of the ideological shrimps to whistle, and provide a few signposts for what may be our last chance of creating a world society.

INDEX